PRAISE FOR *Breakable You*

A *Chicago Tribune* Best Book of the Year

"All Morton's novels have a balance of warmth and acuity; the author sees his flawed characters clearly and still extends them his generous empathy." —*Newsday*

"Heart-rending." —*Chicago Tribune*

"Compelling . . . Moving deftly among his characters' distinctive points of view, Mr. Morton probes dark questions about morality, selfishness, choice, fate and love. *Breakable You* is a bleak book, yet it is written and imagined with a sure touch that achieves a somber beauty." —*The Wall Street Journal*

"Morton milks significance from the finest of perceptions. . . . [He] is especially skilled with subtle humor." —*The Atlantic Monthly*

"[Morton] is a deeply compassionate writer, unafraid to treat the largest themes—love, loneliness, aging, death—in an earnest, generous spirit. . . . *Breakable You* has succeeded in demonstrating, once again, Mr. Morton's appealing and humane gift." —*The New York Sun*

"Brian Morton's novels conjure up a world of smart, sophisticated and surprisingly fragile New Yorkers." —*The Atlanta Journal-Constitution*

BREAKABLE YOU

ALSO BY BRIAN MORTON

The Dylanist

Starting Out in the Evening

A Window Across the River

BREAKABLE YOU

Brian Morton

A HARVEST BOOK | HARCOURT, INC.

Orlando   Austin   New York   San Diego   London

To Heather

—

The Library of Congress has cataloged the hardcover edition as follows:
Morton, Brian, 1955–
Breakable you/Brian Morton.—1st ed.
p. cm.
1. Novelists—Fiction. 2. Psychological fiction. 3. Domestic fiction. I. Title.
PS3563.O88186B74 2006
813'.54—dc22 2006003704
ISBN 978-0-15-101192-6
ISBN 978-0-15-603317-6 (pbk.)

Text set in Garamond MT
Designed by Cathy Riggs
Printed in the United States of America

First Harvest edition 2007
A C E G I K J H F D B

ONE

As she watched her husband walk toward her, Eleanor Weller searched for signs of his recent accident, didn't find any, and wasn't sure whether she was relieved or disappointed. She had expected him to be limping, or walking with a cane, or, more dramatically, listing, like an injured ship, but he looked as brisk and confident as ever.

He kissed her on the cheek. They had been separated long enough for her to find this endurable. Every other time she'd seen him during the past year, she'd held herself stiffly at a distance, sickened by the thought of coming into contact with him in any way.

He took her arm, grasping it too tightly, as was his habit, and led her into the restaurant. She was stunned that she allowed herself to be led in this fashion, after everything.

"You're looking well," he said, but she knew it wasn't true. Since he'd left her she'd been steadily gaining weight, about two pounds a month, and now she had become the kind of woman who wears baggy dresses to mask her girth—a tactic that never, of course, works.

"You too," she said, and this *was* true. Adam had always looked well, and ever since he had left her for a woman who was younger than their daughter, he'd been looking better than ever.

"I'm glad we can do this," he said.

"Do what?"

"Get together. Without hostilities."

"Why?" she said, not concerned about whether there was hostility in her tone.

"Because of everything we've meant to each other. Because of our history. Because of our children."

"Well, fine," she said. When they were seated, she drew a thick file folder from her bag. "Why don't we get started?"

A waiter took their orders, and Eleanor noticed that Adam had changed his style of eating. He'd ordered eggs Benedict with sausages and home fries. He wasn't being careful anymore. When they'd lived together she'd kept him on a low-fat diet to protect his heart.

He looked over the papers her lawyer had prepared. He'd seen them already, but he evidently wanted to make sure that the agreement she was asking him to sign was the same one she'd faxed him earlier in the week.

He read through it quickly. She remembered the first few times she'd watched him reading, more than thirty-five years earlier—remembered how startled she'd been by the sheer speed of it.

In the beginning—for many years, really—she'd been excited even by the way he *read*. She had loved him that much. And yet he'd chosen to throw all that away.

She reminded herself to stay focused. She didn't want to be distracted from what she needed to get from this encounter.

She was unhappy that she wanted to get anything from him, anything at all. It went against her nature. She would have preferred to sever all relations with him, never see him again. But she needed him to keep paying for her health insurance, and she needed him to sign over their apartment to her, and she needed him to supplement her income, and she needed him to make provisions for their daughter.

She disliked herself for all this. Her friends had told her that there was no cause for self-criticism, much less self-loathing. They said she deserved anything she could get from Adam, since she'd prepared the ground for his success by supporting him for all those years. Not supporting him financially, but supporting him by giving him time and space and quiet in which to work, raising the children virtually on her own. And it wasn't as if she were asking for a big piece of what he had: she was asking for far less than what she was entitled to by law.

He finished reading the agreement and put it aside. "The only thing that still bothers me," he said, "is the part about Maud."

"We've been through all that. Just sign it."

"We *have* been through all that, but I still think you're making a mistake. She doesn't need special treatment—and treating her like a person who *does* need special treatment is the surest way to infantilize her."

Infantilize. What a ridiculous word. She had a moment of grim pleasure in noting that even he, the great Weller, could speak in clichés, but it was a paltry triumph, as if catching him in the act of using an awkward word could remedy the imbalance of power between them.

"She needs extra help," was all Eleanor said.

Eleanor and Adam had two sons and a daughter. Their boys, Carl and Josh, were doing well: married, with healthy children, good jobs, rooted in the world. Maud, their youngest—she was twenty-nine—was bright and independent-minded and radiantly lively, but she seemed to be missing something. She seemed to be in short supply of some quality that was mysterious and unnameable, but that was indispensable if you were to navigate your way through life uncapsized.

Maud had had two breakdowns: one during her first semester in college, one just after she'd graduated. She'd been institutionalized on both occasions. Nothing comparable had happened to her since then, and the second one was eight years in the past, but after you've seen your daughter fall apart, you can't stop worrying that she'll fall apart again. You can't, at least, if you're a mother. A father evidently can.

The waiter brought their food. Eleanor had ordered a grapefruit, but when he set it down in front of her she remembered that she wasn't supposed to eat grapefruit. Her doctor had told her that they intensified the effect of the medications she was taking. She hadn't eaten one in months, but this morning she'd ordered it on automatic pilot, since she used to like to share a grapefruit with Adam when they had breakfast together in the old days.

"I'm not going to fight you on this," Adam said, "but I want to put it on record that I think you're making a mistake."

"It's duly noted. Sign it."

He removed a pen from one of the inner pockets of his sport jacket. It was a fountain pen—a Montblanc. A very expensive pen, which must have been a birthday present from Thea. Not a present that made sense for him: he was always losing pens, and he'd surely lose this one within a month. Eleanor had another flush of shabby triumph: *he's left me for a woman who doesn't understand what he needs.*

But she couldn't actually be so sure. Adam *did* look better than he had in years. He was sixty-three but he could have passed for fifty. Eleanor was fifty-nine, and feared she could have passed for seventy.

"What have you been up to?" he said. "How's work?"

Eleanor was a psychologist. She used to tell him stories about her clients, but her sense of professional ethics had grown keener over the years and she'd finally stopped telling him anything. He never seemed to have noticed the change.

"Busy," she said. "Very busy."

"I've been busy too. My little vacation already seems like a distant memory. I would have liked to stay longer in France, but after I broke my ankle I didn't trust French medicine to fix me up. It was a wonderful week, though. We were—"

She put her hand on his.

"Adam. I didn't *ask* you what you've been doing. I don't want to know. You hurt me very deeply, and I don't want to hear about any of your 'wonderful' weeks. I don't want to hear about any of your wonderful *minutes*."

"Fair enough. I suppose there isn't anything left to say, then."

"I suppose not," she said.

Since all of your minutes are wonderful now, she thought.

"I hope you won't mind if I order another cup of coffee."

While he drank his coffee she tried to keep silent, but she wasn't sure she could. She had always played the role of family peacemaker, even when she didn't want to. She found it impossible to let a tense silence go on too long. She could do it with her clients, but she couldn't do it with people she loved, and, despite everything he'd put her through, she still loved Adam. She didn't trust him; she didn't like him; she would never consider getting back together with him; but she had lived the largest part of her life with him, and they were joined forever through their children, and she knew she'd never be able to stop loving him.

"Maud should be getting her Ph.D. in the spring," she said.

"I know. She made me write down the date of the convocation."

"She wants you to be proud of her."

"I *am* proud of her. And I wish I could be there. I haven't had the heart to tell her yet, but unfortunately I'm already committed to this Jewish book festival in Prague."

When Maud graduated from high school, Adam had missed the ceremony, and when she graduated from college he'd missed that one too. He'd had good excuses: lecture tours or book-sellers' conventions or something—she couldn't remember. These events might actually have taken place, and Adam might actually have attended them, but that was of secondary importance to Eleanor. What mattered to her was that she'd learned, long after the fact, that on both occasions Adam had been traveling with another woman.

Not the same woman: it turned out that Adam had been having affairs for years. "Brief and meaningless" affairs, as he'd characterized them during their one wretched attempt at marriage counseling. And although Eleanor, now, was sure that Adam *would* be in Prague on the night of Maud's convocation ceremony, just as he'd said, she also knew that he'd be traveling with Thea.

She realized that there *was* a use for the grapefruit.

"I was wondering why I ordered this," she said. "And now I know."

She leaned across the table and tried to ram the pink pulpy plane of it into his face. If she'd succeeded it would have been glorious, but he saw it coming and pulled back his head, and because she was insufficiently committed to the gesture—committed enough to lean forward but not enough to rise from her seat—she couldn't reach him.

"Very nice," he said. "Very James Cagney. Now let's get out of here."

People were looking at them—as brief as her clumsy attack had been, she'd made a little scene—but she didn't care. Adam called for the check.

Two

They left the restaurant together and walked up Broadway. Adam seemed unfazed by her assault: as always, he was unflappable.

They walked for two blocks in silence. Eleanor was puzzled by how comfortable it felt to walk beside him. She told herself she shouldn't be surprised. During most of their years together, she'd felt secure with him; she'd felt blessedly safe. Since they'd been apart, she'd come to realize that in return for this feeling of safety, she'd given up some of the things that were most important to her. And yet she still had an instinctive nostalgia for the old feeling.

"There's one other thing I wanted to mention," Eleanor said. "Ruth keeps calling me. She says she keeps leaving you messages and you haven't returned them."

Ruth was an old friend of theirs. Her late husband, Izzy, had been Adam's mentor and best friend. Probably his only friend.

"What does she want?" Adam said.

"I don't know. Maybe she just wants to talk to you."

"That would be nice, but it's unlikely."

"Have you been getting her messages?"

He didn't say anything.

"I'll take that as a yes. For Christ's sake, Adam, call the woman. Who knows how much time she has left?"

"Why? Is she sick again?"

"I don't know. All I know is that she wants to talk to you. Have some pity on the poor woman, Adam. She's old, and she's alone, and she's heartbroken."

"No one ever died of a broken heart," Adam said.

"Well, be that as it may," Eleanor said, "I gave her your cell-phone number."

Adam looked displeased, a sight that Eleanor found pleasing.

They said good-bye outside her building. She stepped back quickly to avoid a kiss, but he didn't try to kiss her.

THREE

Eleanor took the elevator to her apartment, the apartment they had shared for their entire married life. It was huge and full of books and beds and windows. They had raised three children here, and lived by themselves for ten years here after the children were gone. And now it was just her.

She hung up her jacket—she had worn a leather jacket for their meeting, in a doomed effort to seem newly hip and liberated, different from the woman he'd known—and closed the closet door. The outside of the door needed a coat of paint. A full-length mirror used to hang there, and now that it was gone, there was a bright white rectangle in the middle of a field of faded gray. Eleanor had taken down all the mirrors except the one above the bathroom sink. She could look at her face when she needed to, but never had to look at her body.

I would have liked to stay longer in France . . . It was a wonderful week.

She felt richly humiliated.

She wasn't sure if it would have been better or worse if she'd succeeded in reaching him with that grapefruit.

The most distressing thing about the encounter in the restaurant was that when he'd mentioned James Cagney, it had made her feel close to him. She'd actually been thinking of James Cagney when she picked up the grapefruit—Cagney grinding a grapefruit into Mae Clarke's face in *The Public Enemy*. Adam was the only person she knew who could have guessed this.

She went into the room that she used as a study. It had been Maud's bedroom years ago. Eleanor had put a desk there shortly after Adam moved out. She'd started keeping a diary in a marbled composition book and was trying to write something in it every day.

Sometimes she daydreamed that keeping a diary would lead to other kinds of writing. Maybe she'd write a book about the craft of psychotherapy—a collection of case studies that would be a little like essays and a little like stories. Or maybe she'd write a family memoir. Or maybe she'd even return to the novel that she began when she was in her twenties.

Or maybe she'd write nothing except a diary.

Eleanor had reached a privileged time of life, a time in which you could just give up, if you wanted to, without harming anyone. No one needed her anymore.

Maybe that made it an awful time of life—she wasn't sure.

For many years, she'd been needed, needed above all by their children. The duties of caretaking had lasted much longer than she'd expected—that was one of the biggest surprises about being a mother. And she had also been needed—or she'd thought she was—by Adam. She'd thought that he considered her indispensable, and at the beginning, perhaps, she'd been right about this. He'd once told her that she was the North Star of his moral life, but that was only one of the roles she played for him. The other roles were more practical. She was his first and most trusted reader, his unofficial editor, his unofficial agent; she was his liaison with the world and his shield from the world.

And now all that was over. Adam had a new muse, or at least a new fuckmate. She used this term bitterly, for the shock effect, even though she wasn't even speaking it aloud and was shocking no one but herself.

Eleanor, at fifty-nine, was going to have to start a new life, even if she didn't want to.

It didn't feel like a season for starting over. It was October, and she often looked out the window at the reddening trees in Riverside Park and remembered lines of poetry that she had read long ago, lines like

> *Now it is autumn and the falling fruit*
> *And the long journey towards oblivion.*

The songs she remembered were not songs about renewal but songs about preparing for death.

She wrote a few sentences about her meeting with Adam, and then she rested her head on the desk. Seeing him had so unnerved her that she had to lie down on Maud's bed and take a nap.

When she woke, she remembered that she'd promised Maud that she was going to call her with a recipe for chocolate-chip cookies. She looked for the recipe, couldn't find it, and then she called Maud, who wasn't home, and left an apologetic message on her machine.

As she closed her diary and put it back in the top drawer of her desk, she wondered whether she was fooling herself. Maybe it was just too late for her to start over.

Starting afresh is the great new myth. It's an article of modern faith that everyone *can*. Books and magazines and TV shows and movies were filled with stories about people "reinventing" themselves. But who among us ever does?

Four

Maud saw Sam from half a block away. He was waiting for her at the entrance of the Café de la Gare, the restaurant in Brooklyn Heights where they'd agreed to meet.

Although it was still two days away from Halloween, she had to make her way through a flock of little goblins before she could get to him. This was unfortunate, because the sight of her wading through all these children would surely make Sam more aware of her bigness.

She wished she could make herself small. To be so much taller than he was made her feel impolite. She was five-ten, and he—well, she wasn't sure how tall he was, but she knew that if they were playing basketball, she could dunk over him with ease.

He was standing stiffly at attention, and when she came near him he nodded hello. He didn't try to kiss her, didn't move toward her, didn't even smile.

They hadn't kissed yet. She had encountered him on five earlier occasions, but this was their first date.

She gave him a crisp military salute. His bearing was so formal that it seemed like the appropriate way to greet him.

No reaction.

"What's your name again?" she said.

He looked unsure of whether to answer her.

"I'm just joking," she said. "It's a joke I always make on the first date."

He held open the door for her and they went into the restaurant. The place was crowded, and as they moved between the pressed-together tables she found herself stooping, as if that would somehow make it easier to pass.

They sat down; a waitress arrived; they ordered drinks.

"It's funny to see you in regular-person clothes," she said. He had been working as a carpenter for her friends George and Celia, so she always encountered him in work clothes flecked with sawdust.

He nodded tensely and said nothing.

He was leaning stiffly away from her. He looked as if he thought she was a hit woman—as if he was nervously expecting her to reach into her handbag and pull out her .44.

Maybe the problem was that she was Jewish. Maybe he hates Jews, she thought.

Maybe I hate Arabs. Maybe *that's* the problem.

She didn't think she hated Arabs, but she couldn't be sure. On the one hand, she wanted peace in the Middle East; on the other hand, when she imagined going to bed with him, she imagined it as going to bed with someone who was slightly greasy. Even though in actual fact he seemed very clean.

Sam had been born in New Jersey and had lived on the East Coast all his life—George had told her that. He was as American as she was. But still, he was an *Arab* American, and she'd never even been friendly with an Arab American before.

Show him you're above all that. Show him you've bravely risen above your prejudices. Show him you're *interested* in him.

"George and Celia told me that you used to work for the Arab American Human Rights League."

"Arab American Human Rights Committee. Yes. That's right."

"Did you enjoy it?"

"I'm not sure if enjoyment had anything to do with it. But it was fulfilling."

"So why did you leave?"

"Things can get old."

"Did you get fired? Was there a scandal?"

She was leaning forward with—she was sure of this—an imbecilic grin. *Was there a scandal?* What a dumb question.

Why, she wondered, do silent people always turn the rest of us into babbling idiots?

"Wasn't fired," he said. "No scandal."

He said this in a voice that was barely stronger than a whisper, so she wondered if there *had* been a scandal.

The waitress arrived with their drinks (wine for her, water for him) and took their order. For the next few minutes, neither of them said a word. He kept his eyes on the table as he sipped his drink.

Mumbling, withdrawn, never looking anyone in the eye—he was like a man on the run from the law. Maybe he was a terrorist. In six months, she thought, I'll see his mug shot in the paper. Everyone will be horrified that he once moved unnoticed in our midst.

This was the oddest date she'd ever been on.

"You don't seem to be enjoying yourself," she finally said. "How come you decided to do this?"

"Do what?"

"Have dinner with me."

"I'm not sure. I'm still trying to figure it out."

He was honest, at least. Grant him that.

But, on the other hand, fuck him.

"Well, if you do figure it out, let me know," she said.

He looked very serious suddenly, grave and sympathetic, like a kindly doctor about to deliver bad news.

"I'm sorry, Maud. I really don't mean to be so unfriendly. But I think I shouldn't be here. I'm not looking for anyone right now, and I don't think I'd be a suitable partner for anyone."

"Who's talking about being partners?" she said. "I'm just thinking it would be nice if we made it to the soup."

He smiled. He had a nice smile.

"That sounds like a fine ambition," he said. "Let's try to get to the soup."

George and Celia had known Sam in college. They'd lost touch with him a few years after graduation, and he'd resurfaced only lately, when they were looking for someone to turn their study into a nursery. Someone had given them the phone number of a guy who was supposed to be a good carpenter, and it had turned out to be their old friend.

George had told her that Sam was one of the most interesting people he'd ever known. But the Sam he described to Maud didn't seem like the Sam she'd met. The person George described was an intellectual and a political activist: he'd received a master's degree in political theory at Columbia and had wanted to promote the cause of civil rights for Arab Americans. Just after college he'd gotten the job that George had told Maud about, with the human-rights group. But now he was working as a carpenter.

He used to work as a carpenter in college, George said, to help pay the bills, but George didn't know why he was working full-time as a carpenter now.

George and Celia had made him sound wonderful: intelligent, responsible, ethical, kind. They'd volunteered to set Maud up with him, and that sounded fine to her, but when they got back to her a few days later, they said it turned out that he wasn't interested in dating. They didn't know why. He wasn't married and he wasn't gay, they said, but he wasn't interested.

That was that, she'd thought, but a few weeks later, when her apartment was being repainted, George and Celia had given her their key and told her that she could use their place as a study if she wanted to, and one afternoon she ran into Sam there. She'd never been attracted to a man who was shorter than she was, but she was attracted to him instantly: his compact, tense, wiry body, the play of the muscles of his arms as he sanded down the crib that he'd built. She tried to talk to him, but he answered in monosyllables. His distance made him even more desirable, and she started showing up two or three afternoons a week—ostensibly to study, but really just to see him—and although he never warmed up to her, hardly ever even smiled, she kept talking to him, stimulated by the challenge, and finally asked him out to dinner, and he, though without much enthusiasm, had said yes. And here they were.

Well, obviously it had all been a mistake. She should have left him alone.

His soup and her salad arrived.

"Well, we made it," Maud said.

"We did."

"Maybe we can try having a conversation. Maybe it would work."

"Stranger things have happened," he said.

"Okay. Let's think of a topic. What did you do today?"

"Today, I finished making a set of kitchen cabinets for a young couple in Manhattan."

"Okay, that's good. That's a start. Did you like making the cabinets?"

"I would have liked it if I'd been alone. But unfortunately, there was the couple."

"What was wrong with the couple?"

"The two of them had very different ideas about kitchen cabinets. They each had a vision."

"That must happen a lot."

"It does. Sometimes I feel like a carpenter, and sometimes I feel like a marriage counselor."

He seemed to be loosening up.

"I can't quite see you as a marriage counselor," she said. "Samuel."

She'd used the formal version of the name just to be playful.

"It isn't Samuel, actually. It's Samir."

"Really? Samir? That's beautiful."

"Thank you."

"Why don't you use it? Why do you Samify yourself?"

"I don't. I only Samified myself for a few years, in college. I was trying to become a typical American. That's what I was calling myself when I met George and Celia. The people I know from college call me Sam; everybody else calls me Samir."

This was more information than he'd volunteered during all the encounters she'd had with him before. He was opening the door to her, a tiny bit.

"Maud is a good strong name," he said.

"I'd like to call you Samir, if that's all right with you," she said.

He didn't say anything, and his expression seemed to indicate that he didn't give a damn what she called him, and the flicker of good feeling from a moment ago was gone.

The waitress returned with their main dishes and said, "Can I get you guys another drink?" After she left, Maud said, "It would be nice if just once you could go to a restaurant where the waiters didn't address people as 'You guys.'"

"That's the kind of thing my ex-wife used to say. It used to drive her nuts."

His ex-wife.

Why hadn't George and Celia told her about this?

"I don't think I've heard you had a wife." Of course I haven't heard, and of course he knows it. Sometimes Maud thought that no one ever says anything casually. Behind the most random-seeming utterance there is always precise intent.

"I had a wife."

"It didn't work out?"

"If it had worked out I wouldn't be here."

She didn't know him well enough to interpret his tone. She wasn't sure if he was kidding around or being hostile.

"Why didn't it work out?"

"Things don't always work out in life."

"I know that. But what I meant was, why didn't this partic-ular relationship work out?"

He didn't say anything, just took a sip of his water.

"Is it a horrible secret?" she said.

"It's not a secret," he said. "But it *is* horrible."

She suddenly felt that she'd walked too far into something that she shouldn't have walked into at all.

"I'm sorry," she said. "I shouldn't have been so flippant."

"That's all right."

He still hadn't told her what had happened, and now she was afraid to ask. Had his wife died?

With the unhappy phone message her mother had left her that afternoon — loneliness encoded within a cookie recipe — and now with this hint of tragedy in Samir's life, she felt sur-rounded by people who needed to be taken care of. She made a mental note to arrange a lunch date with her father. The great thing about her father was that he never *needed* you. That was the deal she had with her father: he won't take care of you, but you don't have to take care of him.

She was thinking that it was a good idea to stay away from people whose wounds are very apparent. Some people carry disaster around with them, and, if you have any instinct for self-preservation, when you come upon such people, you run.

By the time the check arrived, she had made up her mind. She was attracted to him, but she wasn't going to see him again. There was too much in the way. The problem of Arab and Jew; his guardedness; his height; the hint of tragedy in his past— there wasn't just one reason. Her conclusion that it would be better not to see him anymore was "overdetermined," as the insane French philosopher Louis Althusser used to say.

Having decided, she felt freer. He had been praised so highly by Celia and George that even before their first date she had started to feel as if they were engaged.

I don't have to marry this guy. I don't have to marry anyone. I can sit in my apartment reading for the rest of my life.

He paid the bill, and they decided to take a walk on the Promenade, which was two blocks away. It was a cold night, and the wind from the East River was swirling around them in great mad gusts. Manhattan looked glorious in the glinting mist.

As they walked, she felt glad that she didn't have to be self-conscious about her height anymore. She didn't need to stoop, because she didn't need to worry about his feelings.

"I always used to scrunch myself up when I was little," she said. "I was unhappy about how fast I was growing, so I tried to make myself short. I was like a little hunchback."

She didn't even know why she'd said this. It seemed sort of passive-aggressive, maybe. At any rate, it wasn't nice.

"Why were you unhappy about being tall?" he said. "Tall is powerful. Isn't it?"

He thought she had a strong name; he thought tall was powerful. She wondered if she should reconsider her decision about him. It might be nice to be with a guy who saw her as strong.

Maud had faith in the power of her mind—she loved to think and she had confidence in her thinking—but she didn't have much faith in anything else about herself. She certainly didn't think of herself as strong.

"Maybe that's why I was unhappy about being tall. Because people think tall is powerful. Maybe I thought that if I was smaller, people would want to take care of me."

To her own ears, this sounded like psychobabble, but it was true. Sometimes she felt like a wallflower, a little bookworm, trapped in the body of Xena the Warrior Princess.

"I should probably get home," she said. "I should do some work on my dissertation."

In other words, she thought, I've given up trying to chase you.

"Well, it was nice to see you," she said. "I'm glad we could get together. Arab and Jew. A testament to the fact that people can rise above their ancient prejudices."

She was talking just for the sake of talking, because nothing she said mattered, because she was never going to see him again. She felt more comfortable with him, now that they'd gotten a divorce.

"The swarthy Arab and the brainy Jew," he said.

"Brainy but resourceful. Don't forget, we defeated you in battle. Many times."

She leaned against the fence that bordered the Promenade and smiled at him. This might be the last time she'd ever see him. He was a good-looking little man.

He stepped toward her quickly and for one mad moment she thought he was moving with violent intent, angry that she'd bragged about the history of Arab military ineptness. He put his hands on her shoulders and his mouth on hers. The night was cold and the wind from the river was ripping at them and they were wearing thick fat jackets and her nose was numb and he tasted surprisingly delicious.

His hands were burrowing under the many layers of her winter wear. Cold fingers. They were still kissing.

This was the last thing she would have expected.

This is interesting, she thought.

FIVE

Adam hurried away from his breakfast with Eleanor with the feeling that he had narrowly escaped with his life. Eleanor could do that to you. With her unspeakably, almost ludicrously mournful eyes, the eyes of a cow who has been wronged, and with her aura of bravely suffering victimhood, and her talent for long silences, she could suffocate you under the weight of her moral superiority. When you left her, you felt as if you were breathing a freer air.

The thing about Eleanor was that although it was *she* who'd asked *him* to move out, after he did move out she found herself stripped of her identity, and after a brief panicky search for a new identity, she'd found one in being a victim. A brave and plucky victim. *That monstrous husband of hers mistreated her for years and then traded her in for an underage sexpot, but somehow she's found the strength to endure*—this, he thought, was what she wanted the world to say. She wanted the world to regard her with awe because she had remained unbroken—she wanted to transcend her victimhood just that far, but no further. Because if she transcended it further, she risked letting the world forget that she was a victim in the first place. And that would be unacceptable. The world must understand at every moment that she had been wronged, and who had wronged her.

He wasn't meeting Thea until lunchtime, so he went to the gym and spent half an hour in the weight room and half an hour on the treadmill. He felt perfect. His doctor couldn't believe how quickly his broken ankle had healed.

At sixty-three, Adam was in better shape than ever. He could bench-press two hundred pounds and he could run for ten miles. He derived no pleasure from exercising, yet he exercised faithfully, putting himself through his paces with a grim relish.

He flirted with a young woman on the treadmill next to him, and after she left he examined himself in the wall of mirrors and tried to remember how long it had been since he'd been attracted to Eleanor. More than a decade. When he married her, she was a beautiful young woman; now she was covered with rust.

He felt sorry for her, but, with a spirit of indifference that was partly innate in him and partly a quality he cultivated, he was able to derive some amusement from the thought of how things had turned out for the two of them. He was about to head downtown for an afternoon rendezvous with a regal mistress in the full bloom of her youth, while Eleanor, if she should ever decide that she wanted to find someone new to share her nights, would be signing up for golden-years mixers sponsored by the AARP.

An hour later he was at the Algonquin. He was supposed to meet a young academic who'd been writing him literary fan mail, and the young man had suggested they have lunch there. Thea had invited herself along, chiefly because of the location. The Algonquin seemed glamorous to her, because it was a literary landmark, the place where Dorothy Parker and her circle used to convene.

There was nothing glamorous about the place for Adam. The Algonquin wits had never been as witty as they were supposed to have been—for the most part they were mediocrities with good press agents. And in any case, they'd all been dead for decades, and their slightly fraudulent luster had vanished with them. Now the Algonquin was just a run-down hotel with a run-down restaurant in the lobby.

Adam didn't find Thea's naïveté surprising. She was still in her twenties, and she was new to New York. A former high school beauty queen—she'd gone to college on a scholarship she'd earned by winning the title of Miss Junior Wyoming—she had come to the city only a year ago, eager to make a mark. Precisely what kind of mark she wished to make was unclear, but she was intent on making one.

Thea may have been unsound in her literary judgments, but she had other virtues. He checked his coat and glanced into the dining room, and he knew where she was sitting even before he saw her. He didn't know how he knew it, but he always did. He didn't even question it anymore.

She was at a table in the corner with one of her vodka gimlets in front of her. Whenever he had his first sight of her, he had a moment of sheer disbelief that he could be with someone so beautiful.

"Hello, Weller," she said. "You're late."

She liked to call him by his last name because she thought it made her sound cynical and worldly, like Lauren Bacall in *To Have and Have Not*. Thea liked to imagine that in another life she could have been a film-noir heroine.

"Are you feeling all right?" she said as he sat down. "You look a little out of breath."

This too was vintage Thea. She liked to put you on the defensive. She liked to start things off with a jab.

"It's your beauty that's rendered me breathless, my dear."

"You're talking like a book again."

He asked her how her day had been so far, and she told him a story about her job. She was working as an assistant producer for Charlie Rose, with whom she had a love-hate relationship. It was a long story about the incompetence of a booking agent. Adam didn't listen closely to the details; he just let the names swim past him—Tim Robbins, Susan Sarandon, Paul Wolfowitz, Paul Berman—while he took pleasure in looking at her face. He couldn't say he was in love with her, but he hadn't enjoyed a woman's company so much since the early days with Ellie.

He had left Eleanor because of the explosive combination of Thea and Viagra. He'd been having affairs for years, but of steadily declining intensity, and he'd reached a point at which he could almost imagine giving them up. But then the lordly blue pill had entered his life and rendered him magnificent again. Women he had begun to consider out of his league—he could still get them, but he couldn't do much with them once he had them—once again seemed fitting objects of pursuit.

He had never intended to leave Eleanor. After the first two or three flings, years ago, he'd been sure that Eleanor knew about them, had made her peace with them, was merely pretending not to see them. He had assumed that things would go on like this forever, but with Thea it all changed. Thea had asked for more and more of him, and he'd surprised himself by giving it. She didn't ask for money (she wasn't vulgar) and she didn't ask for love (she wasn't sentimental); what she asked for was recognition. His other mistresses—he was old-fashioned enough to use this word—had accompanied him when he traveled, but in public they'd maintained a discreet distance. Thea refused to be distanced. Adam knew many people who might be of use to her in her professional life, and she wanted to meet them all. He'd still somehow thought the affair could go unnoticed—unnoticed, or at least unmentioned, by Eleanor—but one night, sitting in the living room with Eleanor, he mentioned having attended some

July Fourth event sponsored by *The New Yorker,* and Eleanor, who had been pecking at the remote control in search of *Judging Amy,* had instantly put it down and said, "You're seeing someone." He was so surprised—surprised that *she* was surprised—that he didn't have the presence of mind to deny it. And everything followed from that. If he had denied it, Eleanor would have chosen to believe him, and he would still be living with her on Riverside Drive. "I think you should leave," she had said, and, still in a daze because it was so hard to absorb the idea that she hadn't known about all his previous affairs, he took a few things with him and left. At the time he wished he'd been cool-headed enough to deny everything—to tease her a little about mistrusting him—but now he was glad about the way things had played out.

Thea was still talking about Charlie Rose, but now she interrupted herself. "That must be your young admirer," she said.

A young man was approaching the table. Even from a distance he seemed awkward and uncertain. Adam rose and extended his hand.

"Mr. Weller," the young man said. "You don't know what an honor it is to meet you."

"It's overdue. We've been e-mailing for so long that I feel as if we've met already." Adam said this as he searched through his memory for the young man's name.

"You must be Jeffrey Lipkin," Thea said, rescuing him.

Adam had taken the man's measure before he'd even sat down. Jeffrey Lipkin was no different from the dozens of other supplicants Adam had met in the past few years. How familiar the type had become: all with the same tongue-tied eagerness, the same panicky need to please, the same vaguely homosexual hunger for a mentor.

Adam and Thea had already ordered. After a minute of introductory small talk, Jeffrey picked up a menu. "What's good here?" he said. "What's good here that doesn't have meat?"

"Vegetarian," Thea said darkly. "Oh dear."

"Why are people bothered by vegetarianism?" Jeffrey said. "Making fun of vegetarians is the only respectable prejudice left."

"It isn't a prejudice," Thea said. "There's something about vegetarians. Gandhi was the only vegetarian with balls."

One of the things Adam shared with Thea was the pleasure they took in attacking, and one of the things that amused him about her was her habit of attacking anyone anywhere, firing off shots in all directions. He never could have proceeded through the world that way, particularly not when he was young. But a beautiful young woman could get away with it. Could get away with practically anything.

Adam wasn't sure why this young man had wanted to meet him. They had been corresponding for a few weeks, but Jeffrey's purposes were still unclear. Jeffrey was an assistant professor at Rutgers, nervously compiling credentials for his bid for tenure. His area of specialization was Jewish American fiction, so his getting in touch with Adam was understandable, but after one e-mail expressing his admiration for Adam's novels and another asking some quietly show-offy questions, questions designed to demonstrate his intimate acquaintance with Adam's work, he had stayed in touch, and Adam hadn't quite figured out why. At first Adam had thought that Jeffrey wanted to write something about him, but Jeffrey hadn't said anything to that effect.

They talked aimlessly for a few minutes—New York intellectuals, New York restaurants, New York hotels.

"Are you working on a book?" Adam said. "If you're trying to get tenure you probably have to publish something, don't you?"

"I haven't actually started writing, but I am considering something." A small smile, an odd one: Jeffrey seemed to be reaching for modesty but he couldn't quite suppress a hint of a smirk. "Actually, that has something to do with why I looked you up in the first place. I was on leave last semester, and I spent a lot of time in the archives at Brandeis."

As soon as he said this, Adam's mood turned gray. He knew what was coming.

"You want to write a biography of Izzy Cantor," Adam said.

"How did you know?" Jeffrey said.

As if there could be any other fucking reason, Adam thought, for him to be nosing around the archives at Brandeis.

"Izzy Cantor?" Thea said. "Another of your desiccated friends from days gone by?"

Because Adam's mood had changed, he no longer found Thea's manner amusing. In fact, he wouldn't have minded crushing a grapefruit into her face. He should have saved Ellie's grapefruit and used it on Thea. And then Thea could have used it to attack someone else. The grapefruit could travel all over town.

"You don't know of him?" Jeffrey said, gaping, as if she'd said she'd never heard of Chaucer. He looked quickly at Adam, with an expression that seemed to say that it was hard for him to believe that Adam could be seeing a woman who had never heard of Izzy Cantor. Which irritated Adam all the more. You could say that one of the things that Adam looked for in a mistress was that she *hadn't* heard of Izzy.

Jeffrey addressed Thea. "Isidore Cantor was . . ." He turned toward Adam. "But I should let you talk."

"No, no," Adam said. "I'd like to hear what a bright young English professor has to say about the man."

"Isidore Cantor was a writer. Between 1965 and 1992 he wrote five of the strangest, most unclassifiable novels that

American literature has ever produced. In an essay he wrote for *Esquire* in the eighties he said—I think I can get this right—that 'Adam Weller, my oldest friend, is my conscience, literary as well as political. If I didn't know him my fiction would be flabby and my opinions ill informed.' The section about the two of you growing up in the Bronx was one of the most moving things he ever wrote."

"It was a nice article," Adam said.

"How did you become friends? He was a lot older."

"Our mothers were best friends. We were in each other's apartments all the time. He was like an older brother. I worshipped him. He was the first person who ever mentioned Walt Whitman in my presence. Also the first person who ever mentioned Joe DiMaggio."

"And you remained close friends until the end of his life," Jeffrey said, half as a statement, half as a question.

"We did," Adam said quietly. "I was with him the night before he died."

"And, if you don't mind my saying so, the fact that someone like you hasn't heard of him"—Jeffrey turned to Thea as he said this—"is proof of why we need a biography. He was a major writer. Besides that, he led a fascinating life—"

"A writer who led a fascinating life?" Thea said. "Do tell."

Jeffrey had a frighteningly wide grin, as if he'd been wanting to talk about Izzy Cantor for many long years. "In the mid-fifties, after he got out of college, he spent a year in a Zen monastery in Japan, observing a year of silence."

"He never did explain to me why he felt the need to do that," Adam said. "He claimed he just didn't have anything to say."

"In 1960 he played a role in the early Civil Rights movement. He was involved in the lunch counter sit-ins in North Carolina."

"He got his nose broken down there," Adam said. "It improved his appearance."

"And it was only after that, after his return to New York, that he started to take writing seriously. And that was when he began to produce a series of novels that bear the same relationship to the work of his contemporaries that Nathanael West's work bore to the writing of people like Hemingway and Fitzgerald in the thirties. In other words, it was unclassifiable. It wasn't the realism of writers like Saul Bellow and Philip Roth—and Adam Weller." He turned toward Adam as he said this, and Adam was annoyed. He liked to be flattered, but the flattery had to be plausible. It was one of his chronic grievances that no critic had ever placed him on the level of Bellow and Roth. "And it wasn't the pop experimentalism of writers like Barthelme and Coover. It was something all its own. Which is one reason, I think, that history hasn't treated him the way it should have. It's hard to stick a label on his work." Jeffrey looked elated to be talking about all this—overeager, overcaffeinated, overjoyed. He'd already written the book in his mind. "And along the way he had time to teach at Brandeis and Columbia and City College, to launch a literary magazine that did some interesting things before it ran out of funding, and to have high-profile fistfights with Norman Mailer and Alfred Tomas."

"Who's Alfred Tomas?" Thea said.

"Painter," Adam said. "Wild man."

"Well, what do you think?" Jeffrey said to Thea. "Does he sound as if he deserves a biography?"

"It sounds like he deserves a miniseries," Thea said. "How come you've never told me about him, Weller?"

"There are many things I haven't told you about."

Adam was unhappy. Izzy had been a friend of his, but also a rival. Adam had believed he had defeated him, simply by outliving him. But this was the second time Izzy's ghost had appeared that day. It was as if Izzy were a representative of the dead, coming forward to claim him.

But he could outwit him. He could outwit his old dead friend. He didn't know what it was yet, but he was sure there was something in this situation that he could use to his advantage.

"Izzy was a remarkable writer and a remarkable man," Adam said. "He'd be a worthy subject for a biography. I'm not sure what you want from me, though."

Jeffrey's grin, if possible, grew even wider. He looked insane.

"What are you smiling about?" Adam said.

"You keep calling him Izzy. I've seen him referred to as Izzy, in letters. In the archives. But I've never actually met anyone who knew him well enough to refer to him by his nickname."

"Congratulations," Adam said. He wanted this encounter to be over. He wanted to be far away from this young man's ghoulish dampness.

"But to answer your question: what do I want from you? I want your help. First of all, I'd love to interview you. Your memories of him would be invaluable. And I'd like your help in locating people he knew."

Thea snorted. "Locating people? Try using Google. It sounds like you're asking the old man to research the book for you. He has bigger fish to fry."

She put her hand around Adam's bicep. He was glad he had worked out at the gym that morning.

The young man looked embarrassed. "I'm sorry. I mean . . ."

"It's all right," Adam said. "I loved Izzy. Of course I'll do what I can."

Meanwhile he was furiously thinking about how he could steer this project in a direction of his own choosing.

"It's still pretty hypothetical at this point," Jeffrey said. "I need to find the time to work on it. All my spare time goes into preparing for my classes. My course load is brutal." He put his fork into a pale slice of squash.

Brutal, Adam thought. Like working on a chain gang. Poor little professor.

Adam raised his glass and said, "To Izzy. And to your project." Hoping that this project wouldn't succeed.

"I do have a specific question for you," Jeffrey said. "I haven't been able to locate Ruth. I would love to interview her. If she's still alive." Ruth was Izzy's widow. The woman who'd been leaving messages on Adam's machine for two weeks.

Adam rolled his wine around in his mouth and considered this.

"She *is* alive. But she's a very private person. I can speak to her on your behalf, but I can't guarantee anything."

"If you speak to Ruth, that would be great. That's all I can ask."

You're on a first-name basis with her already, you little prick, Adam thought.

"I'd be happy to," he said.

After the lunch was over, Adam went to the men's room and extracted one of his secret blue saviors from his pillbox. Grandpa's little helper. He cupped his hands under a water faucet and slurped enough water to get the pill down. He was hoping Thea would accompany him back to his apartment.

Outside the restaurant, after the young man had left to catch a train back to New Jersey, Adam asked Thea if she was doing anything.

"It's two-thirty. Charlie awaits."

"You can't go back a little later?"

"You know better than that. Charlie can't be kept waiting." She kissed him—insultingly, on the cheek. "But I'll see you tomorrow."

Angular, intense, impersonal, she looked extraordinarily attractive in the harsh October light.

He wondered whether his eagerness to make love came from a desire to assert the rights of the living over the rights of the dead. In other words, a desire to deliver a fat Bronx cheer to his old friend. You are in your final resting place, in the Woodlawn Cemetery, the intimate companion of chiggers and mites, and I'm in a warm apartment, fucking Miss Junior Wyoming.

But that would have to wait. He didn't ask what she'd be doing that night. He didn't want to play the lovesick suitor.

He made a mental note to call Ruth. He hadn't been planning to return her calls—she was a nudnik—but now he supposed he'd have to, if only because it was important to keep tabs on her, to make sure this wan little biographer never found her.

"You seem a little jumpy, Weller," Thea said. "You should take a Xanax." And she hailed a cab and was gone.

He *was* a little jumpy.

When Izzy was alive, reviews that mentioned either of them usually mentioned both. Because they'd been friends since boyhood, and because they wrote about the same terrain, critics could never resist the easy angle of writing about them as if they were the Martin and Lewis of Jewish American writing. (Bellow and Roth being the Hope and Crosby.) In the early 1990s, Adam finally began to feel as if he was shaking himself loose from his old friend, and after Izzy died the liberation seemed complete. Adam had published three books since then and had come to feel confident about having left Izzy behind. But during this past week—with all the phone calls from Ruth, and now with the

appearance of the scholarly vegetarian—he had started to feel
as if Izzy wasn't as gone as he should be. As if Izzy had thrust
his hands out of the earth and was grabbing at his ankles, trying
to pull him down into the land of the dead.

Not yet, old friend, he thought. Not yet.

Six

Samir had arrived early, mainly because he wanted to leave early. Now it was 7:58, and although they hadn't arranged to meet until 8:00, the fact that he'd been waiting so long made it feel as if she were late. He was on the verge of going home, but then she appeared, rounding the corner, and he had that curious feeling he'd had every time he'd seen her. It was two emotions back-to-back: a jolt of desire and then a jolt of something like rage.

She walked with that peculiar gait that he already found unmistakable, and that he already, in spite of himself, found endearing. She seemed to tip forward, her face preceding the rest of her, as if her balance were thrown off by the weight of all the thoughts in her head.

Although it was still two days away from Halloween, she had to make her way through an army of little goblins before she could get to him. They must have been coming from a school play.

She looked like Venus emerging from a sea of schoolchildren. She seemed like a goddess of intellect and sexuality and playfulness and fertility—all of these qualities at once.

Every time he saw her, he wanted to turn himself off to her, but every time he saw her, something about her overwhelmed his intentions.

For some reason, she saluted him.

"What's your name again?" she said.

He didn't know how to react to this.

"I'm just joking," she said. "It's a joke I always make on the first date."

They went into the restaurant. It was crowded, and he found himself annoyed with her, since she'd chosen it. It was a trendy spot, populated by the superficial and the smug. Vapidly glittering women; young men with boxlike heads and lovingly tended hair.

After they sat down, he tried to regroup. He reminded himself of the resolution he'd made that afternoon: to make sure their first date would be their last.

They made small talk while they waited for their drinks. She asked him about his old job. He wished that George and Celia hadn't told her anything about it. It was information about another man, another life.

She seemed a little too interested in his job and why he'd left it. He didn't like being interrogated. She was probably trying to find out if he had abandoned his solidarity with the Arab world. Probably hoping that he had. He considered putting on an act to scare her away—pretending to be a follower of Osama bin Laden, yearning to spill the blood of the Jews—but decided it wouldn't be worth the effort.

When their drinks arrived, he checked his watch. It was 8:20. If he gave this another forty-five minutes, he could leave.

Maud had been showing up at George and Celia's a few times a week and bothering him while he was working. Supposedly she was dropping by to work on her dissertation, but he'd never seen her do any work there. All she did was stand around and try to draw him into conversation. Finally she'd invited him to have dinner with her, and the question had caught him off-guard, and he'd said yes.

If it had been anyone else, he would have said no, but she was so damnably attractive that his circuits had jammed.

He tried not to look at her as he drank his water. He was aware that she was watching him, but he didn't lift his head. She was too good-looking to look at.

"You don't seem to be enjoying yourself," she finally said. "How come you decided to do this?"

"Do what?"

"Have dinner with me."

"I'm not sure," he said. "I'm still trying to figure it out."

"Well, if you do figure it out, let me know."

She was angry, obviously. He could understand that. He could respect that.

It had been inconsiderate to say yes to her in the first place. Dishonest. He shouldn't be wasting her time.

"I'm sorry, Maud. I really don't mean to be so unfriendly. But I think I shouldn't be here. I'm not looking for anyone right now, and I don't think I'd be a suitable partner for anyone."

"Who's talking about being partners? I'm just thinking it would be nice if we made it to the soup."

He smiled at this. She seemed like a sweet woman, and he wished that his life had been different. He wished that he'd met her at another time.

"That sounds like a fine ambition. Let's try to get to the soup."

The soup arrived, and they talked about inconsequential things. She asked him about his work; she called him "Samuel"; he corrected her. She'd been asking him questions since they arrived. Years ago he would have had questions to ask *her*, but now . . . now, he didn't want to know. The world went on, but his soul no longer went out to meet it.

As they spoke and, for politeness's sake, he pretended to be interested in what she was saying, he was thinking about her body. Her body and the way she wore it.

She seemed to be almost unaware of her body—not unaware, but embarrassed, even ashamed. She could have been intensely foxy if she'd chosen to be, but instead she'd chosen the role of the intellectual, awkward and inward, hunching down to make herself less imposing and hiding her face behind her hair. Every time he'd met her, he'd seen her with a kind of double vision. He couldn't help imagining her as she would be if she took advantage of her statuesqueness and her looks, and he created an imaginary, erotically commanding Maud who stood beside the real Maud, and who sometimes, for fleeting moments, inhabited her, and it was dizzying to consider the possibility that he might be the man who could inspire the two Mauds to come together.

Her attractiveness seemed to make her uneasy, but it wasn't the kind of thing you could hide. She had long legs that she wrapped around each other when she sat—she crossed her legs at the knee and then she tucked one foot behind the shin of the other leg. She probably contorted herself in this fashion out of nervousness, but her legs were so incredibly long that it made her look like some sort of snake goddess: it was a gesture that made her seem both demure and overwhelmingly sexual.

When George and Celia had told him about all her virtues (they placed particular emphasis on how smart she was: "It'll be nice for you to be going out with a woman who's smarter than you are," George had said), he thought that even if she was as special as they said she was, he still didn't want to meet her. He had had enough. And then when she dropped by, he'd been immediately . . . well, George and Celia had said that he looked smitten, but that wasn't it at all. It wasn't smittenness: he'd been in the deep freeze too long to feel anything as urgent as that. Rather, when he met her, it was as if he heard a faint sound that reminded him of something, something that had left his life so long ago that he could barely remember what it was.

The waitress appeared and asked them a question. He wasn't listening. After she left, Maud said, "It would be nice if just once you could go to a restaurant where the waiters didn't address people as 'You guys.'"

He remembered the way Leila used to complain in restaurants. She was always getting into fights with waiters. "That's the kind of thing my ex-wife used to say. It used to drive her nuts."

"I don't think I've heard you had a wife."

It was stupid of him to have said that. He didn't want to talk about his old life.

"I had a wife."

"It didn't work out?" Maud said.

"If it had worked out I wouldn't be here."

"Why didn't it work out?"

"Things don't always work out in life."

"I know that. But what I meant was, why didn't this particular relationship work out?"

He didn't say anything, just had another sip of his drink.

"Is it a horrible secret?" she said.

"It's not a secret," he said. "But it *is* horrible."

"I'm sorry," she said. "I shouldn't have been so flippant."

"That's all right."

He could feel her giving up. She'd finally gotten the message.

The waitress brought the bill, he paid it, they went out to the Promenade. A brittle wind blew from the river. Manhattan looked broken and hopeless across the way.

They walked for another minute, talking about nothing of importance — something about how she felt about being tall.

From the first, he had found it weirdly exciting that she was taller than he was, but of course he didn't tell her that.

"I should probably get home," she said. "I should do some work on my dissertation."

She was going home. The experiment was over. This was good.

Probably she would avoid him now: she wouldn't visit George and Celia's again while he was working there. He would never have to see her again.

"Well, it was nice to see you," Maud said. "I'm glad we could get together. Arab and Jew. A testament to the fact that people can rise above their ancient prejudices."

She was smiling sarcastically. Her eyes were alive with sharpness, intelligence, wit. He wanted to find out whether George and Celia were right: whether she really was more intelligent than he was. And also, he wanted to kiss her. But that was just a momentary rush of lust, not something he wanted to act on. What he really wanted to do was to go home by himself and never see her again.

"The swarthy Arab and the brainy Jew," he said.

"Brainy but resourceful. Don't forget, we defeated you in battle. Many times."

She said this with a light braggy flirtatious tone, and now besides being sexually electrified by her nearness, he felt something else: some weird shock of powerlessness, partly because she was taller than he was and partly because she spoke to him as if he were the representative of a defeated people. Why on earth did he find this exciting? It was hard to say why, but—

He didn't know what he was doing and then when he knew what he was doing he didn't know why he was doing it, but he moved quickly toward her and kissed her. Then he kissed her again. She wasn't completely returning his kiss but she wasn't moving away from it either.

Is this the way it's starting? Wanting her because I'm angry at her? Wanting her because she makes me feel defeated? What is going on here? In the cold he was working his fingers underneath the layers of her jacket and sweater. She, tentatively, inquisitively, hesitantly, was returning his kiss.

The kiss was interesting, but something else was affecting him more than the kiss. They were pressed against each other, and he could feel each breath she took: long and slow and steady and calm and deep. His own breathing was growing calmer and deeper in response. He felt as if he was receiving some sort of spiritual CPR. He felt bafflingly connected to her. Breath of life.

What is going on here? he thought. What am I doing?

SEVEN

"You look great," Vivian said.

This was the second person in two days who had told Eleanor this. Fifty-nine, overweight, out of shape, and perpetually worried about her future, she knew it was unlikely to be true.

She thought she understood why they were saying this. When Eleanor encountered old friends or acquaintances who looked awful, she would sometimes feel guilty about noticing that they looked awful, and, as a way of atoning, she would tell them how good they looked.

"I look great, do I?" Eleanor said. "I look great because I've let myself go to hell?"

"You look great because you don't look like you're trying to please anybody anymore. So you've gained ten pounds. Big deal. You look like yourself now."

Vivian was being kind: it had been more like twenty pounds, even before Eleanor got rid of her scale.

Sometimes she felt like an actress who had put on weight for a role. The role of the abandoned woman.

It was easy for Vivian to tell other people not to worry about their weight. She had been gaunt since girlhood. Eleanor knew this, because they had been friends since fourth grade. They'd both grown up in Portland, and they'd found their way to New York within five years of each other.

Eleanor's doctor had ordered her to start exercising, and, not wanting to jog or ride a stationary bicycle or challenge her coordination on one of those moon machines, she had decided to learn to swim. Vivian had offered to teach her, and now, at seven in the morning, they were in the women's locker room of the 92nd Street Y, getting ready for the first lesson.

Eleanor was changing into a one-piece bathing suit that she had bought the day before. She wished you were allowed to swim in street clothes.

She went gingerly down the steps into the shallow part of the pool. Vivian dived in at the deep end and swam toward Eleanor.

"You're such a coward," Vivian said. "You're not going to *drown*." She splashed a little water toward Eleanor, not to get her wet, just to convey the idea of splashing. "Water is your friend."

Patiently and slowly, Vivian introduced Eleanor to the fundamentals of swimming. First they stood elbow-deep in the water and Vivian showed Eleanor how to use her arms in the dog paddle and the crawl. Then she led Eleanor to the edge of the pool, had her hold on to the lip, and directed her to let her legs float up and start kicking.

"Now you've got the parts," Vivian said. "All you have to do is put them together."

Eleanor had news that she wanted to share with Vivian. Gossip. Although is it gossip if it's about your own life? But she couldn't bring herself to talk about it. It seemed too high-schoolish. *You remember that boy I used to like? I got a phone call from him the other day* . . . The fact that it was high-schoolish probably shouldn't have been a problem, since she'd known Vivian since long before high school. But it was.

"How are the interviews going?" Eleanor asked. Vivian, who was a historian, was editing an oral history of women in the labor movement.

"It's eerie. The people I'm talking to were once the most vital people of their generation, and to look at them now . . .

There should be something beautiful about old age. But there isn't."

Vivian put her hands on Eleanor's shoulders and turned her around and said, "Now we swim." She showed Eleanor how to push off from the edge of the pool, and she swam beside her as Eleanor kicked frantically. Eleanor was sure she was doing it all wrong. She felt like a child's windup bath toy, inefficiently paddling halfway across the tub before tipping over onto its side and sinking.

She couldn't spare any thought to the question of how to kick more efficiently because she was trying to make sure that she didn't gulp down any of the disgusting chlorinated water. Stroke with your left arm, twist your neck, feel pain, breathe, put your head back in the water, stroke with your right arm—she kept screwing up the rhythm and breathing when her mouth was in the water and then spitting the water out. Somehow she reached the other end of the pool. She clutched the side of the pool to hold herself up. Vivian was beside her, treading water.

"I think you should know that I'm feeling this urge to drown you," Vivian said.

Without her glasses, Vivian did look a little frightening. She had tight, sinewy, strappy muscles, and a face that was hardened and almost brutal—a face that might have been chiseled by a sculptor who had fallen out of love with the idea of beauty.

Her face expressed her warriorlike will to mask herself, to efface all traces of the defenseless creature she felt herself to be.

For decades, the two of them had been making the opposite choices. Vivian didn't have children, and she'd never had a serious relationship. In order to concentrate on reading, writing, and thinking, she had refused everything else. A long time ago, there had been a man, and sometime after that there had been a woman, but the pull of neither had been strong enough to distract her for long from her single-minded dedication to her calling.

Eleanor admired her friend, but she sometimes thought that she had sacrificed too much. Of course, Vivian probably thought the same thing about her.

For Vivian, the important question about people was what they had done with their professional lives. She seemed to regard raising children as a sort of hobby, not an endeavor substantial enough to deflect a serious person from the duty to make a contribution in the wider world.

Eleanor's contribution had been limited. When she was young she'd had a clear idea of her future: she was going to be a writer and a psychologist. She imagined herself writing novels, short stories, and books about psychology—not textbooks, but case studies, informed by a fiction writer's eye. She met Adam just after she got her BA in psychology, and within six months of meeting him, she was pregnant with Carl. During the first few months of her pregnancy, she looked for a job, but in her third trimester, her doctor put her on bed rest, and she stopped thinking about the work world, and didn't begin to think about it again until many years later, after Maud was born. Eleanor went back to school, got her master's degree in psychology—feeling like Rip Van Winkle because of the way the intellectual landscape of the profession had changed—and set up a private practice. She wasn't yet forty at the time, but she felt perpetually haunted by a sense of belatedness: she was getting started so much later than she'd planned.

She never did return to writing. Trying to pursue a career as a psychologist while taking care of three children was almost more than she could do. She never stopped hoping that she might find a way to turn some of her energies to writing some-day, but she had to place the hope into a sort of dream-deferment plan, where it had remained for almost forty years.

She had never stopped *thinking* about writing. It often struck her as unbelievable that she hadn't become a writer after all; it was as if she were living the wrong life. But as Adam, slow and steady and unstoppable, had become more and more of a suc-cess, her own dreams of being a writer had started to seem child-ish. She had wanted to be a writer long before she had ever met him, but at some point during their marriage she had convinced herself that if she ever did get back to writing, everyone would think that she was pathetically trying to imitate her husband.

When you can't have the life you'd hoped for, the great test of character is what you make of the life you have. The thing she could be proud of was that she'd given herself fully to her life. She hadn't diminished herself by making the mistake that some of her friends had made: unable to live the lives they'd dreamed of, they had ended up stuck in a ghostly limbo, failing to com-mit themselves to the lives they actually had.

For a few minutes they didn't speak, as Vivian tried to help Eleanor learn to float. Floating was harder than making your way across the pool. Vivian gently supported her with her hands while Eleanor lay on the water, feeling tragically heavy, a para-lyzed porpoise, doomed to go down.

"You can do this," Vivian said. "All you have to do is relax. All you have to do is stop *trying*."

Eleanor was aware that this lesson had a conclusion that was foreordained, just as it is foreordained that a romantic comedy will conclude with a marriage. The conclusion was that Eleanor would learn to float, and it would be not only a swimming les-son but a lesson about life. It would be a lesson about letting go (you learn to float only after you've stopped trying) and a lesson about feminist renewal (older woman conquers fears, learns something new).

She was lying in the water with her eyes closed, and Vivian was holding her up gently, one hand on her back and the other under her knees, and Eleanor visualized the beautiful outcome: Vivian, without letting her know it, would remove her hands, and Eleanor would realize only after a minute or two that she was floating on her own, and the realization would blossom into a kind of spiritual awakening, and she would lie in ease and comfort on the water, a woman reborn.

Unfortunately, her body wouldn't cooperate. Every time Vivian let go, Eleanor started sinking.

"Maybe some people weren't meant to learn to swim," Eleanor said.

"That's possible," Vivian said.

After they dressed, they had breakfast in a coffee shop on Lexington Avenue. Eleanor still didn't know whether she wanted to share the thing that she was thinking about, but Vivian had known her too long for her to be able to conceal it.

"You look like you have something to say," Vivian said.

"I do. I have news."

"So what is it?"

"I'm not sure this is a good time to talk about it. I don't think we have time to discuss the ramifications," Eleanor said. It was almost nine, and both of them had to be at work soon.

"You can't tell me you have news and then not tell me what it is."

"I guess that's true," Eleanor said, relieved. "Okay. I got a phone message from Patrick."

"Patrick?" Vivian said.

"Patrick."

"*Patrick Patrick?*" Vivian said.

Eleanor didn't say anything, because she didn't want to keep saying the name Patrick anymore.

"Did he hear you're getting divorced? What did he say? What did *you* say? How *is* he?"

"I don't know. He just left a message. I haven't called him back."

A familiar expression came over Vivian's face, an exasperated-with-her-old-friend look.

"When are you going to?"

"I'm not sure."

"*Are* you going to?"

"I'm not sure."

"*Why* haven't you called him? Don't tell me: you're not sure."

Eleanor didn't speak.

Vivian drummed her fingers on the table, trying, evidently, to think of a question that might yield a different answer.

"What harm could there be in calling him back?" Vivian said. "Don't answer that. Ellie: listen to me. You could turn out to be the love of each other's life. Or, you could have an awkward fifteen-minute conversation and never talk to each other again. In either case, what can you lose?"

"I don't know," Eleanor said. "I don't know what I could lose."

And yet she had the feeling that she could lose something.

"I wonder what he's like now," Vivian said. "I haven't thought about him in about twenty years."

"I've thought about him a lot," Eleanor said.

We love some people because of what we see in them; we love others because of what they help us see in ourselves. Patrick was the only person Eleanor had loved for both reasons. He was not a man who would have impressed you if you saw him on the street or met him at a party. But when she was with him, the world seemed calmer; the world seemed to make more sense. And when she was with him, she felt—well, she had never been able to decide whether she had felt more *than* herself or more *like* herself.

In many ways it had been an unlikely romance. Patrick, when she had last seen him, nearly forty years ago, was well on the way to becoming a labor-union bureaucrat. He represented the third generation of a family of die-hard trade unionists; he was the first member of his family to go to college. He was an idealist, but he was also tenaciously practical and tough as nails. She, at the time, thought of herself as a free spirit, an anarchist, an artist. She wasn't any of these things anymore. She wondered if Patrick had changed as much as she had.

"You *have* to call him back," Vivian said. "If not for yourself, you should do it for me. It would be the most romantic story I've ever heard in my life. He could be your true love."

Someone who didn't know Vivian very well might have thought it odd to hear her talk about romance in this way. But it wasn't. Beneath the cowl of her cynicism, Vivian was a thorough romantic. She was alone in life not because she didn't believe in true love, but because she did.

Eleanor didn't want to believe that Patrick might be her true love, because if that was so, it made the rest of her life one long mistake.

"It's better to let him remain a memory. What if he's become a Republican? I don't think I could handle that."

"Labor organizers don't become Republicans," Vivian said. "You have to call him."

"What if he's become a drunk? Don't tell me labor organizers don't become drunks."

"You have to call him."

When she thought of calling him, she felt excited. But she

was troubled that it excited her as much as this. She hadn't felt this kind of nervous anticipation about anything in a long time, and it disturbed her that the feeling didn't concern her own work, didn't concern any effort of her own toward self-creation, but instead concerned the pie-in-the-sky possibility of getting together with a boyfriend from almost forty years ago.

"Well, I don't know," Eleanor said. "We'll see."

EIGHT

A dam didn't object to the idea that his dead were calling out to him. What he objected to was the idea that they were calling out for him to join them.

He was in the lobby of the building where Izzy Cantor had lived with his wife, Ruth, during the last twenty-five years of his life. It was a brown brick prewar building just off Broadway. The lobby smelled of Jewishness and time.

He was happy to have escaped from all this—from this Upper West Side world, the world of the fathers, the world of late-night conversations about Marx and Freud in homey little delicatessens of dubious cleanliness, the world that had seemed to be his destined burial ground. He took the elevator to the fifteenth floor.

It required a full minute for Ruth to open her door: she had to turn three locks and then slide the chain away. When she finally got it open, he was taken aback by how badly she'd deteriorated. Her skin was an unhealthy blue, like a slice of ham that had been left too long in the refrigerator and had aged oddly. She seemed to have shrunk by a foot. And she had let herself go. When they were younger, Ruth had always reached for elegance; now she was in an old gray bathrobe and slippers.

Adam wasn't sure how long it had been since he'd seen her. Could it have been two years?

Izzy had been seven or eight years older than Adam, and Ruth in turn had been four or five years older than Izzy. Adam couldn't remember anyone's age. When he'd first met Ruth, she'd seemed the archetype of the desirable older woman—mysterious, alluring, possessed of secret lore. She'd lived on a kibbutz in Israel in the late 1950s and for years had retained or affected a slight accent, and although from his current vantage point Adam could imagine few things less appealing than life on a kibbutz—men hectoring women about fine points of socialist ideology; women muscular and without makeup; children running around filthy and snot-nosed because no one person in particular was responsible for keeping any of them clean; and meetings, meetings, meetings—at the time it had lent her an exotic air.

"How are you, Ruthie? You look wonderful."

"How am I? Everything hurts." She smiled and touched him on the arm. "I'm glad you could come."

"Of course. I'm only sorry I couldn't come earlier." *I'm only sorry I never changed my phone number.*

She led him down the long cramped hall. The bookcases that lined it were crowded with books that hadn't quite outlived their time. *The Rise of David Levinsky. Jews Without Money. Summer in Williamsburg. The Unpossessed.* Sometimes Adam would come across a cluster of books like this at a used-book sale, and he would know for sure that another old Jewish leftist had died.

He himself had staged a bonfire at the end of the century. In a rented cabin in Maine he had burned his papers, and soon after that he'd given most of his old books away to a public library. He'd rid himself of the things that had marked him as a member of a dying generation.

It was an enormous apartment, though Izzy had never made a dime. The story of literary New York, Adam thought, was the story of rent control. But all that was over now.

"Will you excuse me for a minute?" Ruth said. "I didn't forget you were coming, but I lost track of the time. I just want to freshen up."

She left him alone in the den.

The smell of the place carried overwhelming evidence of her sadness. A smell composed of many different things: microscopic flakes of skin from a lonely, aged body; dust mites accumulated over several decades; the troubling traceless scent given off by someone who has long been sexually deprived; and the faint scent of cat urine, lingering throughout the apartment even though Lionel, Izzy and Ruth's cat, had died almost a decade ago, just after Izzy died.

But now that she was out of the room, he felt more at home. He wondered how many hours he'd spent in this room with Izzy, bullshitting about politics or gossiping or talking about books. Talking about books, mostly. Adam, now, had reached an age at which he didn't give a damn about literature: writing was a trade to him like any other. But Izzy had never lost the radiant-hearted exuberance of his youth.

When Ruth reappeared he saw that she had made a heroic effort to pull herself together. She wore a white cotton blouse and a long skirt. She was still reaching toward elegance, it seemed.

"You must be wondering why I've been so persistent. I think I must have called you about five times."

More like twenty, he thought. But before he had a chance to say anything, she clasped his hand. "I have some exciting news. News about Izzy."

Has he come back from the dead? Adam thought. That was the only news about Izzy that would qualify as truly exciting.

But of course he knew what Ruth was going to tell him. Somehow she'd gotten wind of Jeffrey Lipkin and his project, and she was giddy at the thought that someone was going to write Izzy's biography.

"Lillian died this past summer," Ruth said. "Did you hear?"

Lillian was Izzy's sister. He didn't know what this had to do with anything.

"No. I didn't know," Adam said. "I'm sorry."

Actually, he didn't care. Lillian had always been a querulous, disagreeable woman; whether she was alive or dead didn't matter to him.

"I never liked her either," Ruth said, and Adam smiled, remembering why he used to be fond of her. "Anyway, her kids were closing up the house, and when they went through the attic, they found two huge chests filled with Izzy's papers. Evidently he'd been storing things at Lillian's for years. I'm not surprised he never told me. Izzy loved his secrets. Why Lillian never bothered to tell me I'll never know."

Adam was still a step behind. He was still trying to see how this connected to Jeffrey, even though he was beginning to see that it didn't connect at all. That maybe Ruth hadn't heard of Jeffrey yet.

"What was in it?" Adam said.

"Copies of his letters, for one thing. I started looking through them but I can't take it for more than a few minutes at a time. They make me miss him too much."

Adam tried to make a sympathetic sound, but what came out of him sounded, to his own ears at least, like a grunt of indifference, which was pretty much what he actually felt.

He was reminded of the reason he'd increasingly found Ruth a good person to avoid. There was something clammy and unappealing about her. She had become a professional widow.

During their marriage, Ruth had been Izzy's greatest supporter. Unlike Ellie, she had never had literary ambitions of her own, so her admiration for Izzy had always been free of any tinge of rivalry. (More than once, during their dinners together, while Izzy was in the midst of telling some story that Adam and Eleanor had heard many times before, a story that Ruth must have heard *hundreds* of times before, Adam had seen Ruth listening in a rapture of attentiveness, as if every word were a revelation.) And in the years since his death she'd become even more obsessively her husband's champion. She had turned all her energy and all her gifts toward the effort to promote his reputation. She wanted the world to finally recognize Izzy's merit, as it never really had during his lifetime. To Adam it seemed like a fool's mission: we die and the world flows on, and the idea that it will pluck your dead husband from the rut of his obscurity and carry his name into the future struck him as impossibly naïve.

Adam was untroubled by the thought that the world would forget him as soon as he was gone, that his reputation would not merely grow dim but disappear. He wanted to hold on to his place in the world while he was alive, and he didn't give a damn what happened after he was gone.

He thought that Ruth, who fancied herself psychologically sophisticated, was evading the evidence of her own vanity. It's Ruth you mourn for, he wanted to say to her: it's your own disappearance you fear. But you can't admit it to yourself, so you make these frantic efforts on behalf of Izzy's memory.

"I don't know what to do with them," she said. "The letters. Brandeis has all the manuscripts, but they've never treated me very nicely. I wonder whether Columbia might want them."

Adam shrugged.

"Somebody must want them," she said. "Izzy wrote the most interesting letters!"

This, surely, was the moment to tell her about Jeffrey. It was Jeffrey who should have them—who should have the first look at them, at least. This was the moment to give her Jeffrey's number, surround her with a congratulatory embrace, and tell her that her dream might well come true. A new generation was going to learn about Isidore Cantor.

But he already knew that he was going to tell her no such thing. If he had any say in the matter, she and Jeffrey would never meet. She would never find out about him at all.

"But this is the thing I've been dying to tell you, Adam. This is the reason I've been calling you. It wasn't just letters. It wasn't just notebooks. There was also a manuscript."

"You're kidding me. They found the book?"

"They found the book."

Ruth was actually standing, as if it was obligatory to rise when the book was mentioned. She was radiant, quivering with awe. The book.

Neither of them needed to name it. There could be no question about what book they were referring to.

During the last ten years of his life, a period in which he had published two novels, Izzy had worked steadily on a third, which he kept saying was the best thing he had ever written. Izzy had been famously self-deprecating, so to hear him speak well of anything he was writing was a surprise. After Izzy died, Ruth had expected to find it in his papers, but she'd found no trace of it.

"Have you read it?" Adam said.

"I've read it. I have. I've read it twice. I read it on Saturday, the day I got it. I started at eight o'clock at night and I read all the way into the morning. And then I read it again on Monday and Tuesday. I wanted to read it more slowly, so I could appreciate all the nuances. I think it really is his best book. I think it's brilliant."

This, Adam thought, was unlikely. Izzy had written himself

out many years ago. He'd had a thin vein of precious ore, had mined it conscientiously, but had exhausted it decades ago.

"That's wonderful, Ruth."

"I really think that this is the one that could do it, Adam. This is the one that could cement his reputation. It's funny. It's the 'breakout' book that his publisher was always asking for and he was never interested in writing. It turned out that he wrote it, even though he never tried to write it. And it's going to come out only after he died."

Adam nodded, seeking to infuse his smile with warmth, seeking to look as if he believed there was a chance that any of this was true.

Many, many years ago, he—well, he'd never been in love with Ruth, but there had been a period when she'd haunted his thoughts. He and Ellie and Ruth and Izzy used to get together often; inevitably the woman who doesn't accompany you home begins to seem more attractive than the woman who does. Ruth, the older woman, had seemed wise and calm and queenly, while Ellie in those days had seemed hectic and distracted, a blur of apologies and nervous jokes. One day when Izzy was out of town, Adam had dropped by, ostensibly to borrow a book but really because he had wanted to be near her. He hadn't actually thought that anything would happen, but he wanted to spend an hour in her orbit, in the charged atmosphere of their desire. She had made coffee and placed a tray on the coffee table, and then she'd sat next to him on the couch and leaned over, brushing against him, toward the sugar bowl, and dropped two sugar cubes into his coffee and said, "You take sugar, don't you? I suppose I should have asked." He didn't say anything, and then she said, "I feel like we're in a movie," and for some reason he knew that this was his cue to kiss her.

He wondered whether all this had happened on the same couch where they were sitting now. It looked old enough. He remembered being surprised by how vulnerable she allowed herself to be—whispers and sighs and little moans.

They had spent the afternoon on the couch, though, come to think of it, he couldn't quite remember whether they'd actually, technically, made love. They'd done something, but he couldn't quite remember what.

How strange that they were once so hot for each other. He couldn't have summoned up any interest in her now, not even if he wanted to. Even if he could reverse the effects of global warming just by getting an erection for Ruth, the accomplishment would be beyond him.

What would she think if she saw him on the street with Thea? She'd definitely have a few acid things to say—about his second childhood or about the unfairness of a society in which older men can take up with younger women while older women are, as Eleanor had once pompously put it, "disappeared."

All these thoughts went through his mind in telegraphic form, in an instant.

"Thank you for telling me about this, Ruth. But is that all? Is there anything you need from me? Anything you want me to do?"

"Yes, there is, Adam. Thank you for asking. There *is* something I want you to do. I want you to read it. I think it's wonderful, but I'm his widow. I'm his wife. I need you to tell me if it's as good as I think it is. And if it is, I would love it if you could help me find a publisher. New Directions was faithful to Izzy, but I don't know anybody there anymore, and I'm not really sure they'd be the best publisher for him at this point anyway."

"Of course, Ruth. Of course I'll read it. And I'll do what I can."

"Wonderful," she said. "I'm so thankful."

She went to the bedroom and returned with a cardboard box and set it on the coffee table. He lifted the cover and took a look inside. The title of the manuscript was *So Late So Early*. He sneaked a look at the last page, not to see how it ended but to see how long it was. Six hundred pages. It would be a chore.

"If you could read it sooner rather than later, that would be a special favor to me," Ruth said.

"I'll try, Ruth, but I don't know. I've got a lecture to give at Bennington next week that I still haven't prepared for, and after that I'm committed to a weeklong workshop in Florence. And after that—I don't even want to tell you all the ridiculous commitments I've made."

"I'm sure those things are important, Adam, and I hate to impose on your time. But if you could read it sooner rather than later, I would appreciate it."

Something about her tone made him want to ask if there was a special reason she felt pressed for time. Ruth had had breast cancer a few years ago. Was she ill again? He didn't ask.

"It's big," she said, "but it's hard to put down. I told you I read it in a night; I wouldn't be surprised if you do too. Maybe I can't judge . . . I thought everything he did was great. But I really think you might end up agreeing with me that it was the best thing he'd ever written."

Doubtful, Adam thought. Doubtful.

"I have a feeling you might be right," he said, wondering if his utter lack of sincerity was obvious. "I'll get to it as soon as I can. This isn't your only copy, is it? I wouldn't want to lose your only copy."

"I have another. Don't worry. Izzy always made a carbon copy of everything he wrote."

A carbon copy! Adam was surprised that he'd forgotten. Though Izzy had lived half a block away from a copy shop, he'd made carbon copies of everything he wrote. For reasons that would remain a mystery, he didn't trust copy shops.

Known to all the world as sunny and sane, Izzy had had an odd obsessive secretive streak. It was so like him to hide his most cherished work at the home of his sister—his unliterary, uninterested sister. He was like some furred and furtive creature hiding bright objects in the darkest place he could find.

Adam looked at his watch. He tried to do it without her noticing, but she noticed.

"Do you have to go already?" she said.

"I wish I could stay, but I have about twelve different places I have to be in a half hour. All at once."

"You sure you wouldn't like to have some tea? I have some strudel, if you like. I can heat it up in a jiffy. I think I have ice cream too."

"I wish I could," he said.

"Then *do*. You just got here."

He imagined having to fight his way past her as she blocked the door. He didn't say anything.

Ruth got the message. "I'm sorry. I won't keep you." She stood up. "Sometimes it just gets so bleak," she said. "I'd say that all I have left is my daughter, but I don't even know if I can honestly say that I have my daughter anymore. I hardly ever hear from her these days."

She walked him to the door. Her excitement of a few minutes ago was all gone.

"I just feel so lonely," she said. "And lately I've been in so much pain that I can barely make it out of bed." For years she had suffered from arthritis. "Sometimes I still don't understand how everything could have ended up like this."

There was a limit to his ability to humor her. He was putting his coat on, and he thought he should probably just leave, but he couldn't stop himself from speaking.

"You're acting like a child, Ruth. It's like you've just found out that there aren't any happy endings. Where have you *been*? Hasn't it always been obvious that everything ends in shit?"

Ruth looked genuinely shocked. "That's a horrible way to look at things."

"Be that as it may. It's the truth."

"It hasn't ended in shit for you. You seem to be happy. You have three beautiful children. You have perfect teeth."

"Yes," he said, "I do have perfect teeth." Two years ago he'd had his mouth reconstructed and his teeth bleached.

"Well then." She was smiling, letting go of her self-pity. "And I hear you have a new girlfriend. With perky breasts."

"That's true too, Ruth. But I know that I'm likely to end up soiling my pajamas every night and not being able to clean myself. And not recognizing my three beautiful children. And by the time that happens, my perky-breasted girlfriend is going to be long gone. Izzy was lucky, when you think about it. He had his mind until the end. And he had you."

She didn't respond to this. In silence she unlocked her three locks. He kissed her chastely on the cheek and was slightly repulsed by her odor, although it was nothing more than the odor of an old woman. He wondered whether his own odor too was repulsive, and wondered why Thea was with him. Could it be that she didn't find his skin and his breath and his hair and his nostrils and his lips and his mouth and his teeth—could it be that she didn't find them repulsive? He held the cardboard box in the air as if it were something he was dying to get to, and said, "I'll call you."

On the street he had an urge to toss the manuscript into a

Dumpster, just because he was exasperated with Ruth. Her illusions, her hopefulness, her woe.

He was irritated with himself for losing control—for saying anything that he actually felt.

After a block or two, he stopped being angry with himself. Nothing about the encounter mattered enough to get upset about. The cardboard box was heavy under his arm. He began to feel half interested in the thing. Adam was going to be spending a few hours in Izzy's company again. He wondered what his old friend had to say.

NINE

Maud could see Samir waiting for her near the monkey bars. Sitting on a bench, unaware that he was being observed, he didn't look the way he usually did. He usually looked tense, uncomfortable in his own skin. Now, breaking off a piece of a pretzel and tossing it toward a bird, he just looked sad.

It was a mild Saturday afternoon and Central Park was crowded. She hadn't seen him since they'd had dinner a week earlier. Nothing had come from their odd groping moment on the Promenade: they had made out for a little while and then, as if mutually bewildered, gone their separate ways. She thought she might never hear from him again, but eventually he'd called her and asked if she wanted to spend this Saturday afternoon together.

He didn't notice her until she was standing over him, casting her shadow over his face. He looked up and smiled at her, but with a touch of remoteness, and she could see that as far as he was concerned, they were back at square one. She didn't want to accept that, didn't want to allow things to go backward, so before he had a chance to stand up, she put her hands on his shoulders and kissed him on the mouth. But his kiss was stiff and held-back.

"Hello," he said.

"It's good to see you."

They were planning to go to an outdoor concert. The Singles, a band that she'd read about in *The Village Voice,* were playing that afternoon at the bandshell.

"Which way?" he said.

They began to walk. It was early November but it felt like the height of spring.

The park was filled with families. They had to walk slowly because of the stroller armadas heading in both directions on the path.

Maud was interested in every child they passed, but her closest scrutiny was reserved for the mothers. Trim, athletic, competent mothers, all of whom, doubtless, were also important figures in the worlds of law, entertainment, finance. The warrior-mothers of Manhattan.

Here in stroller heaven, on this warm afternoon, almost all the families they passed looked happy, and Maud experienced a dividedness that was familiar to her. When she was a girl she'd always assumed she'd be a mother someday. But her two trips to the snake pit had made her reconsider. On the female side of her family, there was a strain of . . . something. Something not quite right. Her mother was unimprovably solid, sane to a fault, but several of the women in the family past had fought losing struggles against a kind of darkness that would probably now be diagnosed as depression, but that had been called madness then. When Maud thought about having children, she worried that she wouldn't be able to hold on to her equilibrium long enough to usher them safely past infancy. She imagined herself sitting in a stunned stupor while her baby howled in its crib.

"Sometimes I feel really happy that my brothers have kids," she said. "They've taken care of the family obligation to bring children into the world. My parents already have all the heirs they need."

She'd said this spontaneously, in the flow of the moment, but it was also true that she'd been planning to mention at some point that she didn't intend to have children. She'd wanted him to know.

Sometimes she dated guys who didn't want children, and it put their minds at rest when she told them that she didn't either; and once in a blue moon she'd dated a guy who *did* want children, and it was only fair to let this kind of guy know that she was one of the rare women who didn't.

She didn't know what Samir made of this information. He didn't say anything.

A man was selling ice cream from a cart, and Maud stopped to buy a Popsicle.

"Seneca wouldn't approve of me," she said to Samir as she tore the wrapper off. "I've been reading him all week and I feel like I'm letting him down."

"You've been letting him down," Samir said. He said this as a flat statement. It was as if he wouldn't even commit himself to asking a question. But she decided to take it as a question.

"He's very severe," she said. "He was the father of Stoicism. I don't know what he'd say about the Popsicle." She started telling him about Seneca. It was easy, because she had been reading him with devotion for years. He wasn't among the two or three philosophers who were closest to her heart, because there was finally something life-denying about his asceticism, but even so, she admired the fierceness, the purity of his thought. The philosophers closest to her heart were those who wrote about how we can find a way to recognize one another, empathize with one another—Kant and Buber and Levinas. But she also needed philosophers like Seneca and Schopenhauer, thinkers with a chillier mission: the mission to remind us all that life ends in nothingness, and that there is no God, no beneficent universe, to confer meaning on our lives from the outside. She needed them to remind her that the meanings we assign to our lives are the only meanings they will finally have.

She didn't want to endure any more awkward silences; she was talking about Seneca just to make some noise. But why was Samir being so withdrawn again? He was the one who'd bolted up at the end of their date last time and launched their make-out session; he was the one who'd called to suggest they get together again. She felt played with. He wasn't even looking at her. He was staring off at a family on a picnic—two kids and two parents, spread out on a blanket. He looked angry.

TEN

It was a beautiful warm afternoon, and the park was filled with families. Samir didn't notice the mothers, because he was too attracted to Maud to notice other women. And he didn't look at the children, because it would have hurt too much. So the only people he noticed were the fathers. Fathers pushing strollers; fathers wearing Snuglis; fathers leading children by the hand. Young fathers, distracted, because they had so much raw animal life in them that they couldn't give themselves over to the task of caring for their young. Older fathers: bearded, balding, considerate, attentive, somewhat emasculated midlife dads.

Samir wanted to kill them all. He wanted to tear their scraggly little beards off, punch their teeth in, put his index fingers in their eyes and watch the retinal jelly pop out like pus.

Maud was talking about philosophy, in the study of which she was absolutely and touchingly absorbed. He didn't know if he'd ever met anyone this pure, didn't know if he'd ever met anyone who lived more genuinely for ideas than she did. Even in their brief and limited and strange acquaintance, he had found this clear.

Pure-minded woman.

But what was the point of being here with her?

"On the other hand," she said, "maybe Seneca himself enjoyed a Popsicle from time to time. In secret."

"Do you think so?"

"I wouldn't put it past him. He was always preaching indifference to worldly pleasures and worldly success, but when you read his biography it turns out that he did everything he could to ingratiate himself with whoever was ruling Rome at the time. He wanted to be with the in-crowd."

"So he was just another hypocrite."

"Yes," she said. "Probably. And some people conclude that that makes his ideas worthless. But I'm not sure. Does that really mean there's something wrong about the ideas themselves? Maybe an idea can be true and useful even if the person who thought of it can't quite put it into practice."

A group of about twenty children, flanked by two beleaguered grown-ups, was converging on the ice-cream cart.

If he were an honest man he would simply walk away. She claimed she didn't want children, but he didn't believe it. He knew that she did want children. She had to. She was a life-giver, a life-giver down to her bones; he could feel that. And so he was sure that he knew what she wanted, even if she herself didn't know it yet.

If he were an honest man he'd walk away, because he had nothing to give her. She was drawn to him because of an illusion. If she could see him as he really was, she would find that he was not a human being at all. He was just a construction, a thing that kept itself going by means of little contraptions: he had a motor in his throat that started turning when he needed to talk; he had several tiny men working machines inside him to make sure that he smiled when he was supposed to smile; he retained the muscle memory to do his carpentry; but it was all shit, and he wasn't sure how anyone ever could miss it, could miss the obvious fact that he was through.

As he looked at the children clustered around the ice-cream cart, all he could think was Zahra, Zahra, Zahra. None of them was Zahra. None of them was his dear one. None of them was his child.

The park was horrible. He needed to get away from all these *people*. Especially these children, but everyone else as well. He changed direction and led her toward a wooded part of the park.

"I think this is called the Ramble," Maud said. "It's about the only part of the park where a person can get lost. I remember once wandering in here as a kid and not being able to find my way out. I was terrified."

But even from here you could hear them, you could hear the children's voices. It was no good.

He turned to Maud and touched her arm. It was the first time he had touched her since he'd mashed up against her on the Promenade.

"I have to go," he said. "I apologize for everything. You seem like a special person, but I really have to go."

Eleven

Okay. Get lost.
    This was the first thing she thought of saying, because she was sick of this, this doomed effort to woo him. But she didn't say it, because she didn't want him to go.
    Don't go. Please.
    This was the second thing she thought of saying, because despite the ample evidence that he had barricaded himself off from human contact, she was weirdly and irrevocably drawn to him. But she didn't say it, because it would have sounded weak. She had no interest in pleading.
    You're not going anywhere.
    That was the third thing she thought of saying. And this is what she said.
    "You're not going anywhere. You know that."
    She moved closer to him. She was looking down at him.
    He was the first man she'd ever been with whom she *could* look down at, and it filled her with a sense of her own power.
    She had always been attracted to tall men. So this was something new. Samir was half a head shorter than she was, and she felt obscurely that the disparity in size was part of the attraction here, part of the mutual attraction, part of why he couldn't quite walk away from her, part of a charm that she could figure out how to work.
    He looked puzzled. But he wasn't walking away. He was

waiting for her to do something. He was waiting for what would come next.

What *would* come next? It was up to her.

She felt the way you do when you've got a key that doesn't fit perfectly in the lock, but you know that if you play around with it a little, the lock will turn.

"I have something to show you." She took his hand and led him farther into the untended part of the park, thick with high wild hedges. The path was faint and unpaved.

She was anxious. The Ramble, she was remembering now, used to be well known as a place to avoid. Prostitutes, transsexual prostitutes, gay men grimly humping. Here under the trees the light was nearly gone.

She found a little clearing that was hidden from view behind a circle of tall bushes. Still holding his hand, she squeezed through a space between the bushes and pulled him after her.

She put her hand on his chest and pushed him back a step, so that he was backed up against a thin young tree. She put her other hand on his belt and undid it. He still had a look of puzzlement, but he wasn't stopping her.

"You never had any intention of leaving," she said. She undid the two lower buttons of his shirt and kneeled and kissed his stomach, which was a good stomach, not too trim—he didn't have "washboard abs," which, to her, would have signaled mostly vanity—but not too paunchy, and then she pulled his zipper down and was pleased to see that he was hard. She licked the tip of the thing, slowly, and then looked up at him.

"You *do* want to be with me," she said. "I thought so."

She felt like some femme fatale from an old movie—Greta Garbo as Mata Hari, although in an X-rated version—which was wildly new to her. She had always felt that her sexual life was unoriginal, uncreative—wholly missionary and *bien pensant*—and it was exciting to find herself sinking so effortlessly into a different role.

She took his penis into her mouth and he leaned back against the tree and closed his eyes.

The blow job, for Maud, had always been problematic, an engenderer of mixed feelings. On the one hand there was something disgusting about it: the ignorant penis, always weird-looking when observed from up close, sporting too many pimplelike things and inexplicable purple patches, smelling pungent and unwashed—a blow job is a man's idea of heaven, but it rarely occurs to a man that a woman might have more interest in putting his penis in her mouth if it was *clean*—and then of course if he comes in your mouth, although it doesn't always taste awful, it never exactly tastes good. It's never as nice as a milk shake. *I could give you that blow job you asked for, but I'd much rather have a milk shake.* But on the other hand there was something she loved about having a man in her mouth like this: his helplessness, the way he falls into a kind of trance when you go down on him. And she also loved the complexity of it. Giving a blow job always made her feel like a supplicant, as if she were unworthy of meeting the man face-to-face, but it also made her feel powerful, because of the hint of primal danger, the fact that you could bite the damned thing off if you felt like it, ridding the world of a penis. Maybe the thing she liked about blow jobs, after all, the reason she continued to give them, was that both participants, the woman and the man, were at each other's mercy.

She had him in her mouth, and he was leaning against the tree, and he was shuddering, he was working his fingers through her hair with a gentleness that surprised her, and she still didn't even know if she even *liked* him, but here she was, taking him in a shady part of Central Park. It was as if the two of them had connected, from the first, on a pre-rational plane; it had been obvious from the first that something in each of them craved something in the other. She had a feeling of mystical right-ness—she remembered Plato's notion that each of us has an other half, whom we search for during all our earthly days—and she knew that she was giving him as much pleasure as he could stand.

Maud Weller, pleasure artist.

But when she looked up at his face, she saw that she'd per-haps misperceived the situation, because even though his cock was hard in her mouth and he seemed, down here, to be feeling as good as a man could feel, his eyes were wide open, and he was crying.

Twelve

She took her mouth away, which was what he wanted her to do, which was what he didn't want her to do. One or the other, but he wasn't sure which.

She brushed her hair away from her eyes and sat back against a tree. She was smiling at him: kindly, puzzled, sympathetic.

"Are you okay?" she said.

He zipped and buttoned and sat down next to her and took her hand.

"I guess I should tell you a couple of things," he said.

"I'd like it if you would."

"I told you I used to be married."

She nodded.

"We had a daughter. She was born with a blood disease. She died when she was three years old."

"I'm so sorry," Maud said.

She looked sincere. Samir could always tell whether expressions of sympathy were genuine or not. Experience had turned him into a lie detector of condolences.

"Let's walk," he said. He gave her his hand and they started back out of the tangled shelter of trees.

Back in the brightness of the park, life was continuing. Families, runners, bicycle riders, friends out for a walk. The beauty of the human body. He felt very tired.

"Do you want to tell me more about it? I want to know, if it's okay for you to talk." She said this in a small voice that he didn't like. Hushed and trembling with concern. A social worker's voice, he thought.

He was aware that he was being ungenerous to her. Even if her voice was a little phony, she was being phony in a good cause. She was trying to show him that she was interested.

He wasn't sure what else he should tell her. The problem was that if he started to talk about it, he might never stop.

He had met Leila just after college, and they were married in their mid-twenties. Within a year of their marriage, Leila had given birth to a girl.

In the cab, on the way to the hospital, Leila had said, "It's like stepping into eternity." He knew what she meant. He felt as if they were taking their place in an endless procession, a procession extending from the darkness of the past to the darkness of the future.

At the hospital, Leila in her labor was out of her mind with pain, but she refused to take anything to make it easier. Standing next to her, holding her hand, he cried uncontrollably without knowing why.

After Zahra emerged, and the midwife brought her to Leila's breast, Leila lifted up her head, smiled with beatified exhaustion, and said, "She's perfect."

But it turned out that she wasn't perfect. On her second day of life, their doctor, concerned by Zahra's yellow appearance, took a blood sample. An hour later he came back to tell them that there seemed to be some irregularity with her red blood cells. An hour after that, he came back again and said that Zahra would have to be transferred to the pediatric ICU for a blood transfusion.

He would never forget the sight of her, sixteen inches long, with an intravenous tube piercing her heel and a bag of blood suspended over her bed. Leila nursed her while she received the blood, and Zahra was able to sleep through most of the transfusion. Samir felt stunned, stupid, and useless. He kept going down the hall to the vending machine and bringing back snacks that Leila didn't want.

Zahra was unable to make healthy red blood cells. The doctors told them that a diagnosis could take months; in the meantime, she needed transfusions to keep her alive. Every two weeks Samir and Leila took her to the hospital, where she would scream as nurses pierced her skin with needles, and then she would collapse into a kind of frightened sleep as the blood dripped into her slowly over a period of many hours. Although the volume of blood she needed was very small, it had to be administered very slowly, so as not to overtax her tiny heart.

In her first year, Zahra endured more physical suffering than he himself had endured in his life. Samir and Leila took her to the hospital once a week to have her blood count checked, hoping every time that it had finally stabilized. Zahra would sit in Leila's lap as the technician prepared the syringe and the tube. Even at six or seven months, she loved nothing more than to joke around, and she would play peekaboo with the technician, smiling at the woman with an expression that seemed to say, "You look nice. Who are you?" She would submit with a smiling curiosity as the technician took hold of her arm, and only when the rubber tourniquet went on would she start to struggle, and then, when she found that her mother was holding her firmly in place, she would finally realize that something bad was happening, and she would start to cry, and when the technician inserted the needle, she would howl, giving out drawn-out cries of anguish and disbelief that Samir would never be able to forget.

He and Leila wondered what it was like for her to be taken by her parents, the people who played with her and fed her and sang to her and loved her, and handed over to strangers who tortured her. The books on child development said nothing about anything like this; and they didn't go in search of books on the psychological development of children with diseases, either because they were so preoccupied by her purely medical problems that they didn't have the strength, or else because they couldn't yet admit to themselves that she was a child with a disease.

Her infant veins were so small at first that the doctors and nurses always had trouble inserting the thick IV needle. They usually had to plunge the needle into her again and again before they succeeded in entering a vein. On one occasion, when she was a little less than a year old, they couldn't find a usable vein in any of the usual sites—not in her heels, not between her toes, not on her legs, not on her hands, not on her arms—and they ended up inserting the IV line into her jugular vein. She saw what they were about to do and she screamed and kicked and struggled and thrashed around madly, and as tiny as she was, it took four nurses to hold her down while the doctor inserted the line.

A person who has had the experience of standing by and doing nothing while watching a group of strangers hold his infant daughter down as she struggles and spits and screams— such a person is never the same again. You pass into a different world. At ten months of age she wasn't close to talking, but when they held her down and forced the tube into her neck, her screams didn't sound inarticulate; she sounded as if she was trying to say something. It sounded at first as if she was trying to appeal for mercy, and then as if she was trying to call for help. She went through her entire repertoire of noises. At first she was yelling, "Nay nay nay nay!" which was a sound she often made when she was in distress, and then she was yelling, "Yi yi yi yi!" which sounded like an animal cry, a plea for help, and finally she started flapping her lips, giving out noises that sounded like little Bronx cheers. It was a sound that she normally made when she was happy. But now she was making the sound in panic and pain and fear. It was as if she was using everything she knew, everything she had, to try to make them stop hurting her.

It is a truism that parents are willing to die for their children. Living with Zahra's illness, Leila and Samir discovered that the tragedy is that you can't suffer for them.

Zahra's illness wasn't all there was to her. When she wasn't having needles jammed into her veins, she was a radiant child. She seemed to have a kind of instinctive generosity. When you were feeding her, she wanted to take the spoon and feed you too; when she was playing with a toy, she would give it to you, and then, after a while, she'd put her hand out, wanting you to share it with her as she had shared it with you.

It was a joy to watch her encountering everything for the first time, to see the world being reborn through her experience of it. A few months before her second birthday, they went to Leila's parents' home in the suburbs to take Zahra trick-or-treating on Halloween. They weren't sure she was old enough to understand the idea of it, but after they had visited the first two houses it was hard to restrain her: she would race ahead of them to the next house, holding out her little red purse. The next day, back in Brooklyn, the three of them were taking a walk, and Zahra abruptly and laboriously climbed the stoop of a stranger's brownstone and tried to reach the doorbell, imagining that she lived in a world in which you could walk up to any house at any time and ask for candy. In the spring of the next year, when the Mister Softee truck started to come around, Zahra wanted to know why it was playing music; Leila, health-conscious, told her only that some trucks *liked* to play music, but a few days later, Zahra, in a tone that suggested she had made a discovery that would excite Leila as much as it excited her, said, "Mommy! I think that truck has ice cream!"

After she had learned to talk and began to make sense of the world, the transfusions became both easier and harder. They were easier because she no longer experienced them as random assaults—she seemed to understand that they were necessary—and they were easier because she allowed herself to be distracted. She was a horse-crazy two-year-old, and Samir and Leila would bring her favorite tape to the hospital—*Cloud Dancer: Stallion of the Southwest*—and she would watch it at least twice, completely absorbed, while the blood dripped slowly into her, hour after hour. There was a scene near the beginning that always thrilled her, in which a herd of wild horses runs through a shallow lake. Even in the hospital, she would get so excited that she'd stand up in her chair and call out, "Mommy! They chase!"

But it was also harder, because now she could look ahead. Around the time she turned two, she started to recognize the hospital, so as soon as they approached the building she would begin crying, and when they lifted her out of the car she would attempt the impossible task of clutching onto Leila and fighting her off at the same time.

She began to have nightmares: tigers were coming to get her. Leila would hold her in her arms and tell her that there were no tigers, that she was safe, and Zahra would whisper, "No tigers. I safe," but she'd continue to glance with a petrified vigilance around the room. During the day they'd stage pantomimes in order to make her feel fearless: Samir would pretend to be a tiger, and Zahra would shout, "Get away, you tiger!" and roar at him, and Samir would cower and retreat, undone by her mighty roar. This always made her laugh, and she would insist that they repeat the performance, and soon she was roaring at the breakfast table, roaring at strangers on the street, roaring whenever the spirit moved her. Samir and Leila loved this: they loved to see her thinking of herself as strong.

One day they were driving to the hospital for a transfusion and Leila was on her cell phone, talking to one of the nurses, and Zahra suddenly understood where they were going. She started to scream: "I don't want any blood! I don't need any blood!" Leila tried to calm her, and after a while she grew quiet. After a minute or two of silence, she said, "Are they gonna give me blood?" Leila said yes. Then: "Is it gonna be done?" Neither Leila nor Samir understood what this meant, and they asked her to say it again. "Is it gonna be done?" And they realized that she was asking whether it was going to be over. She was trying to comfort herself by anticipating the end of the transfusion.

Samir was stunned by this. He never would have believed that he could admire a two-year-old, but he admired her.

It took the doctors almost two years to come up with a diagnosis. Finally they determined that she had been born with a genetic abnormality that caused a disease called Diamond Blackfan anemia. Neither Samir nor Leila had ever heard of this disease, but when he started looking into his family's medical background, he found out about a great-aunt who had died at the age of ten because of a problem with her blood that the doctors had never been able to diagnose.

Some children who have Diamond Blackfan disease can be helped by steroids. After Zahra turned two, they tried a course of prednisone. Samir kept making jokes about all the home-run records she was going to break, but none of them were funny. A ring of hair grew around her face — a sort of Abe Lincoln beard on the lower half of her face and a crown of hair on her forehead — and she became bloated, and her moods grew strange: manic mornings, moaning nights. But the disease continued on its course. She continued to need the transfusions.

Diamond Blackfan is bad enough in the beginning, but it leads to afflictions that are far worse: in the early years it can cause bone deformities, facial abnormalities, and stunted growth, and, in the years after that, diabetes, leukemia, liver failure, heart failure. The only treatment that offers the possibility of a cure is a bone-marrow transplant. Zahra's malfunctioning bone marrow could be replaced by someone else's healthy marrow, which would produce healthy cells. She could be liberated from her transfusion regimen and safe from all the diseases that otherwise lay in wait for her. She could have a normal life.

It took more than a year to find a suitable marrow donor. During that year, Samir kept changing his mind about the wisdom of putting her through a transplant. It would be a terrible yearlong ordeal. It would begin with two weeks of chemotherapy, which would knock out her immune system so the new cells could take root. But it would be months before her immune system came back to full strength, and during those months Zahra would be helpless to ward off infections. She would have no defenses. She would need to spend two months in isolation in the transplant unit, and after that she would need to spend a year in a state of semi-isolation at home. No one who was even slightly ill could be in her presence.

Samir and Leila kept questioning the decision. Zahra was a frail child, small and light and delicate, tired much of the time, but she was also a beautiful girl—a comedian, a philosopher, and an explorer. They loved her as she was, and most of the time she was happy as she was, and it was hard to comprehend how it could be wise to put her through a procedure that carried such risks. But the doctors painted frightening pictures of the life that was in store for her if she wasn't cured. They kept reminding Leila and Samir that she couldn't just go on like this: if she didn't get better, she would get steadily worse. And they painted beguiling pictures of the life she could have after they cured her. If they performed the transplant now, while she was still a toddler, the chances were good that when she grew older she wouldn't even remember that she'd ever had the disease. She could live the life she was meant to live.

So they took the risk.

He had never been able to describe what the first few weeks were like—not to his family, not anyone else. There is no way to describe what it's like to see your child, your curious laughing mischievous strong-willed daughter, transformed by weeks of chemotherapy into something hairless and white-lipped and dull-eyed and brittle and dim. No way to describe what it's like to see her transformed into a listless thing, lying inertly in bed, her face and belly bloated and covered with rashes, not even looking up when you enter the room.

After three weeks, she seemed to be getting better. One afternoon she used her toy cell phone to talk to Cloud Dancer, and she told him that as soon as she got out of the hospital, she was going to ride him.

But two nights later she had a dream that frightened her deeply and that frightened Samir even more. She woke up trembling and wanting to be held. "The floor was breaking, and there were tigers, and I tried to roar back at them, but I couldn't scare them away."

He didn't hear her recount this dream: he had already left for work by the time she woke. But when Leila told him about it over the phone, he closed the door of his office and cried. He hated the thought of her having a dream in which she tried to use her strength but it still wasn't enough. He hated the thought that she couldn't scare the tigers away.

The medical news continued to be good. Her body was accepting the new marrow cells. She didn't develop graft-versus-host disease, in which the new cells go to war against the body. She was getting better, and then she died.

Somehow, despite the fact that she was living in pristine and vigilantly guarded isolation, a cold virus made its way into the room and invaded her body, and she wasn't strong enough to fight it off. If this same virus had infected her six weeks earlier or six weeks later, it would have caused nothing more severe than a runny nose, but coming when it did, despite massive doses of intravenous gamma globulin to protect her lungs and her heart, despite hourly infusions of purified white blood cells to fortify her immune system, it led swiftly to pneumonia, to the shutting down of her lungs, and to her death.

She caught a cold and died. A simple sentence that recorded the destruction of a world.

Zahra was dead. We were trying to save her, but we killed her.

Leila and Samir spent the first night after her death in the funeral home, sitting beside her where she lay in an open coffin. She looked hard and oddly shiny, as if she had been coated with plastic. She didn't look as if she were resting; she didn't look as if she were sleeping. Death is death.

She was buried in her favorite dress, a bright purple jumper, and her Dora the Explorer shoes. Next to her they placed her Halloween purse, into which they had put a small packet of Hershey's Kisses and her favorite plastic pony.

There is no way to explain what it's like to sit through the night next to the open coffin of your three-year-old daughter. Your daughter, who, a week before her death, had told you that she knew she was going to get well again because "if they can't bring ponies in the hospital, I have to get out of the hospital to ride the ponies." Your daughter, who, for your birthday present, had given you "birthday jumps," leaping off the couch onto a pile of pillows, delighted by her own fearlessness. No way to explain what it's like to sit beside her all night when she is nothing.

On the second night after her death, Leila and Samir made love, coming together in a crazy hunger of sorrow and disbelief. On the night after that, they couldn't bring themselves to touch. Each of them took up a thin wedge at the edge of the bed, sleeping as far away from each other as possible. On the next night, after lying in bed for hours, unable to sleep, Samir got up and went into the living room. The things they had brought back from the hospital were still in a suitcase in the closet. He opened it and found *Cloud Dancer: Stallion of the Southwest.* Within a minute or two came the scene where the herd of mustangs storms over a hill and into a lake, and he could hear Zahra's voice clearly in his mind. He could see her standing delightedly on the couch, pointing to the screen and crying out: "Mommy! Daddy! They chase!"

Leila came into the room while Samir was watching the scene in which Cloud Dancer, still a colt, makes friends with a herd of buffalo. Samir was weeping. She went back into the bedroom without saying a word.

Although they didn't separate until months later, it was at that moment that their marriage came to an end. At the same time as Leila was so wild with grief that she felt as if she knew what it would be like to go insane, she knew that she would need to get over it someday—not soon, but someday. And when she came out into the living room and saw Samir watching *Cloud Dancer,* she instantly understood that he had no such commitment, no such wish; she understood that he was not going to be her partner in building a new life.

This, at any rate, was what she told him when they had coffee one afternoon a year later.

She was right. He *had* given up. He had no interest in a new life. The world had ended for him.

Unrecoverable brightness.

He couldn't remember the last words he'd heard Zahra speak. It tormented him, the fact that he couldn't remember them, and he sometimes thought of going to a hypnotist to re-trieve them. But he didn't.

Two days before she died, he came to the hospital from work and entered her room just behind a nurse, who was there to give her one of the sixteen horrible oral medications she had to take every day. Zahra, lying miserably on the bed, tried to push the nurse away and said, "You don't touch me! My daddy won't let you!" The nurse retreated for a few minutes, but then returned and held Zahra down and inserted the syringe between her lips and forced the medicine into her mouth.

"My daddy won't let you." Those weren't the last words he heard her speak. But they *seemed* like the last words he'd heard her speak. Sometimes they seemed to be the last words he had heard anyone speak. There was a slight delay in everything that had been said to him since, as if he were watching a film where the picture and the sound were poorly synchronized. You saw people's lips move, and the meaning came later. Nothing he had heard since then could reach him.

Samir and Maud had walked in silence all the way to the reservoir. The late-afternoon sunlight was spread out across the water.

"I don't know," Samir said. "I think that's all I can say about it right now."

Thirteen

Eleanor opened the door of her office and welcomed her last client of the day. It was a woman named Jenny, whom she'd been treating for almost six months now. It was a good working relationship. Eleanor respected Jenny—respected her honesty, the rigor of her self-investigations.

For a few minutes, Jenny talked about trivial matters: a movie she'd seen that week, an encounter on the bus that morning. It was a way of warming up. Then she turned to the subject that had been preoccupying her lately: her husband.

"Every time I feel myself starting to trust him, I pull back. And I never know whether I'm pulling back for a good reason. He comes home late from work three days in a row. Is that a good reason? I think I catch him looking at women on the street when we're walking together. Is that a good reason? I keep trying to figure out whether he's an untrustworthy person or whether he's just a person."

Eleanor listened closely, even though Jenny had said these things before. It was interesting to her precisely *because* Jenny had said these things before. The things a person repeats contain more hidden material than the things a person tries to conceal.

Eleanor felt locked in. When she was listening to her clients, her mind rarely wandered.

The dirty little secret of the world of psychotherapy is that therapists, like the rest of us, space out. Therapists talk about the problem among themselves, try to find ways to account for it and work with it (they generate theories, for example, according to which one's lapses of attention can help one reach a fuller understanding of one's clients). But underneath all the theories, the raw rude fact remains: the shrink isn't always listening. As one of Eleanor's more candid teachers once put it, if a therapist's session with a client can be compared to a stroll, a walk two people take together without quite knowing where they'll end up, then the patches of inattention on the therapist's part are like piles of dog shit in the path.

Jenny was struggling with herself over whether to leave her husband. A year ago, just after their wedding, she had become pregnant, and although she and her husband had planned the pregnancy, he had promptly launched into an affair with one of his co-workers, and within a week of finding out about the affair, Jenny had had a miscarriage. Her husband had been genuinely sorrowful, had stopped seeing the other woman, and Jenny had remained with him, but she found it impossible to trust him.

"I don't know how much longer I can keep going like this. I have to find a way to forgive him or else I have to leave."

Jenny was on the verge of tears, and Eleanor wanted to cross the room and embrace her, but this was not the kind of thing she would ever do. The days of hugging therapy were over, except in California.

"I keep having these dreams about Andrew," Jenny said. An old boyfriend. "And in every dream, he's my true love. Not Nick. Are the dreams trying to tell me that Andrew really *is* my true love? Or are they just trying to tell me that I don't really want to be with Nick?"

Jenny knew Eleanor too well to expect an answer. Eleanor hardly ever answered her clients' questions. She had long ago reached the conclusion that the answers that matter come from the clients themselves.

What Eleanor tried to offer her clients was the presence of someone who listened. Sometimes she thought it was the only thing she offered them.

Listening well was her passion, her Holy Grail, the name of her desire. Sometimes she thought that the effort to listen well occupied precisely the space in her soul that the struggle for clarity of language and suppleness of form would have occupied if she had followed her youthful plan of becoming a writer. Listening was her art, as challenging and beautiful and impossible to master as any art worthy of the name.

If you're a therapist, and if you're conscientious about listening, you soon come to realize that you can never listen well enough. Because it involves impossible combinations. You must clear your mind of everything except the words that your client is speaking; when random thoughts stray across your mind, you must not let them distract you. Yet at the same time, you need to pay attention to the random thoughts, because sometimes they aren't random: sometimes they can give you the key to a deeper understanding of the person you're listening to. At the same time as you need to "be here now," you need to remember everything your client has told you in the past; and you need to remember as much as you can about comparable situations that other clients and other people you know have been in; and you need to remember everything you learned in your training. You need to forget the world and you need to have the world in the room with you.

She was like an acolyte of listening; it was a passion that she pursued with a religious intensity. She hadn't written anything, hadn't added anything to the literature of psychology; she hadn't come up with any groundbreaking theories, or any theories at all. She had been an ordinary working therapist, nothing more. But though her professional life had been smaller than she had expected it to be, she sometimes thought that she had fulfilled herself to the limits of her gifts, and that that was enough.

One reason she had never made much of a living at her trade was that she simply couldn't work with too many clients in a single day. She could handle four clients in an eight-hour day, perhaps five. After that, she was too tired. She kept several blouses in the closet of her office because sometimes the sheer effort of listening would leave her soaked with sweat.

"The thought of staying with him scares me. But the thought of leaving him doesn't make me happy either. We have so much together. And the thought of starting off again with another man . . . the thought of trying to learn to *trust* another man . . . I talked to my brother on the phone the other day and he said I should come out to New Jersey and stay with him for a while. He's just about the only man I *do* trust. But I don't think I trust his girlfriend."

In the six months they'd been working together, Jenny had avoided the subject of her own past. She had told Eleanor about the years she had spent in some sort of religious community in Oregon, but she'd never gone back much further than that. She referred to her father only with dismissive jokes, and when she talked about her mother, she talked in such an exaggerated way about how much she loved her that it was clear there was trouble there.

Eleanor believed that Jenny would eventually wish to explore her own past. She worked her questions through very slowly, but she seemed to be committed to working them through.

"And meanwhile," Jenny said, "I don't know if Nick has any idea what's going on inside me. The one-year anniversary is coming up, and I don't know if he's been thinking about it or if he just senses it, but he's being sweeter to me than he's ever been before. And I start to think, 'He behaved horribly, but he's a good man, and I've got to get over this.' And then we'll be walking down Broadway and I'll catch him staring at some bimbo, and I think I should just walk away from him on the spot."

Eleanor didn't feel sure about what would become of Jenny and Nick. She had a hunch that they would keep going, and that things would get better between them. Nick, from Jenny's account, seemed genuinely to want to grow, and to grow within the relationship. Eleanor's impression was that he was just as Jenny had described him: a good man who had behaved badly. But Eleanor wouldn't say this. She didn't want to give advice, and if she said it, it would be a piece of advice masquerading as a description.

There were about two minutes left in their session.

"There's one thing that scares me, though," Jenny said. "We still have sex once in a while, you know, and I keep getting this urge to throw my diaphragm away. Like, put it in, but then go to the bathroom and take it out again. Not because I want to have a baby right now. I think it would be terrible to be pregnant again when I'm not even sure I want to stay with him. But I keep having this strange impulse to do what I can to get pregnant. It's almost like I want to punish him. Or test him."

"Have you actually done it?" Eleanor said. "Taken the diaphragm out?"

"Just once."

Eleanor didn't know precisely why Jenny would want to do something that had such a high probability of leading to more misery for herself, but it didn't surprise her. It's what we all do, she thought.

She wanted to say: *Don't do it. Don't blow it. Don't fuck up your life*. But, for better or for worse, she didn't.

Clients often wait until the end of their session to come out with the things that most deeply disturb them. It was hard to know why. Was it simply because the things that were hard to say always came last? Or was there some sort of test involved—were they testing their therapists to see if they'd relax their boundaries and let the session go on?

Eleanor never relaxed her boundaries. She looked at the clock and said, "It's time," and stood up.

After Jenny left, Eleanor spent a few minutes drawing together her thoughts. She tried to do this after every session. Jenny, from the beginning, had posed a particular challenge. Eleanor had to monitor herself constantly to make sure she wasn't reading her own life into Jenny's. It would be so easy to superimpose Adam's features over Nick's, and to start rooting for Jenny to leave him, as she herself should have left Adam years ago. And it wouldn't be hard to go the other way and idealize Nick, to see him as a man who had made one mistake and was prepared to pay for it—to imagine him, yes, as a flawed man, but, in contrast to Adam, a flawed man who was in love with his wife. Her job, part of her job, was to help Jenny paint her own picture of her own life, not to paint one for her.

She put Telemann's Trio in E Minor in the CD player. At the end of the day she liked to listen to something by Telemann or Mozart or Vivaldi or Bach, something to remind her of the possibility of happiness. Freud had famously told a prospective client that he couldn't say that psychoanalysis would make her happy; all he was offering her was the chance to exchange her present misery for an ordinary unhappiness. Given the human condition, he thought, one could hope for nothing more than that. Eleanor thought he was right. But it was good to be reminded of the *idea* of happiness.

After half an hour, she gathered up her things and started

out for home. Her apartment was only fifteen blocks away from her office. It was nice to walk in the coppery light of the autumn afternoon.

This was the round of her life now, ever since Adam had moved out. During the day, people came to her and she listened to them, wondering, all the while, whether she was listening well enough, creatively enough, intelligently enough, responsively enough. And at night she tried to listen to herself. She would come home to an apartment that was too large for her, have dinner and a drink, open her notebook, and resume the effort to understand her own past and to make out the shape of her future.

Fourteen

During the walk she stopped at a grocery and picked up a chicken breast and some asparagus, intending to cook herself dinner, but when she got home she abandoned the plan. This happened pretty much every night. She would briefly think about transforming herself into a "strong, proud woman living alone," the kind that her friend Vivian would approve of, and making a meal for herself always seemed like a necessary first step. But then she would decide she was too tired, and she'd pick up the phone and order Chinese food, which was one reason she had gained so much weight over the past year.

After deciding to have some food delivered, she would always tell herself that she was going to read while she ate. But when the food came, she would still feel tired, too tired for the exertion of reading, and she would eat her broccoli with garlic sauce in front of the TV.

After turning on the TV, she usually tried to remain respectable by watching *The NewsHour* on PBS, but after ten minutes she would inevitably switch to a rerun of *Friends* or *Law & Order*. Tonight she watched *Law & Order* for half an hour, wondering idly, as she always did, whether Sam Waterston was unattached.

She cleaned up the kitchen, turned off the TV, and finally managed to drag herself into Maud's room and start writing. She started by describing her sessions with the clients she'd seen that day, and somehow this led her to return to the subject of what it had been like to see Adam. Writing randomly, directionlessly—just trying to keep her pen moving across the page for a few more minutes—she found herself writing about the day she met Adam, in 1966. Thirty-seven years ago. She thought it might be interesting to write down everything she could remember about that day.

She was still writing when the phone rang. Through caller ID, which still seemed like magic to her, she knew who it was. It was Patrick.

She didn't answer. She wanted to talk to him, but she didn't want to talk to him now. She wanted to wait until she was feeling stronger, more whole.

The phone stopped ringing. He didn't leave a message. A minute later it rang again. It was him again.

There never is a right time, of course. It wasn't as if she could wait for a time when she'd feel whole again. That time would never come.

She picked up the phone.

"Hello, Patrick."

There was a pause, as he took a moment to understand how she knew who was calling.

"It's really you," he said.

"It's really me. More or less."

There was a silence.

One of the things she remembered now about Patrick was that he wasn't a talker. She who believed in the talking cure had been in love with a man who never talked.

"How are you, Ellie?" he finally said.

"That's a big question to answer after thirty-seven years."

"I guess it is."

"Are you still a union guy?"

"Still a union guy. Are you still a writer?"

"No." It made her sad to say no. Made her feel as if she'd let him down.

"How's Adam?"

She didn't know if she wanted to tell him that she and Adam weren't together anymore. It was presumptuous, she knew, for her to feel sure that Patrick was reaching out to her in more than just a friendly way, yet she did feel sure. Telling him about Adam would be like opening the door to him, and she didn't know if she wanted to open the door. What she and Patrick had had was so far back in the past that they weren't even quite the same people anymore. At least she wasn't quite the same.

She didn't know if she had the strength to heave her heaviness—her bulky body and her bulky soul—into the effort to begin a new life. *Now it is autumn and the falling fruit . . .*

"Adam is doing well. At least he seems to be. We separated a year ago."

"I'm sorry," he said, but she knew he wasn't.

"Are you still with Diana?"

"Yes. We're still together. Sort of. It's a long story."

She was disappointed.

"I'm happy to hear from you, Patrick," she said, "and I'm also curious about why you're calling me now. What's going on?"

"My daughter's going to NYU. My older daughter. She's a freshman. I'm going to be visiting her soon. I thought that if I was in New York, maybe we could finally have that cup of hot chocolate. It'd be a little late, but . . ."

She wasn't sure she wanted to see him. More precisely, she wasn't sure she wanted to be seen. Patrick was surely imagining her as the reedy soft-souled girl she'd been at twenty-two. She didn't know if she wanted him to see her as she was, round and saggy. A human beanbag.

A picture of what it would be like to see him flashed across her mind. She saw him waiting on some street corner, smiling and eager, and, then, on first catching sight of her, looking stunned, and struggling to hide his disappointment.

Of course he would try to take account of the years — try to draw a mental portrait of her, like one of those computer images produced by the police, depicting the likely appearance of a suspect who hasn't been photographed in decades. But she was sure he'd be getting it wrong. There was no way he could imagine her as the ruin that she was, the testament to the power of gravity, with a face that was all wrong: wrinkled in the places where she once was soft, soft in the places where a woman who had lived her life right, a woman who had done more to define herself, would be sharply chiseled.

He told her when he was going to be in the city. She felt a panicky wish to get off the phone.

"I might have to be away then. There's a conference." She didn't care whether she sounded plausible.

"Well, maybe I can call you when we get a little closer to the date."

"That sounds good. Look. I have to go. I have a call coming in." A lie: she didn't even have call-waiting. "It's good to hear from you, Patrick, but I need to go."

He said good-bye, and she said something, and he said something else; it was all rushed and hazy; and they got off the phone.

The teacher who had been her mentor many years ago — the same man who had supplied the useful metaphor for therapists' lapses of attention — used to say that every choice we make is either a growth choice or a fear choice. She wasn't sure that he was right about this: she found it a painfully strenuous way to look at life, a way of looking at life that never let anyone just relax. But she was sure that getting off the phone so quickly had been a fear choice.

After a first flush of self-loathing—she was supposedly a student of the human soul, and she'd acted like a child—she tried to be gentler on herself. Even though Patrick was still with his wife, it felt as if he were asking her out on a date. And she hadn't been out on a date since her first date with Adam, all those years ago. In terms of her romantic life, she *was* a child. It was natural that she'd acted like one.

Part of the problem was that, after the turbulence of the past year, she was no longer used to having good things come into her life. Whatever Patrick's situation, even if she and Patrick were going to be "just friends," his calling her was indisputably a good thing. She may have simply forgotten how to welcome the good things.

Here is a good thing, she thought. And this is my task. I have to learn how to welcome it.

Fifteen

Adam was sitting alone on his couch with a glass of scotch in his hand. It was the first peaceful moment he'd had in a week.

He enjoyed being alone in this apartment. Everything in it was new. Except for his clothing and a few other personal items, all of his things—his furniture, his books—were in the old place, with Eleanor. This new place was soulless, but comfortable. This suited him fine.

He was twelve floors above the traffic on Fifty-seventh Street. It was a busy street, but he had double-paned windows. Everything was quiet here.

Izzy's manuscript lay untouched on the coffee table. Adam hadn't had time to read the newspaper lately, much less take up a burdensome obligation like this.

Adam looked at the first page with a familiar mixture of affection and exasperation. Izzy should have bought a new ribbon before he typed this thing.

Adam knew the characters made by Izzy's typewriter in the way someone else might know a friend's handwriting. Izzy had claimed that computers made things too easy—writing *should* require a physical effort—and near the end of his life he was still pounding gamely away at the tanklike manual IBM that he had bought in the 1950s. He must have gotten the thing repaired a hundred times. He was forever heading down to Osner Business Machines on Amsterdam Avenue to drop it off or pick it up.

Adam fingered the manuscript and took another sip of his scotch.

He knew in advance that it wouldn't be very good. Before Izzy died, Adam had come to realize that the problem with Izzy's writing was the problem with Izzy. He didn't have enough of the devil in him. Izzy always wanted to be the nice guy. He wanted to take care of everybody. This made him a wonderful husband and father: steadier, more responsible, more caring than Adam had ever dreamed of being. But it had made him a bland writer.

In his books, he always took care of his characters too much. He never wanted to believe that any of them could be evil. So if one of his characters did something morally reprehensible, Izzy would never just go with it; he would surround the action with context, explanation, extenuation. It was as if he couldn't decide whether he wanted to be a novelist or a social worker.

Adam wasn't eager to be immersed again in the vague skim-milky kindness of his old friend's world.

He lifted up a stack of pages and read a couple of sentences from somewhere in the middle of the manuscript. Then he read a page or two from an earlier part.

It was set in the 1940s and 1950s and 1960s, the era of Izzy's youth, the era of his own. It was the same era, coincidentally, in which Adam's new novel was set, the novel Adam had been working on for the past few months. But this was unremarkable. Two old men turning back to the days of their youth.

Flipping through the book, he came upon a few things—a sentence or a situation—that had been taken directly from Izzy's life. A young married couple, weighed down by new re-sponsibilities; one night after the children are asleep the woman says to the man, "Honey, if I ever wanted to have sex, it would be with you." Adam knew that Ruth had said this to Izzy a few months after their daughter was born. He remembered Izzy smiling ruefully as he quoted the line.

He turned back to the first page and started to read. Adam had always been a quick, greedy reader, gulping down the books of teachers and rivals, keeping his eye out for anything he could steal. He read the entire book in less than three hours.

In part, it was what he'd expected. He'd expected an elegiac book about growing up in the last generation before the Jews became part of the American mainstream, the last generation in which secular American Jews could feel as if they belonged to a world apart. And this *was* part of its subject. But everything else about it was surprising.

The first thing that was surprising was that it was an energetic book. Izzy, in the last few years of his life, had been anything but lively, but this was the liveliest book he'd written. It was as if he'd been saving all his powers for one last ride.

And it was free of the narrative curlicues that had always been Izzy's trademark and his crutch. In this new book, each scene proceeded swiftly toward its target.

Most impressive of all, it was a tougher-minded book than its predecessors. It was free of cheap uplift. And Adam felt that he himself might have had a hand in this. He wasn't sure it would be obvious to anyone else, but it was clear to Adam that the main character, though he was mostly based on Izzy, had little bits and pieces of Adam thrown in. There were a few scenes that came directly from Adam's life, scenes that cast the main character in a not very favorable light, and these touches of not-so-goodness gave the character a distinctiveness that most of Izzy's protagonists had lacked.

Even before he'd reached the middle, he saw that this new book was stronger than anything Izzy had written since his thirties, when he was in the full bloom of vitality and ambition.

Maybe Ruth was right: maybe it *was* the strongest thing he'd ever written.

Adam read the book with a rising feeling of admiration. The old bastard had come through in the end, Adam thought. He'd tottered up to the plate on busted-up legs in the bottom of the ninth inning and hit the thing out of the park.

Adam had another drink and thought about his old friend's triumph. It was actually possible, he thought, that this novel would bring Izzy the success that had eluded him in his lifetime.

It's hard to comprehend that the dead don't care. We know it in our heads, but it's hard to *feel* the truth of it. Dead parents don't care whether we visit their graves; dead writers don't care about their reputations. Emily Dickinson died in the same condition as anyone else who writes for himself, any furtive unknown diarist; Herman Melville, at the end of his life, was just some local loser, not the awe-inspiring author of *Moby-Dick;* neither of them was ever to know the dimensions of their future success. Yet there is something in us that makes us think of Dickinson and Melville as conscious somewhere, taking pleasure in their readership, glad to have at last been understood.

But when the dead writer is someone you knew, it's easier to grasp the fact that he can't take pleasure in a revival of interest in his work. Adam had known Izzy for more than forty years. He remembered sitting next to him at the counter of Dave's Luncheonette on Canal Street in 1953 while Izzy waved his spoon around and talked excitedly about *The Adventures of Augie March.* He remembered the long walk they took in 1960 or 1961, when Izzy was trying to figure out whether he wanted to marry Ruth. He remembered Izzy's wedding, the birth of his daughter, his funeral. And he knew that no matter how much praise might be lavished on Izzy's last novel, the news would never reach the precinct that was now his home.

An artificial light was burning in Adam's fireplace, bright and heatless. It was a Friday night, and the city was doubtless full of manic life, but in his apartment, behind his reinforced windows, everything was silent.

His admiration for Izzy's book wasn't unstained by the despondency that can come over you when a friend succeeds. In a way, it would have been better if the book had stunk.

He heard the lock turning in his front door, and then the sound of Thea walking in. Her heels on the hardwood floor sounded brisk and confident. He was infatuated even with the way she walked.

And then there she was. The long and noble line of her, even if she herself was not particularly noble. It was midnight, and tonight, as on any other night, he had no idea what she might have been up to. He wouldn't have been surprised to learn that she was visiting a sick friend, and he wouldn't have been surprised to learn that she was stealing a sick friend's job.

"Hello, old man," she said.

Adam's scotch was sitting on top of the manuscript. Thea picked up the glass and finished it.

"How's your friend's book?"

Dead though Izzy was, he remained a rival, and Adam didn't, at the moment, feel like praising him.

"I haven't had a chance to look at it yet," he said.

Sixteen

Maud shook the bottle of perfume too vigorously and instead of sprinkling a few drops on her throat, she gave herself a bath. When I go outside, she thought, bees will descend on me.

She started making up a song:

> *No matter how crowded the barroom*
> *I know that he can find me with ease*
> *'Cause I'm always wearing a perfume*
> *That can drive a horse to its knees.*

She chose a dress that was both low-cut and short. She looked through her stockings and didn't find any that she wanted to wear and decided not to wear any. A phrase came into her mind: *I want to overwhelm him with skin.*

She was meeting him in ridiculous Brooklyn. The Brooklyn Academy of Music was showing a compilation of short films by Maya Deren, a surrealist dancer and filmmaker from the 1930s and 1940s whose movies Maud had read about but never seen. She had arranged to meet Samir at his apartment, for the sole reason that if she snooped around a little, she'd have a clearer idea of who he was.

When he opened his door, he was wearing an eye patch.

"Ahoy there, matey," she said. Although it wasn't what she would have expected of him, she thought he must be kidding around. "Topscuttle me bamberger."

"This isn't a joke, unfortunately," he said. "I scratched my cornea this afternoon. I was planing a table and I was too lazy to put on my goggles. I have to wear this for two days."

"Bummer," she said. "Does it hurt?"

"It hurt before I saw the eye doctor. It hurt every time I blinked. But he put something in it and now I have to keep it closed. That's what the eye patch is for."

"I always wanted to be seen in public with a pirate," she said. "I think it would be good for my image."

"Actually, I was trying to call you. I wish you had a cell phone. I'm sorry that you made the trip all the way out here, but I don't think I feel up to going out tonight."

She was disappointed, but not completely. She was also relieved. On the way over, she'd been sour-stomached with ambivalence, and now she was glad to think she could just go home.

It was hard to admit this to herself, but what he had told her the other day about his daughter had spooked her.

She sympathized with him fully: she could imagine nothing more terrible than the death of your child. But at the same time, it made her want to run from him. People whose lives have been marked by disaster seem to carry the stink of it on their bodies, and it attracts further disasters their way. Disaster may make its first entrance into your life by pure bad luck, but after that first visit, it loses its randomness. It knows your address. Lightning *always* strikes twice.

She wished she could have had a more purely "feminine" reaction to his revelation: she wished she purely sympathized, without the self-protective recoil. But there she was.

"Well I have to sit down for a minute. Mr. Kant here weighs a ton." She was rereading *The Critique of Pure Reason,* which felt like a brick in her shoulder bag. "Dude had a lot to say." She swung her bag in the air. "Also good for fending off muggers."

"I'll take your coat," he said, and when he went down the hall, she had a chance to get the lay of the land.

She had never seen a place so bare. It was as if someone had gone through it and removed everything that suggested a past, everything that suggested a spiritual or intellectual life. There were no books. She knew that he'd read a lot at one point in his life, and he *seemed* like a reader, so she assumed his books must be in the bedroom. But when she took a few steps to look into the bedroom, she saw no books there either.

There were no photographs on the walls. She had expected to find photographs of Zahra.

The only thing in his apartment that implied someone was actually living there, an individual with a personality, was the furniture. The table and chairs in the kitchen and the rocking chair in the living room were sturdy and graceful. Probably he had made them himself.

When he returned, she said, "No books."

"No books."

"That surprises me."

Samir didn't say anything. She sat on the couch.

The only thing on the living room wall was a clock, flatly functional.

"You have a clock in the living room."

He looked up at it as if he'd never noticed it before.

"It seems strange to me," she said, "but I'm not sure why it seems strange." She thought about it for a moment. "I guess I think that kind of clock belongs in the kitchen. It's a clock you expect to see in a diner or something. It's a clock from the world of work. And the kitchen is closer to the world of work than the living room."

He didn't respond.

He isn't charmed by me, she thought. My quirky musings.

He's too sad to be charmed. But he's . . . something.

She had an effect on him; she could feel it. She hadn't been able to feel it the first few times they'd met, during those awkward attempts at conversation at George and Celia's. But now she could feel that her presence discomfited and excited him at the same time. He was kind of tilted away from her, as if he were next in line at a limbo competition.

She felt large in his small apartment, but for the first time in her life she felt gorgeously large. She felt as if she had a large personality. She felt like a force to be reckoned with.

"Is it just vanity that makes you want to stay in?" she said. "Because if it is, you should know you look kind of dashing in that eye patch."

"I just don't feel up to it."

He was impassive; he was giving her nothing. He was a one-step-forward-two-steps-back kind of guy, and tonight he was stepping back.

She wasn't going to let him keep his guard up. "Come here for a second, will you?" she said. "Look at this." Still sitting on the couch, she put out her hand and looked at her palm as if there were something on it. He walked toward her—he looked as if he were hypnotized—and when he was standing close enough, she undid his belt buckle and unzipped his pants. "Unfinished business," she said, and pulled out his penis and took it into her mouth.

It was soft, of course, and there was a moment when she was afraid it would remain soft, which would be humiliating for both of them—if he didn't get hard she would probably have to leave, because the encounter would be too silly for their relationship to survive. But then it began to get hard, like magic, like those Sea-Monkeys she once sent away for in elementary school, using a full two weeks' allowance: "Just dip them in a glass of water and watch them grow." Except that she wasn't dipping anything into water. So this wasn't like those Sea-Monkeys at all.

She wasn't really *enjoying* this, not on a sexual level, at least. But she *was* enjoying it in some way. She was in the grip, not of desire, but of a desire to possess him.

At the Ramble the other day, before she'd looked up and seen that he was crying, there was a moment when his legs were trembling, when she felt a long tremor passing along his entire body, and she had thought, If this went on too long he could die from it; if I kept him at this peak without letting him come I could kill him. And although killing him was the last thing she wanted, it had made her feel powerful. And she wanted to get that back. She wanted to get back that moment when she had him in her mouth and he was trembling.

A friend of Maud's who'd recently broken up with a long-time boyfriend had told Maud that the boyfriend was constantly complaining that she never woke him up in the middle of the night with a blow job. Her friend was a brilliant and witty and lovely woman, and doubtless the boyfriend had loved all these things about her, but he had also wanted her to be a sexual fantasy. When she heard the story, Maud thought the guy was a pinhead, but now, with Samir's cock in her mouth, she was thinking, Why not? It would take so little, really, to play the role of a man's sexual-fantasy woman, since most men's fantasies were so crude. Maud and Samir were on the floor, somehow, and she already knew him well enough to know that he was close, and he wasn't crying, which was progress, and now his fingers were in her hair, fluting, tapping in an almost coherent way as if he were typing a letter, and then he was arching his back, and then she could feel him starting to come, something she had to brace for, the curiously unholy taste of come, here it was, but his come wasn't so bad, didn't taste quite so much like chlorine as some other men's, and he was still coming, and her thoughts had already leaped ahead to the next act, because it's one thing to give a guy a blow job and quite another to make him want you to stay around after the blow job is over.

Back in college, she had become all too familiar with this sequence: you have an hour or two of intense, soul-sharing communion in bed with a guy, and then he asks you to go home, explaining that he likes to sleep by himself. How to make sure that that didn't happen now? The perfect strategy to employ with most guys would be to get out of bed as soon as he comes, grab a couple of brews from the fridge, and ask if he'd mind if you turned on the hockey game. But Samir didn't have any brews in the fridge, and she was sure he didn't give a damn about the hockey game. The wisest thing, she thought, might be to leave without saying a word: the element of surprise; the element of keep-him-guessing; the strategy of keep-him-wanting-more. But that would be ignoble — cowardice teased up into a style. Something more active was called for here, even if it was more of a risk.

So as soon as he had come, as he lay there with his head turned away from her, so that he could be hidden, so that he could deny, in a way, what had just happened, she unbuttoned her dress and made herself naked and crawled up the length of him and said, "Smell this," and then, "Taste this," and he complied, putting his mouth on her, and she could tell instantly that he was inexperienced at this and furthermore that he didn't have much of an instinct for it. "Most men don't know how to do this," she said, "but I'm going to teach you." And she told him what to do, showed him, as best she could, leading him on a guided tour, until he got a sense of what he should be after, and she talked him through it, trying to keep the element of humor out of her mind (trying not to compare this to *Airplane!,* with the doughty air-traffic controller talking the hapless pilot through the landing).

She landed successfully, with a climax that was pleasurable and long. It had been a kind of do-it-yourself experience, but she felt good. The key to having satisfying sex with a man, she thought, is that you have to masturbate.

He was hard again. She liked this: she was glad to see that giving her pleasure made him hard. She lay beside him and put one hand over his face, so he could be only half here if that was what he wanted, and with her other hand she stroked him slowly until he had come again.

After a moment she returned to the idea of leaving early. At this point, she thought, it would be a good move. Now that he's spent.

She kissed him on the mouth, gathered up her things, and left without saying a word.

She needed to pee, but she didn't want to dilute the drama of her exit by using his bathroom. She regretted it once she reached the street, because she *really* needed to pee. Luckily, there was a coffee shop about a block from his apartment, and she used the women's room there. When she got out, a slight but aggressive waitress demanded that she order something, so she got an egg cream to go, and drank it on the subway while reading Kant.

SEVENTEEN

He kept wanting each time to be the last time. But she kept coming back.

The truth was, he kept asking her back.

It was like living within a dream of sex. She would come to his apartment in the evening, close the door, and unbuckle his pants. Sometimes they reached his bedroom, sometimes they ended up on the couch or the rug or, once, on the kitchen table, as if they were a meal. Sometimes they would talk a little before they fell asleep, and sometimes they wouldn't: there were times when she stayed through the night without either of them speaking a word.

During the first few weeks of their acquaintance, when she kept making those awkward attempts at conversation with him at George and Celia's place, he didn't have the slightest interest in getting to know her, but he constantly daydreamed about getting to know her body: kissing her, smelling her, biting her, swarming all over her with his hands. And now he couldn't believe that she had turned out to be exactly the sexmate he'd dreamed about. He couldn't believe he'd found a woman who wanted the same thing he did: sex without commitment, sex without conversation.

This kind of faceless sex had never been his fantasy in his former life. He would have considered it adolescent and uninteresting. But now the thought of getting to know anyone repulsed him.

During his time alone, his sexual hunger had never died, but he hadn't been able to satisfy it, because he hadn't found a woman who wanted nothing but sex, and he'd come to believe that such a woman probably didn't exist. He had no interest in the commercial varieties of sexual experience — prostitutes or lap dancers or phone sex. He wanted a real, non-fee-charging woman. But he didn't want to *talk* to anyone; he didn't want to hear anyone's life story or tell his own. He'd come to think that he'd never have sex again, and he'd grown almost resigned to the need to starve his sexual impulse to death.

But now there was this. Here was Maud, and here was fucking. It was sex without affection, sex without connection, sex without conscience, sex without soul. It was just what he needed.

There were many things about her that would have reached him deeply if he'd met her years ago — her reflectiveness, her curiosity, her humor — but he didn't care about any of these things now.

They were seeing each other several nights a week. She would show up at his door with a satchelful of books that she was reading for her dissertation — Kant and Hegel and all the small fry in between — but none of the books ever made it out of the satchel.

When he was around her he somehow felt both more alert and more sluggish. He felt alive to every flicker of her mood, but at the same time all he ever wanted was to lie down with her and be animals together.

Her height transfixed him. He had never felt this before, never suspected it, but there was something erotically stimulating about standing on level ground with a woman and looking up at her. It was as if she could contain him — so it was as if the sexual act was implicit in every moment, even when they were just standing next to each other, fully clothed.

Maud wasn't overweight, but she had meat on her bones. All the other women he'd been with had been recovering anorexics. "I'm not sure I have a body," Leila had once said. Maud most definitely had a body. As she moved around his kitchen wearing one of his button-down shirts, wearing only that, she seemed to be too much for the room: she seemed to carry too much aliveness in her to be contained in such a small space.

It wasn't as if their sex was some delicious delirium in which everything simply flowed. He went down on her all the time, but he sometimes felt that he didn't know what the hell he was doing down there. He used to feel like he knew what he was doing with Leila, but it turned out that giving a woman pleasure was not like riding a bicycle. Uncovering the mysteries of one woman's responses had nothing to do with uncovering the mysteries of another's.

He was ashamed of how little he understood her sexually, when she seemed to understand everything there was to know about him.

Sometimes when she touched him he felt panicked, because it felt *too* good. She had hands that made him think she should have been a sculptor. He felt as if he were being created by her touch. It wasn't that she was finding out what he liked; it was that she was teaching him what he liked.

With her large beautiful body, which she operated with the delighted abandon of a shy woman who had decided to let her shyness go, she would maneuver herself on top of him, lower her face to kiss him, and her hair would fall over his face and he would feel as if he were losing himself, losing himself within her. There was something weirdly compelling about this, about the feeling of simply letting go.

After three weeks of getting together at his place, they decided to have an evening at hers. When he showed up, she had a cup of tea ready for him, and as she brought out a tray with both sugar and honey on it he experienced a wild desire to punch her in the mouth.

"How are you?' she said.

"I'm fine," he said. "How about you?"

"I'm well," she said.

I'm well, he thought. What pretentious bullshit. Can't you just say, "I'm good," like everybody else in the world?

He hadn't hit anyone since sixth grade, and he hadn't *wanted* to hit anyone since then, but now, with Maud, the urge to do violence was starting to overwhelm him.

Why did he want to attack her? He wanted to attack her because she was Jewish. He wanted to attack her because she was so persistent, had been so persistent from the first. He wanted to attack her because he was so drawn to her.

He would leave her apartment and walk home and fall into a rage-demented silence. He wanted to kill her. She was a Jew and she was doing this to humiliate him.

Doing what? Making herself irresistible to him. Making herself indispensable to him.

He would walk home quickly, gritting his teeth with the desire never to see her again, but before he had passed out of the island of Manhattan his rage would burn itself out and he would begin to think about her longingly: her full mouth, her long, strong legs, her genius hands; and after he thought about her longingly he would think about her tenderly. He would think about her mind, about the way she somehow combined intellect with innocence. She was strong and she was soft, and the combination moved him. And every time he caught himself thinking about her tenderly, he had to wrench himself back into indifference.

He didn't want to grow with her. He didn't want them to evolve into a condition where they were renting videos together and telling each other the names of their childhood pets. He wanted to keep fucking her, and he didn't want anything to change.

Except something *was* changing. Something began to change after the time he stayed over at her apartment. When they were getting together at his place, she seemed to be taking her cue from their surroundings: he had eliminated every ornament, everything that wasn't functional, and they had fucked with a zeal that in its silence and its one-dimensional intentness was almost grim. But in her apartment, which was filled with books and papers and paintings and photographs and plants and flowers and souvenirs and figurines and tiny treasured toys and little knickknacks, something about their sexual encounters began to change.

The first thing that changed was that she began whispering. She would put her mouth close to his ear and talk to him, and the things she said made him crazy. Or maybe it wasn't the things she said; maybe it was just her voice. She would talk, and keep talking, and he had the feeling that he was being led downward into a place where their sex was even more private, even more unlike anyone else's. She was guiding him into some other region, guiding him there with her talk, dark wet slippery slithering bed talk, unsayable in the light. The things she said to him made no real sense, didn't mean anything when he thought about them later, but in bed they seemed to be the things he'd always wanted to hear someone say, and her voice was the voice in which he'd always wanted to hear them said, her low and confident voice, sliding around him in the darkness. Binding him. One night lying in bed in her apartment he woke up in the dark and thought of leaving, just getting out of there and getting home, because they had been waking up too much together lately, waking up and having breakfast, and he didn't want what they were doing to evolve into a normal life, and as he lay in bed resting for one last minute before getting up, she stirred and put her hand on his stomach—she was still sleeping but it was as if she had intuited his thought—and then, without opening her eyes, she began to touch him, slowly, and after she was done he fell asleep again, and when he woke again it was morning and he had his arms around her and their fingers were intertwined. They had been holding hands in their sleep.

Maud liked to have dessert with every meal, and, for some reason, she liked to have the dessert at the beginning. When they went out to breakfast, she usually started off with a cupcake. This habit charmed him, even though he didn't want to be charmed.

During one of their breakfasts—the only time they really talked about anything—she told him a little bit about her dissertation. She was working on the problem of recognition.

"Kant's categorical imperative," she told him, "says that we have to treat other human beings as ends in themselves, not as means to our own ends. I'm trying to trace the development of that idea in some of the thinkers who have held it since Kant."

"Like who?"

"Martin Buber. Jürgen Habermas. Emmanuel Levinas."

"Do you look at the political implications of the idea?"

"No. I mean, they're implied. But I don't write about them."

"So you don't point to the contradiction between the fact that these last three are distinguished Jewish thinkers but the Jewish state has done its best to render its neighbors, the Palestinians, into nonpeople."

He wanted to pick a fight with her, but she wouldn't fight.

"That won't be in the dissertation," she said. "Maybe when they turn it into a movie."

There was a plate of eggs and toast in front of him, but he didn't touch it. If she wouldn't give him the satisfaction of fighting with him, then he wouldn't give her the satisfaction of eating.

He felt like an eleven-year-old.

He hated being drawn back into life.

Even when they were making love, he hated it. At the same time as he was hungrily putting his mouth on her and smelling the powerful weird smell of her sex, he was hating it, because with every moment in which he was drawn more fully into life, Zahra was being delivered more fully into death. Running his hands over Maud's body as they lay on his small bed, he felt as if the two of them were conspiring to murder his daughter all over again.

He didn't want to admit anything new into his life, anything that Zahra wouldn't recognize. He wanted his life to be a hollowed-out place of worship, a house of memory, and he was afraid that any new experience he had would make his memories of her grow faint. He didn't want to forget anything. The memory of her learning to crawl, face lit up with a remarkably sophisticated mixture of determination and pride, as she fought her way across the floor, gurgling and drooling, in an attempt to reach a ball Leila had laid down for her. The memory of her learning to talk—of the first time he heard her put two words together. One afternoon when she was one and a half, she sat on Samir's lap for a while as he read the paper, then climbed down and said, "Bye," and then, after taking another few steps, she turned around and said, "Bye, Daddy," the first time she had ever put two words together, and she smiled a little slyly, as if she knew she had accomplished something special, and then she continued on her way to the living room.

When she first learned to talk, "horse" for some reason was "wahwah." The first time they took her to Prospect Park to ride a pony, Leila and the young attendant had put a helmet on Zahra's head and strapped her to the saddle, and then Leila stepped away and joined Samir on the other side of the fence, and the attendant led the pony slowly around the little ring and Zahra looked at them and in an exultant voice cried out, "I riding! I riding a wahwah!"

How could all this have been taken from the world?

"I love your chest," Maud said, and it seemed irrelevant, and he needed to get away from her, needed to be alone again. "I love how hairy your chest is," she said.

The day before she went into the isolation unit to begin receiving chemotherapy in preparation for her transplant, they took her to the park. They had been told that after she got out of the unit she wouldn't be able to go to the park again for at least a year. At the Prospect Park stables, she rode her favorite pony, a small bedraggled creature named Too Tall. At the end of the afternoon she patted him and said, "See you next week." They had tried to explain to her that she would be in the hospital for a long time, but it hadn't really gotten through. She was just beginning to understand the concept of time: for her, everything in the past was yesterday, and everything in the future was tomorrow. Of course she never saw Too Tall again.

So as he was tussling in bed with Maud he wanted to leave her and he wanted to kill her and he wanted to kill himself and he wanted to fuck her into unconsciousness and he wanted her to immobilize him with her sexuality, whatever that might mean, and where, he wondered, in all this mess, was there any room for affection? He didn't think there was any. "How does this feel?" she said, and it felt good, but what did it mean when he had lost the person he had been born to protect?

She had suffered terribly in her last two months, day after day after day. He could never blot out the memory of her agony when she woke up in the recovery room after they inserted her ports. Before the bone-marrow transplant, they inserted tubes, "ports," in her chest, threaded them into the arteries near her heart, so they could give her medicines and remove her blood for testing without repeatedly pricking her with needles. When the doctors had explained this he had thought that the ports would be barely noticeable, hidden beneath the skin, but instead they were long tubes that dangled down her chest, tubes with brightly colored plugs at the ends. They looked like stereo cables; she looked like you could plug her into your speakers and listen to *The Goldberg Variations.* She was three. Leila and he had tried to prepare her for the surgery, inserting tubes in the chest of one of her teddy bears, but Zahra didn't really understand. After the operation, Leila and Samir weren't allowed into the recovery room until she was awake—which meant that they couldn't go in until they heard her crying and screaming. She was lying on the gurney screaming with shock and pain and anger and disbelief: "I don't *like* these things! I want you to take them out!" Later that night, when Leila's mother visited, Zahra told her that the doctors had "made a mistake," because they'd left these things inside of her. At three, she had come to understand that the transfusions and the blood draws were necessary, but this—waking up in pain and finding long tubes coming out of her chest—was something that she had no explanation for. The next day she asked Samir if he used to have tubes in him when he was little. He said that he hadn't—he said that different people needed different things, and told her about a sort of cast that he'd had to wear over his nose after he'd broken it in a fight in ninth grade. "Did Mommy have the tubes?" she asked, and he had explained that she hadn't, but that she'd had to have something in her mouth—he explained braces to her, trying to make her believe that having braces was the same as having ports. She had listened intently as he had tried to paint a picture of a world that was a democracy of suffering, in which everyone had his own distinctive way of suffering, his own distinctive way of being violated, but in which all of us were violated, all of us bore some foreign extrusion upon our bodies. She had listened intently, and after he was finished she didn't say a word. He wondered at the time, and wondered still, whether she had any suspicion that he was lying to her: that the world is not a democracy of suffering; that some of us suffer unendingly while others hardly suffer at all; and that the ones who are singled out for suffering are singled out for no reason.

And here he was with this woman, this woman who had nothing to do with his life, pushing his cock into her anus, something he'd never done before with any woman and had never wanted to do, but with Maud he wanted to do everything, but he didn't *want* to want to do everything with her, because Zahra had never met her, because she had never met Zahra, had never loved Zahra, and he didn't want to fall in love with a woman who had never loved his love.

Someday I will die and Leila will die and all memory of her will vanish from the earth. How can that happen?

One night he got out of bed to go to the bathroom and when he came back he stood in the doorway, watching Maud as she slept. She slept effortfully, as if she was troubled. He had no idea what she was troubled by, and didn't want to know.

He thought that it might be a good idea to leave her, right this minute, and never see her again. Leave. Leave with your life. He picked up his shoes. He would leave her apartment stealthily and put his shoes on in the hall.

Even as she slept, she possessed some kind of force, in his imagination, at least. Even as she slept, he could still feel the pull of her: her largeness, her innocence, her brilliance, her naïveté, her instability, her fear, her seductiveness, her hopefulness.

Leaving—now, in the middle of the night, while she slept— wouldn't be the right thing to do. If you are seeing a woman who spends all her time grappling with the problem of how we can learn to treat each other respectfully, a woman who is dedicated above all to exploring the "I and Thou" relationship, it would not be a nice thing to sneak out of her life without saying good-bye.

He wanted to leave her, but there was no reason to do it in such a hurtful way.

He stood there in her bedroom doorway, with his shoes in his hands, listening to her breathe. This was the last night he would be with her. He would see her again, to tell her that he couldn't be with her anymore, but he would never again hear her breathe in her sleep. So he stood there and listened. He listened for a long time.

Zahra used to talk in her sleep. When she was three, and they were putting the needle into her arm every night while she slept, one night, without even waking up, she had murmured, "Be very careful."

Eighteen

Sitting in the library on a Wednesday afternoon, trying to read Richard Rorty's *Contingency, Irony, and Solidarity,* Maud couldn't concentrate. She was eager to see Samir again and return to their sexual carnival. That was how she thought of their encounters.

At the same time as they excited her, something about them made her sick at heart. If you're beginning to see a man whose life has been blown apart by the death of his daughter, and if you offer him a love life, then the love life you offer him, she thought, should be something pure and true and spiritual, something that brings together body and mind and spirit. That wasn't what she was offering him, though. What she was offering him—it was as if she'd taken him to a pit and dumped him into it and jumped in after him, a vat of sticky murky brackened blackish broth.

She struggled with the book until five, not happy with Rorty's argument that we naturally feel sympathy for people we know, people in our own tribe, before we feel it for "the other," and that a humanitarianism that tries to deny this will inevitably be delusional. She didn't like the thought that we're naturally clubby, hardening our hearts to those not our own. Rorty wasn't a pessimist—he thought we could gradually enlarge our idea of who is included in the category of "our own"—but the minimalism of his short-term expectations distressed her.

After a while she put down the book and tried to write in her diary. She'd kept a diary ever since she was a girl, writing in small notebooks that fit into her back pocket or her purse. For days she had been trying to write about what it was like to see Samir, but she kept being stymied by the problem of language. The problem of how to refer to the sexual organs. *Penis* and *testicles* and *vagina* and *clitoris*—these words seemed so clinical that when she used them it made their sex acts seem stilted, inhibited, constrained, and they were anything but that. But on the other hand, words like *cock* and *cunt* and *clit* seemed leering and adolescent. There were no nouns that didn't sound slightly off. Everyone on the planet was preoccupied with sex, yet no one quite had the vocabulary to describe it.

When it got dark she left the library and headed to Samir's.

On seeing his expression—businesslike and dry—she knew that there would be little or no conversation again tonight, if he had his way. She sat on his couch, and instead of sitting next to her, he sat in a chair.

He was infuriatingly held-back.

"Why are you over there?" she said.

He didn't answer.

She worked off her shoe and put her foot on his fly and started moving it up and down.

"Do you think I'm smarter than you are?" she said.

"I don't know."

"You must have thought about it."

She was still working on him with her foot, so there was no danger that either of them would take the conversation too seriously.

"I think you're probably more profound than I am," he said.

"What do you mean?"

"There's more to you."

"What do you mean?"

"I don't know."

She had always been proud of how dexterous she was with her feet. When she was in her teens, after seeing the movie *My Left Foot,* she had tried to type a book report with her feet, and she hadn't done too badly. So now, still sitting casually on the couch, she was taking down his fly.

"And that's it? You haven't thought about it more than that?"

"I think you have more intellectual energy than I do."

"And what does *that* mean?"

"It means that when you get hold of a thought, you don't let it go. You follow it all the way, wherever it takes you."

"How do you know that about me?"

"I don't know."

"So when you add it all up," she said, "you do think I'm smarter than you are."

"Probably."

"That's good. I think so too."

In reality she had no idea who was smarter; she didn't think it was a useful or interesting question. But she liked talking this way with him. She liked playing the part of someone utterly self-assured.

Maud had never been comfortable with herself sexually. She had always felt too large, too loose: her legs were a thousand miles long, her breasts were udders. And she was not, in general, a champion of the human body. Sometimes she thought she would be happy as a creature of pure thought, a creature from a science-fiction movie — a giant pulsating brain in a glass shell.

She had always fumbled around in bed with men, not knowing what they wanted, not knowing what she wanted.

But with Samir, something was different. She felt the way a safecracker must feel in the moment when he hears the tumblers ease into place. He was a furious grief-stricken being, affronting the air when he walked; his smallness made him feel no match for the world, and even when their sex was violent, even when he was doing things to her that could be construed as sadistic, she knew that what he was wanting above all was to lose himself to her, to give himself up to her, to let her surround him and hold him and contain him. Small proud rageful sentimental dev-astated broken boy.

He was leaning back in his chair now, his eyes starting to close. She still hadn't moved off the couch.

He wanted her to take the lead in this relationship. And she thought: I can do that. I can move this thing.

In the morning he looked as if he was ready for her to leave, but she said, "You're going to take me out to breakfast today. There's a diner I like on Seventh Avenue."

He didn't look enthusiastic.

"Get dressed," she said.

She felt weird, being always on the verge of bossing him around, being sort of dominatrix-y, except that it was so obvi-ously not what she was. What was happening, she thought, was that she was responding to some need he couldn't express and probably couldn't admit to himself. He needed to be dragged back into the world.

Nineteen

He had thought he'd just have a cup of coffee and get out of there, but after they sat down he realized he was hungry, and he ordered fried eggs and sausages and orange juice.

"Where did you get it from?" he said.

"Get what?"

"The idea behind your dissertation. Why is it so important to you?"

"I think I got it from my mother. When I was growing up, she was just starting to work as a therapist, and I loved to hear her talking about what she did. I once read that there are some therapists who want to tell you who you are, and some who want to find out who you are, and she's definitely the kind who wants to find out who you are."

"That's a good quality."

He was alarmed at himself, to be participating in one of these how-did-you-get-to-be-the-way-you-are conversations. Not just participating in it, but initiating it. He didn't know the source of this awful mellowing. But the fact was that sitting across from her in the diner, with the sunlight splashing through the window and making it difficult, at moments, to see her, he felt relaxed, and the question he had asked her was one that he'd been wondering about for weeks.

Years ago, a friend of his had described what went on in his mind when he met an attractive woman at a party: "You know you're gonna have to do all this *talking*. You know you're going to have to listen to her *ideas*. But it's all just a game, because you know, and if she has any brains at all, she knows, that listening to her is just the price you pay for taking her home and fucking her. It's like paying a toll."

His friend had said all this with a know-it-all smile, as if he was sure that every man felt this way. But Samir had never felt this way. He had always felt something like the opposite: if he didn't love to listen to a woman, he had no desire to take her home.

During these last few weeks he had tried to be like his old friend, but it had been an effort. He kept wondering about Maud, wondering about her thoughts, her goals, her life. He kept thinking about her and then forcing himself not to. But he felt his indifference faltering.

After breakfast they took a walk through the park and they passed a kid pulling another kid in a red wagon and somehow she was telling him about the tonsillectomy she'd had at the age of four.

"My parents told me I'd be going to sleep for a while, and after I woke up I'd have ice cream. The last thing I remember was being in a red wagon in the hospital with a nurse wheeling me down the hall. I was sitting there waving to my parents. Very excited. And then I woke up in the morning and my throat hurt. And they didn't have any ice cream. They said the hospital ran out."

He was looking at the ground as she spoke. He was moved by her story, more than she could ever know. He saw her as a little girl, hopeful, ready to be treated well, ready to trust.

He glanced up at her and saw that her face was bright red.

"You must think I'm an idiot," she said.

"I don't know what you're talking about."

And then he did. She didn't think she had a right to tell this kind of story, to dwell with a nostalgic sadness on her childhood disappointments, when his own daughter had suffered and died.

He would have liked to tell her that it was all right: she was allowed to talk about her life without testing every word against the greater sorrow suffered by his daughter.

He didn't say this, however, because he didn't want to speak of these things.

She still had bright red blotches on her cheeks and throat. A woman who blushes, at this late date. At this moment in history. Astounding.

To reassure her, he took her hand.

Her brother Carl was coming to visit that weekend, and she was telling Samir about her niece and nephew. "When I spent a week with them over the holidays last year, my entire picture of human nature changed."

"How?"

"I used to think that people were good. Plato and Aristotle believed that. They believed that everyone seeks to do good, and that the problem is just that we don't always recognize the good. I believed this, because I *wanted* to believe it."

"And your niece and nephew made you see that people are basically evil?"

"They made me see that everyone starts off as a bundle of possibilities, and that goodness isn't there from the start. It's something that has to be learned."

"What were they doing that made you see that?"

She answered him at length, as if reciting a philosophical argument, and as he listened he experienced a peculiar elation. He loved the way she took everything so seriously. She threw herself headlong into ideas; she *lived* them. When she bought a Popsicle, Seneca was beside her, contemplating the act; when she visited her niece and nephew, Plato was there, and she and Plato were disagreeing. If she were just a tiny bit different, he might consider all this pretentious, but he could see that there was nothing forced about it, nothing self-conscious: she wasn't pretending to think this way, she really did. He wasn't sure he'd ever met anyone who lived her ideas out in this way.

He was surprised by what he was feeling.

It was a beautiful day—it was a week away from winter, but the landscape seemed to be on the verge of blooming—and although it was hard for him to admit this, it wasn't just sex anymore. He wanted this. He wanted her. He wanted to be here, walking through the park with her, holding her hand.

TWENTY

Patrick looked ill at ease. He looked like someone who had never set foot in the big city before.

"Eleanor Levin, I presume," he said. He kissed her on the cheek.

"Eleanor Weller," she said—because she liked her married name better, and because she wanted to remind him that she wasn't the girl he had known all those years ago. She was that girl—she had that girl inside her—but she also wasn't.

Not that she really needed to remind him. She weighed about fifty pounds more than that long-ago girl had weighed, and her hair, once brown and flowing, was now gray and close-cropped. As he took her hands, she watched his face, super-alert for any sign of disappointment. But she couldn't find any.

He hadn't aged that well either. In his youth he had been rugged, athletic, prematurely weatherbeaten, but in a pictur-esque way. Now he looked beery and tired, and his face had the unnatural redness that comes with decades of addiction to nicotine.

They had arranged to meet at Rockefeller Center, near the skating rink. Jewish to the bone, she nevertheless found the Christmas season exhilarating, and this spot, overlooking the skaters and just beneath the enormous illuminated tree, some-times seemed to her the most glamorous place in the world.

"This city is incredible," he said. "I feel like a country bumpkin."

"You look like a country bumpkin."

"Really?" He looked down at himself. "Is it the tie?"

He was wearing a string tie, which did, now that he mentioned it, look absurd.

"I feel like I'm on a date with Gene Autry," she said. "The singing cowboy."

"I think Roy Rogers was the singing cowboy."

"Gene Autry could carry a tune."

She took his hand.

"Are you ready for that hot chocolate?" she said.

It was a hot chocolate with a history. Thirty-eight years ago they'd planned a ski trip, but Patrick broke his leg the week they were supposed to go. She kept asking him to go with her anyway, trying to paint a romantic picture of evenings spent drinking hot chocolate and reading in front of a fire, nights spent holding each other under a stack of blankets in the brilliantly chilly night. But he hadn't wanted to go there if he couldn't ski, and she'd ended up taking her sister.

They walked north on Sixth Avenue. She didn't know exactly where the proposed hot chocolate might be.

She felt terribly self-conscious, self-conscious about being old and fat and in no way the fox that she had once believed she had at least a chance of being.

"I'm glad I gave myself an extra hour to get lost in," he said. "You told me to get the subway on Sixth Avenue, and I walked and I walked and I couldn't *find* Sixth Avenue, until I finally stopped on the Avenue of the Americas, which I'd walked past around fifteen times, and asked somebody where Sixth Avenue was, and he told me I was on it."

She said something, but a moment later she had no idea what she'd said, because she couldn't stop thinking about how she'd let her body go to pot. She remembered how attracted to her he used to be. There was no way on earth he'd feel that powerfully attracted to her now.

He stopped at a souvenir stand. "I promised Maggie I'd get her one of these," he said, and bought a T-shirt with a photo of John Lennon, himself wearing a T-shirt, which read NEW YORK CITY. Maggie was the second of his two children, a high school sophomore still living in Oregon. "When John Lennon died she wasn't even born yet, but she's a Beatles fan now, and John is her favorite Beatle."

They found a café on Central Park South. The waitress was a beautiful young woman with a French accent that might have been real. She was wearing a skirt with a slit down the side. She gave them their menus and swayed away.

Eleanor wished that she didn't have liver spots on her hands. She laid the menu down and put her hands under the table.

"It's really good to see you," Patrick said.

"It's good to be seen," she said, which was an old Steve Allen joke, but she meant it. She had always remembered him as someone who tried to see her as she was. Whether this would still be true, she had no idea.

She was hoping that he would view her charitably. She was hoping that he would see her not as the battered bag she had become, but the woman of spirit he had known when they were young. She was hoping that he would look past the cruelty of the way she had left him and see that she was not a cruel person but a kind person who had committed a desperate act.

As soon as these hopes passed through her mind, she wondered whether what she was thinking about herself was true. Was she still vital in her spirit? Was she a kind person? These are probably questions one can't answer about oneself. They can be answered only by others.

He was looking at the menu. "What's the difference between

a café au lait and a cappuccino?" he said. "I've never been able to figure it out."

At the same time as she was hoping that he would see her charitably, she was trying to see him charitably.

He looked so provincial. He looked all wrong for New York. He looked like an elderly fur trapper who had ventured into the city in search of a wife. His suit looked as if it was made out of Dacron: it was probably a wash-and-wear suit from Sears. She was trying to stop her mind from noticing these things. She was trying to stop her mind, her critical evaluating mind, from criticizing and evaluating him. She had to remind herself that there was no reason he should have known that the Avenue of the Americas was Sixth Avenue. New Yorkers tend to forget that knowledge of the city's geography is not innate. There was a part of her that was thinking, despite herself, that if he hadn't known this, then he was stupid.

She had to stop evaluating him, had to stop noticing, for example, that his teeth were very yellow, much more so than she'd remembered. Decades of late-night negotiating sessions fueled by coffee and cigarettes.

She tried to change her perspective. If he were a New Yorker he probably would have bleached his teeth by now, in anticipation of the moment when a reporter for *Eyewitness News* might stick a microphone in his face and ask him his opinion about some episode of "labor strife" in the sanitation department. Like everyone else in New York, he would have wanted to be ready for his close-up. She tried to see the fact that he hadn't as a sign that he wasn't interested in playing careerist games. She tried to see his teeth as nobly yellow.

She felt herself being buried under a mass of trivial and ungenerous thoughts.

"Cappuccino . . . I'm not sure," she said. "So you're here for a week?"

"I wish. That was the original plan. Katie went to the trouble of setting up a whole week's worth of activities. But I got a call this morning that they just took a strike vote out at United Paper, and the rep who's been working with them is just a kid, so it looks like I have to go back on Monday."

"That's a drag," Eleanor said, feeling relieved. When he had told her on the phone that he was coming out for a week, she had been nervous about the idea of seeing him more than once. Once was enough: manageable, contained. She would be able to carry the experience back to her apartment and meditate on it. A single nugget of experience was as much as she could digest right now, would nourish her through the winter.

"Yes. But that's the life of a union rep."

They were at a moment where the conversation could go in either of two ways. They could speak from the heart, about things that were real, or else they could stay on the surface. And perhaps everything that would flow from this moment would take its shape from the choice they made.

She opted for the surface.

"Do you still believe in your work as much as you used to?" she said.

It wasn't entirely a superficial question. One of the things she had admired about him had been his commitment to his work. He was as passionate about the labor movement as any artist she knew was passionate about art. But in asking it she was making a choice to avoid the subject of their own past.

"Even more so," he said.

"I wouldn't have thought that was possible."

"This country has gotten so much worse. So much more

cruel. I always knew the labor movement was important, but now I think it's more important than ever. Did you see *The New York Times* this morning?" He reached into the breast pocket of his jacket and brought out an article he'd clipped from the paper. "It's part of their series on poverty in America. Forty million Americans don't have health insurance. Ten percent of American children are going to bed hungry. It amazes me that we think of ourselves as a civilized country."

"That's sad," she said.

She had forgotten about his habit of clipping newspaper articles, producing them in the middle of conversations, and quoting important statistics. It was a habit that she had not been entirely in love with.

"It is sad," he said.

"I'm glad to know you haven't changed. Every once in a while, when I've felt like things are just getting worse and worse, it's been a little bit of a comfort to know that you were probably still out there, going town to town, patiently talking to one person at a time about the idea that things might be different."

"Still out there," he said. "Still talking union. Still sleeping in fleabag hotels and getting up at five so I can be at the factory gates when the night shift is getting off, so I can buttonhole one or two of them and take them out for coffee and find out if they want to get organized."

He sounded weary, but she felt sure it was the mock weariness of someone who loved what he was doing and wouldn't dream of doing anything else.

They talked about their jobs; they talked about their children; and after a while they were silent.

She couldn't put the serious things off forever.

"So what's this complicated situation with Diana?" she said.

"Diana." He took the salt shaker out of its holder and nodded slowly, as if it had given him secret instructions. "We're together, we're not together, we're together. It gets to the point where even we have trouble keeping track."

"What was it when you last checked?"

"When I last checked. When I last checked we were together."

The waitress swept over and gaily refilled their water glasses. Eleanor wondered how the two of them looked to her. Oldsters reminiscing about days of yore.

"Do you know what you want?" she said.

"I do. But . . . thirty years is a long time."

"These things are hard," she said. "I sympathize with you."

Profound, she thought. *Give that woman an honorary doctorate.*

He took off his glasses and closed his eyes and rubbed them.

"I don't know whether you'll really want to hear this," he said, "but I've never loved her the way I loved you."

He opened his eyes and looked directly at her. Without his glasses, his eyes looked naked.

Her liver-spotted hands, still on her thighs, were trembling.

She'd probably wanted him to say something like this, but now that he'd said it, it disturbed her. It made her sad for him. It was like a confession that he hadn't grown.

But had *she* grown? Hadn't she spent decades avoiding the truth about Adam, because she hadn't had the courage to leave him?

The café was filled with young people, having hip and witty conversations, presumably. They looked like young conquerors. She wondered how many of them, even now, were making the mistakes that would hobble them for the rest of their lives.

"That was a long time ago," she said.

Is it possible, she thought, for a person to get *two* honorary doctorates?

"Sometimes it feels that way," he said. "Sometimes it feels like it was yesterday."

The afternoon declined into awkwardness and small talk. Journeys end in lovers meeting, she thought, but not always.

He was meeting Kate at the Metropolitan Museum. Eleanor accompanied him into Central Park. The broken beauty of winter in New York. They were walking in a chilly wind; she pulled her collar closer around her throat.

Somewhere in the middle of the park, he took her hand, and they walked that way. Her hand was sweating madly.

When they reached Fifth Avenue, he asked if she wanted to meet Kate. He looked at his watch. "She's usually no more than forty-five minutes late."

"I'd love to, but another time. It's been an emotional day."

"Can I get you a cab?" he said.

"Thank you. But I think I'd like to walk."

When they said good-bye, they embraced, and then he took a step back, to look at her. The way he looked at her made her worries about her appearance fade. For a moment she felt like a desirable creature, rather than the shapeless old handbag she knew herself to be, the woman in a dress that was like a circus tent. He had once told her that she was the light of the world.

Twenty-one

She walked for a minute or two, and then, as soon as she was sure that she was out of his range of vision, she stopped and waited for the crosstown bus. She'd had no intention of walking all the way home; she'd told him she wanted to walk only in an effort to seem like a poetic being, someone who lived outside of the world of subways and buses and cabs.

Amazing that on the verge of sixty, you still put on such airs.

When she got home she took off her jacket and sweater and scarf, went to Maud's old room, and started writing. Suddenly she had a lot to write about.

If Patrick were to be believed, he had spent nearly forty years longing for her. As she sat writing about their afternoon, she had to admit to herself that she hadn't felt the same way about him. He had remained in her mind as the person she respected most, the man who had more integrity than anyone else she'd ever met, but she hadn't spent all these years pining after him.

We wish for a symmetry of feeling, but we rarely get it. It is painful to be the one who loves more, and painful to be the one who loves less.

Patrick had never known the real story of what happened when she left him. He had thought she left him in a kind of delirium after the death of her sister. He didn't know that she'd been planning to leave him even before Joanna died. She'd already met Adam, and she'd already decided that she was going to marry him.

Thinking about it clearly and seriously, she admitted something she'd never admitted to herself before. Although she had loved Patrick as she'd never loved Adam, the choices she made when she threw Patrick over, took up with Adam, and accompanied him to New York, were choices she would make all over again, even knowing, as she knew now, that Patrick was the better man. She had probably known it even then. She hadn't been in a state of temporary insanity when she chose Adam. She had chosen Adam with her eyes open.

For years she had been telling herself that the only reason she didn't regret the choices she made back then was that her marriage to Adam had produced their children. But now she admitted to herself that there were other reasons as well. When she made the choice, she wasn't just choosing a person; she was choosing a life. She had thought that Adam could introduce her to a wider world than Patrick could. And she'd been right. She didn't want to stay in Portland and be a labor organizer's wife. She didn't want to listen to stories about negotiating sessions and the effort to get a cost-of-living clause inserted into the contract of the United Brotherhood of Pulp Mashers; she didn't want to socialize with labor organizers and their wives. She respected these people completely; she thought that the work they were doing was as noble as any work in the world. And yet she hadn't wanted to live out her life among them. Their nervous grasping for respectability—they were always saying, "Between you and I," or, after using some perfectly ordinary profanity, "Pardon my French." She believed that their concerns were broad and serious: the fate of working people, the future of equality, the effort to wrest a measure of fairness from an unfair system. And yet their concerns had always felt small to her. Not small, really, but drab.

In her twenties, Patrick, as much as she cared for him, was Portland; Patrick was the provinces. Adam was the promise of New York.

At twenty-two, when she had imagined a life with Patrick, she had imagined living a closed-in life that hardly changed from year to year. When she had imagined a life with Adam, she had imagined parties, literary gossip, the drama of Manhattan, a never-ending sense of the new. In choosing between two men, she had chosen between two lives, and the life she had imagined was not too far from the life she had gone on to live. She had enjoyed the world that Adam had given her: she had enjoyed the trips to Paris and London and Amsterdam, the monthlong residencies at Bellagio; she had enjoyed meeting Norman Mailer and Susan Sontag and Joyce Carol Oates. She might not have loved Adam as genuinely as she'd loved Patrick, but she'd found him more exciting.

It was still exciting, even now, to remember her first weekend in Manhattan with Adam. She was officially still seeing Patrick, but she'd sneaked off to New York to be with Adam during the week between Christmas and New Year's. Adam introduced her to his writer friends; he took her on a carriage ride in the park; and on New Year's Eve he took her to dinner at the Rainbow Room, with the city glittering below them. It was the middle of the 1960s, but although Adam was only a few years older than she was, he seemed to belong to a different era, and he seemed to be offering her some timeless New York, where the streets were rain-washed and glistening and the soundtrack wasn't Jim Morrison and Mick Jagger but Cole Porter and George Gershwin. It was as if he were lifting her up out of her life. As the new year came in, they were dancing, and it felt as if life's most extravagant promises could come true, and she closed her eyes and put her head on his shoulder and pressed closer to him, as the band played "Embraceable You."

She spent about an hour at the desk in Maud's old room, writing about all this. She would have stayed there longer, but her fingers had started to lock up.

It was an hour, but it was also thirty-seven years. The woman who rose from the desk had a different past than the woman who had sat down in front of it.

TWENTY-TWO

Thea, across the room, with a delighted expression, was talking to a young man, laughing at something he'd said. Her head was thrown back, offering him a view of her brilliant throat. The man looked pleased, but also unsure of himself, as if she was laughing at a remark that he hadn't intended to be witty.

This was Thea: she could make you feel flattered and insecure at the same time.

Adam handed his coat to the cloakroom attendant and started toward her. He didn't mind seeing Thea flirting with other men. He rather enjoyed it.

It was an end-of-the-year party given by the *Los Angeles Times Book Review*. They held one party in LA and another in New York. Adam had been going for years; Thea had never been to one before, and she had been excited about it all day.

He gave her a wide berth. He didn't know who the man was, but Thea was clearly, as she liked to put it, "working him"— he was obviously someone who could be useful to her, and Adam knew enough not to interfere. So he just stood with his drink and took in the scene.

The room was dotted with celebrities from the world of literature and performance. E. L. Doctorow, remote behind his air of suave imperturbability, was talking to Laurie Anderson, who was, as always, carefully disheveled, and Lou Reed, who had the pruny monkeyish face of somebody's grandfather, but who was imperishably hip—the hippest man in the room, in any room, by definition.

Philip Levine, the poet, was holding forth to two attractive young women. Levine was wearing a baseball cap and a duck-hunting jacket. He had grown up in Detroit and had worked briefly in an auto factory, and although he'd spent the last fifty years exclusively in academic and literary circles, he still cultivated the image of a rough-hewn member of the laboring class. If you didn't know better you might have thought that he'd come straight to the party from the assembly line.

Adam noted this not in a critical way, but with admiration. Everyone, he thought, needs an act, and Levine's had served him well.

Adam's own act had never been so elaborate. His height had done a lot of the work for him, and Ellie had done the rest. She had been so relentlessly nice—so generous, so warm—that he was able to be laconic and ironic and unapproachable without anyone considering him a shit. Ellie was gone, but Thea had replaced her—she'd much more than replaced her: she was like a young actress who had stolen a role from a faded star and infused the entire production with new life. The production being Adam. Thea made him seem, not exactly younger, but more contemporary.

Her work completed, Thea joined him, kissing him on the cheek.

"Have you been enjoying yourself?" he said.

"I always enjoy myself."

"That's what I like about you."

"Have you noticed?" she said. "Your young striver is here." She indicated a man across the room. It was Jeffrey Lipkin, the professor who had the literary crush on Izzy Cantor.

She caught his eye, and Lipkin walked over to them.

"Jeffrey," Adam said. "So good to see you. I've heard about your good news. Congratulations."

A few weeks ago, *The New York Observer* had run a story about the Gellman Foundation, an old, distinguished Jewish philanthropic organization, and its vigorous new president, who wanted to give more attention to the arts. As one of his initiatives, he was launching a program whereby literary prizes would be awarded yearly to Jewish writers and visual artists. To Adam's surprise, Jeffrey had been one of three people appointed as permanent judges for the literary prizes. "That little nerd is going to be controlling hundreds of thousands of dollars in awards?" Thea had said when Adam showed her the article. "That's why one must always be cordial to everyone, even little nerds," Adam had said.

Now, at the party, Thea raised her glass to Jeffrey. "You must be feeling pretty good," she said. "You're a kingmaker."

"I wouldn't say that," Jeffrey murmured. "I'm just happy to have this chance to do something for Jewish culture. For the culture as a whole, really." He seemed to be impressed by his own modesty.

"I guess I'll have to stop making fun of your eating habits," Thea said. "So give us the inside scoop. Who's getting the big prizes this year?"

"I'm not at liberty to say."

"Can we guess? And you'll tell us if we're right or wrong?"

"We don't have to guess," Adam said. "If you're giving out two prizes, they're going to Bellow and Roth. Three, then it's Bellow and Roth and Ozick."

Jeffrey was silent, with a happily owlish expression. Glad to be important enough to have a secret.

"Bellow and Roth," Thea said, and, with one of the occasional outbursts of vulgarity that never ceased to surprise him, she stuck her index finger down her throat and mimed the act of vomiting.

"What's wrong with Bellow and Roth?" Jeffrey said.

"The patriarchs," she said. "Between them they've put out something like a hundred books, and in all those years of chatter, all those forests laid to waste, neither of them has been able to come up with one lifelike woman character."

"I don't know if that's true," Jeffrey said. "Certainly women aren't their strong suit. But the daughter in *American Pastoral*—she's a destructive force, but she's also very human. She's not *nice,* but she's very real."

"First of all," Thea said, "that's debatable. And second, even if it's true, it proves my point. You can only point to one example to make your case, and she's an example of woman at her most destructive."

What Adam found especially impressive about Thea at this moment was that he knew that, other than *Portnoy's Complaint* and a few pages of *Herzog,* she hadn't read a word by Roth or Bellow.

Thea's way of flirting with men was to fight with them. It was a quality Adam found appealing. His previous mistress had been a young woman who ostentatiously deferred to power and status: she would treat Adam's every utterance with astonishment, as if he summed up in each casual phrase some idea she had been struggling to articulate for years. It was flattering at first but soon grew tiresome.

"Let me know when the decisions are announced," Thea said. "Maybe I can get you on Charlie's show. You and one of the patriarchs."

Jeffrey looked intoxicated. A beautiful woman was inviting him to appear on TV. This was probably his idea of heaven.

"At least if it's a slow news day," she added.

Thea's beauty was something she used; it was a tool that she wielded in an impersonal way. When she was growing up, she'd once told Adam, she had been quite plain, and she'd grown used to being ignored. When she blossomed, suddenly and startlingly, during her sophomore year in high school, she'd already had too many years' experience of being plain to make the mistake of identifying herself with her looks. Suddenly boys were talking to her. *Men* were talking to her—whenever she was out in public, grown men, men who had wives and children and careers, were drifting over and trying to strike up conversations. But she knew she was the same person she'd always been.

She had once explained to Adam that when life started to change for her, she quickly resolved that she wasn't going to make the mistake her mother had made. Her mother had been born beautiful, and the way she was treated all her life made it easy for her to believe that she possessed a kind of natural royalty. When her beauty faded, she was left without resources. She hadn't made adequate provision for the cold second half of her life, and she spent her last years in a baffled haze, convinced that one more session at the hairdresser's or one more tiny pinch of plastic surgery would return her from her exile, would make the world bow down to her again.

Thea, by contrast, knew that her attractiveness was a card that couldn't be played forever. It was a magic ticket that provided entrée practically everywhere, but a ticket with an expiration date. She was going to use it while it could be used, but she intended to make sure that she had other, more durable assets, long before it was gone.

"Have you had any time to work on your biography of Izzy?" Adam said.

"Not really," Jeffrey said. "I didn't have any free time in the first place, and now with this gig with the foundation, I have less than no free time."

This gig: he was trying to sound as if it were something he took casually, but he was obviously excited by his newfound power. It was clear that his sense of his own worth had ballooned since they had seen him last. His movements were slower and more rounded, and there was a new quality of ripeness in his way of speaking, as if he were listening to himself through head-phones. He was trying on the part of the distinguished man.

When he excused himself to say good-bye to a friend who was leaving the party, Adam and Thea just looked at each other. Adam felt sure that Thea knew what he was thinking.

He was thinking that there must be a way to exploit Jeffrey's new position. Adam had won most of the fancy prizes, but he hadn't won anything lately. He had won two Jewish awards, but it would be good to win another.

"Prizes," Thea said.

Adam nodded.

"Prizes are for old men who are finished," Thea said.

Adam shook his head. "Prizes are good."

"Would you like me to help?" she said. And then: "Silly question." Meaning that of course he would.

And she was right. Adam himself couldn't make the case that he deserved an award. There were some people who could do such a thing, but Adam couldn't. During the years of being Ellie's husband he had lived under a regime of enforced high-mindedness, and had gained a reputation as someone who didn't grubbily grab for things, didn't blow his own horn. It would not be wise to endanger that reputation at this late date.

"Have you told him about the book yet?" Thea said. She was referring to Izzy's novel.

"I'd prefer that he didn't know about the book. Not yet."

He knew what she was thinking: she was looking for something he might offer, something he might dangle in front of Jeffrey's nose. But it was a delicate matter. She couldn't tell Jeffrey that if he gave Adam a prize, Adam would give him something that would turn a biography of Izzy into a "literary event." She couldn't, that is, try to bribe him explicitly. She had to find a way to imply it.

"I wouldn't mind letting him know about Izzy's letters," Adam said.

"His letters."

"Yes. Izzy made copies of all his letters. Which could use a suitable editor, if they're ever going to be published in book form."

"That's good," she said.

"If I had to leave soon," Adam said, "Jeffrey probably wouldn't be disappointed."

"Probably not."

They both knew that Thea could do more for him if he was gone.

He had complete faith in her. He knew that she wouldn't stain the conversation with any vulgar implication of reciprocity. He knew that she would play her part perfectly.

What he anticipated was something like this. She would lead Jeffrey into a conversation about Adam, suggesting that he would be the perfect person to receive a Gellman award. Not a boringly obvious choice, like one of the patriarchs, but not a controversial choice either. And then at some other point in the conversation she would mention that Adam had been looking through Izzy's letters lately, and that a few scholars had already been in touch with him about them, hoping to put them together in a book.

She would put these ideas out there, and that would be all. She would scatter the seeds in Jeffrey's mind, where they might or might not grow.

This might not be the way Thea would act if she were trying to get something for herself. She might be more direct, more brutal. She liked to blow the doors down. But she knew Adam well enough to know that that wouldn't be the way to get something for him. If she wanted to help Adam she'd have to do it in the style that he himself preferred. And she had observed him closely enough to be familiar with his style of manipulating people.

Adam was a cheerful manipulator. One of the things he had learned about manipulating people is that you can't be too attached to the results. If this gambit didn't succeed, there was no harm done; he wasn't going to sit around lamenting the injustice of it all. Because there wouldn't be any injustice.

Adam never took anything personally. People who took insults and disappointments personally, he believed, were people who made the mistake of thinking that something was owed them in the first place. Adam didn't think that anything was owed to us except suffering and death. If good things did happen to you, they usually happened because you were lucky or because you'd stolen them. He had set out to steal as many of the good things as he could, but it was part of his code to be clear-eyed about what he was doing. He knew that he was stealing them, so when his efforts didn't work out, he was never offended or hurt. He accepted defeat gracefully, as he tried to accept everything gracefully.

"Thank you, my dear."

His relationship with Thea was entirely one of convenience, and both of them knew it. There was no crudely concrete quid pro quo in their relationship, but each of them was using the other, frankly and unapologetically. For Adam, their infrequent excursions in bed together were gratifying, but what was actually more gratifying was being seen with her in public, and if he had to choose one or the other, it was the public element of their coupling that he would choose.

And in turn he had introduced her to a wider world. She had gotten the job with Charlie Rose through connections she had made because of him. He hadn't made them for her, but he'd smoothed the way.

Adam and Thea found Jeffrey again near the bar. Adam shook his hand. "I used to be a night owl," Adam said, "but I can't seem to stay awake past ten anymore. It's time for me to go."

"I'm still awake, though," Thea said to Jeffrey. "And hungry. I need someone to take me out to dinner."

Jeffrey looked unsure of how to respond. The party was still in full swing.

"Have dinner with me, Lipkin," Thea said. "The old man left me his credit card. It's all on him."

"She's right," Adam said. "It's on me. In celebration of your new stature."

He shook Jeffrey's hand and kissed Thea, and was off. At home he got into a pair of pajamas and made himself a cup of hot cocoa. It was delicious to be inside and alone and warm on a cold December night, while the incomparable Thea was working on his behalf. Life was good.

TWENTY-THREE

S amir wasn't sure whether the difficult part was over or was just beginning. A month ago, he would wake up every morning thinking that things with Maud were starting to get too heavy, and that he would have to break up with her, and every evening his cock would be in her mouth. Had that been the difficult part, because he'd felt so torn? Or the easy part, because sex was the only thing they'd had?

Now things were not so clear. They were still having sex every time they got together, but they were also spending time together before and after sex, and it was then that the complexities came in.

He felt himself coming alive, and it was painful. It was like a scene in a movie, where the klieg lights are thrown on one by one, illuminating more and more of the set. First his sexual life had come alive. Then his intellectual life: he became more and more interested in the things she had to say.

And then his tenderness. He kept remembering the story she'd told him about her tonsillectomy—waving at her parents as she was being wheeled away in a red wagon, with no idea that she was headed for something that would cause pain, and waking up in a strange bed the next morning, and telling her parents, in a tiny, scratchy voice, that her throat hurt.

One night a few weeks after she told him this story, they were in his apartment, and he was making something for dinner and she was reading on the couch, and he craned his neck to see what she was reading and he saw that it was something by Fichte, and he marveled, as he always did, at the difficulty of the thinkers in whose company she spent her time, and thought about her essential purity—the purity of her interests, the purity of the way she pursued them—and her purity seemed a kind of innocence, and he was struck, more powerfully than he'd been at the moment when he'd actually heard the story, by the image of her sitting in the red wagon, waving good-bye to her parents, happy and proud, unaware of where the wagon was going to take her. The thought of her innocence, the thought that she had been misled by the people who loved her—all of it made him wish he could step into her past and protect her from harm, or at the very least be there when she woke up after her operation with the ice cream that had been promised to her.

These feelings caught him by surprise. He had never felt this kind of protectiveness toward anyone except his daughter.

She looked up from her book and smiled at him. "Whatcha lookin' at, big guy?"

"Just looking," he said.

He remembered the title of a poem he had read in college. "Surprised by Joy."

During these weeks, as he felt himself changing, Samir sometimes observed the process with a sort of detached curiosity. He was curious about what he would become. Curious to find out whether his new self was going to be his old self reclaimed, as if he'd left it in storage for a few years, or whether it was going to be something entirely unknown. He wondered, for example, whether his interest in the world would return—his old passions, his old anger.

In his old life, he had worked for a series of human-rights organizations, and finally at the Arab American Human Rights

Committee. He'd liked the job, and he never really thought about leaving.

When he went back to work after his daughter's death, he fulfilled his obligations on automatic pilot, dutifully putting out bulletins and research reports and "AAHRC Action Alerts!" He might as well have been writing beer commercials for all it mattered to him, but he thought that if he just went through the motions for a while, he would eventually start to care again.

On a Tuesday morning a little less than a month after Zahra's death, he was working from home, transcribing an interview with a Palestinian American academic that he'd recorded the month before, when his phone rang. He heard his grandmother's voice on the answering machine, talking about something she'd seen on CNN. He turned the volume down, intending to call her back after he'd finished working.

His grandmother was a sad creature. She had spent the fifteen years of her widowhood sitting in front of the television. She would come alive during those periods when the entire country was supposedly riveted on one event: she would click avidly from CNN to MSNBC to Fox News and call Samir several times a day to give him updates. As she delivered these updates, Samir would leaf through the newspaper or check his e-mail and pretend to listen.

On that morning, she called a few more times. He could hear her voice faintly on the answering machine but he couldn't hear what she was saying. Finally, after the fourth or fifth call, he picked up.

When she said that he had to turn on the TV because two planes had flown into the World Trade Center, he was annoyed. He visualized two light planes, gliders or four-seaters. A sad event for the people involved, but of no importance whatsoever compared to the larger things that were going on in the world.

Exactly the sort of thing that the all-news networks like to milk for days.

"They're gone," she said.

"What's gone?"

"The World Trade towers. They're gone."

"What do you mean they're gone?"

"Haven't you been listening to me? They crumbled. They disappeared."

This was how he heard.

He called his office, thinking they'd need him, but everything was in such confusion that his boss told him to stay home. Leila came home in the middle of the day and the two of them sat in front of the television and neither of them could take it in. He understood with his rational mind that it was an event in the world, out there, but the event was so huge as to punch a hole in the wall that separated the rational mind from the dream mind, and in the dream part of his mind he felt as if this was the world's attempt to do justice to Zahra's death.

He even felt, in some remote corner of his brain, a touch of *satisfaction*. During the previous days he had hated the world's indifference, its obvious belief that it need not stop, need not kneel, to mark the death of his daughter. So after the towers fell, amid the welter of his other feelings, there was a small note of something oddly like vindication, because much of the world was now plunged into a mourning to match his own.

That was an immediate, unthinking response. In the next few days, other responses followed. It ceased to feel as if the world were bowing to Zahra's death. It began to feel like the opposite. The world's indifference had grown even larger. It was as if Zahra's death had been robbed of its meaning. No one he spoke to, even old friends, had a thought to spare for her anymore.

On the day the towers fell, he hoped that it was the work of anyone but Arabs. He wanted the culprits to be crazed Americans, Timothy McVeigh–ish inveighers against the CIA, the FDA, the Trilateral Commission, the blacks, the Jews, and fluoride. He was angry when the television commentators, within hours of the attacks, had all nominated Osama bin Laden as the probable "mastermind." And he was despondent when it began to seem as if, this time, they were right.

He was sure that the possibility of peace between Israel and Palestine, never very strong to begin with, had been extinguished now. And he anticipated a pogrom against the Muslim American community, a response that would match the insanity of the incarceration of Japanese Americans during the Second World War. His organization, dedicated to fighting against discrimination against Arabs in American society and culture, was going to be faced with the biggest challenge of its existence. If his job had been important in the first place, it was doubly important now.

The only problem was that he didn't care. He didn't care about Israel and Palestine, and he didn't care about the Muslim American community. He wasn't even sure he still believed there *was* such a thing as the Muslim American community, but if there was, he didn't care about it. He didn't care about anyone he didn't know. The only thing he cared about was Zahra.

It wasn't just that politics had ceased to matter to him; it was that politics—his own politics, at least—had come to revolt him. He had come to believe that he was a hypocrite. He had never been a hypocrite in his words or actions, but he had been a hypocrite in his thoughts.

For many years, in many contexts, he'd had occasion to write about terrorism. In college and graduate school he'd written papers on the subject, and since he'd been working with the AAHRC, whenever there was a suicide bombing in Israel he'd written an article or press release with the organization's response. He'd written more of these than he cared to remember.

He had always approached the subject in the same way. In response to suicide bombings, for example, he would write the same three paragraphs. He would begin by denouncing the bombing. Then he would denounce all forms of violence against civilians. And finally he would assert that Palestinian violence against Israel was dwarfed by Israel's violence against Palestinians. He would argue that when a Palestinian teenager sets off a bomb on a bus in Jerusalem, the U.S. government and media rightly condemn it as a terrorist act, but when the Israel Defense Force bombs a house in Jenin, in an attack ostensibly aimed at a Palestinian militant but one that results in the deaths of innocent people, the U.S. government and media look the other way.

He still believed that this argument, in its basic outlines, was accurate, but what he admitted to himself for the first time after Zahra's death was that at the same time as he had always condemned the suicide bombers, he had always, in his secret heart, admired them. He admitted to himself that whenever he'd written his three paragraphs of boilerplate condemnation of violence in the Middle East, the only paragraph that he truly believed was the third one, the one in which he argued that Israel's crimes were far worse than those of the Palestinians, and that, although he never put it on paper, he had always believed that the history of Israel's violence against the Palestinians was the true cause of the suicide bombings, and that therefore they too were Israel's fault.

When Zahra was alive, he had sometimes, in order to stoke his rage against Israel and the United States, imagined her as the victim of an Israeli raid in Palestine. To his shame, he now realized that he had never imagined her as the victim of a suicide bombing in Israel.

His organization expected him to write a press release responding to the World Trade Center attacks in the same old terms: condemn the attacks, and then condemn the larger injustices that give rise to terrorism. He couldn't do it. He could no longer write anything that would subtly excuse the killing of innocents by putting it into some anodyne "context." When he walked through Lower Manhattan and saw the posters taped up on the walls and bus shelters and street signs, posters with the faces of the missing, every face he saw was Zahra's face.

The response of friends to September 11 sent him reeling. People he had always considered comrades were — in private, in secret — celebrating. His own grandmother had celebrated. His parents, born in New Jersey, thoroughly assimilated, had been as horrified as anyone else, but his grandmother had actually been gleeful. When they talked on the phone on the night of September 11, he was disgusted by her reaction, but not surprised. While he was hoping that the authors of the act would turn out to be Americans, his grandmother was hoping that it had been planned by Yasser Arafat. "The old man has finally come through," she kept saying. (Later she changed her tune: she came to be certain that "the Jews" had planned the attacks. Every time they talked about the subject, she would tell Samir solemnly that she knew for a fact that no Jews had shown up to work at the World Trade Center that day.)

His grandmother was a simple woman. Far worse than the responses of the simple were the responses of the clever. Noam Chomsky, whom he had always admired, wrote on September 12 that Bill Clinton's bombing of a factory in Sudan in 1998, in which one person had been killed, had been an atrocity worse than the attacks on the World Trade towers. Edward Said, the most articulate and intelligent defender of the Palestinian cause, a man who had always been one of Samir's heroes, condemned the attacks in language so exquisitely evasive that it was hardly clear whether he was condemning them at all. In an essay written shortly after September 11 he wrote, "No cause, no God, no abstract idea can justify the mass slaughter of innocents, most particularly when only a small group of people are in charge of such actions and feel themselves to represent the cause without having a real mandate to do so." So it must follow that if a large number of people are in charge of such actions, and do have a real mandate to represent the cause, the mass slaughter of innocents might be okay. The thinkers Samir had always admired now filled him with loathing.

The thinkers on the other side were just as bad. He still hated the writers who apologized for the violence of Israel and the United States. Although the cause was different, the contempt for others was the same. When the United States invaded Afghanistan, Christopher Hitchens, the former leftist who was now a newly minted friend of the Republican party, dismissed critics of the war with the remark that the Pentagon had adhered to "an almost pedantic policy of avoiding 'collateral damage.'" As if the U.S. had taken a bit too far some quirky reluctance to murder noncombatants. A sentence this morally shallow, Samir believed, could have been written only by someone who had never endured the loss of a loved one. If Hitchens ever *had* endured the loss of a loved one, so much the worse for him.

The partisans on both sides made the same lazy gestures to conceal their root belief that the murder of innocents is justified in the name of tomorrow's greater good.

Samir tried to find a political thinker who seemed truly to grieve over the death of innocents on the "other side," who seemed truly to feel compassion for his enemies. He found the note he was searching for in the writings and speeches of Nelson Mandela, and Martin Luther King, and Gandhi. He found it in the memoirs of Primo Levi, the survivor of Auschwitz, and in the articles of Sari Nusseibeh, a Palestinian theorist of nonviolent activism whom Samir always used to consider a bit of a clown. But for the most part the world of political thinking now filled him with disgust.

He couldn't do his job anymore. He could no longer be the partisan of a cause. When he heard of an opening for a position as a writer and researcher at Amnesty International, he applied for it, and when he got it, he quit his job. Amnesty didn't take positions about ideological or theoretical questions, about forms of government or economic systems. It stood for a few simple things: it was against torture, it was against the killing of civilians, it was against cruel treatment of prisoners, it was against capital punishment. It fought against certain measurable forms of cruelty. This was the kind of thing that he had once scorned about the organization. It wasn't militant enough; it had no historical perspective; it had no critique of the deep structures of political and economic oppression. But it was precisely what he valued about it now. It was against cruelty, and that was enough.

He didn't last long. It was a job that required that you be obsessed—obsessed with the fate of the individuals whom it was Amnesty's goal to defend—and Samir could no longer be obsessed with anyone's fate. He knew that each of these people, the jailed poets, the disappeared student leaders, the tortured dissidents, was a world; he knew that each life was as valuable as Zahra's; but this knowledge could not fill him with the zeal you had to have if you were going to lead campaigns to help them. He didn't care that much about anyone anymore.

He left the job respectfully, making clear his admiration for the organization and the work it did, and then he set out to make his living as a carpenter. He had worked his way through college by way of carpentry and student loans, and he was skilled enough that it didn't take him long to begin to make a living at it again.

It was the only possible work for him, in his new state of mind. The demands of simple honest craftsmanship kept him sane.

For two years he kept his life scrupulously empty. At first he spent his evenings reading, but he rarely finished any of the books he began. History and politics seemed like part of a life he had left behind, and fiction bored him. Fiction was just writers showing off. He would read five pages of a novel and then come across something that was obviously fake, and then he would put it down.

He never watched television. If he did make the mistake of turning it on, he would inevitably come upon one of those made-for-TV movies about dying children, families bravely struggling to cope. Each of these movies concluded in a glow of heartwarming acceptance, as if the death of a child were the best thing that could happen to a parent.

Once a week he would stop at the library and pick out one or two books of photographs, and he would sit at a long table, looking at faces. The faces in the Mathew Brady photographs from the Civil War; the faces of Palestinians; the faces of the Israeli pioneers, from the generation of 1948; the faces of people who had been distinguished by nothing, touched by no large fate. He preferred old books of photographs. He preferred to gaze upon the faces of the dead.

And that had been his life, for two years. Until now. Until Maud had come along and dragged him back into the world.

He still had moments of resentment, of resistance. Still had moments when he was horrified by the thought of abandoning

Zahra. But in the wisest part of himself, he knew that he wouldn't be doing justice to Zahra by holding himself back from life.

So he was allowing it to happen. He watched the lights inside him go on, one by one, and he didn't do anything to stop them.

Twenty-four

In January, during Maud's winter break, she and Samir took a trip to New England. They stayed for two nights in Rockport, Massachusetts, where her family used to go every summer when she was a kid. She had always loved it and hated it. She hated it because her parents would always rent the same tiny cottage and she and her brothers would get crammed together in one room, and as the smallest child and the only girl she always suffered the gravest indignities. But she had loved it because of the ocean, and because of the starkness of the weather, boiling in the day and freezing at night, and because of the romance of Bearskin Neck, which was one long street that ran the length of a skinny peninsula, extending into the ocean like the finger of a giant, a street filled with candy stores and bookstores and knickknack shops, down which, after supper, she and her family would stroll, and where her parents would buy her a different kind of penny candy every night. Now, as she walked there with Samir—the place was unchanged, its glamour, to her eyes, undiminished— she was touched with the flutter of mortality. She missed her childhood: the time when she knew her father simply as her father, not as a public man, a man renowned for his literary achievements and his indefatigable interest in chasing youthful tail. The time when she knew her mother simply as her mother, a being complete, rather than a woman who, like the rest of us, was struggling and baffled and half born.

But of course she wouldn't trade her old naïveté for her present knowledge. Knowledge is always a good thing, even when it makes us unhappy. This was one of the beliefs closest to her heart.

It was good to be an adult here, to be a grown woman with her lover. When she used to come here with her family she was a cog, a squished little fish, voteless.

They went to the end of Bearskin Neck and sat on the huge rocks near a lighthouse, and though it was too dark to see the ocean below them, they heard it, battering forever against the rocks.

"Thank you for taking me here," he said.

"Why?"

"It's good to see a little more of your life."

She knew that his happiness was still a guarded happiness, a happiness with a wound, but she marveled at how far he had come, and she thought that with enough time and enough love they would knit their lives together, and although he would never "move on," if moving on meant ceasing to mourn his daughter, he would finally be free to take her, Maud, all the way in.

There would be no fairy-tale ending here, because life wasn't like that; there would always be the fact that his child had died. But there could be something rich and strong between them. Sometimes when they were making love they would keep their eyes open. This was new for her. Sex always used to be something to be done with eyes closed. What was different now, she thought, was that there was no break, no separation, from the flow of feeling between them when they were in bed and the flow of feeling between them when they were out in the world.

We have the world and we have the bed, she thought. We have everything.

They sat on the rocks near the lighthouse, bundled up in the frigid night. The light at its tip revolved slowly, sending its thin long beam into the black.

After Rockport they drove north and stayed in little towns they'd never heard of. There were moments, sitting beside him in the rental car, when she felt lonely and estranged. Because he was still mysterious to her. He seemed to have made himself a creature who existed in the moment only. He rarely talked about his daughter, he rarely talked about his parents, he rarely talked about his past: he didn't "share," in the conventional sense. Yet he was entirely present, entirely engaged. She thought he was the most alert person she had ever met. He listened to her in a full, undistracted way, as only her mother had ever listened to her before.

"You're a little like my mom," she said as they drove up the coastal highway in Maine.

"Thanks?" he said.

Being with him made her feel powerful. She knew that he thought of her as strong, and it made her feel strong. Two or three times they talked about the Middle East, and didn't agree, and she loved the feeling of being able to fight him. He wasn't sensitive; he could take whatever she could dish out. She felt like she did years ago when she took a "Model Mugging" class, where you learn how to defend yourself by fighting a man who is so wrapped up in protective gear that you can punch him and kick him as hard as you like. When she argued with Samir she could let herself go; she didn't have to hold back so as to seem feminine or nice. She loved the feeling of the full force of her mind meeting the full force of his.

In a hotel room in Maine, as she got ready to take a shower before dinner, Samir emptied out his pockets at the dresser, picked up his key ring, and looked at it. When she got out of the shower, he was sitting on the bed, holding the key ring in his hand. He seemed to be studying it.

He worked two keys off, looked at her solemnly, and gave them to her.

She recognized them. They were the keys to his building and his apartment.

"I'll probably regret this," he said.

"No you won't," she said.

On the last night of their trip they stopped in Cape Elizabeth, Maine, a town that neither of them had ever visited before. They ate dinner in a fancy restaurant and then, wrapped heavily in layers of clothing, walked down to the beach. It was late at night and no one else was there.

The night was clear and filled with stars. The moon was brightly shining, almost full, very low, browsing over the dark ocean.

Samir closed his eyes, trying to remember something.

"'If the stars should appear one night in a thousand years, how would men believe and adore; and preserve for many generations the remembrance' . . . I can't remember the rest."

"What's that?"

"Emerson. I read it in college."

Apart from their talks about the Middle East, it was the first time he had opened the door on his intellectual life, the first time he had admitted being moved by anything he'd read.

The moon and stars are our testing ground, she thought. In a place like this, any trace of dishonesty in your life feels shabby and shameful. Looking up at the purity of the night sky, she felt as if she were being urged to find a kindred purity in herself and to let herself be guided by it. If you're with another person in a place like this, it should be someone you love without reservation.

She felt happy to be here with Samir.

She wanted to say something to him, something like, "It's right between us." She didn't, though: it was still too early, he was still too skittish, for her to say anything like this. It didn't matter. It was right between them. She was sure.

On their first night back in New York, they stayed in his apartment. The next morning he left for work early and she slept in. After she showered, she started looking through his desk. She didn't feel good about this — she wasn't exactly respecting the categorical imperative — but he was still so mysterious to her, still so hidden, that she felt parched for information.

She couldn't find anything personal. No diaries, no letters. She hadn't really expected to: it was impossible to imagine him keeping a diary. But it was still a disappointment.

Finally she came upon a box of photographs.

She had never seen pictures of Zahra or Leila before.

If she had been the person she wanted to be, she would have looked at the pictures of Zahra first. But she didn't. She was the jealous rival before she was the tender friend.

Leila, she was relieved to discover, wasn't much. She was stick-thin and chilly-looking; she had features that might have been pretty in someone who was relaxed and gentle, but she looked brittle and tense. She looked like the kind of person it was good to get away from.

And then Zahra.

Maud had assumed, without having asked herself why, that Zahra had been a beautiful child. She didn't think Samir had ever described her that way, but she had assumed it. The truth was that she hadn't been beautiful.

Her disease had marked her. After Samir had told Maud about his daughter, Maud had spent some time reading about congenital blood diseases, and now she remembered reading that they sometimes led to facial deformities. Zahra's cheekbones and forehead were bulging and large. If you hadn't known she had a disease, she would probably have looked no more than a bit unusual, but once you knew it, you could see how it had deformed her.

Zahra must have been two or three when the picture was taken, but she didn't look like anyone's idea of a carefree toddler. There was something very complicated in her eyes. Maud tried to think of the words she might use to describe them. The first three she came up with were cautious, evasive, haunted. This little girl had known pain; it had taken up permanent residence within her. But there were other qualities in her expression: playfulness, certainly, and maybe something like irony. If you encountered a little girl with eyes like this, Maud thought, you would be fascinated by the thought of what she might become. You could imagine this girl becoming numbed, stunned, rendered stupid by years of physical and emotional distress, or you could imagine her becoming the most enthrallingly complex person you'd ever met.

When she saw Samir that night, they made love, and as they made love, she started to cry. She loved being with him, she was beginning to think that she hoped she could be with him forever, but it had suddenly occurred to her that she wouldn't be here with him if not for the death of his child. If she could have chosen, she would have chosen not to have met him, if it meant that his child would still be alive.

She didn't say anything, and there was no way he could have understood that she was crying because of his grief, his daughter, but when he realized that she was crying, he started to cry as well, and they made love this way.

Twenty-five

"Paul Auster," Thea said, "makes me wet."

"Is that so," Adam said.

They were meeting for a quick drink in the Oyster Bar in Grand Central Station. Each of them had multiple appointments that day. Thea was having a martini with three olives and Adam a glass of wine.

"I never liked his books much," she said. "I read that trilogy, *City of Glass,* and I thought it was phony from the first word to the last. Bloodless. But in person! He was on Charlie last night to promote his new book, and . . . wow. I felt like I was in eighth grade again, having my first crush."

This was part of the price one paid for being with Thea. She liked to remind you that she desired other men, and she liked to remind you that other men desired her. Adam didn't know why she delighted in this.

"You should get together with him," Adam said. "Help him put a little blood in his books."

Thea was always making you pass little tests. She would say things that were certain to upset you and then she would watch what happened.

Usually Adam operated on the assumption that the way to pass the tests was to remain unruffled. But sometimes he thought that he was doing it all wrong, and that the only way to gain her respect would be to slap her around for a while. He had never hit a woman in his life, though, and it was too late to get started now.

"In other literary news," Thea said, "I ran into the power-wielding vegetarian at the Gotham Bar and Grill last night."

"Jeffrey?"

"The man himself. We were both waiting for people so we had a drink at the bar. And I'm sorry to say that he said that he'd thought over my suggestion, and it's a nonstarter." She was referring to the suggestion that he steer one of the new Gellman prizes Adam's way.

"That's too bad," Adam said. "Thanks for trying."

Adam hadn't been counting on anything, and the prize didn't mean that much to him. It would have been nice, but not getting one didn't sting.

Thea sucked the pimientos out of her olives and popped the olives into her mouth, one by one. Then she licked her fingertips. She looked as if she had something more to say. She looked as if she was saving the best part for last.

"He said that as much as he admires your early work, you haven't done much lately, and the prize is only given out to mark some major recent achievement."

This did sting.

Thea had said it smilingly, and he wasn't sure whether she actually was testing him, finding out whether he would show that he was wounded, or whether she was oblivious to the effect her words would have on him. Was that even possible? He had a fit of longing, brief but fierce, for Ellie: her sympathy, her tact.

"Maybe you're just not major anymore, old man."

Thea's eyes glittered with amusement. Adam had been cruel often enough in his life, when cruelty was required as a means to some end that he wished to bring about, but he'd never had any fondness for cruelty for its own sake. Nor did he have any fondness for being the recipient of the cruelty of others.

"They should give it to Paul Auster," Adam said. "Anyway, major is as major does." He wasn't quite sure what this was supposed to mean, but he thought it sounded okay. He took out his wallet, put a twenty-dollar bill on the table, and stood up and kissed her on the cheek. "Let's talk later in the week," he said.

As he left he wondered whether the price of being with Thea was starting to be too high.

Out on the street, he turned his cell phone back on and saw that he'd gotten another call from Ruth Cantor. He'd have to call her back soon. He'd dodged her successfully for quite some time, but in her last phone message she'd said something about health troubles, and although he knew this was the same ploy his mother resorted to when he wasn't returning her calls—his mother, who was still alive at ninety, in Miami Beach—he was programmed, nice Jewish boy that he was, to respond.

He had been dodging Ruth because he didn't want to talk to her about Izzy's novel. If he told her it was a masterpiece— which it was—then he would have no excuse not to start showing it around. And he didn't want to show it around. He had worked long and hard to leave Izzy in the dust, and he wanted him to stay there.

Particularly now that it had been established that it had been decades since he himself had written anything "major."

If Izzy's book were published, it would harm him—Adam— without helping Izzy, since Izzy could neither be helped nor harmed. If, for instance, despite the obvious literary brilliance of this novel, Adam, far from attempting to arrange for its publication, were to deposit it in the garbage can in his kitchen, and, after covering the book up with coffee grounds and eggshells and soiled paper towels and snotted tissues and the bitched-out butts of Thea's cigarettes, were to tie the bag closed and take it into the hall and drop it down the garbage chute into the enormous Dumpster in the basement, from where it would be carried to its final resting place, crushed under twenty tons of waste matter in the Sullivan County landfill—if Adam were to ensure in this fashion that no one ever laid eyes on the novel, it would not represent a betrayal of Izzy, for the simple reason that Izzy didn't exist.

Would it be a betrayal of Izzy's *memory,* though, even if it wasn't a betrayal of the man?

The idea, Adam thought, was meaningless. There was no way to be kind to Izzy now and no way to be cruel to him. One could no sooner betray him than one could betray the planet Mars.

The only person it mattered to, the only person whose fortunes might be improved by Izzy's posthumous rehabilitation, was, of course, Ruth.

To Ruth it would matter a great deal. As a literary widow, tending to whatever remained of her husband's reputation, she had been more faithful to Izzy's memory than the most fanatical Christian martyr had ever been faithful to God. During the past ten years—with her loneliness, with her illnesses—her life had been a thing of gray on gray. If Izzy's book were published, and if it turned out to be a success, then it might radically transform Ruth's last years. It might reverse her sense of the course her entire life had taken. It would give her the peace of a happy ending.

Twenty-six

Ruth was so excited that she seemed unhinged. She was fluttering back and forth in her small kitchen, bumping into herself. She put two frozen crullers in the toaster oven; poured water into her Mr. Coffee; removed two more crullers from the freezer and opened the door of the toaster oven, and looked flustered by the magical appearance of the first two, and watched with helpless dismay as water, rather than coffee, began to drip into Mr. Coffee's carafe — she'd forgotten to put any coffee into the cone.

"Coffee. Coffee." She was peering into one cupboard after another. "I think I'm out of the Zabar's. Would instant do?"

"Instant would be fine."

She spooned some instant coffee into two cups, added water, put the cups into the microwave, pressed start, and then the lights went out.

"Oh, goodness," she said.

Adam found the circuit-breaker box in the hallway and flipped a switch and the lights came on again.

"How do you know how to do that?" Ruth said.

Ruth brought the crullers and the coffee cups into the living room on a tray. Adam, on the couch, reached for a cruller.

"Well?" she said. "What's the verdict? I'm so excited. I can't stand the suspense."

Adam had thought about this moment many times. But when the time came to speak, he found it difficult.

"What did you think?" she said.

He picked up his cup and brought it toward his lips, but then he noticed that the rim bore traces of lipstick, and he put it back down. The touch of irritation that he felt made it easier for him to begin.

"Ruth, you know how much I respected Izzy. You know how much I loved him."

She could already see where he was heading. He thought he saw her eyes starting to well up. He hoped he was wrong. He didn't want to deal with her tears.

"I wanted this book to be good," he said. "I wanted it with all my heart. But . . . Ruth. It wouldn't be smart to try to get it published. It really wouldn't be smart."

"Why wouldn't it be smart?"

She could barely get the words out of her mouth. She looked like a stunned child.

"Well, first of all, I very much doubt whether anyone would want to publish it. I could send it to Paula Cohen. I know she was never Izzy's editor, but she admired him, and she might be interested in looking at it for sentimental reasons. But no one publishes anything for sentimental reasons, not anymore. Publishing has become a business and nothing but a business, even for someone like Paula."

"But you could show it to her?"

"I could. I could. But my concern is that, even if, by some miracle, someone did publish it, it wouldn't do anything to help Izzy's reputation. I think it would have the opposite effect."

"Why is that? Why would another book hurt his reputation? It's a great book. It's vintage Izzy."

He smiled in a way that he hoped looked rueful, warm, and knowing. "You could say it's vintage Izzy. You could say that. But that isn't the way the critics will see it. They'll see it as Izzy repeating himself. You know how much Izzy always added to the last draft. Who knows what he could have done with this if he'd had another two years. He might have turned it into a wonderful book. It certainly has the seeds of a wonderful book inside it. But as it is . . ." He gestured at the manuscript in a helpless, resigned way.

"Didn't you think parts of it were beautiful? Didn't you think the beginning was fantastic, with the way they meet on the Brooklyn Bridge? And what about the ending? Didn't you think the ending was special? It was so filled with hope. Real, genuine hope, after everything that had happened with those people — when you thought they had no hope left at all."

"I did think parts of it were beautiful, Ruth. But . . . trust me. You're reading it with the eyes of love. I read it with the eyes of love myself. You know that. But part of my responsibility — to Izzy and to you — was also to read it with the eyes of critical judgment. And, Ruth, I need to say it plainly. Readers who don't already know Izzy, who don't love Izzy, will not be moved by this book."

Ruth was crying now, full force. An inarticulate sound escaped her. She picked up her napkin and hid her face and continued to cry.

Adam was glad she was hiding her face. Most women, he thought, look so foolish when they cry. Eleanor always looked like a melon.

But he had to hand it to Ruth: she had remarkable powers of resilience. By the time she took the napkin away from her face, she had collected herself. She was still snuffling, but she seemed composed.

"I thought he really got it this time," she said. "But then again, I guess I thought everything he wrote was a work of genius."

"Izzy was a wonderful writer," Adam said. "And he couldn't have been the wonderful writer that he was if you hadn't supported him so beautifully. He couldn't have done what he did if you hadn't believed in him."

"I did support him," she said. "I did believe in him."

"I know you did," he said. "It made him strong."

He pushed the plate of crullers toward her, but of course she didn't touch it. When women are suffering, they can't even look at food. This is the main difference between the sexes, he thought. A man can always chow down.

It was time for gentle humor, Adam thought. Fond and loving reminiscence.

Adam reminded her of the time Izzy had asked her to swear to him that she considered him a better writer than Tolstoy. She laughed, and told an Izzy story of her own, and for the next ten or fifteen minutes they shared memories of him, and Adam's lies floated lightly in the air, dispersing now, and she would never know that he had lied to her.

He was at peace with what he had done. He had never claimed to be a good man. He had never claimed to put the needs of others over his own.

For a few days, after he had been informed that he had written nothing major in decades, he had considered destroying Izzy's manuscript. But he decided not to. He cared too much about literature for that. He had loved Izzy, but now he was gone, so there was no point in talking about treating him well, but he also loved literature, which was not yet gone, and he wanted to preserve this sparkling thing that his friend had brought into being. He would put it among his papers, and when he too was dead, it would be discovered, and if posterity judged that Izzy was the better writer of the two of them, so be it.

As for Ruth, it was a pity that he needed to disappoint her, but it couldn't be helped. And he was going to try to be good to her in another way.

"I've also been looking through his letters, Ruth. And I think they really are remarkable. I think I might be able to arrange to have them published. And, who knows? It could lead to a redis-covery of his work. Unless you have any objection, I'd like to start looking into it right away."

"No. Of course I have no objection. I'd love that."

He intended to see this through. If Jeffrey wasn't interested in editing the letters, he would find someone else to do it. He might even take on the project himself. And in that way, Ruth could have her happy ending. She could die believing that her husband's work had a chance, at least, to survive.

Ruth seemed to have recovered already. He was relieved about this. He hadn't done her any permanent harm. They talked for a few more minutes, and then he said he had to go. At the door, he kissed her on the cheek, noting with distaste how she had let her cheek become faintly, whitely hairy, and prom-ised to see her again soon. As the elevator doors closed, he won-dered whether he'd see her again at all.

After Adam left, Ruth picked up the dishes and the coffee cups and the utensils and put them in the dishwasher. She wiped the table clean with a sponge. She thought about turning the radio on, but decided not to. She worked in silence.

Adam's verdict had left her deeply sad. When she was read-ing the novel, she'd felt as if Izzy had laid out the truth of their lives, her life and his, rendered it indelibly, immortalized it. And it had made her feel less afraid of dying. She had felt as if she could shed her body now with no regrets, knowing that the two of them would live forever in the pages he had written, in the full strong bloom of their love.

It was shattering to realize that this wouldn't happen. No one would read these pages; no one would be nourished by the beauty of what she and Izzy had had.

It never occurred to her that Adam might not have been telling her the truth. It had been a long time since she'd considered him a good man, but she knew that he loved Izzy—his love for his old friend was one of the few indisputably good things about him.

She decided that she would call Paula Cohen herself. She didn't want to bother Adam any more by asking him to make the call for her. Paula had always liked Izzy, and she'd probably be happy to take a look at it. But Ruth believed she already knew what she'd say. If Adam thought that she was deluding herself about the value of this book, he was probably right.

She washed her face and brushed her teeth and changed into her nightgown and got into bed. Izzy had felt so present, so close, for weeks now, but Adam's verdict on the book had pushed him back into the dark. It was as if he had come back into her life for a few days, and now she had to let go of him all over again.

She closed her eyes and thought about the dream she'd had a few nights earlier. Izzy had been in the dream, but it had broken off before she'd had the chance to talk with him.

She was meeting him in a park. She had come with a gift. In the morning she could no longer remember what the gift was; all she could remember was that she was holding it in a brightly wrapped box. Izzy was walking toward her from across the park. He was young, as young and striking and wild-looking as he was when she'd first known him. But she herself was her true age, which made her more than twice as old as the young Izzy who was making his way toward her.

He was still on the other side of the park, and she wasn't sure how clearly he could see her. She wasn't sure if he could see that she was old. She stood there waiting for him, nervously clutching her gift, wondering whether he could still love her.

TWENTY-SEVEN

Eleanor was in Maud's room, writing. The phone rang. She let the machine answer, and then she heard the old unmistakable voice.

"Ellie. It's Patrick."

When he spoke, he always sounded as if he had a pebble in his mouth. He spoke in a measured way that made you think each word cost him dearly.

He didn't say anything else. He was thinking.

The answering machine, concluding from his silence that he was no longer there, cut him off.

A few minutes later, he called back, but he didn't say anything.

The same thing happened a minute after that.

He lived in a simpler world than she did, a more naïve world. How could he not know that when you call again and again like this, repeatedly engaging an answering machine, there's a better than even chance that the person you're calling is home, listening to you make a fool of yourself?

Then he called again and began speaking.

She remained at her desk. She felt no impulse to pick up the phone.

A few months ago, when she had refrained from taking his calls, she had done so because she didn't have anything going on in her life. She was afraid that if she started talking to him again, he would quickly become, in the little circus of her life, the main attraction. Now she refrained from taking his call only because she was immersed in what she was doing.

"I'm going to be in the city again soon," Patrick said. He told her when. "I'd love to see you."

She reached for her pocket calendar and circled the date.

The machine cut him off again before he had a chance to say good-bye, and she went back to the thing she was trying to write.

If she was immersed in her writing, it was partly because of the afternoon she'd spent with him. Their meeting had shaken something loose in her. It had made her past more urgent, less simple, and from that day to this, she had spent almost every evening in Maud's old room, writing about the world she had grown up in.

When she was young, she'd begun a novel about her family, but she'd stalled out, not too long after she met Adam. Now she was returning to the subject, almost forty years later. Maybe it was the only story she had to tell. But she wasn't trying to write it as fiction anymore. All she wanted to do was put something of her past down on paper.

It had been strange, during the past weeks, to be spending part of every day with the ghostly presences of her parents and her sister. To have these people who were long dead as her companions, her familiars.

It was painful to experience Joanna anew, to remember fully what the loss of Joanna had meant for her. When Joanna was alive, Eleanor had always felt protected, both because her sister took it upon herself to protect her and because her sister had gone through every experience first, so that every experience, no matter how scary, had been domesticated and demythologized by the time it was Eleanor's turn to attempt it. Joanna had fought her way through every thicket, and when Eleanor followed, the branches had been pushed back and the path was clear.

Although Joanna was frozen in her youth, Eleanor still thought of her as the older sister. Twenty-seven-year-old Joanna still seemed older than fifty-nine-year-old Eleanor, and if Joanna were to reappear today, Eleanor would still look up to her.

Sometimes, in writing and thinking about her sister, Eleanor felt as if she had found the key to her own loneliness. She had been separated from her other half. Experiencing things when Joanna was alive had been like experiencing them twice, since Joanna was always there, counselor and co-conspirator, to think them over with. Eleanor could almost believe that the loss of Joanna was the reason that she herself moved so slowly through life, slow to choose, slow to change. She had to think things over before she acted, think things over for an inordinately long time, because when she was young she'd always had her sister there to help her size everything up and plan everything out.

Remembering the night of the day she died. Remembering the phone call. Joanna had died in the morning, and that night Eleanor had gone into Joanna's apartment and sat amid her things and felt overcome by the thought that she was still living in a day in which Joanna had been alive, and that she never again would be living in a day in which her sister had been alive.

She had slept on Joanna's bed that night. She had lain down there just for a moment—she had felt sure that she wouldn't be able to sleep that night. But she did sleep, and she woke up in the morning, astonished, into a day that her sister would not see. How had she let the previous day go so easily? Simply by waking up into this new day, Eleanor thought, she had failed her sister.

She had sat up in her sister's bed and moaned like an animal. It wasn't something that she chose to do to relieve her grief; it was just something that came out of her, that poured out. It was like vomiting. Or no, it wasn't like vomiting: it was like something being born from her. It was as if she were giving birth to her sister's death.

Twenty-eight

*H*asn't *done much lately.*

The phrase was still worming around in Adam's brain. Because he knew it was true.

Adam still sat down to write every day of his life. He had always been guided by a private gospel of productivity: amid all the distractions, all the parties, all the traveling, he had always sat down and written his one good page a day. Sometimes it took fifteen minutes, sometimes it took five hours; he wrote the page until he got it right and then he moved on. He might revise the page a hundred times on the day he wrote it, but he never revised it again. This was easy for him because he always had an outline for his books before he began them, and he never deviated from it. He didn't know any other writers of "literary" fiction who worked by this method: most of them strained and stressed and wrote very rough drafts of their novels and then started over from the beginning, often with a new conception of what the novels were about, and in that anguished, stumbling way, every three or four or five or six years or so, managed to complete a book. The only writers Adam had met who worked in the same brisk, efficient way that he did were people who wrote mysteries and thrillers. When you unshackle yourself from a superstitious reverence for the mysterious god named Literature, you can get a lot of work done.

But it was true, and he knew it, that for more than ten years now he'd been on cruise control.

He was at his desk, writing, when he received word that Ruth had died. It was nine in the morning. He had already been working for an hour, but he had barely written a word. He had been distracted for weeks now—*hasn't done much lately*—and he had spent most of the morning looking himself up on Google and thinking about creating new e-mail accounts, with fanciful names, in order to write favorable reviews of his own books on Amazon.com.

He got the news from Ellie, who had gotten it from some member of her shadowy society of women, the righteous society of brave, plucky women living alone. Ellie had never liked Ruth: the quality of Ruth's devotion to Izzy had always struck Ellie as doglike. But after Izzy left Ruth by dying and Adam left Ellie by leaving, Ellie had embraced her, a new and honored member of the sacred female order of the insulted, the injured, and the ignored.

Evidently Ruth's cancer had returned several months ago, and she'd never told anyone about it.

"I guess there'll be a memorial service," Adam said.

"I guess so. I suppose you'll speak. I suppose you'll be the star."

It was too early in the morning to be subjected to her bitterness. He said good-bye and hung up.

No more Ruth.

He wondered if Ruth would still be alive if he'd been truthful with her.

Twenty-nine

Maud was standing in front of the classroom when everything changed. Her breasts had been aching for three days, and she had been thinking it was because she and Samir had been a little rough that weekend. She was listening to one of her students talk about the "Adam Smith problem"— the contradiction between the ideas of human nature implied by Smith's two major works, *The Wealth of Nations* and *The Theory of Moral Sentiments*—when she realized that she was pregnant.

I can't be pregnant.

Of course I'm pregnant.

The basic question was whether individuals are motivated primarily by self-interest (*The Wealth of Nations*) or by sympathy (*The Theory of Moral Sentiments*).

"It was like he wasn't communicating with himself," the student said. "It was like on one day he didn't know the things he knew the day before."

"That can happen," Maud said. There was a silence. Perhaps her students were expecting her to say something wise, but she had nothing wise to say.

After class she went to Rite Aid, bought a home-pregnancy-test kit, walked back to campus, locked herself in a stall in a women's room in Butler Library, and opened the package. The kit conveniently came with three testing strips, and she tested herself three times. She was pregnant the first time, and then she was pregnant, and then she was pregnant.

I'm pregnant.

She tried to think about it further, but that was about as far as she got.

THIRTY

Two days later, Maud still hadn't told anyone her news. She needed to talk to someone, but she didn't know who.

She placed her books in her backpack, left the library, and walked through the Columbia campus toward Broadway.

She sometimes thought this campus was her favorite spot on earth. The wide calm walkways; the grandeur of the structures; the long green lawns. Sometimes when she walked here on a quiet night, she felt as if she were walking through history. William James had lectured here, and John Dewey, and Alain Locke, and Horace Kallen.

Passing in front of Low Library, with its long stone stairway, she felt connected to the past, to the ghosts of these thinkers, men and women who had hurled themselves against the inexpressible, and to the shades of future thinkers, people who would devote their lives to serious thought in the decades and centuries after she herself was gone.

She found it stunning to contemplate the idea that she had become the host of a two-celled organism that, if left to develop unhindered, would become a human being. She had never believed in God, but she did believe in a sort of divinity of everyday life: the sheer mystery of human consciousness, the fact that mere *matter* somehow gave birth to mind, called forth from her an intense reverence. So the idea that something was taking place inside her that would yield a being with a consciousness was not one that she could easily dismiss.

But at the same time, she didn't *want* to have a baby. She didn't want to have to take care of anyone else. She didn't know if she could handle it.

She felt lucky that the man it had happened with was Samir. Thank God it hadn't happened to her during her promiscuous years. When she thought of all the dopes she'd been with, all the jerks who'd lurched into her yurt—when she thought that it could have been one of them who had fathered her child, she felt disgusted.

Who could she talk to?

She couldn't talk to Samir. Not yet. Not until she had a clearer idea of what she wanted.

She was a little afraid of him. Afraid of how he'd react. He might go down on his knees before her, or he might throw her out the door.

She couldn't tell her mother, because her mother would be so worried—worried about her well-being—that she wouldn't be able to give any sensible advice.

Anyway, she was pretty sure she knew what her mother would think. Her mother would have trouble coming right out and saying it, but she'd want her to have an abortion. Her mother would think she couldn't handle having a child.

She couldn't talk to her father because she wasn't even sure he'd be interested.

Either of her brothers? Nope.

She thought of a friend of hers, Sally Burke, who would probably have some good things to say. Sally was a woman in her forties whom Maud had met in a tai-chi class. For some reason Maud thought that she would understand what she was going through. But it had been a long time since they'd spoken, and it would be too awkward to call her up out of the blue to talk about being pregnant.

George and Celia, the people who introduced her to Samir? No. Conflict of interest.

The only person she wanted to talk to, the only person she *could* talk to, was her old friend Ralph.

She had met Ralph on the very first day of college. They'd become friends quickly and had remained friends ever since. She trusted him as much as she trusted anyone in the world.

She didn't call him. She just took the bus to the East Side. He lived alone in a huge apartment on Park Avenue. Whenever she visited she felt as if she should hand the doorman her card, but she didn't have a card.

The doorman called upstairs, and Ralph asked him to let her up. When she got out of the elevator, Ralph's door was open and he was waiting for her in his wheelchair.

He'd been diagnosed with muscular dystrophy seven years ago, and had been steadily ceding ground to the disease. He hadn't needed a wheelchair until a year ago.

If possible, he looked even more purified, more abstract, more ephemeral, than he had the last time she'd seen him. Less made for this world. More ready to leave it.

"To what do I owe the . . . Maud. You look like you've . . . what's going on?"

"Can I talk to you? Do you have time?"

"Of course."

He nodded toward the living room, and remained in his wheelchair while she sat on the couch.

"Tell me everything," he said.

She was about to speak, was trying to figure out where to begin, when she lost control of herself. She put her head in her hands. She couldn't have expressed how relieved she felt, just because of his willingness to listen to her. She knew him well enough to be sure that he would listen to her without judgment.

She had a moment of sadness about her mother, who listened for a living, but who, Maud was sure, would not be able to listen to her, not about this. She'd have advice, worries, opinions. That wasn't what Maud wanted now.

She talked for a long time, in too much detail. What it came down to was that she didn't know if she was strong enough to be a mother, and that she hadn't known Samir long enough to know if she could raise a child with him.

Ralph listened, his patient, small, slightly monkeyish face twisted in an awkward expression of sympathy. His disease had deprived his face of some of its mobility, so that all the nuances of his delicate and expressive nature now had to find a way to manifest themselves in stiff and brittle features.

"What do you think?" she said. "Doc."

"I think four things. The first thing I think is that I'm sorry this is so hard for you. The second thing I think is that I've never seen you as serious about anybody as you are about him. I've never seen you this interested in anybody except . . . Immanuel Kant."

"That's true," Maud said. "I've always had a crush on Immanuel Kant."

She noticed only now that he had a new wheelchair, a luxury model. A padded seat and a complicated panel of buttons on the side.

"That's a nice wheelchair," she said. "Looks like it has a lot of options."

"Thank you," he said. "I always wanted you to admire my wheelchair."

"But what if it's just infatuation, and once it burns out I'll look up and realize I don't even like the guy?"

"That could happen. But it never happened with Immanuel Kant, did it?"

"No. That was an infatuation that turned into true love."

"Maybe this one will too."

"I don't know. This is a real person. This involves bodies and mutuality." Mutuality. Who ever uses a word like this in conversation? She felt like a hopeless academic. "It's easy to have a relationship with a dead thinker. But a real live person who . . ."

"It's true that the fact that you fell head over heels in love with him isn't really a sign that this will last. But . . . you did fall head over heels in love with him. There's no way you can take that as a bad sign. You're not the type of person who falls in love with people who are bad to you. I think you kind of prefer people who can be good to you."

"I guess I'm an old-fashioned girl in that way."

"What you are," he said, "is a complicated girl with simple needs. You need your books and time to read, and you need a few friends, and you need someone, not to take care of you, but to care for you. If you have all those things, you'll always be all right."

"What's the third thing?"

"The third thing is that I do think you're strong enough to take care of a child. I know you are. I think you'll be a wonderful mother."

"You really think so?"

"I wouldn't have said it if I didn't."

He had a confidence in his voice, a quiet authority, that made her almost believe it.

"So you think I should do it. You think I should have the baby. You think I could live happily ever after with my Arab boyfriend."

He didn't say anything.

"You know, I don't think you've ever told me what I should do," she said.

"I respect you," he said simply. She knew that what he meant was that respecting someone means wanting her to make her own choices.

He worked his wheelchair over to the cabinet. "Would you like some tea? I have every kind of tea there is. Herbal teas, black tea, green tea, chai. Yogi tea. Teas for the hippie, teas for the common man."

He was having trouble moving his wheelchair to the sink, so he turned on the motor, and it got him over there quickly.

She still had trouble believing he needed a wheelchair. It was terrible to see the illness conquering him inch by inch.

"It's not so bad," he said. Sometimes she had the uncanny feeling that they could read each other's minds. "I feel kind of spiffy in this thing."

"Are you working on anything interesting these days?" she said.

Ralph was a restorer of paintings. A difficult, delicate task that was getting more and more difficult for him as his illness progressed. He started to tell her about a painting in the Philadelphia Museum of Art that he had just worked on. He had a very clear way of talking about his work, so that she never got lost in the technicalities, but today she wasn't taking any of it in. She was just admiring him.

It would be terrible to lose him. Even putting personal considerations aside — the consideration that she loved him, as she loved few others — it was sad to think of all this beauty passing from the world.

More than anyone else she knew, he represented, in Maud's mind, a spirit of personal refinement, moral beauty. When his illness was discovered, shortly after they graduated from college, Maud was only half surprised. He had always reminded her of some doomed tubercular poet from the nineteenth century, too delicate to survive.

Even back in college, when most of the people she knew were fucking like monkeys, Ralph had been close to celibate. Inevitably some people thought he was "really" gay, but hadn't admitted it to himself, or secretly gay, but hadn't come out of the closet. Maud didn't think that either of these conjectures was true. If he was secretly anything, she'd always thought, he was secretly an angel.

There had been a moment during their sophomore year when she thought they were going to get together, she and Ralph. One afternoon they were sitting in his dorm room listening to music and talking, and then they both fell silent, and suddenly these two people who for the past twelve months had been carrying on a nonstop conversation about everything under the sun had nothing to say. It was as if they hadn't been introduced. Then he had leaned over and kissed her, and she'd thought, It's beginning. The love of my life. But somehow everything was wrong—his lips felt wrong; the way they were touching each other felt wrong—and finally they just lay there, not saying a word, with a feeling of strangeness and defeat, and after a little while she left, and they were awkward with each other for the next few days. Gradually, during the weeks that followed, their friendship returned to its glory, and they had never talked about those ten strange minutes from that day to this. Maud didn't think they ever would. She had never understood what happened, and never really regretted it. She loved their friendship; she felt lucky to have a friend like him.

Now, in his apartment, at the end of the evening, she said, "So are you giving me your blessing?"

"I'm giving you my blessing no matter what you decide to do. Why are you smiling?"

"I'm thinking about something Jean-Paul Sartre said."

"That's what I love about you, Maud. Most of us smile because we're thinking of things like what we're going to have for dessert. You smile because you're thinking of something Jean-Paul Sartre said. What did he say?"

"Jean-Paul Sartre said that when you ask someone for advice, you've already decided what you're going to do, because we know the advice each of our friends will give, and when we choose who to ask we reveal that we've already chosen what to do."

"Are you saying I'm predictable?"

"I'm saying that you're the only person I know who would tell me that anything I do will be all right."

"Wouldn't your mother?"

"I don't know. She would want to say that. It's what she would say to one of her clients. But I'm not sure she'd be able to say it to me."

She gathered up her things, but then she stopped.

"What was the fourth thing?"

He was fiddling with the control panel of his wheelchair. He looked as if he hadn't heard her. She didn't repeat the question. She knew, of course, what the fourth thing was. The fourth thing was that he was sorry that life hadn't gone differently. Sorry that he wasn't the one this had happened with.

THIRTY-ONE

Adam did speak at Ruth's memorial service, and he *was* the star. He had done so many of these events that he had it down to a science. At memorial services, people want to hear stories, and they want to laugh. He told a few stories about Ruth's early life, making everyone remember what a faithful and energetic friend she'd been, and he told a few amusing, gently chiding anecdotes about the zeal with which she devoted herself to Izzy.

After the service, people clustered around him, many of them people he knew from the old days, hadn't seen for years, and would have been happy never to see again. Bent-over, bad-toothed do-gooders from the Upper West Side.

Ellie had been at the service, sitting in one of the back rows. Afterward she patted his arm, said, "You did good, Weller," and left.

The only person Adam was glad to see there was Paula Cohen. Paula had been his first editor, when both of them were young.

"Ruth called me just a couple of weeks ago," she said. "I hadn't heard from her for years. When my assistant told me she'd called, I remember thinking that I hadn't even known she was still alive. I never did get back to her. I feel so awful."

Ruth must have wanted her to look at Izzy's manuscript. *She didn't trust me,* Adam thought, with an indignation that, given the circumstances, verged on the insane.

Ruth and Izzy's daughter, Shelly, a kindly, bedraggled social worker, with a face unattractively red and puffy from weeping, told him that he had "really brought Mom into the room."

Adam didn't care for Shelly, for the reason that she hadn't read her father's books. He remembered Izzy once saying, "She just hasn't gotten around to it," and smiling that mild, helpless smile of his. Izzy, at root, probably expected as little from people as Adam did, but where the knowledge of how frail and wavering and unreliable people were had led Adam to become cynical, it had led Izzy to become more tolerant, more compassionate.

Adam accompanied Shelly to Ruth's. She wanted him to collect Izzy's papers as soon as he could so she could clear out the apartment. Ruth had been her husband's literary executor; years ago, she had asked Adam to take over the role if he survived her.

The last visit to the old place. About twenty people were milling around by the time he got there. Ruth had had more friends than he'd realized. Some of them he recognized vaguely; some of them he'd never seen before. He leaned against the wall eating a slice of babka and drinking weak coffee while a couple of Ruth's old friends coyly asked him if he remembered them. He felt as if his presence made the gathering more stimulating, more charged; if he left the apartment now, there would be a sense of letdown throughout the room. Everyone would find the gathering a little flatter and less interesting.

Except for the young. Ruth's niece, Leslie, was there, along with her daughter, Morgan, and Morgan was extraordinarily attractive. She had thick dark hair and blue eyes that you noticed from across the room. She was wearing a black dress that was probably a little too short for the occasion.

At one point Adam found himself near her at the table where the refreshments were laid out. She was examining the tea bags. Finally she chose something herbal. Peppermint Sunrise or something like that. Insipid.

The coffee and hot water were in large silver urns, so he couldn't gallantly pour water in her cup for her.

"I'm sorry about your great-aunt," he said.

"Thanks." She was hunting for something on the table and didn't bother looking up at him.

"We were very old friends. I grew up with your great-uncle."

She glanced up at him and then resumed her search. "That's nice."

She was even more beautiful from this distance. A dark-haired, sleepy-lidded, long-limbed beauty.

"Are you looking for something?" he said. "Can I help you with something?"

"Nope. Found it." A jar of honey, hidden behind a column of plastic cups. She put a spoonful of honey in her tea and then headed back to her mother.

Either she didn't know who he was, or she knew and didn't give a shit. And why should she give a shit? Young people today, if they read at all, tended to read no one older than Dave Eggers or Lorrie Moore. Even if she does know who I am, Adam thought, to her I'm just another dead white male.

And he'd published his last ambitious book eight years ago, when she was probably barely into her teens. The three things he'd published since then had been trifles. A collection of essays; a slim collection of four autobiographical lectures that he'd given at Duke; and an even slimmer book of short stories.

Hasn't done much lately.

He sat next to Shelly on the couch.

"How are you holding up?"

"I can't believe she's gone. My mommy. I guess I thought she'd be around to take care of me forever."

Rolling one's eyeballs at the bereaved, or suggesting that she might consider growing up, was probably not the appropriate response in a situation like this.

He squeezed her elbow wordlessly and arranged his features into a sympathetic configuration. Lips pressed together in some sort of "I-share-your-pain, keep-your-chin-up" mode.

"I guess I should show you the things she wanted you to have," Shelly said.

She led him to Ruth's bedroom. Near the window were two large black trunks, the kind of things a seafarer would bring along to the ship.

"There you are," she said. "Everything he thought was worth keeping. It doesn't look like much, does it?"

"Your father was his own toughest critic. I have a hunch that all the things he saved were gems."

"Maybe. Even if they were, I wouldn't be able to judge. My dad's writing was always over my head. A while ago my mother said she found something of his she'd never read before, and she said it was great. But she thought everything he did was great."

"Did she show it to you?"

"By the time I got here she was already in the hospital. I haven't been to New York in three years. I kept wanting to visit, but I've been so busy."

"Of course," Adam said.

"I really don't have the strength to go through my father's old papers right now. If you could just take it all and do what you want with it, I'd really appreciate it. I just don't have the time right now."

Or the interest, he thought. Maud was the only one of his children who was the least bit literary, but all of them had read his books.

"I can't believe they're both gone now," Shelly said. She sat on the bed, head down, arms hanging limply. She looked like an abandoned marionette. "I'm an orphan now."

Adam sat down beside her and placed his hand on her back. Consolingly. He said something about how she could count on him, and not just on him, but on the many people who had loved Ruth and Izzy. What he was thinking was: When did I leave the human community? When did it happen? There was a time when I could have listened to this without wanting to throw her out the window—a woman in her late thirties talking about feeling like an "orphan." If I stay a little longer, I'm sure I'll have the privilege of listening to Shelly talk about her "inner child." Is there anyone left in America who truly wants to be an adult?

Maybe the human community, he thought as he walked home, has left *me*. It was early evening. Broadway on the Upper West Side, from the nineties to the seventies, was a haunted avenue, a promenade of the dead and the missing. In the cold and brittle air, the ghosts of the people he had lost were more real to him than the living figures who passed him, hunched over, faces muffled in scarves.

He had arranged with Ruth's super to have the trunks delivered to his apartment. They arrived later that night. They didn't contain any surprises. One trunk contained letters that Izzy had received and carbon copies of letters he'd written, all of them meticulously organized by date. The other contained the manuscripts of Izzy's published stories and novels and the carbon copy of *So Late So Early*.

It had been a few months since Adam had looked at the manuscript. He sat at his kitchen table and leafed through it.

It was as strong as he'd remembered. Stronger, perhaps. It was a book that became deeper, richer, the more you considered it. Adam couldn't get over his astonishment that his old friend had managed to write this well during his last years.

Adam hadn't done any work yet that day. He went to his computer, wrote a few sentences, played around with them, wasn't satisfied.

He thought of the blank indifferent look that had been given him by Izzy's grandniece Morgan.

Hasn't done much lately.

He wrote another sentence, played around with it, wasn't satisfied.

He went back to the kitchen and read another page of Izzy's novel. It seemed more and more clear to him that the main character was partly based on him. Several things he had told Izzy in confidence had ended up on the page. Adam noticed this without being troubled by it. It's just what a writer does. If you believe that anything you tell a writer will truly be held in confidence, then you're a fool.

The main character was so much like himself as a younger man that people might almost believe that he had written it.

The main character was so much like himself as a younger man that people might believe that he had written it.

Why not?

If he published this book under his own name, no one would know.

It was a perfect solution to two problems: the problem of Adam's temporary lack of inspiration, and the problem that if his rivalry with Izzy prevented him from trying to publish the book, the world would be deprived of a fine novel.

It didn't matter to Izzy; it didn't matter to Ruth. The only person it mattered to was Adam. If it was published as Izzy's book, his own life, Adam's life, would be changed—changed for the worse. Reviewers would begin to compare them again, and some of them would decide that Izzy had been the better writer.

If it was published as Adam's book, on the other hand, his life would be changed for the better. It would be called one of his best books—a book as strong as the things he wrote in his forties. It would be hailed as a literary comeback.

So if one put aside all sentimentality, acknowledged in a clear-eyed way that nothing mattered to the dead, it was obviously true that the only person who would be affected by this was Adam. Therefore, it made no sense to publish it under Izzy's name, and all the sense in the world to publish it under his own.

He brought Izzy's manuscript to his desk, sat down, and began transcribing it into his computer. Even in the first few paragraphs, he changed a word or two, making it more his own.

THIRTY-TWO

Eleanor met Patrick at the arch in Washington Square Park. When she arrived, he was waiting for her, leaning against the arch with a wry smile.

"Both times I've seen you, you've wanted to meet in public," he said. "If I didn't know better I'd think you were afraid I was trying to bump you off."

She didn't have a witty reply to this, so she didn't say anything.

She took his arm and they walked through the park. The smell of marijuana was thick in the air.

"I'm paying forty thousand dollars a year for Kate to go to college here," he said.

Thompson Street was blocked off below Washington Square. There were long trailers taking up half the street, tables filled with Gatorade and platters of sandwiches, huge klieg lights like creatures from outer space. Two techies in headsets prowled the end of the block, self-importantly shooing people away.

"Street's blocked off. Try MacDougal."

"This is a public street," Patrick said.

"Office of the Mayor says it's not a public street tonight. We've got a scene to wrap here, dude."

"I've never been called 'dude' before," Patrick said to Eleanor.

"Gotta move, gotta move, gotta move," the techie was saying to another man, a nerdlike figure in a short-sleeved shirt who was holding an ice-cream cone and standing on tiptoes, scanning for the faces of the famous. "Gotta book, dog."

"I wonder why I was dude and he was dog," Patrick said.

"It's hard to say," Eleanor said.

The short-sleeved man was following the techie. "What are you filming?"

"Sean Penn, Angelina Jolie," the techie said. *"Help Wanted."*

A child actor who didn't look familiar to Eleanor was being filmed as she walked down a flight of steps outside a brownstone. When she reached the street, the cameras were turned off, four or five men came together for a huddled conference. One of them broke off and talked to the girl, who walked back up the steps, waited as two women attended to her hair, waited further as a squad of men adjusted the lights, and walked down the steps again.

Patrick shook his head and laughed. "Jesus. With the amount of money they're spending here, they could feed Ethiopia."

He seemed solid, substantial, sure of his values. He was perhaps the one person she knew who, if offered a day's work as an extra in this production, whatever it was, would have no interest. Everyone else she knew would find it hard to pass up the chance to get a close look at Angelina Jolie. Including herself.

They walked down to MacDougal and finally stopped at the Caffe Dante. It was crowded. Two girls in front of them on line kept calling everything "awesome." Patrick looked amused. Not condescending, not uncharitable, but amused.

She was reminded of an old TV series about a cop from Texas or Nebraska or somewhere who comes to New York to solve a case and ends up staying. Marching around in his cowboy boots and ten-gallon hat: the hick who keeps outsmarting all the city slickers.

After their coffee came, Patrick said, "I saw Kate's show last night."

"Kate's show?"

"The reason I'm here right now? Kate? My daughter?"

"That's right. I forgot about the show. How was it?"

"I understood about two percent of what she was getting at. Even after she explained it to me. But I was amazed. I know she's my daughter, so I might not be very objective, but I really think she's brilliant. She made these things . . . they look like half trees, half people. I don't know if I've ever seen anything like them before. The only thing I can compare them to is—well, Diana and I went to Florence a few years ago, and one museum has these unfinished sculptures by Michelangelo, *The Slaves,* where the people seem like they're emerging from rocks, or getting swallowed up by the rocks." He stopped and smiled at himself. "Yes, friends, take it from me. My daughter and Michelangelo."

Eleanor looked down into her coffee cup, purely because she wanted a minute to savor this. This was a father who wanted his children to succeed. He wasn't competing with them. She'd almost forgotten that this was the way it was supposed to be.

She asked him what his other daughter was like.

"Maggie? She's like a bomb. She'll say anything, anywhere, anytime. She's a one-girl truth patrol."

He told a few stories about his one-girl truth patrol. He was proud of her. Eleanor didn't want to ask about Diana, but she had a feeling that he was proud of her too.

I'm a fool, she thought.

After she'd seen Patrick in December, when she went back to her apartment and wrote about her memories of him, she'd admitted to herself that if she were sent back to her youth and once again given the choice between Adam or Patrick, she would once again choose Adam—not because of the man but because of the life. She had chosen Adam because she knew he could introduce her to a larger world, and she would choose him again for the same reason.

But now she wondered about this. What *was* the larger world? Adam's idea of the larger world was . . . what? Parties. Fame. Getting ahead. Dreaming of ways to triumph over his rivals.

Patrick was a born appreciator. He used to make her feel important, and he still did. He used to make her feel interesting, and he still did. She couldn't regret the choices she made, because the choices she made had brought her children into the world. But she wondered what she herself might have become if she'd chosen him.

"I feel lucky that you called me last fall," she said.

He smiled oddly.

"What?" she said.

"It wasn't entirely luck."

"How's that?"

"When Vivian was back in Portland last year to close up her mother's house, I ran into her. I asked her about you, of course, and she told me you were free. I asked her for your number. I said I wasn't even sure you'd remember me, with your big-city life. She said she thought you probably would."

Vivian had never even hinted at this. Eleanor was amazed by her friend's capacity for deception. But, really, it was just like her. The secret romantic, working behind the scenes to bring Eleanor together with the man who, in Vivian's eyes, she should have been with in the first place.

"Vivian always liked you," Eleanor said.

After they had coffee they walked downtown, toward his hotel. "When you first moved here," Patrick said, "I'd sometimes go to the photography section of the bookstore and look at books about New York. I used to imagine you on every street."

He turned and put his hands on her shoulders and kissed her, and she put her arms around him, trying to remember the last time she had kissed anyone but Adam. The last time she'd kissed anyone but Adam, she realized, was when she had last kissed Patrick.

She put her head in his jacket, half as a coy show of affection, half to slow things down.

"And what's happening with Diana?"

"It's still the same."

"You're together, you're not together, you're together?"

"That's about it."

He put his arm around her waist and they continued walking.

"I don't think that will work for me, Patrick."

He nodded. He looked as if he already knew this.

"I'm not asking you to leave her. All I'm saying is that I don't want to be the other woman."

"I respect that."

"You do?"

"It's not like I haven't been thinking about it. My conscience has been trying to tell me more or less the same thing."

"But you weren't listening?"

"I wanted to kiss you. So I told my conscience to take a hike."

They were walking through Soho. Young people on parade. Most of them, to Eleanor's eye, looked slightly manic.

It's good, she thought, not to be young.

"I don't know if Diana and I can split up while Maggie's still living at home. I don't want to be seeing my daughter at a pizza parlor once a week."

She could understand that. She was glad that it mattered to him.

"Is there any chance that you and Diana can work it out?"

"I don't think so. We could stay together. We could accomplish that. But we've been having the same fights for the last thirty years. I think both of us are ready for different fights."

They reached his hotel too soon.

"I won't ask you to come up," he said. "I think you might be the most moral person I've ever known."

"I hope not," she said.

When she got back to her apartment, she opened her notebook and began to write.

It wasn't an abstract sense of morality that had made her tell Patrick that she couldn't see him if he was still with Diana. It was something more specific than that.

Eleanor had been continuing to write about her old life. During the last few weeks, she'd been writing about the period when she met Patrick.

It was disturbing to revisit those days.

Eleanor's sister met Patrick before Eleanor did. He and Joanna were in an antiwar group together. Eleanor could still remember the way Joanna talked about him: smiling with an unselfconscious radiance, bringing up things he'd said with an air that would have made you think she was quoting George Bernard Shaw.

When Eleanor met him, she wondered whether she would have found him attractive at all if Joanna hadn't advertised his merits beforehand. Eleanor, in her twenties, was a kind of snob—she only liked smart people—and she might have mistaken his deliberateness for a lack of intelligence, his solidity for an absence of fire.

One day he and Joanna were supposed to go over a statement the group was putting out, but when he showed up in the evening, Joanna was still at work. Eleanor invited him to wait for a while on their porch and brought out a pitcher of iced tea and two glasses, and they talked until it got dark, and finally he had to leave, and she never quite told him that Joanna had called that afternoon to say that she wouldn't be able to make it home until midnight.

She still had a clear memory of sitting on the porch with him—although in truth, her picture of herself was clearer than her picture of him. She was barefoot and wearing a sleeveless sundress; she set down his glass on a table next to one of the wicker chairs and sat across from him on the swing seat; and, because this is the kind of thing you know about yourself when you're twenty-one, she knew just how nice her legs looked as she kept lightly, slightly swinging, pushing herself casually off the floor.

When she and Patrick got together, a week or two after that, Joanna acted as if she were happy for them. Joanna had never quite admitted that she was interested in him. She was such an innocent that it was conceivable that she hadn't admitted it to herself.

Joanna and Patrick were both straightforward people—honest, commonsensical, free of guile. Free, even, of irony. They might have been perfectly matched. And Eleanor had stepped between them, for no reason, really, other than that she could. And had left him shortly afterward for a man she thought could give her a more exciting life.

The taking of Patrick. If Joanna had lived, it might have been just one contest in a long and mostly loving rivalry, something not of much importance in the scheme of things. But because Joanna had died that same year, it had been the last thing that passed between them, and in Eleanor's mind the two events, the taking of the man and the death of the sister, were twisted together.

Over these past few decades, Eleanor had grown comfortable with an idea of herself as a virtuous woman: a forgiving wife, a patient mother, a caring therapist. Revisiting the past had reminded her that she had once been a different creature. The discovery wasn't entirely unwelcome: it isn't a bad thing to remember that you have some wildness in you, that not every inch of your soul is honorable and responsible and presentable and tamped and tamed. But at the same time, remembering how she'd taken Patrick away from one woman, she couldn't give herself permission to take him away from another.

THIRTY-THREE

Maud let herself into Samir's apartment. She could hear him snoring from the front hall.

A grown man who is sleeping is almost always an unlovely thing. Even if you love him. There's something heavy and dull about the sleeping body of a grown man, something strangled and death-gripped about the sounds he makes. And Samir slept more charmlessly than most. Over the past few months, he had become happier than he thought he could be — he had told her this, and she believed it — but whenever she watched him sleeping, she thought that unhappiness was the root condition of his soul.

She felt as if she were about to drop a bomb on his life.

She should probably just leave, without waking him. Leave, schedule an abortion, never tell him. And then they could go on as they'd been going, getting to know each other slowly.

Let him live, she thought. He doesn't need this. The love of his life was his daughter. His mourning is his home. Don't bring someone new into his life.

He stirred and opened his eyes.

"Good morning," he said. "Come to bed."

She didn't think it would be fair to get into bed. She wanted to tell him what was happening, and it wouldn't be fair to tell him while they were making love, or just after.

She didn't move.

He sat up.

"Are you all right?"

He still often did his best to seem like an insensitive man, but he was incapable of hiding who he really was. He was astonishingly attuned to her.

"Maybe we should take a walk," she said.

Thirty-four

After she told him, he had to force himself to keep walking normally. *Lift this leg. Then that leg.*

This was one of those soul-making moments that come very seldom in life. What they did and said in the next hour would go a long way in determining not only what the two of them were to each other, but what the two of them were. It's probably true that you're forging your own character during every minute of every day, with every decision you make; but there are some moments in which this is much more clear than in others.

She hadn't yet told him what she wanted, and he had no clue. Nor did he have a clue what he wanted himself.

It was Saturday morning. It must have been about six o'clock. The streets were quiet. They walked to the Promenade, passing without comment the spot where he had kissed her on that first night.

This moment might have been beautiful. If her news had excited them both, rather than confused them, this moment, as they walked down the Promenade while the city began to come to life across the river, might have seemed holy.

But the moment did not feel holy. He had a bad cold, and he felt sluggish and awkward, and he didn't know what he wanted, and *Zahra Zahra Zahra.*

"Don't worry," he said. "We'll figure this out."

"We will?" she said. "Is there a 'we' here?" she said.

He could say, *Come to think of it, there isn't.* In asking him the question, she was opening a door, and he wanted nothing more than to walk through it, out of her life, out of the land of *we* and *ours* and *us.*

"Of course there's a 'we' here," he said.

He didn't know if he believed this but he had to say it. He didn't know what he believed.

But the thing to do was to try to react with his kindest impulses and then wait until later to figure out what he really thought and what he really wanted.

He brushed a strand of hair away from her eyes.

"Isn't there?"

Thirty-five

O f course there's a 'we' here," he said.

He brushed a strand of hair away from her eyes.
"Isn't there?"

She expected him to follow this up by saying, "Isn't we?" but of course he would never say anything as playful as this. He was not a playful man. She wasn't sure he had a sense of humor, actually. Can I be with a man who doesn't have a sense of humor?

"Maybe we should get something to eat," he said.

They walked toward a coffee shop, and she tried to think of it as walking, rather than trudging.

"I wish I hadn't spent the last couple of weeks reading Schopenhauer," she said.

"Why not?"

"He has this very persuasive way of explaining that life is hell."

"Every life?"

"Every life. He says that life consists of little more than suffering. He says that life would make sense if it *were* hell. He says that it's as if all of us are being punished for crimes that we can't remember committing."

"He's probably right," Samir said. "But he doesn't sound like much fun."

She would never have imagined that Samir would say that— that Schopenhauer didn't sound like fun. She wouldn't have thought that the word *fun* was in his vocabulary. In recent months they'd had passion, and exaltation, and maybe love, but she wasn't sure they'd had anything that could have been described as *fun*. So his use of the word now was a reminder that he was a man who could change. A man who had. And being reminded of how much he'd changed helped her look upon the prospect of a transformed life with less dread.

"You're right," she said. "He probably wasn't."

A word can change the world. If she were finally to give birth to this child, this last minute might turn out to have been decisive. Eighty years from now, this child, this Jack or Jill, would spend a mellow last Thanksgiving surrounded by children and grandchildren, and none of them—the Jack or Jill, the children, the grandchildren—would know that all of them owed their existence to a single utterance of the word *fun*.

Was that crazy?

She had thought more about going crazy in the last ten hours than she had in the previous five years.

THIRTY-SIX

Y ou amaze me," Candace said. "You amaze me."

Candace was Adam's editor.

Adam just smiled and had another sip of his martini.

"You really think it's that good?" Thea said.

"I don't just think it's that good. I think it's astounding."

Thea squeezed Adam's arm. "It sounds like the old man came through."

"I would love this book if I'd never heard of the author," Candace said. "But having read everything you've ever written—I can't say it makes me love it *more,* but it makes me love it in a different way. Because I think you've transformed yourself. You're writing about the same things you've always written about—the same places, the same people—but you're writing about it now with a tenderness I've never seen in your work before. I'm really stunned."

Adam smiled modestly. "I'm glad you like it," he said.

No one in the world knew the truth. No one but Adam. Over the course of twelve intense days he had retyped the manuscript onto his computer, making improvements along the way—playing with the language and the placement of scenes, shading characters a little differently. At the end of the process, he almost felt as if he *had* written it.

After typing the last word, Adam had made good use of the fireplace in his apartment by destroying both Izzy's typewritten manuscript and the carbon copy. Even if someone someday suspected the truth, some scholar with too much time on his hands, no one would ever be able to prove it.

"I don't like it," Candace said. "I love it."

She shivered slightly in her chair. It was kind of sexy—a swaying little shiver dance.

"It's weird. I've been working with you for twenty years, and I've loved everything you've written . . . but all of a sudden I feel kind of intimidated by you."

"That's excellent," Adam said. "I've always wanted to intimidate you, Candace."

Candace had never displayed the least bit of sexual interest in him—she'd always seemed to regard him as a father figure—but now, he was wondering . . .

Even Thea seemed awed.

"I'm afraid to read it," she said. "I'm not sure I'll be worthy of it."

"The people in sales can't believe it," Candace said. "They're all going crazy. Dean says he hasn't seen anything like this since *Ragtime*." Dean was the head of the sales department, a man with a long memory. "He says that it's only about once a generation that you see a book that appeals with equal success to people who want to be challenged and people who want to be entertained."

"I've always liked Dean," Adam said.

After lunch, Adam saw Candace into a taxi while Thea stayed behind on the sidewalk. When he returned to her, she said, "What now? What are you doing this afternoon?"

Thea, who was always running off because "Charlie can't be kept waiting," suddenly had time on her hands.

Adam took her hands in his. "I have a few appointments. I wish I could get out of them, but I can't." He had no appointments at all, but Thea had been cock-teasing him for so long—

it was a considerable accomplishment, really, to be cock-teasing a man even while you're sleeping with him—that at this point the satisfaction of disappointing her was greater than the satisfaction of fucking her. He kissed her on the cheek, offered to get a cab for her, and got one for himself when she declined.

In the cab he turned his cell phone on and checked his messages. The only message he had was from Maud. She didn't say anything in particular, just hello. But she sounded needy.

This would be as good a time as ever to call her. He liked making phone calls from cabs.

She answered on the first ring, and sounded disappointed to hear who it was, then happy to hear who it was. There was someone else she'd wanted to hear from more, but she liked hearing from her father.

He employed a tone of insistent buoyancy to ask her how she was, hoping either to force her to share his own high spirits or, if that failed, at least to make it clear that he didn't want to listen to an account of why she couldn't.

"Okay," she said.

"What are you up to?"

"Just reading."

"Who are you reading?"

"Still reading for my dissertation. Schopenhauer."

Schopenhauer, who believed that the only way we might achieve our aims in life was by aiming for misery and suffering—because misery and suffering, no matter what we aim for, is what we will get.

Why did she always go for these sadsack philosophers; why was she always drawn to the work of the prematurely defeated? Her mother's influence, doubtless.

"Maybe you should broaden your reading," he said. "Maybe you should read a little Nietzsche."

"What?" she said. Their connection was bad. He heard three short beeps and then they were cut off.

He called her again.

"There you are," she said. "What were you saying?"

"Nothing."

Surely she had read Nietzsche, and surely she had barred him from her personal pantheon. His project of gloriously un-apologetic self-creation probably left her cold. She probably only liked philosophers who were *nice*.

"Are you in a spaceship or something?" she said. "You sound all . . . futuristic."

"Taxi on Lex. Is that futuristic enough for you?"

Again he heard the series of beeps, and again the connection failed.

It was as if technology had gone backward. In the old days, when a telephone was a bulky thing that stayed plugged into your wall, you could actually *hear* the person on the other end of the line. Now you could take your phone anywhere, but you couldn't actually talk.

But he had come to like cell phones for just this reason. The phone cuts you off and you don't have to call back. It was as if the capriciousness of the cellular phone had enabled us to admit that we don't want to talk to one another at all.

THIRTY-SEVEN

Something was wrong with Maud. Eleanor felt sure of this, but she didn't know what it was.

She felt sure of it not because she saw any change in Maud, but because she felt a change in herself. She was a little more concerned than she should have been about whether Maud was going to eat her pie.

Maud was sitting at Eleanor's kitchen table on a Saturday afternoon, and Eleanor had just served her a slice of apple pie.

During her teenage years, Maud had never eaten enough. She was horrified by how quickly she was growing—in sixth grade she was taller than any of the boys in her class—and she tried to slow her growth by starving herself. It had been an anxious period for Eleanor, and ever since then, she'd found it gratifying to see Maud eat. It made her feel as if Maud were saying yes to being alive.

It had been a long time since she'd felt anxious about Maud's eating habits, and she wasn't sure why she was feeling so anxious now. It made her wonder whether she'd picked up on some feeling of unease or unhappiness from Maud without even being consciously aware of it.

Eleanor went to the refrigerator and got out eggs and butter and milk and mushrooms and cheese. She was cooking Maud an omelet for lunch. She'd served the pie first in keeping with Maud's odd tradition of starting off with dessert.

"So how are you?" Eleanor said. "How are things with my baby?" She was trying to find a light tone.

A flutter of displeasure crossed Maud's face, and Eleanor wished she hadn't used the word. She remembered how her own mother used to crow, "No matter how old you are, you'll always be my baby," and how much it used to annoy her.

"How's your dissertation going?" Eleanor said, as a way of acknowledging that Maud was much more than her baby.

"I haven't been able to concentrate on it that well lately," Maud said.

"Why is that?"

"I don't know." Maud was looking glumly at her pie. "I mean, what's my dissertation *about*? It's about the way people should treat each other. But is there really any point in writing about what different philosophers have thought about the subject?"

Eleanor's first impulse was to reassure her—writing about what philosophers think is more important than curing cancer!—but experience had taught her that smothering Maud with reassurance never helped.

"Well," Eleanor said, "what *is* the point?"

"I used to think there was a point," Maud said. "Maybe I'll think there's a point again. But at the moment it just seems so abstract."

During Maud's first semester in graduate school, she'd had a lot of similar doubts—*studying-philosophy-is-a-cop-out; I-should-be-doing-something-in-the-real-world* kind of doubts—but Eleanor thought she'd made her way beyond them long ago.

Maud's two plunges into depression had taken place years ago, but Eleanor could never rid herself of the fear that she was going to go under again. The smallest sign that Maud was unhappy could put Eleanor into a full-blown panic.

Eleanor put the omelet and the toast on a plate and placed it in front of Maud.

"What do you mean it seems abstract?"

Maud just shrugged. Eleanor waited, and then tried another avenue. "So how's the new guy?" she said, with all the casualness she could muster.

"He's good," Maud said. "He's good. He's not that new any-more. But he's still good."

"When do I get to meet him?"

"We'll see, Mom," Maud said. "We'll see."

Eleanor didn't press, and tried not to feel slighted. It was im-possible to know, she thought, whether Maud is reluctant to in-troduce us because my opinion means so little to her, or because it means so much.

"What do you like about him?" Eleanor said. "Or is that an intrusive question?"

"No. That's not intrusive. He's really smart."

Eleanor was about to say, *That goes without saying.* All of Maud's boyfriends had been smart. But she didn't want to inter-rupt her daughter's train of thought.

"And he feels things deeply," Maud said. "And he's never fake. He may not tell you everything he's thinking, but he never pretends to be thinking one thing while he's thinking another. I don't think he'd be capable of it. Why are you smiling?"

"I'm smiling because he sounds like a good person. And I'm smiling because everything you've said about him could also be said about you."

"Thank you," Maud said quietly.

But she still seemed uneasy.

"Are you okay?" Eleanor said.

"Sure."

"Really?"

"Really."

It was frustrating to be shut out of your child's life.

Eleanor was sometimes amazed by how little she remembered of her children's infancy, but one of the things she did remember was the feeling that she knew everything about them, that they had no secrets from her. Of course it had never been true, but it had *seemed* to be true, for years.

And then they grow away from you, and then they leave home, and then when they reappear they seem to have less to do with the world you once shared with them than with the world they've left you for. Their friends understand them better than you do. They're like one more piece of modern technology that you don't know how to operate.

"I noticed that you've turned my room into a study," Maud said. "Does that mean you've been writing?"

"A little bit." Eleanor couldn't help smiling. She felt as if she were confessing to something scandalous.

"Does my room inspire you?" Maud said.

"It does."

Which was true, Eleanor thought, although she couldn't have said exactly how.

"What are you writing about?"

"I'm writing about my family. My mother and my sister. Not so much my father."

"You've written about them before. Right?"

"I've tried. I've never gotten that far."

"How's it going?"

"A little better. I think. I hope."

"That's great. Do you know why it's going better?"

"I don't know. I'm older?"

"That doesn't explain anything by itself. Does it?"

"Probably not," Eleanor said.

"Then what else could it be?"

Maud never let you get away with a lazy answer. After you answered her questions, you usually had a better understanding of what you'd been thinking in the first place.

She would have made a good therapist, Eleanor thought. Maybe better than I am.

"If I really had to point to one thing," Eleanor said, "I guess I'd say it has something to do with my work. You spend twenty years at a job, and it changes you."

"How has being a therapist changed you?"

"It's made me see life in a different way. When I was in my twenties, I wanted to be a writer, but I didn't believe in plots. I didn't think life *had* plots. So everything I wrote petered out after twenty or thirty pages."

"And you believe in plots now?" Maud said.

"I do. After twenty years of listening to people tell stories about themselves, I sometimes think that life is nothing *but* plot, if you think of plot as the choices we make. You could say that neurosis is a condition in which we think we don't have choices. And you could say that the goal of therapy is to help someone see that he's already making choices, and that he could be making different choices."

Maud put her head down, to think. Eleanor became aware that what Maud thought mattered to her. She wanted to pass the test of her philosopher-daughter's scrutiny.

As Eleanor went to the refrigerator for a carton of apple cider, Adam appeared in her mind, wearing a mocking smile. Adam had recently told her that he'd finished a new book. His ninth. He was probably at his laptop, writing, at this very moment. While she, having published precisely nothing, was sitting in the kitchen pontificating about art and life.

Eleanor put two glasses on the table. Maud still seemed to be thinking about what Eleanor had said, still seemed to be pondering the question of choice in human life. As she poured the cider into Maud's glass, Eleanor had a dizzy spell—which might not have been a dizzy spell at all, but simply an excess of emotion. She was overcome by an appreciation of Maud's kindness, her essential goodness.

Maud, if she ever had a child, would be a wonderful mother. She would be the kind of mother who treated her children's thoughts with seriousness and respect. Eleanor suddenly felt sure of this.

She had no idea why she was thinking about Maud's possible future as a mother. The thought had come out of nowhere.

After Maud left, Eleanor cleared the kitchen table. Maud had barely eaten anything. It was only when Eleanor noticed this that it occurred to her that they'd never gone back to the subject of how Maud was doing.

Eleanor had told herself that she was going to find out why Maud was unhappy, and had then become distracted by the sound of her own voice.

She made herself a cup of coffee and, although she wasn't hungry, had a slice of pie.

The small ways we fail one another, every day.

THIRTY-EIGHT

Samir spent three days in Bethesda, working on a high-paying remodeling job that he'd made a commitment to several months earlier. He'd wanted to postpone it, but Maud had told him not to. With the frankness he admired, she'd said that she stood a better chance of figuring out what she wanted if they were apart for a few days.

He assumed that she was talking to her loved ones—her old friends, perhaps her brothers, perhaps her mother. He knew she found it helpful to consult the people she trusted.

He himself had only one person he needed to consult.

He got back on a Thursday night, and on Friday he visited the cemetery. It was the first time he'd been there since he'd begun seeing Maud. It had rained that morning, and the grass was still damp. His feet made little sucking sounds as he made his way up the hill.

Zahra's grave was unembellished. There were three lines of writing on her gravestone. On the first line was her name; on the second, the year of her birth and the year of her death. On the third line were the words WE WILL ALWAYS LOVE YOU. That was all.

He stood at her grave for a long time, letting random thoughts pass through his mind. Remembering how eager she always was to "help Daddy." When she helped Daddy perform some task, it took three times longer, but that was a small price to pay for the privilege of witnessing her excitement. When she earnestly tried to fold one of his shirts as he was getting ready for a trip, or when she stood on tiptoes on a kitchen chair, stretching over the table as far as she could, so she could blow on his cup of tea in order to cool it, or when she carried the newspaper to him in the morning after Leila had picked it up from their doorstep, she always looked so proud, so important.

Remembering the first time she accompanied him to the laundry room. How stunned she was by the dryer: "Daddy! My clothes go round and round!"

Remembering the stories she used to love, stories about how she triumphed over the animals.

Without deciding to do this, he sank slowly to his knees in front of the gravestone.

The wetness of the grass seeped through the knees of his pants. He wished he were so pure-minded as not to even notice this, not to be detained, not even for a moment, by the thought that the pants might in the future be unwearable because of grass stains. He wasn't that pure-minded, however.

On his knees, he leaned forward and touched his forehead to the stone. Then he shifted his position and lowered his forehead to the earth.

His daughter was a few feet beneath him.

Even if the universe lasted for another billion years, Zahra would never come again. Zahra would never see another day. No one would ever hear the sound of her laughter.

It would not do to pretend that if he welcomed the new life, the new life that he and Maud had created, Zahra would remain undisturbed in the place she now occupied in his mind. His memory of her would grow dimmer. If he became accustomed to the laughter of another child, his memory of Zahra's laughter would grow uncertain. If he welcomed the new life, he would be pushing Zahra further into the land in which everything is finally forgotten.

His daughter, his poor daughter, in the earth, never to breathe, never to see snow, never to see light, never to see anything again. If the universe lasts billions and billions and billions of years, there will never be another Zahra.

"I don't want to live without you," he said.

He remembered her howling, howling, howling, at the age of ten months, as they pressed the needle into her jugular vein. He remembered her howling, at the age of three years, when she woke up in the recovery room after having tubes implanted in her chest. He remembered what she said about her dream: "I tried to roar back at them, but I couldn't scare them away." He remembered how she told the nurse: "My daddy won't let you!"

I wanted to protect you, my love. I wanted to protect you.

How can you do it? How can you contemplate having another child when she's gone?

He knew that he was going to embrace the new life. If he refused the new life, he wouldn't be honoring Zahra. The only way to honor her was to live.

But there would be a cost to this. It would not do to pretend there would not be a cost. The more completely he gave himself to life, the more her memory would fade.

He had been kneeling; now he simply lay down on the earth. He spoke softly into the grass.

"Forgive me," he said. "Forgive me, my love. Please forgive me."

THIRTY-NINE

H ow was your week?" Maud said.
  "It was interesting."

Interesting, she thought. A word that meant nothing.

It was a Saturday afternoon, his second day back in New York, and they had gotten together in Riverside Park, near the Soldiers' and Sailors' Monument. They were walking near the water.

It was threatening rain. The river was gray and unmajestic, humping along in little dull lumps. It looked like thousands of moles stitched together.

She was unhappy about the fact that he hadn't called her until the morning of his second day back. She didn't know what he'd been doing on his first day.

"How was *your* week?" he said.

"Just a week. Taught classes, worked on the monster."

And stopped drinking coffee. And stopped drinking diet soda. And stopped eating tuna, because of the mercury levels. And constantly did mathematical calculations in my head, she thought, trying to imagine how many cells now composed this alien life-form growing inside me. But she wasn't going to mention anything about this—not until he did.

"That was all?" he said.

"What else is there?"

She wasn't pleased with herself for being so snitty, if that was a word. But she couldn't help it. He should have come straight to her door after he returned, stopping only to dash into a flower shop, and appeared at her threshold with an armful of roses, and told her that she was his destiny.

They were walking past the Boat Basin. A colony of house-boats. Maud imagined raising her child alone, out here on the Boat Basin. *In landlessness alone resides the highest truth.* The two of them, Maud and her child, nobly seasick.

"When I was gone," he said, "I did some thinking."

At last, he was getting to the subject.

"What did you think about?"

She was afraid that he was going to say he wanted to go ahead with this, afraid that he was going to say he didn't.

"I thought about you," he said. "About us. About the baby."

"What did you think?" she said.

But she already knew. You don't say "the baby" if your wish is to dump the thing in the trash.

It made her happy and it made her afraid.

Just south of the Boat Basin was an abandoned baseball field where people walked their dogs. You had to be careful where you stepped.

"I want us to be parents together," he said.

Here we are, she thought. We're grown-ups.

They walked along in silence for a while.

She remembered walking along this same path with her first boyfriend, Daniel, on a late-summer day almost twelve years earlier, just before she went off to college. Before her first break-down. At seventeen she'd thought that her life was good and that it would only get better. She hadn't had an inkling of the troubles that lay in wait for her: her breakdowns, or her parents' divorce, or the many splintered relationships she was destined to endure, or the subtle fogging of her mind through years of un-happiness, or the subtle fogging of her mind through years of medications prescribed to keep the unhappiness in check. She had anticipated none of these things. Whenever she visited the park, she remembered that walk with Daniel, and whenever she remembered it, it seemed to represent a utopian moment, a state of high possibility to which she had no chance of returning.

But now, as she walked beside Samir, she thought that there was a chance that she might return to that state of grace after all. There was the possibility of a good, sane, productive, fulfilling life. She could see herself in ten years: teaching philosophy, happily married to Samir, happily raising children together.

Happily married, she thought, and she asked herself what this idea meant to her. What it meant to her was that they would still be enjoying each other and still be challenging each other.

She knew that she wanted to be with him. The feeling of rightness that she had with him was bone deep. And although she had always worried that she wouldn't be strong enough to raise a child, she believed that she *could* be strong enough if she was doing it with Samir.

A minute or two had passed since his pronouncement, and she thought it was probably time for her to respond.

"That makes me happy," she said.

She had to force the words out of herself, because her throat was constricted by fear. But despite the fear, despite the fact that she had to force them, the words were true.

Samir smiled at her. His smile was quizzical, but kind. He seemed to understand that she was struggling.

Maybe, she thought, the two-minute pause was a tip-off.

"*Does* it make you happy?" he said. He didn't sound hurt; he didn't sound as if he were interrogating her. He sounded as if he wanted to know.

"I think so," she said.

The sky was gray and grave and grim and the river was dull
and humped and hunchbacked, yet she found all of it stirring,
because the day was anything but bland, but at the same time as
she was glorying in it, in the large-souled moodiness of nature,
she had to keep glancing down to make sure that she wasn't
about to step in dog shit, and she tried not to think of this as a
metaphor for the human experience.

"I hope we can both embrace this," he said. "But I want you
to take as much time as you need. I don't want to force you into
this."

She stopped walking and turned to face him. It seemed important to be facing him when she said what she was going
to say.

"Thank you," she said. "I appreciate your saying that. But . . .
you couldn't."

"I know that, actually," he said.

He took her hand, and he didn't seem to mind that her hand
was sweating like mad, and for the first time she felt that she
could do this, that they could do this, that it was going to be all
right.

FORTY

Maud hadn't yet introduced Samir to anybody from her world. She was a little bit afraid to.

For one thing, she was afraid that people just wouldn't *get* him. He'd come a long way during the past several months, but he was still perennially reticent, perennially serious, perennially uninterested in small talk. As they used to say in nineteenth-century novels, he wasn't clubbable.

And she knew he wouldn't try to *help* anybody get him. He'd opened himself up to her only after she'd devoted months to the effort to crack the code of his guardedness. And the only reason he'd been willing to spend those first months in her company was that she gave such irrefutable blow jobs. It had worked for them, but it would be an impractical way for anyone else to get to know him.

As far as she and Samir had come, she still couldn't imagine them living a normal life together. She couldn't imagine them spending weekends visiting friends and family. So far they'd spent almost all their time alone. She had no doubts about his essential nature: she knew that he was intelligent and interesting and solemn and serious and kind; she knew that he'd be faithful; she knew he'd be a good and careful father. But she didn't know if he'd ever want to let other people into his life. Sometimes she envisioned a future in which it was just the two of them and their child, or their children, against the world, a future in which she saw her friends by herself or with the kids, but never with Samir. She feared that life with Samir was going to be a hard life.

When she examined her own reluctance to introduce him to the people in her world, she also wondered if it had anything to do with the fact that he was an Arab. It wasn't that she was afraid that he and the other people in her life would get into arguments. She wasn't afraid of arguments. But it was all too easy to imagine some bit of casual anti-Arab prejudice escaping from the lips of her friends or family, or some scrap of casual anti-Semitic prejudice from his.

But now they were going to have a child together, and she needed to let him into her world.

When Ralph called her one Friday afternoon, suggesting they do something the next day, she knew it had to be him.

The three of them got together on a cool afternoon in March. She had suggested that they go to the Met. Ralph was waiting for her and Samir, sitting in his wheelchair, near the fountains outside the building.

Ralph looked terrible. She had seen him just a few weeks ago, and she actually wasn't sure he looked any worse; it might just have been that it had been a long time since she'd seen him in the sun. When she saw him in his apartment, amid the paintings and the sculpture and the nineteenth-century novels and the art books, his pallor never seemed out of place. Outdoors, in the bright day, he looked ghastly.

Holding up one hand to shield his eyes from the sun, Ralph smiled up at Samir. "I've heard a lot about you."

Samir just nodded. Maud wanted to brain him with her purse, and suddenly this encounter, which she'd been telling herself she shouldn't feel tense about, seemed like a test. If he flunks it, she thought, he's out. If he can't be nice to Ralph, then he's not worth keeping.

They walked slowly through the museum, and she kept trying to take her mind off her own anxiety. Ralph had no shortage of things to say—he was in his element here, and he was playing the part of the genial tour guide—but Samir remained firmly committed to silence. Maud felt herself growing perky and cheerleaderish, to keep things light. After Ralph said something about Pisarro's use of the color gray, she nodded enthusiastically, and ten seconds later realized that she was still nodding. She had a vision of herself as someone else might see her— head bobbing up and down with an inane vigor. *Maud Weller,* she thought. *The bobble-head doll. At toy stores everywhere.*

When they were ready to leave the museum, they took the closest elevator, a freight elevator with a heavily scuffed floor and gray industrial padding on the walls. When you left the museum the usual way, walking down the white stone steps on Fifth Avenue, the experience had a kind of grandeur. They had no choice but to leave the way they did—Ralph couldn't make it down the steps—and yet the dismalness of the elevator and the way it dumped them at a side entrance at the mouth of the parking garage made it feel to her as if they'd been kicked out. It was as if the museum had been a test for all three of them, and they'd failed.

They decided to get something to eat. Maud suggested a coffee shop she knew on Madison Avenue. It wasn't built with handicapped people in mind—Ralph had trouble getting through the entryway—but once they were in, the waiters courteously and efficiently cleared space around a table to give him enough room.

"I used to come here with my dad when I was in high school," Maud said. "We'd go to the museum and then we'd have a snack. The only problem was that there was this literary critic who used to eat here once in a while, and my dad couldn't stand him. So there would be a lot of glaring going on."

"What critic?" Ralph said.

"Irving Howe?" she said.

"I remember him. Why didn't your father like him?"

"He didn't like my dad's books. He gave *Daybreak* a terrible review."

"I guess that would do it."

Samir was smirking.

"What?" she said.

"Irving Howe. I didn't like him either."

"Did you know him?" Maud said.

"No. I mean I didn't like his work. I don't know anything about his literary criticism, but I never liked his political things."

"Why not?"

"He wrote a lot about the Middle East. And . . . how shall I put it? He was not a friend of Palestinian aspirations."

"Irving Howe?" Ralph said. "I thought he was a dove."

She saw a series of thoughts cross Samir's face. At first he looked as if he was going to say something cutting; then he looked as if he'd decided against it.

"In the American political climate, he was the kind of person who passes for a dove. Why don't we just leave it at that."

"I can understand how you might feel that way," Ralph said. "I can't say that I've ever given much thought to how our media coverage of the Middle East must look to an Arab American."

She was touched by her old friend's graciousness—by the steady friendliness he'd shown Samir all afternoon, by the way he'd remained undeterred by Samir's coldness.

But still, the afternoon had been a disaster. All she wanted to do was go home by herself.

Their food arrived. Some kind of meat things for the men, and for Maud, a grilled-cheese sandwich.

Samir had to go back to Bethesda to finish the job he'd been doing there. While Maud talked with him about the logistics of the next few days, she noticed that Ralph was watching a baseball game on the TV that was mounted over the cash register.

"Baseball?" she said.

"Spring training."

"I didn't know you were a baseball fan."

"I'm a born-again baseball fan. I used to love baseball when I was a kid. Then I gave it up for around fifteen years. Now I've become a baseball fan again."

"Why?"

"I'm feeling so tired these days that I can't really read for more than twenty minutes at a time. And the Mets have a couple of new players who are fun to watch. I think they're going to do pretty well this year."

"Don't bet on it," Samir said. "The Mets will always break your heart."

"You too?" Maud said.

"Me too. Just in the last week or so, I've been listening to the game sometimes when I work. I used to be a fan a long time ago."

"Mets?" Ralph said.

"Yeah. In the eighties. Gooden, Strawberry, Hernandez."

"Mookie Wilson," Ralph said. "Lennie Dykstra. That was a great team."

"I bring together two of the most serious men I know," Maud said, "and the thing they have in common is baseball."

"Baseball is serious," Ralph said.

"An intellectual who likes baseball," Maud said. "How does it feel to be a cliché?"

"Feels all right," he said.

Samir and Ralph spent the next ten minutes talking about baseball. She kept uttering little noises of disapproval, but of course she was delighted that they'd found something to talk about.

Sometime in the middle of the conversation, while Samir was talking, Ralph removed a vial from his jacket and took two pills. Maud saw the label: they were painkillers. He hadn't said a word about being in pain today.

Ralph knew how much this meeting meant to her, so he was trying to put aside his own troubles and make the occasion successful. It struck her that there were many opportunities for heroism in life. You don't need to fight in a war to find out who you are.

They left the coffee shop and walked through Central Park. She and Samir took turns pushing Ralph's wheelchair. Samir and Ralph were still talking about baseball.

It was a pleasure to see Ralph and Samir warming up to each other, but a complicated pleasure. For Samir, the fact that he was watching a ball game now and again was a sign that he was returning to life, beginning to accept life's pleasures, large and small. For Ralph, it was a sign that his vitality was waning, perhaps forever.

She tried to brush this thought away in the beauty of the afternoon.

FORTY-ONE

I'm feeling awfully bored with myself these days," Arthur said.

And I'm feeling awfully bored with you too, Eleanor thought.

She had never fired a client; she had never wanted to. But now she was wondering.

"I feel so bored with myself I'm afraid Willa's going to get sick of me. I'm starting to think she's planning to dump me."

She'll have to stand in line, Eleanor thought.

But this was unprofessional.

It was difficult to listen patiently to Arthur when there was so much noise inside her own mind.

She'd violated one of her own rules by taking a phone call just five minutes before a session. She'd established this rule for herself years ago, on a day when she'd picked up the phone, had a fight with Adam, and then found herself unable to concentrate on a client.

But today she hadn't been able to help herself. She hadn't heard from Maud in a while, and she'd been concerned about her, so when her phone rang and her caller ID told her it was Maud, she hadn't been able to stop herself from picking up.

"But sometimes I feel bored with Willa too," Arthur said, "You know how they say that the thing you like about someone at the beginning is the thing that drives you nuts in the end? I used to admire Willa because she was so bouncy. So optimistic. But my boss's wife just died, and Saturday we went over to make a condolence call, and she's grinning and telling him to look on the bright side!"

Ditch the wench, Eleanor thought. Stop paying her Nordstrom's bills. Let her find the bright side of that.

She should have just cancelled this session. How could she think about Arthur when she'd just found out that Maud was pregnant?

Maud pregnant.

If the conditions were right, if Maud had the kind of security she needed, she'd be a wonderful mother.

If the conditions were wrong, Maud could really be in trouble.

And Eleanor had no idea whether the conditions were going to be right or wrong.

On the phone Maud told her that she'd thought it through, that she wanted this, that Samir was a good man.

It was impossible to feel thrilled by the fact that your daughter is going to have a child with a man whom, up until now, she hasn't even wanted you to meet.

"If she still wanted to sleep with me once in a while," Arthur said, "that would make a difference. But she doesn't. It's like she barely notices me anymore."

Huh? Eleanor thought. Did you say something?

She was angry because Maud had taken so long to tell her, and angry because, once she'd decided to tell her, she'd blurted it out like that, even though Eleanor had said that she had only a minute to talk.

Maybe Maud had timed her call precisely: maybe she didn't *want* to have more than a minute to talk.

Arthur was saying something. But what?

Eleanor wasn't sure she'd ever failed a client as miserably as she was failing Arthur now.

"And I wish I could stop wanting to have sex with her. But I can't. She's got this hot little rocket body . . . When I was ten, before I ever touched a girl, I was in love with this girl in my class, and I thought that the proof that it was really love was that she was the only girl I ever thought of when I jerked off. And I'm in the same situation now. I know I'm still in love with Willa because she's the only person I think about when I jerk off."

Eleanor was still trying to form a mental picture of a hot little rocket body.

She had seen Arthur only three times before today. She hadn't started to piece together his story yet.

But what was *Maud's* story? That was the question. If it had taken Maud all this time to tell her—well, Eleanor wasn't blaming herself for being angry about it, but her task now was to empathize, to understand that Maud's inability to talk to her must mean something.

She doesn't feel comfortable with me. I should stop feeling angry and start trying to understand why.

It was two o'clock.

"We'll have to end now," she said.

"Thank you, Doctor," Arthur said, though she wasn't one. She had corrected him after their first two sessions and didn't bother to correct him now.

She only had a few minutes before she had to see her next client, Jenny Mitchell.

Eleanor drew the blinds and closed her eyes and tried to pull herself together.

Maud is pregnant.

The phrase kept repeating itself in her mind. Nothing more than that.

Eleanor heard the door of her waiting room open and close. She got up and opened the door of her office.

Jenny came in and they sat in their accustomed places.

"I'm feeling like a chucklehead today," Jenny said.

The Chucklehead's Tale, Eleanor thought.

Then, with an effort, she cleared her mind, and began to listen.

FORTY-TWO

Maud glanced up from her book. She realized that Samir had put his newspaper down a while ago and had been looking at her.

"What?" she said.

He smiled.

"The day I met you I tore up all my maps," he said.

He sounded as if he was quoting something.

"Beg pardon?" she said.

"It's a line from a poem I read in high school."

"You read poetry in high school?"

He'd never told her anything about high school. She'd always pictured his high school self as grimly serious—a boy with no time for the arts.

"I never read a word of it until tenth grade, and then for a year or two I hardly read anything else."

"What made you change?"

"It was that poem, actually. I still remember the moment when I read it. I was in the library. The Sparta public library. I was writing a history paper about Palestine, and I wanted to use an epigraph from a Palestinian poet named Mahmoud Darwish. Epigram? Epigraph? Anyway, I went to the poetry section, for the first time in my life, and found a book of Arabic poetry, and I happened to open it to a poem by Nizar Qabbani. It was about a poet whose life has been overturned by love."

"And that one poem turned you into a poetry reader?"

"It did more than that. I think it changed my life. My parents wanted me to be an engineer, and I never really questioned it. It was practical. But I read the poem—I think it was just called 'Poems'—and then I read another, and then another. I think I spent the whole day in the poetry section, and everything seemed different by the time I left. I didn't think I was going to be a poet, but I knew I wasn't going to be an engineer."

She had so many questions that she had no idea which to ask first. She wanted to know how this had led to a political science degree and a life that was mainly devoted to politics. She wanted to know if he ever thought about going back to a job that involved working with words. She wanted to know what his parents thought about his choices.

She decided not to ask any of these questions. She had time enough to find out everything she wanted to know.

"What was that line again?" she said.

"'The day I met you I tore up all my maps.'"

He was looking at her steadily.

"I can still remember what I was thinking when I read that line," he said. "I remember wondering if love was really like that. I remember wondering if I could ever feel that way about anyone."

He didn't need to say more.

FORTY-THREE

Samir spent two days in Bethesda, finishing his remodeling job. Around midnight on the second day, he was finally through. He'd already made a reservation at a Days Inn, but at the last minute he decided to drive back to New York. He wanted to see Maud. He didn't want to wait.

He talked to her on the phone for a minute before he started out.

"You know," she said, "I was thinking that we should let the baby choose its own name. That would be more democratic. Don't you think?"

"When would this happen?"

"When the time comes."

"And when would that be?" he said.

"If it's a girl, twelve. If it's a boy, eighteen."

"Sounds good to me."

"You don't have to come back tonight, you know," she said. "I'm going to sleep in a couple of minutes."

"I want to wake up with you," he said.

There is nothing quite like the pleasure of a long night's drive — a long night's drive on empty highways when you're alone and relaxed and excited about where you're heading, and you have music that you love in the tape deck. He had a tape of two of Beethoven's late sonatas, which were always described as "difficult," but which had made sense to Samir as soon as he heard them and had become steadily more interesting and more challenging to him the more he had listened to them.

He wished he'd remembered to buy a cup of coffee, though, before he'd started out.

When he was a boy, his family used to go to Chicago every summer to visit his father's old friends, and his father always liked to begin the drive at night. Samir remembered the cozy feeling of being in pajamas in the backseat while the car moved along in the late-night silence.

Much of parenthood, he thought, consists of efforts to re-create the experiences you had as a child. He and Leila used to go to the Adirondacks every summer. By his choice, they would start out late. Zahra, in her pajamas, would sleep in her car seat in the back. But it never felt the way he wanted it to feel. He had imagined that it would make him feel like the incarnation of the idea of fatherhood: confidently guiding the car through the night while his family slept, feeling honored to be entrusted with the responsibility of protecting them. But it never felt that way. He was never able to forget that he couldn't protect Zahra at all, because the forces that were menacing her were inside her.

I tried to roar back at them, but I couldn't scare them away.

He wondered whether the same experience, two years from now, would be a perfect joy. Himself at the wheel, Maud asleep in the front seat, and their baby, democratically unnamed, asleep in the back.

He was excited about the life that he and Maud were going to have together. He had emerged, finally, into a sort of clearing, where he could welcome life again, where he could welcome the future. He wanted a future with her.

This is one of the strangest things about life, he thought. If I'm being honest with myself, I have to admit that I love Maud more than I ever loved Leila. I think Maud and I can grow together, over the long haul, in a way that Leila and I would never have been able to. I think this is my first real chance at fulfillment with a woman, mind and body and soul. But if Zahra had remained alive I never would have met Maud.

Maybe, he thought, you don't have to hold the two thoughts together. You can miss your beloved child, miss her every day of your life, and you can treasure the joy of finding this beloved woman, and you don't have to connect the feelings, because when you connect them they destroy each other. Who was it who said, "Only connect"? Sometimes it's wiser not to.

He was tired. If I pass a rest stop, he thought, I'll stop and rest. Not stop and rest. That's not what I meant. I'll stop for a cup of coffee. One cup in the restaurant, one cup in the car. That will keep me buzzing until I get there. The only rest stop whose name he knew was the Vince Lombardi, but that was far from here, on another highway. "Winning isn't everything; it's the only thing." That was the only thing he knew about Vince Lombardi. It was a saying that was supposed to be significant— Lombardi was the George Patton of football or something like that. But I've never known what it means, he thought. I don't see the distinction.

He passed a billboard with a grinning Michelin Man. Why are they trying to sell a beer with a cartoon character who's so *fat*?

No: that's Michelob.

The sonata was cresting. It had begun on such a mild note, like a person walking quietly into the room. The music started out as a person and turned into a god. The vastness of Beethoven's mind.

The need to *use* the mind. The friends who refuse to believe I could be happy as a carpenter. No one believes that a carpenter has to use his mind. But you do. Conscientious craftsmanship, tenaciously practiced over weeks and months and years, is something to be proud of. Because there's no showing off. The mind must enter the wood.

The mind must enter the wood? The kind of meaningless thought you have when you're tired. Or maybe it's not meaningless. I'll have to think about it again tomorrow, when I'm fresh.

Thoughts keep flowing off when you're tired, not caring where you want them to go. But isn't that always the case? You never control what you're thinking. You send a thought in a certain direction and see what it does. How does that happen? How do we think? I'll have to ask Maud. Do philosophers have to study the brain these days? Do they have to know about science? Funny that I've never asked her.

Last night in bed he realized that her body was already changing. Her breasts and her belly seemed to be wider and softer. He'd had a feeling of reverence as he touched her. How does *that* happen? Two cells join and set something in motion that can bring forth a Beethoven.

What must it feel like to the woman, to her? The quickening. That's a good word for it.

Their fucking was as intense as it had ever been, but it was also newly tender.

Maud was sleeping by now, in her bed. Zahra was sleeping under a hill. Not sleeping, just lying in the dark. Our future baby is inside Maud, working through the night, laboring to become a human being. Baby: listen to me. Someday I want to tell you about Zahra, your half sister.

Fuck the "half." Your sister.

The tape popped out of the tape player. He'd listened to the whole thing, evidently, but he hadn't heard much. He wasn't sure what he'd been thinking about for the last hour. He wondered if he'd passed any rest stops without noticing.

Coffee. I should have taken a thermos. What was that joke Howie told me in high school? The guy who said the thermos was the greatest invention. "When the coffee is hot, it keeps it hot. When the coffee is cold, it keeps it cold. How does it know?"

His eyes jerked open. He had been back in high school, in Howie's kitchen, listening to his old friend tell the joke. It was as if he had actually *been* in Howie's kitchen. He had driven perhaps ten yards in a dream state. Ten yards and fifteen years.

Howie's kitchen. Not where you want to be at sixty-five miles an hour. He forced himself to keep his eyes wide open.

Don't keep your eyes wide shut. Never saw that movie. Couldn't bring myself to go to a movie with such a stupid name. Why does Tom Cruise always remind me of Mickey Mouse? Nicole Kidman was sexy, though, in the commercial.

There's something to be said for keeping your eyes on the road. One little blink can bear you away. One night when he and Leila and Zahra were lying around watching a video, probably something like *Dance with the Teletubbies,* Leila, after a hard day of lawyering, was falling asleep, and she said, "When I close my eyes I see blue lights," and Zahra said, "Where? I don't see them!" So disappointed because she couldn't see the lights her mother saw.

It's not that hard to stay awake on the road. You keep the need to stay awake at the center of your mind, like a bright white light, and then you let the other thoughts wander off where they will. You can think about anything or nothing, or just watch the lights on the highway, one after the other after the other, or the Michelin Man or that girl Michele from kindergarten, that brainy chatterbox who moved away the summer before first grade. It's funny how your thoughts can skate off in different directions. Magical. You can be looking at the road and pondering the na-ture of cognition and remembering the smell of your kindergarten classroom and coming back to the road and then rising and watching the road from the sky and then rising higher into something that seems unselfishly unsubject to time. What does that mean? Nothing. The mind on skates. Roller skates or Rollerblades or whatever you find on your feet. And now they belong to the library. Not anyone's property anymore. Because a library is like socialism. Or the socialist dream. Ordinary murmurs can't be heard when you find so *wild* the lights, as if the pictures added up to a conscience, because the whole tradition wanted to be there first, which is not what a tradition *does*. It's funny how

FORTY-FOUR

After the funeral, everyone seemed lost. The ceremony had been brief and spare, just as Samir would have wished, but it had been *so* brief and *so* spare that when it was over, no one seemed ready to leave the funeral home.

It was the first time Maud had met his parents. They could barely speak. Before the service, Samir's father had embraced her, and his mother had not. His mother seemed angry. Maybe she blamed Maud for his death. If I was his mother, I'd blame me too, Maud thought, although she wasn't sure why she thought this.

Ralph attended the funeral, looking lost inside a suit that had fit him a few months earlier. Celia and George were there, dressed in weirdly casual and sporty clothes. Maud's mother and father were both there. It was strange to Maud to see them standing next to each other. For a second she wondered whether they'd end up together again, after everything, but she didn't have enough mental energy to pursue the thought.

Maud had been hoping that her brothers would show up. She wasn't particularly close to them, and they were far away—Carl lived in Tucson, Josh in Los Angeles—but she kept thinking that one of them would suddenly appear. They were big strong men, and she would have liked to be held in their arms.

After the service, Maud saw a small slim dark woman giving Samir's mother a long embrace. Leila. She thought about going over to talk to her, but she didn't know if she wanted to. The decision was made for her when Leila slipped quickly out the door.

"What are you going to do now?" Ralph asked her.

At first she thought he was asking about the pregnancy, but then she realized he was only asking about the afternoon.

"I'm going to the cemetery," she said. "I'd ask you to come but his parents don't want too many people."

What *am* I going to do now? she thought.

Better to stop the pregnancy right now, because I can't do this without him.

Better to have the baby, because when he was alive we agreed to have the baby, and to change my mind would be to give death a double victory.

While Samir's parents waited for the limousine to take them to the cemetery, most of the other mourners stayed with them in the lobby. His mother, sitting in a chair that was too small for her, kept repeating that her baby was gone. Maud and Samir had once wryly commiserated over the fact that each of them had a mother who was fond of declaring that "you'll always be my baby." He'd said he was the only Arab man on earth who had a Jewish mother.

When the car arrived, Samir's mother lifted herself slowly out of her chair. As she walked toward the door, she put her hand against a wall to steady herself.

She's falling apart because her baby is gone, Maud thought. And I have to keep it together because my baby is coming.

Maud wished that she could allow herself to fall apart. All she wanted to do was what she had done when she first heard the news: sit on the floor and moan and call his name. But she couldn't give in to her grief. She didn't know what she was going to do about this pregnancy, but for now, she had to be strong.

She wanted the being taking shape inside her to have a chance to flourish.

Maud's mother took her hand and they walked out to the limousine. When they got in, Samir's parents barely looked at them. Maud had the feeling that they didn't think she should be there.

She had the terrible thought that Samir might have agreed with them.

Maud felt as if she'd been a very small part of Samir's life. She imagined a map of the things that had mattered to him: some of the territory would be covered by the struggle for a Palestinian state, some of it by his marriage to Leila, and some of it—most of it—would be taken up by his love of his daughter and his bereavement after her death.

If the soul lives forever, she thought, and if it has memories, then a few thousand years from now, his daughter will be the only thing about his earthly existence that his soul will remember. His soul will not remember me at all.

This is what she was thinking, but she was wrong. Samir had known her for only a little while, but duration means nothing. Souls know no time. She had revived him, she had redeemed the idea of the future, and if he'd never met her he might have died of old age without having come back to life. The map of his life had been redrawn before he died, and she was at its center. She was at its heart.

FORTY-FIVE

During the ride to the cemetery, no one spoke.

Maud and Eleanor sat across from Samir's parents in small bucket seats. The limousine was cramped, and their knees were almost touching, but no one spoke. Maud felt as if there were two teams here.

Samir had reserved a plot for himself next to his daughter's grave. Maud had never been to Zahra's grave before. She felt as if she loved this little girl.

Samir went into the ground.

FORTY-SIX

Eleanor and Maud took a taxi back to Manhattan. Maud wanted to walk for a while, so they had the driver let them out near Riverside Park.

It was a gorgeous day at the end of March. The river was so blue it seemed to be breathing.

"Spring is screaming its bloody head off," Maud said.

Maud was moving in an odd way, sort of dragging the left half of her body along. If Maud had been older, Eleanor would have wondered whether she'd had a stroke. But she knew that this was not a stroke, just a peculiar physical manifestation of her grief.

Grief is like an artist, immersed in the particular, transforming each of us in a different way.

Eleanor felt terrible about the boy—she couldn't help thinking of Samir as the boy—but the weight of her concern fell entirely on her daughter.

She hadn't yet asked Maud about her pregnancy. If Eleanor hadn't had three grandchildren, she might have had mixed feelings, but as it was, what she wanted was for the pregnancy to go away. Making it through the brutal seasons of mourning would be hard enough. Maud didn't need the burden of a child.

When they got to her apartment, Eleanor made tea. Maud sat at the kitchen table, mashing her tea bag with her spoon until it broke and deposited clumps of wet leaves on the table.

"Poof," she said. "Just like that."

Eleanor put a loaf of coffee cake in front of Maud, though the chances that she'd have a slice were roughly equivalent to . . . Eleanor couldn't finish the thought.

"How can it be?" Maud said.

"I don't know," Eleanor said.

"I feel so juvenile. I've been studying philosophy for more than ten years, and reading about the meaning of mortality—reading everybody's opinion from Plato to Camus—and now he's dead and *I just don't understand it*. He had such a good mind. All those thoughts in his head—where can they *be*? How can they just vanish?"

"It's not juvenile," Eleanor said.

She wanted to put her hand on Maud's but she didn't know if Maud would welcome that. Maud didn't always like to be touched.

Eleanor took the risk—small risk—and did it anyway. Maud smiled, but her smile was strained, and in a minute she said she needed sugar, and got up to get the sugar bowl from the cabinet, and perhaps the point of all of it had been to free her hand.

She sat back down.

"What happens next?" Maud said.

"What happens next," Eleanor said, "is that you live. You go on."

"I go on," Maud said. "Why is that again? Why is it a good thing to go on?"

Stay calm, Eleanor thought. *Breathe.*

She needed to resist the impulse to lecture her daughter on the goodness of life. No lectures.

Can she be thinking about suicide? My Maud?

Why is it a good thing to go on? Eleanor was so fearful that she couldn't think of a response. Maud didn't seem to expect one.

"You can stay here tonight, if you like," Eleanor said.

"Really?"

"Of course. Not just tonight. You can stay as long as you want to."

"Wouldn't I get in the way of your love life?"

Maud evidently meant this as a joke. The idea of Eleanor's having a love life was funny.

Which offended Eleanor slightly.

She found it odd that she could be irritated at her daughter for an offhand joke just hours after they'd buried her daughter's boyfriend.

Maud drifted into the living room and turned on the TV. Eleanor followed her.

Dr. Phil was laying down the law to a shamefaced couple. "Something's wrong here," he said. "There's something wrong with this picture."

"What am I going to do?" Maud said.

Eleanor wished that she could step between Maud and grief; that she could ward off its blows. But this of course was impossible. She could wrap Maud in her arms, if Maud allowed it, and hold her with all the strength she had, but it wouldn't do any good. The thing that might destroy Maud was inside her.

"You're going to mourn for him, for a long time, maybe forever. And you're going to honor him, by continuing to be the strong, brilliant, thoughtful, loving, curious, sensitive woman he fell in love with."

"I guess that's one possibility," Maud said.

FORTY-SEVEN

Adam sat beside Eleanor at the funeral. He found it comforting to be near her. He hadn't known anything about Samir—hadn't even known that Maud was seeing anyone—but Eleanor had filled him in when they'd talked on the phone. It had shaken him to learn that Maud's boyfriend had died, and it had shaken him to learn that Maud was pregnant.

Neither Eleanor nor Maud invited him to spend time with them after the funeral, so he understood that his presence was not desired.

He thought of going to the gym, but decided against it. Instead, he just went home.

For an hour or two, Adam forgot himself. For an hour or two, he forgot to think about the fate of his forthcoming book, about the awards he was hoping to win, about the question of when he might have actual sex with Thea again, as opposed to another of the cock-teasing sessions she so enjoyed—he forgot about most of the things that concerned him during the course of a typical day.

The only photograph on display in his apartment was one of Thea. He looked in his files until he found a few photographs of his family.

He found one of Maud at the age of eight or nine. She was in a sailboat with her brothers, screaming with a kind of delighted terror as it tipped.

She had always been the most ingenuous of his children. The most vulnerable, and yet the most forgiving. It had always been so easy to make her happy.

FORTY-EIGHT

Maud couldn't seem to get warm. In the days since Samir's death, the temperature hadn't fallen below seventy degrees, but she was always freezing. She got her winter blankets out from the closet, and she slept under three of them and kept a portable heater at the foot of the bed, but it didn't really help.

A few years ago, Maud had told a friend that she didn't know what loneliness was. As long as she had her books, her philosopher companions, she never felt alone. Now she was discovering what loneliness was.

Maybe she was lonelier than she might have been. Maybe she wanted to be lonely. Her friends kept calling, asking to see her, but she preferred to be alone, because when she was alone she could entertain the fantasy that Samir was with her.

Nothing made sense. Because just one moment had gone wrong, Samir was gone, and would be gone forever. If one moment on the highway had been different, the two of them might have grown old together.

He hadn't kept a diary. He hadn't even sent her any e-mails. There was nothing of him to hold on to.

She woke up every morning feeling miserable before she remembered why.

His death threw its pale light back on everything they had gone through. It was as if they had known at every moment that he was going to die, and had coupled with such intensity because of that knowledge. But she knew it wasn't true.

How could this be happening?

Would killing herself be a good solution?

In death, he seemed so tender, so vulnerable, so exposed. She pictured him as trapped somewhere. He wanted to be with her. He wanted to get across to the other side. But he couldn't. He was being held back. They were holding him back. He seemed so weak in death, so sad.

Maybe the reason she didn't want to see her friends was that she was angry at them. She knew that they genuinely felt for her, but she also knew that they could feel for her only in flashes. How could it be otherwise? She knew that even Ralph, her dearest friend, was thinking of her only sometimes. His life was continuing on its course, with its own pleasures and trials. Ralph was still going to museums, still ordering obscure foreign movies from Netflix, still worrying about the decline of his physical powers.

There *was* one person who, she was sure, was living almost hourly with her pain, feeling it almost as strongly as she was. Her mother, of course. But that was a problem too. She didn't *want* her mother to be living inside her head like this. It had been a long hard labor, taking up all of her teen years and most of her twenties, to get her mother *out* of her head, a labor that had succeeded only after she'd gone in a direction, intellectually, where her mother didn't have the time or energy to follow. But now she had been stripped of her thinking self. She was only her unhappiness; and her mother could intuit every nuance of it, every ache.

After a week she went back to work and taught her classes again and didn't tell her students anything about what she'd been through. She didn't want their sympathy. The classroom was a place where she could escape from her grief for a few hours a day.

It was a relief to spend time in the company of people who

didn't particularly care about her. She suspected that some of her students had heard about Samir's death, but no one said anything, and if she'd changed at all, in her appearance or her manner, she didn't think that any of them had noticed it. College students are not the most perceptive tribe. There's so much stirring and breaking and peaking in their own lives that it's hard for them to notice other people.

But the classroom was not solely a place of escape. It was also, as it always had been, a place where she could talk about the things that mattered most. Shortly after she returned to work, she did a week on Albert Camus with her class. Usually, when she taught Camus, she taught *The Rebel,* his book about social change, violence, means and ends. But this year she decided to teach *The Myth of Sisyphus,* his argument against religious belief. Camus urges us to find the courage to admit that the universe is indifferent to our fate. Sisyphus is the hero of the book—a Sisyphus who doesn't delude himself with the belief that he'll succeed in pushing the rock to the top of the hill. Condemned to his task and refusing to deceive himself about its outcome, he gives himself to it with a sort of joyful scorn.

This book had never meant much to her before, because she'd always taken the nonexistence of God for granted. But suddenly it meant a lot to her, because for the first time in her life, she felt tempted. Even against her will, she kept searching for reasons to believe that something of Samir had lived on.

She'd lost ten pounds in the week following his death, and men were looking at her on the street in a new way. They had always looked—men always look—but now they looked longer. The misery makeover plan.

She forced herself to start eating again. While she tried to figure out what to do about her pregnancy, it was better to eat than to starve.

She had been pregnant for eight weeks. If she was going to have an abortion, she would need to have it soon.

She was doing everything she could to keep her mother at arm's length, but it was difficult. It was like a full-time job. Whenever she saw her mother or spoke to her or sent her an e-mail, she tried to be vaguely cheerful. She didn't want to show her mother that she was despondent, but she didn't want to try to seem *too* cheerful, because her mother would have seen through that.

Eleanor called on a Saturday night when Maud was reading and weeping.

"How are you?" her mother said.

"I'm okay."

"What does that mean?"

"I don't know."

"What have you been up to?"

"Teaching. Reading. Watching TV."

"Have you been seeing your friends?"

Like many of her mother's questions, this posed a paradox. If Maud were to tell her that she hadn't been, her mother would get even more worried than she was already, and would want to come over. If Maud were to tell her that she *had,* her mother would feel excluded, and would want to come over.

Maud gave her an answer that was as vague as she could make it, and somehow it worked. Her mother went on to the next subject.

"What else have you been up to?" she said.

Which, thought Maud, meant, *Have you made an appointment for an abortion yet?*

Her mother had actually been very tactful—she'd asked about the pregnancy a few times, but, in keeping with her habit of not giving unsolicited advice, she had given no advice, because Maud hadn't solicited any.

But Maud could feel the pressure of her concern, the pressure of her wanting to know.

Sometimes she felt as if her little apartment were under siege. It was as if her mother were some vast creature, as unfightable as fog, surrounding Maud's building, sniffing at the windows, nosing at the locks, searching for a way in.

It's sad when the people who love you are the people you have to ward off.

Forty-nine

Eleanor called Adam and they made an appointment to get together for lunch. They met on neutral ground, at an outdoor café on Broadway and 112th. She didn't want him back in her apartment and there was no way she would ever set foot in his.

"How's she doing?" Adam said.

"I don't know. It's hard for me to tell," she said. "We need to strategize. I need your help."

"Tell me what I can do."

"You can help her with money," she said. As soon as she said this, she wished she hadn't led with it. Nothing about him visibly changed, but she felt him harden. "If she needs it," she added.

Each of them ordered a drink, though it was barely noon.

"I'm so afraid that she's going to go under again," she said.

"She's been okay for years now," Adam said.

This was true, but for Eleanor, Maud's last breakdown felt like it had happened yesterday.

Adam seemed impatient, and Eleanor felt like a fool. She had thought it would be comforting to get together with him and share her worries about Maud. At Samir's funeral, Adam had seemed positively human, and Eleanor had thought that the shock of his daughter's sadness might have jarred something loose in him.

"Would it have bothered you if Maud had ended up marrying an Arab?" Adam said.

He was wearing a conspiratorial smile. She'd actually wondered about that question herself, but she didn't want to be his co-conspirator.

"No. Why? Would it have bothered you?"

"Of course it would've."

"Why 'of course'?"

"Show me a Jewish father who *wouldn't* be bothered to see his daughter marry an Arab," he said, "and I'll show you Noam Chomsky."

He finished his drink and called for another, looking pleased with himself.

"I just hope she gets the abortion over with as soon as she can," he said.

"What do you mean? Have you talked with her about it?"

"No. I figured that was your job."

"Then how do you know she's planning to have one?"

"What's the alternative?" he said.

"The alternative is this little thing called 'having a baby.'"

"You don't think she'd be foolish enough to do that now?"

Eleanor didn't say anything. She was reproaching herself for being here with him at all, for having dreamed that he could change.

"Ye gods," Adam said. "That would be a pretty picture."

When Eleanor spoke to Maud that night, Maud said that she was going away for the weekend.

"Where?"

"I don't know. I just want to rent a car and drive for a while."

This sounded ominous.

Don't panic. Or at least don't let her see that you're panicking.

"Will you call me when you get wherever you're going?"

"I'll call you or send you an e-mail."

"Are you taking your computer?"

"I don't think so."

"So how will you be able to send me an e-mail?"

Even as she asked this, Eleanor knew it was a stupid question, but she was brain-locked.

"Just trust me, Mom. It can be done."

When they got off the phone Eleanor had to exert all her self-control to prevent herself from crying. It was hard to be sure what was affecting her more: her worry about Maud or her frustration that Maud wasn't letting her in. She remembered the days when her daughter used to say, "I want to marry with you, Mom," and she'd had to explain to Maud that girls don't marry their mothers.

FIFTY

Maud rented a car, drove north, and spent three days visiting the towns in Massachusetts and Maine that she had visited with Samir in January. On her second night, when she reached Cape Elizabeth, Maine, she checked into a motel and just before midnight she walked down to the beach.

She stood under a clear black sky, under thousands of tightly packed stars, thinking the same thoughts that everyone thinks when looking up at the vast nightlit sky. She tried to comprehend the idea that the universe might go on forever in space and time, and she tried to comprehend the idea that it might not. Both were incomprehensible. How can the universe go on forever? How can it stop?

She remembered lying on a hill in Vermont with her brothers—she must have been eight or nine—and learning that some of the stars she was looking at may have died millions of years ago. This was as hard to grasp now as it had been then.

She wasn't troubled to be thinking the thoughts that everyone thinks. She had no desire to be original. At a moment like this all you can do is wonder, and the fact that all of us wonder about the same things struck her as comforting.

When she thought about the vastness of the universe in time and space, the question of whether she carried the child to term did not seem very significant. The universe would roll on, unaffected by her choice.

And yet she had to choose.

Under a sky like this, humility was an appropriate response; but it would be wrong, she thought, to undervalue ourselves *too* much. She was in awe under the blazing battering time-traveling light of the stars. But the light that we send out from ourselves, the light of consciousness, is even more mysterious, even more miraculous, than the lights we behold when we look up at the night sky.

Maud, a light of consciousness, held another light within herself, a light in waiting, and, standing on the beach where she had stood with her lover, she knew, for the first time, what she wanted to do. She wanted to let the new light come.

FIFTY-ONE

And yet everything got harder.

It was spring, but her body had decided it was winter. Her lips were cracked and her palms were cracked and the soles of her feet were cracked, and the heaviness of her body as it grew did not feel in any way miraculous. The heaviness of her body was accompanied by a heaviness of mind. No one had told her that when you are pregnant you feel, more than anything else, *stupid*. The quickening made her slow.

She kept trying to rediscover the sense of the miraculous that had come over her during that walk on the beach, but she couldn't do it.

A sense of the miraculous, she finally decided, was too much to ask for. All she could ask of herself these days was that she find a way to keep it together.

She received permission to put off her dissertation for a full year, but this didn't give her the relief she'd hoped for. All it meant was that she now spent as much time worrying about her dissertation as she used to spend working on it.

She was still teaching her classes, though it was growing harder. She was just so *tired* all the time. She felt like herself for only about three hours a day, but she needed to keep teaching as long as she could. She needed the money. The chair of her department was being nice to her, and he told her she could take a leave whenever she wanted, but she wanted to put it off until the baby was born.

She knew she had a safety net—her parents would never let her go under—but she didn't want to rely on them any more than she needed to.

She kept telling herself that she needed to stop worrying. She needed to stop worrying about how she was going to afford this child; she needed to stop worrying about becoming dependent on her parents again; she needed to stop dwelling on lurid visions of herself a year in the future, pop-eyed with fatigue and dragging along a baby whose howls were unlike the howls of other babies, because they were the howls of a baby who had been disenfranchised before he was born, a woeful slice of doomed fatherless meat.

Sometimes she felt as if she hadn't absorbed the fact that he was gone. She kept thinking of things she wanted to tell him.

Each step she took brought fresh news of his death. When she passed the park, she remembered their first day together there—the sunlight, the families, the Ramble. If she had to consult a subway map, she tried to avoid looking at Brooklyn, because she didn't want to be forced to remember their nights in his apartment.

Celia and George kept inviting her to dinner at their apartment. Most of the time she begged off with vague excuses, but when she did see them, she arranged to meet them in restaurants. She couldn't bear to return to the place where she'd first met him.

They hadn't had time to marry, but she felt wedded to him nevertheless. Before she'd met him, she was sure the idea that each of us has a soulmate was sentimental nonsense; after she met him, she was sure he was hers. Even during their first few weeks together, when the only thing that kept them coming back to each other was sexual attraction, she'd been sure of it; she'd been sure that what seemed like sexual attraction was in fact something deeper: it was their souls conspiring to bind them until both of them realized that they were each other's fate.

Eleanor was visiting all the time. Eleanor was always underfoot. Maud was glad to have her mother around, but then again, she wasn't. There was something infantilizing about it, about having your mother drop in carrying hot meals from Zabar's because she's afraid that you haven't eaten that day—and having her be right.

Her mother had hinted, several times, that it would be a good idea for Maud to see a shrink. Maud had seen someone for five years, whom she'd liked a lot. But she didn't want to go back to him now.

Maud wasn't reading any books on motherhood. Instead, she read her old mainstays—some of them, at least: Kant and Buber and Levinas—as she continued to work doggedly on her dissertation. Sometimes she felt as if her dissertation was the only thing that was keeping her in one piece. The importance of it became more and more obvious to her: of the simple idea that we must treat other people as ends in themselves, that we must remember that everyone is the center of his or her own universe. Keeping this idea in her mind, going more and more deeply into its implications, seemed like the best way to prepare for being a mother.

She didn't have a social life. She taught her classes, had conferences with her students, went home.

More and more, she was pretending that Samir was still with her. She didn't talk to him; she didn't come close to deluding herself that he was actually with her. But she liked to sit in her easy chair and close her eyes and imagine that he was in the room with her. She felt warmer when she imagined him in the room.

Her body seemed to be changing every day. She was not enjoying it. She was sick all the time, and she felt misshapen. It was astonishing to remember that this body so recently had given and received pleasure.

Sometimes she lay in her bed and put her hands on her belly and tried to imagine how she would feel about her body if Samir were alive. She felt sure that if he were still here he would find her beautiful. She felt sure that he would still be attracted to her. She lay in her bed with her hands on her belly and thought, If he were still alive I would find my own body beautiful. If he were still alive he would be touching me right now. He would be touching me with desire.

FIFTY-TWO

The only person whose company she enjoyed was Ralph. They got together every Friday. They always met at his apartment and had their dinner delivered from a Japanese restaurant down the street. It was convenient for him, because getting in and out of restaurants was such a chore. He probably thought Maud was being considerate when she told him that staying in the apartment suited her fine. But that had nothing to do with it. For Maud, Ralph's apartment was a refuge, a place of quiet and calm.

One soggy Friday night in late April, a month after Samir died, it was cold enough for Ralph to make a fire. He put three logs in the fireplace. It didn't look easy, doing it all from his wheelchair, but he had practice.

"How are you?" he said.

She sipped her drink—a ginger ale—and said, "I've been having a hard time."

Ralph lit a long wooden match and applied the flame to the crumpled newspaper he'd stuffed under the logs.

"It's a relief to be able to say that," she said.

"Why is that?"

"You're the only person I don't need to pretend with. Every-one is so invested in making sure I'm all right that it's like I can't let them down."

He maneuvered his wheelchair so that he was facing her. Experience had taught her not to try to help.

"I'm invested in making sure you're all right too," he said.

"I know. But it's different. I know you care about me. But if I say I don't feel like I'm doing that well, you're not afraid to hear it. It might make you concerned, but it doesn't seem to make you nervous."

"I'm glad you feel that way."

"But?"

"But I do want to ask you—very un-nervously—if there's anything I can do to help."

"You're doing it," she said. "You do it."

He called the restaurant and ordered their meal. They had the same thing every week. Visiting him here had the aspect of ritual, and he seemed to understand, without her having told him, how comforting their rituals were to her.

"I wish I could believe in God," she said.

"Why is that?"

"I could believe things happen for a reason. Samir once told me that when his daughter was getting her bone-marrow transplant, he met a lot of parents whose children were going through the same thing, and almost all of them were religious. The parents. Not the kids. He said God had it easy. When the children were admitted for their transplants, the parents would be saying that God was going to heal them, and when the kids died, they'd say that God had taken them to a better place. If you were cured, it was because God loves you, and if you died, that was because God loves you too."

"Can't quite imagine you going for that," Ralph said.

When their food arrived, Ralph gave her his credit card. Long ago he had made it clear that he would never allow her to pay for their dinners or even chip in. Maud met the deliveryman at the door.

Ralph wheeled his way over to the dining room table and allowed her to set it and lay out the food.

"So has the experience affected your philosophy of life?" he said. "That's not the right way to put it. What I mean is, has it changed what you believe in?"

He didn't say any of this in an ironic tone. He wanted to know.

"I think I just believe more intensely in the things I believed in the first place."

"For example?"

"That there is no God, and that the universe doesn't give a flying fuck about us. That's probably it."

"And does that imply a code of behavior? The universe doesn't give a flying fuck about us, and therefore . . . ?"

Ralph was a friend who asked the second question. She thought that this might be one of the definitions of true friendship. If you have a friend who pays enough attention to you to ask the right question, you're lucky; if you have a friend who listens to the answer, thinks some more, and asks the second question, then you're blessed.

"There is no therefore that I can find. No universal therefore. I still believe the same things I always believed, but it's a choice. Life doesn't care about us, everyone gets pulverized sooner or later, and therefore we should take care of each other. But I believe that because I choose to believe that. If it's a therefore, it's just a personal therefore."

She looked into the fire for a while.

"As long as I'm telling you things I can't tell anybody else, can I tell you one more thing?"

He didn't bother to say anything. He didn't need to.

"Sometimes I feel certain that I'm harming this child even

before it becomes a child. I'm so sad so much of time that I'm afraid I'm poisoning it. This thing is supposed to be getting a warm, nurturing nine-month bath, but instead it's getting . . . misery."

He opened a bottle of wine. Maud wasn't drinking, but Ralph, during the last year or so, had been in the habit of finishing an entire bottle by himself.

"Any response?" she said. "Aren't you going to tell me I'm being ridiculous?"

"Do you want me to?"

"Only if you really think so."

"On the one hand, I think you probably don't have anything to worry about. The human body usually knows what it's doing. There's probably a built-in mechanism to protect the baby from—"

"Crack-ups. From Mommy's crack-ups."

"Right. So I think it's probably okay. But really, who knows?"

She respected him for not offering false comfort, but at the same time she wished he'd said something that could magically take her worries away. It was hard to stop thinking about how she might be fucking up this child. She had lurid pictures in her mind of what was happening inside her. A tiny helpless thing, a diaphanous floating thumbnail, slowly being sickened by the toxins of its mother's grief.

"Any other ground to cover?" he said. "We've established that life is horrible, and we've established that you may be poisoning your unborn child. Any reflections about the inevitable death of the universe?"

"That's old hat," she said.

She took the dishes away and put them in the dishwasher, and then they watched a movie he'd rented. She barely paid attention to it. It was some Asian mood piece, with two yearning lovers who never quite touched. She didn't much care for Ralph's taste in movies, but it was nice just to be here.

At the end of the night he was slowed down by tiredness and wine, but he suddenly perked up.

"I forgot about the taste test."

Taste tests were an old tradition with them, dating back to college, when they'd read an article that said that all brands of vodka tasted alike and had spent four hours in a bar assessing this claim. Their taste tests were milder now.

"I got two kinds of crackers from a health-food store. They're like Ritz crackers, but with no trans fats. Could you help me out of this thing?"

She could have gotten the crackers herself, but for some reason he wanted to get them, and she didn't question it. Neither did she question why he wanted to walk to the kitchen instead of using his wheelchair.

She stood next to his chair. He gripped her forearm with his left hand and lifted himself up.

"If you can just . . . ," he said. He shifted his position so that one arm was draped over her shoulder, and they walked toward the kitchen.

She was taller than he was, and she'd probably always outweighed him; now she must have outweighed him by twenty pounds.

When you saw him in his wheelchair, you could forget how thin he was, how frail. But now, when she was pretty much carrying him across the room—carrying him in a way that maintained the fiction that he was actually walking and she was merely helping him out—his lightness and fragility were shocking. He was sweating: the smell was heavy and not pleasant, and it made her realize how much effort it required for him to move in his normal limited way—sitting in his wheelchair, opening the wine at dinner, tending the fire. The smell somehow jarred her into the realization that he was not an angel, wispy and insubstantial because he was a creature formed entirely of the materials of spirit, but a man who was struggling, a man who was being defeated, a man whose body had gone wrong. He stank, really. Poor Ralph stank.

It would have been easier on both of them if she'd gotten the crackers out herself, but if what dignity meant to him, in that moment, was making his way across the room without a wheelchair so he could get two boxes of crackers for a taste test, then she was going to help him do it, even if she had to carry him there.

They performed the taste test, and they agreed about which of the two crackers was better. She drank more soda and he drank more wine. They were both silent for a long time. He dozed off in his chair for a moment, and she watched him sleep. Or she might have just dreamed this, because she dozed off for a moment herself.

She'd stayed too long. He looked fatigued. Next time she would be more considerate, more observant.

She got up and fetched her coat from the closet. Ralph wheeled himself into the hall.

If she hadn't been so tired she just would have said goodbye. But as she looked at him wheeling his way ahead of her, the thought that he, like anyone else, could be gone before morning, made her frightened.

"If you die too," she said, "I'm finished."

"You won't be finished," he said. "I have faith in you. But I'll try to hang around as long as I can."

Fifty-three

And then after the sonograms and the amnio and the buying of a contraption to listen to the sounds the child was making in the womb, and after the childbirth classes she attended alone (because it would have been somehow humiliating to attend them with her mother and logistically difficult and anyhow wrong-seeming to attend them with Ralph, and because Celia was starting to annoy her and—well, it was just easier to do it alone), and after the visits to the doctor and the visits to the midwife and the visits to the doula, and the decision that even though she could probably use a doula, the word *doula* was just too stupid for her to want to have one of them in her life, and after the attempts to plan her life post-baby, even though it felt like planning someone else's life, and after the emergence of pains in her back and pains in her hips and pains in her legs, pains that reinforced her belief in the rock-bottom *unnaturalness* of this, the unnaturalness of being the host within which another being took form (though multitudes of people believed that pregnancy was the most glorious experience a human being could have, to Maud the hosting of another being within your body seemed like something that happened in science-fiction movies, not something that happened in life), and after the growth of a mental muzziness that she attributed to the growth of the fetus, as if the thing inside her, gathering up its vital forces, were draining hers, and after weeks of false and teasing contractions—after all this, on a cool gray day in October, her

contractions assumed a different quality, and she took a taxi to
the hospital and called her mother, who met her there, and after
six hours of more pain than she would have imagined the world
itself could bear, six hours of weeping and shouting and trying
to follow the directions given in an infuriatingly patient voice by
the midwife, directions that made no sense to her (the midwife
kept telling her not to push when her entire being was shrieking
at her with the primal need to *push this thing out*), her child was
finally born, her child, the child of the love that she and Samir
had shared, and her mother told her that she had a beautiful new
boy, and someone picked the child up and put him on Maud's
breast, and the child yowled, and it was hard to see him clearly
when he was so close to her and she was still in such pain, but
from what she could see he was patchy and slimy, a slimy purple
bag of lips and limbs, and although she couldn't see him clearly,
in his nearness she had a strong sense of him, and what she
sensed was that he was a creature with a frighteningly developed
will—she wouldn't have been too surprised if he had leaped off
the bed and slithered quickly out of the room—and he lay on
her breast, howling, and the midwife moved him closer to the
nipple, but he didn't take it; poor creature, he didn't know what
to do.

FIFTY-FOUR

She named him David. Although Islamic tradition had meant little to Samir and Jewish tradition probably meant even less to her, she liked the idea that their son would have a name that had meaning in both. If he wanted to call himself Daoud when he grew up, that would be fine with her.

Maud and David stayed with Eleanor for a week after they left the hospital. Eleanor wanted them to stay longer, and Maud was tempted, but after a few days she found it hard to breathe. Her mother was constantly on top of her, constantly asking faux-subtle questions designed to find out how Maud "really" was. The unexamined life, as Socrates said, is not worth living, but the life in which your mother is examining you every minute of the day is hardly life at all.

She'd always heard that it wasn't hard in the beginning. In the beginning, everyone said, they just sleep. But he didn't just sleep. He slept and he screamed. He slept and he shat. He slept and he screamed and he shat. He slept and he screamed and he shat and he screamed and he shat and he screamed and he screamed and he shat and he slept and he screamed and he shat and he shat and he shat and he shat. In the beginning, she'd heard, your life doesn't have to change much: you mostly just do your thing while the baby sleeps. She was so sleep-starved that she could barely remember if she *had* a thing to do.

She spent half her time worrying that she was going to damage him and half her time worrying that she already had. Twice she forgot to support his head when she picked him up and it flopped backward as if it had been lopped off. At night she slept with him in her bed, and she kept worrying that she'd crushed one of his fontanels with her elbow one morning when she was half awake — she kept checking the soft squishy center of his head for the imprint of her elbow. If she'd crushed one of his fontanels, she kept thinking, she might have caused him irreversible brain damage.

It was terrifying to think that he had a soft skull, vulnerable to the slightest pressure. And in the same way that it's impossible to walk across a bridge without imagining yourself jumping, she kept imagining herself pushing her fingers deep into his soft, gooey skull.

She kept worrying that his head was lopsided. She was sure it was her fault. She had read that a certain degree of lopsidedness was normal in newborns, but that the condition could get worse if the baby spent too much time in one position. She was always worrying that she wasn't paying enough attention to the position of his head, and that the claylike bones of his skull were being pressed into the wrong shape.

A week after he was born she'd bundled him up and taken him on the bus, and a woman in her eighties had scolded her for letting the flap of his little hat fall over one of his eyes. "Don't you know anything about child development?" the woman had said. "He has to learn how to use his eyes." Maud had fixed his hat and gotten off at the next stop, though she was a mile from her destination. She waited at the bus stop and took the next bus.

But she could keep it together. She could do this.

Life can be dealt with if you just resolve to keep it together. You keep it together by breaking things apart. Complicated problems can be reduced to simple component parts, and then you can deal with anything.

In the morning you feed the baby, then you change the baby, then you change the baby again, then you feed the baby, then you change the baby again. Then you go for a walk. Then you feed the baby. Then you change the baby. Then you remember you haven't eaten yet and you make breakfast for yourself while you hold the baby in one arm.

Make things simple. This, Maud thought, was how you avoid a nervous breakdown.

In addition to her two breakdowns, Maud had had two near breakdowns. During the near breakdowns, she had warded off the worst by simplifying life, just as she was simplifying it now. That was how she had kept it together.

But the problem was this: during the two episodes in which she had *not* been able to avoid the snake pit, she had tried to protect herself the exact same way. It had worked for a while, but she hadn't been able to stop it from going too far. Soon she had found herself concentrating on each individual step as she walked to work, and trying to brush her teeth one by one, and then she had found herself concentrating on each individual breath, as if her body would stop breathing if she didn't remind it, and shortly after that she had found herself in the psychiatric unit, engaged in a humiliating form of art therapy, concentrating on each individual crayon.

Sometimes she felt nostalgic for her old breakdowns. In memory, her old breakdowns seemed like vacations. Because she'd had no one else to care for, she'd been able to surrender to them completely. But now there was this new person, dear, doomed David, and she had to stay strong for him.

During her pregnancy she could stay home and try to lose herself in the fantasy that she was still with Samir, that he was invisibly beside her. That fantasy was gone. David was physically tiny but massive, roaring, and totalitarian in his needs. He left no space for fantasy. He left no room for philosophy. He seemed to occupy her entire apartment. There was no room for any competition. There was barely room for her.

He was still having trouble nursing. He would grope with his lips for the nipple but no sooner would she maneuver it into his mouth than he would lose it and start wailing again. Her pediatrician told her that this wasn't unusual, but Maud took it as an indictment of both of them. A bewildered mother had given birth to a bewildered child.

FIFTY-FIVE

George and Celia came to visit. Maud met them at a restaurant, because she didn't want them to see her apartment, which was becoming more disheveled every day. Sometimes her own apartment struck her as a cry for help.

"No Zoe?" Maud said. Zoe was their daughter—the child whose crib Samir had been building when Maud met him.

"We shipped her off to my mom's for the night," Celia said. "We need some alone time."

Maud had brought David. She was wearing a carrier. He was sleeping, and she held his head up with her left hand while she ate. Don't let it flop.

Maud hadn't been in touch with George and Celia for months. They had undergone an alarming transformation. They'd recently been through the Forum, a self-help course that had left them with an unquenchable optimism, a new vocabulary, and a strange desire to proselytize their friends.

"Do you find that you're *always already listening*?" Celia said.

Maud didn't know what that meant. Celia seemed to be speaking in code.

Evidently Celia took Maud's silence as assent.

"You could get rid of that," Celia said. "You could really become unstoppable."

Although Maud didn't feel very unstoppable at the moment, she was glad to think her friends thought she had the chance to become so. As the conversation went on, though, she found that the belief in personal unstoppableness was the coin of the realm for those who had been through the Forum. I'm unstoppable, you're unstoppable: that seemed to sum it up for them.

Celia and George seemed completely, cutely, cuddlingly in love. She had grown chubbier and he had grown thinner, which suited them both. Celia was a cupcake now, and George was a candle. They held hands as they ate — she was a lefty and he was a righty, so they could pull this off — and they kept verbally adoring each other and giving each other succulent kisses.

It was hard to believe that these were her friends, hard to believe that these were the people who had introduced her to Samir. They didn't mention him once. She had known them to be considerate people, and she was sure that their silence had something to do with their newfound philosophy. Perhaps the Forum held that it was bad to dwell.

They ordered salads and appetizers and steaks and a bottle of wine; Maud, budget-conscious, had a salad and a glass of club soda. When the check came, George suggested that they keep things simple by splitting it three ways.

She got home and put David in his crib. The change in her friends had left her shaken. They were the only people in her life who had known Samir. It's not that she had wanted to talk about him, but she'd thought that she would feel closer to him after she spent some time in their presence. Instead she felt further away.

It was worse than that. By behaving so inanely, they were cheapening him. She was afraid that if she continued to see them, Samir would come to seem a trivial person, a lightweight.

She knew, of course, that that wouldn't happen. Nothing could make him seem trivial. But the evening had made him seem further away.

David was fussing. She picked him up and walked around the room and he quieted down.

She kept remembering the florid things she used to whisper to Samir in bed. You're my animal. I claim you. You're my mate.

Florid, silly, but also true. He *was* her animal; she *had* claimed him; he *was* her mate.

She remembered how powerful she used to feel when she was with him, how powerful he made her feel. In bed with him, especially, she used to feel like a commanding presence. She no longer felt that way. She had claimed him, but then death had claimed him, and the claim of death had been stronger than her own. Death had shown her how weak she was.

Fifty-six

The next day she got together with her father. She wanted to see him for the most rational of reasons: in a month or so she would be broke, and she was hoping he could help her out. She didn't like the idea of asking him for money, but this was a special circumstance.

She also wanted to see him for irrational reasons. In some deep-rooted part of her mind he was still Daddy, imbued with all the magic and authority we confer on our fathers, and without really admitting it to herself she was holding on to the hope that if he saw her, saw how badly she was struggling, he would find some way to make everything work out.

She was meeting him at his apartment, which made her nervous. She didn't want to run into his girlfriend. She hoped they weren't actually living together, but she wasn't sure.

She waited with David at a bus stop on Broadway. When the bus came, the doors opened and the driver pushed a button to make it kneel, and it lowered itself slowly, like a noble elephant, and, wearing David in his carrier and a diaper bag over her shoulder, she climbed on.

Her father's building was intimidating. The lobby itself, an assemblage of inanimate objects, somehow seemed hipper than you could ever be. The doorman was a young man with a gleaming shaved head and a fierce goatee. He seemed like someone who could procure anything—a combination of athlete, actor, gigolo, medicine-runner, and pimp. He sat behind an elevated desk and you had to crane your neck to talk to him.

Her father met her at his door, kissed her on the cheek, and moved the collar of David's sweater so he could see him.

"How's the little fullback?" he said.

Her father was all dressed up, in a tie and jacket. Obviously he had plans. He wouldn't have dressed like this for her.

She hadn't given any thought beforehand to the way he'd be dressed, but she was disappointed to see him like this. When he was dressed casually, padding around his apartment in slippers, she occasionally got glimpses of the man he used to be, or, at any rate, of the man she used to think he was.

"How's he doing?" Adam said. "Healthy, I take it?"

"He's perfect," Maud said.

"You must be living an impossible life these days," he said, with his rich and sympathetic voice. "Are you still teaching your classes?"

"I took a leave."

"That's great that they let you do that," he said. "You were wise to enter the academic life. One of my old teachers, Daniel Bell, once said that there were three reasons why he had chosen the academic life."

June, July, and August, she thought. He had said this many times before.

"June, July, and August," he said.

He had photographs on his mantel—of her, of Josh with his family, of Carl with his. There weren't any photographs of her mother. In the center, in the place of honor, there was a photograph of Thea, a studio portrait in which she looked simultaneously glamorous and goofy. Maud had met Thea only once, by accident, in front of the foreign-cheese display at Fairway.

She had not been impressed. There was something ill fitting about Thea, Maud thought, that she couldn't really get rid of— she could show all the cleavage she had, and all the leg, and through this could distract people for a long while, but inevitably there came a time when you would look at her face, and there you would see an ineradicable trace of mere doofiness.

Maybe, she thought, my father hasn't gotten around to looking at her face yet.

"I've taken the liberty of ordering some lunch," Adam said. His dining room table was already set; in the middle were takeout cartons from a Chinese restaurant.

Maud arranged some pillows on an easy chair and made a nest to hold David while she ate.

"Mu shu vegetables?" Adam said. "Behold the master." He spread a line of vegetables and sauce onto a thin pancake and folded it up evenly and expertly. "I learned how to do this in the sixties," he said. "So my experiments weren't entirely wasted."

"Ah," she said. "Your experiments."

"Yes. I spent the sixties conducting experiments on the effects of long-term marijuana use on the youthful brain."

Her fortune cookie told her that he who hurries cannot walk with dignity; his told him that the wise man sayeth little.

"When did fortune cookies stop telling your fortune?" he said. "Someone should write an essay on the decline of the fortune cookie."

He made two cups of tea and brought them to the table.

"The two of you seem great," he said.

"It's actually been pretty hard, Dad," Maud said. She got up to pour herself some water. She didn't bother telling her father that she wasn't having caffeine while she was nursing.

"I'm sorry to hear that. Of course having a child has to be hard. And bringing a child up by yourself has to be . . . very hard."

"I know. It is."

"I'm sure your mother has been a great help."

"She has been," Maud said.

"Well, that's good. No matter how hard it's been, it sounds as if you've been doing beautifully."

What was stopping her from saying, *I feel like I'm falling apart, Dad. I feel like I'm falling apart again*? She didn't know, but she couldn't say it.

Now was the time to ask him for help. But it was so hard to ask him for anything. He had always bestowed his gifts at random. You never felt you had the right to request anything; rather, if he felt like giving you something, he gave it to you. To actually ask him for something would be to cross some uncrossable line.

After they had cleared away the dishes, Adam announced that he had to go. He was taking a cab and he offered to give Maud a ride home.

When they stopped for a light on Broadway and Sixtieth, a man walked up to the car and started mopping the windshield with a dirty rag.

"The squeegee men are back," Adam said. "Christ. I miss Giuliani."

"Why?"

"He was good for the city. The squeegee men are back, the graffiti is back on the subway. For one brief shining moment, it felt as if the grown-ups were in charge."

There were only a few minutes left in which to ask a favor of him.

She didn't know if he had the slightest sense of what she was going through. Though he'd had three of them, she wasn't sure he knew how much work it was to take care of a child. When she was little, her father was represented to her mainly by the closed doors of his study. Sliding doors that fit together nicely.

They were three blocks away from her apartment. Adam looked down at David and nodded approvingly.

"He's such a beautiful child," he said. "You're very fortunate."

"It's not easy."

"You make it seem easy. That's a gift. In the great game of motherhood, you're Joe DiMaggio. You're a class act."

"I don't know," she said. "It doesn't feel that way."

"I know that parenting has its burdens," he said, "but everything's relative. I think it's a lot more pleasant than publishing a novel, actually. People say that publishing a novel is just like having a baby. But that would only be true if, when you had a new baby, strangers came up to you on the street and said, 'What an ugly baby! Why'd you even bother having that baby! It's not as good as your other babies!' If that were the case, giving birth to a baby would be comparable to giving birth to a book."

He seemed pleased with this formulation. He was doing this purse-lipped thing he did when he'd uttered a phrase he'd liked, but modestly wanted to conceal the pleasure he took in his own wit, but wanted you to see that he was modestly concealing it.

"Dad?" she said, with one hand on the doorknob.

He leaned over and kissed her on the forehead.

"Stay safe, kitten," he said.

She cradled David's head carefully as she worked her way out the door, and waved at her father as the cab drove off.

FIFTY-SEVEN

H ave you eaten anything today?" Eleanor said.
"I don't know. I think I had some toast."

Eleanor was about to say, "You should eat," but then decided that it would be a good idea to go easy on the shoulds.

"Why don't I make you something?" she said.

She looked in Maud's refrigerator, but there was hardly anything there. Peanut butter, maple syrup, halvah.

Eleanor was growing more alarmed every day. She kept expecting Maud to snap out of this, and it kept not happening. Maud stayed in with David most of the day, watching TV.

Eleanor stopped herself from saying, "Your child needs light. He needs fresh air. You're starving him." Instead she said, "Why don't we all go for a walk?"

It was an unusually warm Saturday in November, and Broadway was crowded. Everyone looked free. There was no way that Eleanor could wish David out of the world—she was already fiercely attached to him—but for the thousandth time she thought it would have been better for Maud if she'd never gotten pregnant, if she'd never met Samir in the first place.

David was in his carrier, riding between Maud's breasts. The bumpiness of the ride must have disturbed him, and he spat up. Maud wiped the liquid off his face with a tissue. There was a garbage can on the corner but it was already overflowing. She put the tissue in her hip pocket.

"I've always loved New York," Maud said. "I've always thought I couldn't live anywhere else. But it's starting to disgust me."

It was hard for Eleanor to take her eyes off her grandson. The tininess of every part of him was astonishing. She could look at his eyes and feel astonished by how small they were, then look at his lips and feel astonished by how small they were, then look at his fingers . . .

"I can't even remember when you kids were this small," Eleanor said. "It seems to last so long when you're living it, but then it feels like a dream."

She was thankful to be out of Maud's apartment. It was crazy there, with unwashed dishes stacked high in the sink, newspapers strewn about, humid full-packed diapers piled in the bathroom's overflowing trash can.

But New York *can* seem hideous when you have an infant with you. Central Park was a dull brown, and there were signs taped to the trees, signs with skulls and crossbones, warning that the lawns had been treated with rat poison.

"Enjoy the park," Maud said. "Side effects include seizures and vomiting."

They sat on a bench. Maud discreetly draped a thin nursing blanket over David's carrier and unbuttoned her shirt.

"Let's try this again, big guy."

He fed a little and then spat the nipple out.

"Better than nothing," Maud said. "You're getting there."

They were sitting near a part of the park that Eleanor loved, a beautiful wooded enclave that encouraged aimless meandering.

"That's the Ramble," Eleanor said.

Maud looked vaguely at the trees.

"It doesn't look like I remember," she said.

Her eyes were welling up.

Eleanor had never spanked her children, but she thought that Maud might benefit from a good sharp slap right about now. To be thrown into despair by the sight of the Ramble! It was too much.

FIFTY-EIGHT

L et me take this guy," Eleanor said. Maud took off her carrier, lifted David out, and handed him to Eleanor.

It felt good to bear the weight of this creature in her arms.

"You don't think his head is lopsided, do you?" Maud said.

"His head is perfect," Eleanor said.

"I know it's normal for their heads to be a little lopsided at
first. But his head seems more lopsided than . . ."

"Than what?"

"I look at lopsided baby heads on the Internet sometimes."

"His head is fine," Eleanor said, but Maud continued to look
fretful.

Maud was decomposing into a thousand worries. It was almost as if she were indulging her worries, nurturing them.

David was sleeping. Tiny fingers, tiny lips. Yet like any infant
he exuded an enormous indefinable force.

"This little guy needs you," Eleanor said. "He needs you to
be strong."

"I know that," Maud said.

"And even if he *didn't* need you to be strong—you *are*
strong. You're stronger than this, Maud. It feels like you're giving in to something. You don't have to."

Maud turned her head away. "I don't know if I can do this. I
just don't know if I can do this." Her voice was clogged.

The sound of your daughter trying to speak through tears.
Your daughter telling you she's going under. Eleanor had had

more than twenty years' experience of helping people in trouble, and somehow it had all disappeared. What was the right thing to say? She had no idea. It was as if the experience of helping people had been stored in a discrete section of her mind, and that section had been removed.

"You can *fight* this," Eleanor said. "You have an amazing *mind*, Maud. You can *think* your way through this."

She had no idea whether this was the right thing to say. Maybe she should have told Maud to *stop* thinking so much.

But Eleanor had always loved her daughter's mind, always loved her willingness to use it. Maud's mind was a great shining thing. Eleanor closed her eyes and imagined it as a shield, a fallen shield, and she hoped that her daughter would have the strength to pick it up off the ground.

"Every night I think I'm going to do better the next day," Maud said. "But then there *is* no next day. He wakes me up about every ten minutes, and when morning comes around I feel more burned out than ever." She closed her eyes. "Sometimes I think it might be a good idea for me to spend a week in Holliswood."

Holliswood was the psychiatric facility where Maud had spent two weeks during her second breakdown, just after she graduated from college.

"Do you think you can get anything there that you couldn't get from a week in a hotel?" Eleanor said.

The American Psychological Association would probably frown upon the suggestion that a psychiatric hospital would be less helpful than a Holiday Inn. But she didn't want to see Maud go in again.

"I thought they had a good team there," Maud said.

"You could stay with me again," Eleanor said. "You could stay as long as you like."

Maud didn't answer.

FIFTY-NINE

Adam was watching television when the doorbell rang. He looked through the spyhole and was surprised to find that Eleanor was in the hall.

He opened the door and let her in.

"I never thought I'd see you here," he said.

"I never wanted to be here. But these are extraordinary circumstances."

"Sit down. Can I get you a drink?"

"No thanks."

"I hope you won't mind if I fix one for myself."

He busied himself at the liquor cabinet, wondering what this was all about. He was expecting Thea within an hour, and he wanted Eleanor to be gone by the time she arrived.

"How can I help you?" he said.

"How can you help *me*?"

Her jaw dropped open.

Her jaw dropped open: this was a phrase he would never have allowed himself to use in his fiction. It's the kind of description that lazy writers use, along with "He turned pale with anger" or "She was breathless with excitement." But in fact Eleanor's jaw did drop open. Letting her jaw drop was something she did habitually, when she was outraged by something—for example, when she was stunned by some incredibly thoughtless remark that someone, usually Adam, had made.

How glad he was that he was no longer involved with her,

that he no longer lived in the eternal tropics of her suffocating virtue.

"Yes," he said. "How can I help you?"

"I didn't come here because I want you to help me. I came here because I want you to help your daughter."

She was thrusting her chin at him in a childish show of defiance. But he couldn't understand what she was being defiant about. She acted as if she expected that he'd refuse to help.

"Of course," he said. "What can I do for her?"

He wanted to sound obliging but already he was feeling the chafe of constraint. He hated it when he was expected to do things. He didn't mind being charitable, but he hated to be *expected* to be.

"You can call her every day and remind her she isn't alone. You can remind her that you love her. You can offer to help her out financially."

There it is, he thought. The rest of it is bullshit.

"How much does she need?"

"I don't *know* how much she needs. *She* doesn't know how much she needs. But she's in trouble. She doesn't make a lot of money and she's going to have to be paying for clothing and diapers and wipes and doctors' visits and help around the house. She can't do this alone, Adam. She needs you to be there for her. She needs both of us."

Eleanor was in her glory. The tendons of her neck were protruding as she made her appeal. Her earnestness, her self-righteousness, made her radiantly, triumphantly ugly.

He felt a headache coming on. He imagined grabbing her by the elbows, pulling her off the couch, and giving her the bum's rush out the door. It had been so blissful, during the past two years, to be free of her. Free of her demands. Free of her *needs*. Free of the self-righteousness of her needs.

Thea was different. Thea didn't have needs—not in this wussy way. Thea was one of the few women he knew who was contemptuous of feminism, yet Thea was the most feminist woman of them all. Because she didn't *need* you.

He was not going to be dragged back into that now. He was not going to be dragged back into the world of women's needs.

"I won't be sitting around her apartment holding her hand," he said. "Let me know what she needs, and I'll try to accommodate her. But I'm not going to be changing diapers and reading *Pat the Bunny,* Ellie. It's just not going to happen."

Again the look of indignation, righteous disbelief, disbelief that she could be dealing with such a monster.

"Get over yourself, Ellie. It's the same arrangement that's always suited you in the past. You can take care of the heavy emotional lifting, and I'll do what I can to foot the bills."

Eleanor stood up. Thank God, he thought.

She picked up her purse and clutched it in both hands. She looked like a nun. If she hadn't been born Jewish, he thought, she would have ended up a nun.

"I hope you're better than you're pretending to be, Adam. I hope you're capable of being more than this. There are times in life when we either become better than we've ever been before, or worse than we've ever been before. When there's no third way."

Be all that you can be, he thought. The slogan of the U.S. Army. Ellie was trying to recruit him into the army of the virtuous.

"I love Maud as much as you do," he said. "And I intend to keep helping her. But she has her own life and she's going to have to meet her own challenges. And I'm not going to give you the authority to judge whether I'm succeeding or failing as a human being. So I strongly suggest that in the future you dispense with the lectures. I'm not interested in hearing about where I stand on your moral scorecard."

She was already in the hall, and she was giving him one of her silent looks of wounded comprehension—you had wounded her, but she was going to find a way to forgive you, and in forgiving you she was going to prove once again that she was superior to you. He had the feeling that she would have liked to have stood there giving him this look for ten or fifteen minutes, but he closed the door.

SIXTY

Thea was wearing a long black leather coat. Normally Adam helped women off with their coats, but now he stood in his foyer and watched.

With Thea, even taking off her coat was a performance. It wasn't quite like stripping, but it was exciting in its own way.

"Look what I have."

Her bag was at her feet; she reached down into it and removed a book. Rather, something that was not yet a book: a copy of the bound galleys of his novel.

Months before a book arrives in bookstores, its publisher produces a limited amount of early copies, which are called bound galleys. These go off in all directions: to writers who might supply blurbs for the back cover; to book-review editors; to the buyers at bookstores who decide what new books to order and how many; to overseas publishers and movie agents; to Oprah's people; to Oprah's people's people; and to who knows who else.

"Scribner sent five copies to Charlie, so I snagged one for myself."

"Five copies?" he said.

"I've seen these things all over town. It's a status symbol. The new Weller. 'Have you read the new Weller yet?'"

Thea was not generous with compliments or flattering reports, so this meant a lot.

He already knew that his publisher was pushing the book hard. People he ran into were congratulating him as if he'd won the Pulitzer Prize. And the book wasn't even out yet.

All this felt new to Adam. He'd never gotten the royal treatment before. There had been strong "prepublication vibes" around *Daybreak,* twenty-five years ago, but it was hard to compare the two experiences. The publishing business was much more modest then. It had not yet begun to wish it was the movie business. The clothes were slicker now, the restaurants glitzier. So when a book became a "publishing event," it *felt* much bigger now, it was an event on a grander scale—even though it was over more quickly, since there was a new publishing event every week, a new novel that was being universally hailed as "astonishing."

Adam had no nostalgia for the old days, when the publishing industry had been populated by pompous old codgers with comb-overs and bowties. The new style, more brazen, was more amusing.

He knew that this book was going to succeed. He had such a calm and confident clarity about this that it made him feel like a mystic.

The fate of most books depends on circumstance—on whether they happen to get reviewed sympathetically in *The New York Times* or on whether the author knows someone who can get him onto *Imus in the Morning.* But some books are bulletproof: no bad review or publishing-industry mishap can stop them from their appointment with success. He had felt that way about *Daybreak,* and that was the only one of his previous books he'd felt that way about. It was the book in which he'd worked most effectively within his own limitations, the book in which he'd turned his limitations most successfully into virtues. In that book his temperamental lack of charity had been perfectly suited to his subject and his theme. His habitual coldness was exactly what that book had needed. Writing it, he had been like a surgeon, of whom we don't require empathy but only the knowledge of how to cut.

This new book was something else. It was a departure. It was just as intelligent as any of his other books, but it was warmer; it was more humane.

It was not, of course, his. But after working through it patiently, testing every scene and every sentence, delicately restitching almost every phrase, he *felt* as though it were his. The question of its authorship rarely came into his mind anymore.

"So what happens to the other four copies?" he said. "Do any of them get to Charlie? Does Charlie read?"

"Charlie reads vociferously. I mean voraciously. And he reads whatever his brilliant young producer tells him to read. He'll be taking *So Late So Early* to the Hamptons this weekend."

Somehow the thought didn't fit: the book's cast of striving, idealistic young Jews, yearning for the true and the beautiful, traveling out to the Hamptons in Charlie's Jag.

"That's one copy. Another goes to Krissa, and another goes to Steve." Two other people who worked for the show. "And for the last copy, I decided, since you're probably too proud, to send it to Mister Unexpectedly Connected."

"That would be?"

"Jeffrey Lipkin, of course. The man who keeps the medals."

"Lipkin?"

"The one and only."

"Christ."

"Don't look so rattled, Weller. This will be your greatest triumph. When that little vegan was saying you were played out, you were working on the best book you've ever written. He'll kick himself, because if he had given you the Gellman prize already, people would be calling him a genius in the art of prize-giving. Little nerd though he is, he's more plugged in than anyone else I know."

This was complicated.

Adam had known that Jeffrey would read the thing eventually, of course. But he'd put the thought out of his mind.

Jeffrey, who had studied Izzy's work with an obsessiveness that Izzy himself would have found frightening, was probably the only person on earth who might be able to expose this book.

Sometimes you can feel like a cartoon character: you've run off the cliff without knowing it, and now you realize you're running in midair. And then you fall. Adam's faith that this book would be his crowning achievement had been based on a colossal act of forgetting. He'd managed to forget that Jeffrey Lipkin would inevitably read the thing and expose him for the fraud he was.

He cycled quickly through the possibilities: would it be better if it happened now, before the book was published, or six months from now?

It would kill his career either way, but it would probably be worse if it happened after the book was out. The scandal would be bigger.

So Thea had done him a favor after all.

Adam had been born with an uncommon resilience. Within a few minutes he was purely curious, pondering with something like enjoyment the question of whether Jeffrey would see the book for what it was. Enjoying the risk. If he could slip past Jeffrey undetected, he was free.

SIXTY-ONE

M aud had resumed her tradition of weekly dinners with Ralph. Early one Friday evening, carrying David in a fancy new sling her mother had bought her, she took the crosstown bus at Eighty-sixth Street and got off at Park Avenue.

The doorman in Ralph's building, Brendan, had known her for years. He called Ralph on the intercom. He waited. He tried again. He got no answer.

"That's weird," Maud said.

After David was born she'd bought a cell phone. She got it out and called Ralph, in case his intercom was on the blink. No answer.

"I'll try him again in two minutes," Brendan said. "Maybe he's in the shower."

"This isn't like him," she said. "Did you see him go out or anything?"

"Didn't see him. But I just got on an hour ago."

Maybe he'd gone out on an errand that had taken longer than he'd expected. Maybe he was in the shower. Maybe he had collapsed, and was lying on the floor of his apartment, unable to crawl to the phone.

Samir's death had changed the way Maud thought about the future. It wasn't that she always expected the worst; it was that she never expected anything.

But something bad must have happened. Their Friday dinners were as sacred to him as they were to her. Ralph would no more forget one than the sun would forget to rise.

She didn't want Ralph to die alone. Poor brave lonely Ralph deserved something better than that.

She was about to ask Brendan if they could get into his apartment, when her cell phone rang. The number was one she didn't recognize. It turned out to be Ralph.

"I'm so sorry," he said. "I'm up in Westchester. Somebody called me to take a look at her father's estate. He left behind a lot of paintings. I just lost track of the time."

Long before children know what a telephone is, they hate to see their mothers talking on one. David, who had been quiet, started to shriek.

"I'm so sorry," Ralph said. "I was really looking forward to seeing you."

"Yeah," she said. She heard the tone of her own voice—dead, except for a trace of sarcasm—and couldn't believe it. This was her most loyal friend, and she sounded like a disaffected teenager, pissed off at one of her parents.

"Can we get together tomorrow?"

"I don't think I'm free tomorrow," she said. "This whole week sucks, actually. Why don't we just get together again next Friday?"

Of course she didn't have anything to do the next day, or the day after that, or the day after that. Her calendar—she didn't even have a calendar anymore.

"Are you sure?" Ralph said.

"Of course I'm sure, Ralph. And if I happen to be in Westchester next Friday, maybe it'll occur to me to give you a little jingle, half an hour after I'm supposed to be here."

"Maud, I really am sorry."

"Do you know what it's like to drag David across town on the bus? Do you know that I'm standing outside your building right now? Just about to drag him back?"

He didn't say anything, or if he did, she didn't hear it. David was still wailing.

"Sorry," she said. "It's okay. I'll see you next week."

Brendan was reading a book, acting as if he hadn't heard anything.

It was early enough for her to walk home through the park. She walked slowly, with her hands cupped under David in his sling. A five-week-old being carried by a five-year-old, she thought, if what we're talking about is the emotional intelligence of the two parties.

She still couldn't believe that she had been *that* angry at Ralph. It wasn't like her.

Or maybe it was like her, and she just didn't want to admit it to herself.

Walking on East Eighty-sixth Street, she saw a scary-looking homeless woman inside a Rite Aid, and then realized that what she was seeing was her own reflection in the window.

When she got back to her apartment, she changed David's diaper, nursed him again, and lay down on the bed with him, hoping that he'd fall asleep quickly so she could have some time to herself. Instead, he started screaming. Lately he'd been refusing to go to sleep unless she held him in her arms and walked with him. If she tried to put him down—even if she lay down next to him; even if she laid him on her stomach—he screamed, and wouldn't stop screaming until she gave in.

His scream was loud, furious, high-pitched, effeminate, and very drawn-out: he could hold a note longer than Pavarotti. Some of the books advised you to let the child scream himself out in a situation like this—when he isn't hungry or in pain. But she couldn't. His scream was pitched to her deepest frequencies. It pierced directly to the panic center of her brain, leaving her unable to think.

She lay down next to him, admiring him and wanting to strangle him at the same time. What she admired was his sheer insistence on having his own way. It gave her faith in humanity. She knew about humanity's well-documented tendency to obey authority, but alongside this was an inborn cussedness, an aversion to being controlled.

Finally she picked him up and began to walk back and forth in her bedroom, and he calmed down. She knew from experience that he would start screaming again if she (a) stopped walking, (b) tried to read anything or talk on the phone or watch TV while she was walking him, or (c) tried to hold him in a different position. He liked to be held low, down around her hips, as if he were a football and she about to hand him off. If only there was somebody to hand him off to. It was uncomfortable — she ended each day with a backache — but it was the only position in which he'd keep quiet.

Her dissertation was on the desk, unfinished.

But what was the point of finishing it, really?

Misery doesn't leave the world untouched. It lays its hand on everything. Until a moment ago, she'd thought of her dissertation as a solid piece of work. Whether or not she'd done justice to the subject, she felt sure that the subject was worth writing about. The question of how we should treat one another is the central question in personal relationships and the central question in world politics. It's *the* question.

This is what she had thought. But now she saw she was wrong.

All of her time in graduate school had been spent on this — this mincing meditation on how we should treat one another.

And it had all been a mistake. She'd inherited the good-girl gene from her mother: the gene that makes you too ethical, too aware of the needs of others, too nice. Her mother had thrown away her life. She'd made a fetish out of caring for others because she lacked the courage to take care of herself. It was as if Maud had taken the mistake her mother had made with her life and turned it into a philosophy.

If each of her parents had been a little bit more like the other, then each of them might have become a complete human being. Her father would have had some feeling for other people and her mother would have had some drive.

Maud had fucked up, by building a temple to her mother's weakness.

The reason it was a fuckup, the reason it mattered, was that the ideas that had consumed her for the past three years had left her unequipped to handle what she was feeling now. What she had felt when Ralph stood her up. What she was feeling right this minute.

What she was feeling right this minute:

1. The urge to throw this baby out the window.

2. The urge to put this baby on someone's doorstep and ring the doorbell and run.

3. The urge to grab this baby's head and dig her fingers into his skull.

She'd never known she had this kind of aggression in her.

All of her reading and thinking had not prepared her for the way she felt, had not given her a framework in which to place it. Maybe she'd been in the wrong field. She should have been getting a Ph.D. in psychology, reading Freud and Reich and Klein, people who would help her understand the depth of sheer aggression in the human animal, the pure hot vibrancy of the need to hate. People who would help her come to terms with the part of her that wanted to drop her son out the window.

She thought of the times she'd read about people who'd killed their babies and had told the police that they'd done it because the babies wouldn't stop crying. She used to wonder how people could do such things. Now she wondered why it didn't happen more often.

SIXTY-TWO

I have some news," Patrick said. "It's insignificant compared to what you've been going through, but it's news."

She was sure she knew what it was, but she was still excited to hear it.

"Diana and I have been living apart for a month now."

She wanted to say, *That's wonderful*. Of course she said no such thing.

She was glad that they were on the phone instead of face-to-face. She was glad he couldn't see her smiling.

She'd somehow felt sure all along that he would leave Diana. She'd been sure he'd leave dull Diana, now that he knew she was free. This confidence had made her feel the way she used to feel in her twenties: desirable, super-foxy, the fetchingest girl in town. After decades of earnest selflessness — helpmate, mother, therapist — it was a thrill to learn that she could be selfish on occasion too.

"How are you doing?" she said.

"Well, it's hard. It's been harder than I thought it would be. Even though I'm sure it's the right thing."

"I'm glad that it's been harder than you thought."

"You're glad? Why is that?"

"You lived together for thirty years. You have two children. It should be hard. What would it say about your lives together if it weren't hard?"

"I've thought the same kind of thing myself."

She was also glad that he'd waited a month before calling her. It made it seem more real.

"How are your daughters taking it?"

"My daughters never cease to confound my expectations. Maggie's taking it serenely. She didn't seem surprised, and now she just glides through the new arrangement. She stays with me three nights a week, and as far as I can tell, she's happy. Kate, however, is furious. I've already been to New York once for a peacekeeping mission, and I'll be coming out soon for another."

She was hurt to learn that he had been out here once without calling her, but on second thought, she thought it was a good sign.

"I'm going to be in the city for a week. I was wondering whether you might be free."

The thought of seeing him was exciting. The thought of sleeping with him was frightening.

"I should warn you about one thing," she said.

"What's that?"

"I intend to play hard to get."

"You've been playing hard to get for a while now. That doesn't put me off."

After she got off the phone, she tried to write. She was still working on her memoir about her family, her effort to excavate her old life. Sometimes it was hard to stay with it, in the midst of everything that was going on. But she had the superstitious idea that they needed her—her mother, her father, her sister— the idea that she had been charged with the responsibility to leave behind a record of their lives.

Many years ago, Adam had remarked that a piece of writing is only worth doing if you're a different person at the end of the process than you were at the beginning. Much as Eleanor disliked thinking that anything he'd ever said was worth remembering, she often thought about his words, because over the last year, she had begun to feel like a different person.

The more Eleanor wrote about Joanna, the less Eleanor felt like the younger sister. It was the first time that Eleanor had called upon herself to walk around Joanna, to think about her critically, to put her in the context of her time and place, to think about the choices she'd made and the choices she'd never made. During the past months, what had come to seem most prominent about Joanna were the choices she'd never had the chance to make. She had never been a mother, never worked at a challenging job, never had to face the death of her parents, never had to chart the unexpected paths a love affair takes when it has endured past the four-year point that Wilhelm Reich once said was the natural term of any erotic relationship.

Joanna had begun to seem like a child. A child, and a child of her time. Before computers and VCRs and ATMs and cell phones; before Ronald Reagan and George Bush the first and George Bush the second and the United States' awful turn to the right. Eleanor had always had a rich dream life, and in her recent dreams her sister had appeared in a guise different from any she'd worn before. She was a mere girl, hesitant and shy.

Eleanor sometimes felt like she was becoming a grown-up—"differentiating," in the lingo of her trade—at the belated age of sixty. It wasn't entirely pleasant. She was growing out of an identity she'd become comfortable with.

Eleanor had lost the ideal older sister, the invisible protector, whom she had always carried around in her thoughts. Really, she had lost her family. The more she wrote about the past, the more she understood that she herself had been the family darling, and that Joanna had suffered for this.

A year ago, when she'd finally begun to write, she'd thought that writing about her family would make her more connected to them. That wasn't the way it had turned out.

Over the past decades, whenever she'd daydreamed about going back to writing, she had thought that it would bring her a harmony and wholeness that she'd lacked. She had thought it would make her feel closer to her essential self. But the opposite had happened. It had led her to understand that she had no essential self; it had led her to understand that she was a much more impure creature than she had believed. And instead of restoring her family to her, it had taken them away. She had written her way into a profound solitude.

Sixty-three

Eleanor took a long breath through her mouth. She was trying not to breathe through her nose, because Maud's apartment stank. Soiled diapers were everywhere — on top of the TV, on top of the toaster oven, next to the kitchen sink. Maud used disposable diapers, of course, but she was neglecting to dispose of them. A pile of dirty laundry was slumped like a dead body in the corner of the bedroom. All the windows were closed and the shades drawn.

Eleanor asked Maud when she'd last been out of doors.

"I think it was Thursday. Or maybe Wednesday."

"What have you been doing?"

"Nursing. Reading. Watching TV."

"Anything else?"

"Not that I can think of."

"Maud," Eleanor said, "this is bad."

"I know."

It was raining outside so Eleanor couldn't make Maud go out for a walk.

David, in his crib, started to cry. Maud put him on his changing table, took his diaper off, and cleaned him. On the television, two of the cops from *Law & Order* were talking to a female suspect.

Maud watched for a minute. "I think that's Julia Roberts," she said.

Maud turned back to David and, as Eleanor watched, she took a soiled diaper from a shelf next to the changing table and put it on him.

"Maud," Eleanor said.

"Yes?"

"What are you doing?"

"What do you mean?"

"You've just put a dirty diaper on your son."

"I did?"

Maud took the diaper off again and looked at it.

"How did I do that?"

She carried both diapers to the trash. Then she cleaned David again and put him in a fresh diaper. She picked him up and held him in one arm and unbuttoned her blouse.

"I don't think I can do this, Mom," she said.

Eleanor was watching David nurse. "You're doing fine. He knows how to find the nipple now."

"That's not what I mean," Maud said. "You wouldn't happen to know if Michael Bergman is still connected to Holliswood?"

Bergman was a therapist Maud had worked with for years. Holliswood was the place where she'd found him.

"I don't," Eleanor said. "I can find out."

"I think that would be good," Maud said. She ran her hand over David's soft, feathery hair. "But what am I going to do about the dumpling?"

"I can take care of him," Eleanor said. "I can take care of him until you feel better."

"How would I pay for it?"

"Your health insurance will probably pay most of it. Whatever's left over, I could take care of."

"How?"

"I have a secret fund. For a rainy day. And anyway, even if I couldn't, your father would help out."

"Who?" Maud said. At least Eleanor thought she said it. She said it so softly that Eleanor wasn't sure.

SIXTY-FOUR

Eleanor was making daily visits. For a few days Maud seemed to be doing better. She seemed to be trying, at least. But one Thursday, Eleanor arrived early, with coffee for herself and herbal tea for Maud, and while she was still in the elevator, not yet at Maud's floor, she could hear David shrieking. As she walked down the hall toward Maud's door, the loudness of it seemed unbelievable.

She rang the doorbell, tried the door, and found it unlocked.

David was in his crib. He was lying on his back. He was still too young to turn, too young to lift his head. He was red-faced, pissed off, screaming.

Maud was sitting in a chair across the room. She was sitting erect and still, and Eleanor's first impression was that she didn't care that David was crying. But when Eleanor came closer, she understood that this wasn't true. Maud's face was changed. Something was gone.

David's wailing still filled the room, but for a moment Eleanor almost forgot about him. Her daughter was suffering, and that was all that mattered.

"I can't do this," Maud said.

SIXTY-FIVE

Thea ordered a glass of champagne.

"The time has come, the walrus said."

She looked as if she was in particularly high spirits, and Adam was eager to hear what she had to say. She looked as if she was going to tell a story about some new triumph.

It was early on a Saturday afternoon. They had met for lunch. Later that night Adam was going to take her to a party at the home of a friend of his who worked at *Harper's*.

As by a gentle breeze, he was refreshed by the thought of how glad he was not to be living with Ellie. Ellie had never liked *Harper's*: she thought it specialized in snobbishness and snark. She had always tried to make him feel guilty about appearing in its pages.

"What are the many things we should talk about?" he said.

She looked down into her champagne and then abruptly looked up, smiling brightly, and said, "Here's the thing. I think we should stop seeing each other romantically."

Remain calm. It was essential to appear calm.

"Splendid," he said.

He was about to ask why, but he restrained himself.

He had been a writer and a reader all his life, but in moments of pressure he tended to draw on the movies for guidance. This moment was no exception. Humphrey Bogart wouldn't have asked why, and neither would Cary Grant. All the way across the spectrum of maleness, from the laconic tough guy to the urbane wit, the impressive response was not to ask.

And if he did ask, what kind of answer would he receive? Either she would tell him that there was another man, or she would tell him that there wasn't. In either case, the truth was that there *was* another man. Knowing Thea, he was sure of that. And knowing Thea, he was sure that she had traded up: she'd found someone who could be of more use to her than he could.

"That's all you have to say?" she said.

"What else *is* there to say?"

"I didn't think it would be this easy," she said. "Thank you for making it this easy."

"I've had a wonderful time with you, my dear. So I thank *you*. For everything. I always knew that this day had to come. I'm just glad that I could be of use to you for a while."

"You've been of *great* use to me," she said. She seemed moved, and he saw that she hadn't heard the irony in his remark. "You've brought me into the world."

He was trying to figure out who the new man was. It would have to be someone he'd heard of. Some young writer, someone who was all the rage? Someone she'd met on the set of *Charlie Rose*? Or maybe it was Charlie Rose himself?

He couldn't get over how stunning she looked. But she wasn't stunning for him anymore. Her high color, her vivid brightness, hadn't been a sign of how happy she was to see him. It was, perhaps, a sign of how tense she felt, how frightened she felt at the thought of breaking up with him. Or perhaps it was a sign of how exhilarated she felt at having a new man in her life.

Adam finished his drink. "Excuse me," he said, and slid out of the booth and went to the men's room.

He was glad to find that the restroom was empty. He ran the

water in one of the sinks, caught some of it in his hands, and splashed his face.

When he had looked at himself in the mirror before leaving the apartment to join Thea, he had seen a vigorous sixty-four-year-old, a man who had grown steadily more attractive as he had aged. Now he saw a man who was many years past his prime.

He would have liked to sneak out of the restaurant and go home. Maybe he could. He could leave through the back entrance.

But that wasn't the way. He had to face her.

Continuing the meal as if she hadn't hurt him would be a small act of class. He wanted to perform this classy gesture, but he didn't want to do it all day. He had his cell phone in his jacket pocket. He had the number of Maud's clinic. The front desk of Bedlam.

It took a few minutes to reach her: someone had to find her; she had to come to the phone. She sounded happy to hear from him.

"I was wondering if you wanted a visitor. Would it be all right if I came over in a little while?"

She sounded genuinely excited. "That would be great, Dad. But they have this complicated visiting schedule. I'm not sure they'll let you in."

"I've never yet met an establishment that wouldn't let me in. I'll see you in about an hour."

When he returned to the table he sat down and said, "Did you see the new *New York Review of Books*? Your hero David Foster Wallace seems to have laid an egg."

"He's not my hero," Thea said quietly. Then, even more quietly: "You are."

He knew what she was feeling. She had come into the

restaurant as if she were wearing a suit of armor, prepared to defend herself against his arguments, his bitterness, his insults. And
now she was stunned and full of gratitude because he hadn't
given her a hard time. While she had been preparing to fight herself free of him, she'd walled herself off so thoroughly from her
affection for him, that now, when it turned out that she didn't
have to fight him, all the affection for him that she did have —
genuine affection — had been released. She was probably experiencing a moment of regret, wondering if she should stay with
him after all.

"I hope we can still be friends," she said, which was unworthy of her.

It was tempting to hope that through repeated demonstrations of his inner strength, repeated demonstrations that he
didn't need her, he would be able to win her back. But he knew
that if he tried to play it that way, it would lead only to heart-
break. She had announced her intention to leave him, and
whether she carried it out now or six months in the future, she
would inevitably carry it out. There was no way around that one.
She had hurt him, and he wasn't going to give her the opportu-
nity to do it again.

"We'll see. But let's give it a little time, shall we?"

He signaled to the waiter and paid the bill. He stood up
and she remained seated. She was wearing a skirt with a slit in
it. He took a last glance at her long legs. "Good-bye, Gams,"
he said.

A nickname for a film-noir heroine. She smiled: a fond,
misty, jazz-saxophone-in-the-distance kind of smile. "You know
me so well. How am I ever going to find anybody who knows
me so well?"

He put on his coat, clasped her hands, and let go. He didn't understand why he should be put in the position of comforting *her*.

They went out to the street together. He called her a cab, and, shutting the door, said, "You'll do fine."

Then he called a cab for himself and went out to Holliswood, to see his daughter.

SIXTY-SIX

The cab ride made him nauseous. He didn't have a great deal of sentiment about Thea herself, and yet her leaving him was a blow. He didn't know what his chances were of attracting anyone else like her: so young, so vibrant, so obviously in a hurry.

Just as Ellie had for years lent him an air of compassion that he did not in fact possess, Thea had lent him an air, not of youthfulness, but of something like *currency*. She had made him appear to be someone who mattered to the young. She had made him seem to be a creature of the contemporary world, rather than a fossil from a bygone age when Jewish intellectuals walked the earth.

At Holliswood the receptionist, or guard, or whatever the young man was, told him that afternoon visiting hours were over and evening visiting hours would not begin until eight. Adam refrained from telling him what he was thinking: that he wasn't in the habit of allowing his desires to be overruled by people in rented uniforms. He politely asked to speak to a supervisor, politely told the supervisor a few lies—he said that he was flying out of the country later that night and this was his last chance to see his daughter until the next month—and was allowed into the unit.

He found Maud in the lounge area. The drab linoleum floors, the long tables with built-in benches: it was as if she'd been demoted to elementary school.

She was wearing her own clothes, which surprised him: without actually having thought about it, he had imagined that she would be wearing a hospital gown.

"Hello, my dad," she said. She gestured vaguely around the room. "An unhappy turn of events for the young philosopher."

"Nothing more than a rite of passage," he said. "You probably can't even *be* a philosopher if you haven't spent some time in a sanatorium. Nietzsche, Wittgenstein . . ."

"I know. I just was hoping that I'd served all my time already."

There were two other women in the room, watching a reality show in which people were eating live maggots. The television was mounted high on one of the walls, so that you had to hold your head back in an awkward position to see the screen.

Adam only glanced at the women, but he was disturbed by what he saw. Both of them were obviously *off*. One of them was marked by an air of dullness or vacancy or vagueness—you looked at her and you imagined a history of shock therapy, neurons fried to a crisp—and the other seemed to be afflicted by some other kind of faulty wiring: she was keeping up a running commentary on the program, in a shrill and spittle-flicking way.

He didn't want to believe that his daughter belonged here, in this community of the damaged and the dull. But it was hard to ignore the evidence that she did. She looked both frantic and lethargic, somehow. She kept touching her nose, and she was blinking in a weird rhythm, as if she couldn't speak freely here and was trying to signal to him in Morse code.

"How is it here?"

"It's not that bad. At least I don't have a roommate."

But maybe everyone belonged here, in the community of the damaged. If he had visited her yesterday it would have seemed like an alien land, but now he wasn't sure.

Yesterday he had felt like a distinguished writer and a sexually vital man. Now he felt nothing but old. No one had ever left him before. He had always been the leaver.

There were two books on the floor near Maud's chair. One of them was *A Short History of Ethics,* by Alasdair McIntyre, and the other was *Contingency, Irony, and Solidarity,* by Richard Rorty.

"You're still reading philosophy."

"Of course I am."

A little gargoyle of a man entered the room pushing a food cart and distributed small cups of ice cream to everyone, with plastic spoons. "Chocolate for you, my man?" he said to Adam, with a wink. "Hope you like it, 'cause it's all we got left."

"The food here," Maud said. "It's unbelievable. It's like eating old boots."

He thought of asking her if visitors were permitted to bring food. He could bring her an assortment of things from Zabar's. He seemed to remember that she liked the tofu spread; he seemed to remember that Ellie always used to be sure to have some on hand when Maud came home on vacations from college.

"What do you do here all day?"

"Mom's been visiting every day, with David. And my friend Ralph's been coming by."

He had no idea who Ralph was, but he didn't bother to ask.

"And then for the most part, they try to fill up your time with activities," she said. "They like to keep us occupied. Group therapy, rec therapy, art therapy. In art therapy you sit around drawing with crayons."

"Really?"

"No. Not really. Watercolors. It's almost as bad."

"I'm sure you've done some fine watercolors. If you give me one or two I'll hang them on my refrigerator."

"With little magnets? That will be nice. Just like you used to do when I was in kindergarten."

He was glad that he could joke with her, at least.

A woman entered the room. Probably in her mid-thirties, she was tall and slender, with dark brown hair and brown eyes. She was clearly a therapist or a visitor, not an inmate. She looked as if she'd just beaten a roomful of men at poker. She walked up to the silent, stunned woman, who gained a flicker of animation when she saw her guest.

Adam could tell a lot about her at a glance. She had been raised in a wealthy family: he could see it in her air of confidence, her ease. A wealthy family, but one of those old-style wealthy families that were dedicated to the idea of service. He could see this because although her blouse and skirt were obviously expensive and chosen with care, they were demure, drawing no attention to themselves, and because the only jewelry she wore were pearl earrings and a necklace with a single pearl.

He could hear her suggesting to the shell-shocked woman that they take a walk. The two of them left the room, and he was able to concentrate on his daughter again.

"Do they let you check your e-mail when you're here?" he said.

"You can't use the Internet at all. They used to have Internet access but apparently the men were always using it to visit porn sites."

"Not being able to check your e-mail doesn't seem like a bad thing," he said. He had about a hundred unanswered messages in his in-box.

"That's true. It's kind of a relief. But I'm in this online philosophy discussion group, and I'd give anything if they'd just let me get on the computer long enough to read the posts once a day. It's not just a bunch of graduate students talking out of their hats. Last month they had an online debate between Richard Wolin and Richard Rorty. But they won't let me do it. You can sit here watching *Fear Factor* until you feel sick, but Internet access is strictly forbidden."

"Can't someone just print out the discussions and bring them to you?"

"Mom's the only person I'd feel comfortable asking, and . . . you know Mom and computers. A couple of weeks ago she said she thought she needed to get her computer repaired, and I took a look at it, and the only thing wrong with it was that the mouse wasn't plugged in."

Adam had been using a computer for more than twenty years. He'd been using one when most of the writers he knew, wedded to their Selectrics or their Parker pens, were piously swearing that they would never go near one, since it might wreck the delicate cadences of their art. He was about to tell her that he could print the discussions and bring them to her every day. This was his first visit in the five days she'd been here, but that didn't mean he couldn't change his pattern. She was his daughter.

He stopped himself from telling her, though. There was no point in making promises. She probably wouldn't have believed him if he had. You are what you do. He could come back tomorrow with a care package — the computer printout and some actual food. She'd be stunned.

He asked her how to find the Web site. "If I get a chance, maybe I'll print something out and send it to you." He wanted to sound casual.

He kissed her good-bye and went out into the welcoming day.

If he had visited her the day before, he would have considered his obligations fulfilled. But now he could see that his obligations went deeper. He was going to come back the next day.

He was going to come back every day until Maud felt strong enough to leave.

Adam had long ago grown sick of the conventions of fiction, whereby a narrative gains a sense of completion when the characters "change" or "grow." He had long ago decided that this convention was a comforting lie. People hardly ever actually change or grow once they're past the age of twenty or twenty-five.

But now he saw the matter in a different light. Maybe a man *can* change. It helps when you've been injured, when you've been dislodged from the complacent routines of your life. Sometimes it takes an injury to make you see what you share with others.

SIXTY-SEVEN

Maud didn't know if this was the end or not.

It was nighttime, and she was lying in her bed in her room in Holliswood.

Traditionally, the third time is the last time. A drowning man comes up three times and then goes under.

Before she'd left her apartment, she'd put some things in a bag. Toiletries, clothing, and books. Tonight she was looking through one of the books she'd brought. The parables and aphorisms of Franz Kafka.

"One must not cheat anybody," she read. "Not even the world of its triumph."

She found this haunting, although she wasn't sure what he meant.

She'd also brought her diary, thinking that it might help her organize her thoughts, but although she wrote for twenty minutes at the end of every day, nothing she wrote came close to capturing what she was going through.

This didn't surprise her. She'd learned in the past that you can't describe the experience of misery—that she couldn't, at least. It was as if misery lived below the level of language. Years ago she'd read William Styron's book about depression and found that he couldn't really describe any of it either. He spoke of howling caverns and yawning depths, which she supposed was as close as you could get to describing it, but it wasn't really very close.

She didn't know what other people's depressions were like. Hers was like a blank white wall. It didn't reside in the moments when she wanted to kill her son, but in the moments when she didn't care whether he lived or died. Before her mother had arrived that day, she had spent the morning carrying David around the apartment, feeling like his prisoner, because he wouldn't let her put him down. Finally, because she needed to rest for a minute, she had put him in his crib, and as soon as she let go of him, he started to scream. He screamed, and kept screaming, and she sat down not far from him and watched him as he lay there, his screams interrupted only by gasps, as if he were drowning, and although she knew he'd quiet down if she went back over to him and picked him up, she couldn't imagine why she should want to do that. As she sat there listening to him, she was a thing without feeling. She was no longer someone who could imagine killing a child in anger; she was someone who could imagine allowing a child to die, simply because she didn't care to save him.

She was hoping that if she got a little time to rest here, she might return to a state of being she could recognize as her own.

SIXTY-EIGHT

In the taxi, on the way toward Patrick's hotel, Eleanor was thinking that life brings you everything at once. You can be in misery because of the misery of your daughter at the same time as you're exhilarated by a new romance, a romance that feels like the first act of a new life.

Her friend Vivian was taking care of David for the night. Her thoroughly unmaternal but good-hearted friend Vivian. She had been holding David when Eleanor left, and she'd looked as if she were holding a skunk. Eleanor had had to reassure her that as long as she didn't drop him, she could consider the night a success.

When Patrick opened the door of his hotel room, they didn't kiss. It was almost as if they were afraid to. Nothing stood between them anymore, and this made them shy.

His room was on the fifteenth floor. The wall that faced east was one huge window. The East River was shimmering; the cluster of illuminated bridges to the south looked like creatures of a great and ancient dignity; and Brooklyn looked almost glamorous in the dark.

"This city of yours . . . ," Patrick said.

The hotel room was clean and large. It had a minibar, an entertainment console, a TV with a VCR, a couch, a dinner table, and a desk, upon which sat a card trumpeting the wonders of the high-speed Internet connection available in every room. As she took it all in, she noted, with a gloomy self-awareness, that it was important to her that the room was nice—in other words, that it was expensive. Without really thinking about it, she had been afraid that the hotel room would testify to the cranky frugality of a lifelong radical, a man who distrusted wealth and all its trappings.

It had always been easy for her to imagine herself untainted by any interest in material comforts, untouched by the sordid world of getting and spending, but only because life with Adam had surrounded her with luxuries.

Patrick was talking about his older daughter and the outcome of his peacekeeping mission.

She'd had a weird taste in her mouth all day. Before she left home she'd brushed her teeth three or four times, scraping the back of her tongue until she gagged, but the taste hadn't gone away. She hoped she wouldn't taste weird to him, if he kissed her.

She had once read that you can tell what your breath smells like by licking your skin, waiting ten or fifteen seconds, and smelling it. Sitting in the back of the cab on the way over here, as the driver, wearing a headset, chatted in excited Hindi to a friend, she had licked her forearm, smelled it, and hadn't been able to tell. It smelled pleasant, but she didn't know if she could believe that that was really what her breath smelled like, and even if she could, she didn't know if it would seem equally pleasant to Patrick. When she was little, one of her friends had pronounced that people secretly love the smell of their own farts.

Patrick poured a sherry for her and a scotch-and-water for himself. They sat on the couch side by side.

He was through with his story about his daughter. She hadn't heard a word of it. Will this be on the test? she thought.

"Here we are," he said.

What happens now? she thought. They were free. There was nothing holding them back.

But nothing holding them back from *what*? If they were young they would have hurled themselves at each other now. But she was sixty and he was sixty-two. It wasn't as if the erotic impulse had vanished, but it had changed. It was subtler now.

This was how it was for her, at least. She had no idea how it was for him. All she knew was that at this moment, she didn't feel a hint of a glimmer of sexual desire.

He put down his drink and brushed a strand of hair away from her face.

She took his hand in both of hers, examined it, kissed it.

"You're more beautiful than ever," he said.

Of course she knew this wasn't true, and of course he didn't believe it himself, unless he was suffering from an as-yet-undiagnosed brain tumor. But he looked at her as if he meant it.

"It's a serious thing we're doing," he said, "but I'm glad that we're doing it."

She hoped he wasn't going to kiss her. She wasn't comfortable yet.

He leaned toward her and kissed her. As he kissed her she was half in the room, experiencing it, and half remembering their first kiss, at the end of their first date, nearly forty years ago. It had been an unusual kiss. Light but long. An auspicious kiss, it had seemed at the time, a kiss that was opening the door to a lifetime, but it hadn't been. She'd left him within a year.

But maybe it had been. Here they were.

She was relieved to find that he didn't taste like anything in particular. He didn't have foul old-man breath. But she was still worried that she might have foul old-woman breath.

She wanted to tell him that she needed to stop, needed to pause for a little while at least. But she didn't trust herself. They'd been waiting for almost a year now, and maybe it was time to take the plunge.

They were necking on the couch, and in the pushing together of bodies she thought she could tell that he had an erection, and she wondered if it was purely him or if it had been aided by Viagra. Not that it mattered, except that it would be flattering if it was purely him.

This man wants me. As broken a creature as I am. As a well-preserved sixty-two-year-old, he could have had his pick of all sorts of women ten or fifteen years younger. Merry widows and gay divorcées. And yet he wanted her. With her sheepishly fallen breasts and the twenty pounds that she'd put on for the part, she was somehow still desirable to him.

Can you take the whole of me? A line from a half-remembered poem. He seemed to want the whole of her, and this was so different from what she had known for decades that she was amazed.

And what about her? Could *she* take the whole of *him*? She didn't know if she could promise it. She had too many burdens: her children and her grandchildren came before him, and that would never change.

Maud in the psychiatric hospital. Maud on the bench, crying at the sight of the Ramble. How strange. Poor David, who could never quite keep the nipple in his mouth. It was as if they were here too, sitting on the couch at Eleanor's side.

I don't have the strength for this.

Although they were still kissing, it had become obvious to her that she could not embark upon a love affair. She didn't have it in her. The struggles ahead of her were different struggles: trying to help Maud, trying to help Maud's child, trying to keep alive the creative spirit that she had only recently begun to rekindle.

Their lips were making juicy smacking sounds. It sounded unreal. It reminded her of the way it used to sound when at the age of nine she would engage in kissing sessions with her own arm, practicing for the day when she'd be called upon to kiss a boy.

Patrick pulled his head back and put his arms on her shoulders. "Hey," he said.

"Hey."

"What's going on?"

"I'm sorry, Patrick. I can't do this. I have so many things to worry about right now."

"This doesn't have to be one of them." He went to get a hard-backed chair, placed it near the couch, sat down, and took her hand. "This can be the thing that's worry-free."

"What world are you living in, Bub?" She said this softly, affectionately, and lightly made a fist and hit him on his chest.

It couldn't be worry-free. She knew that. But it might be the last chance she would ever have for love, grown-up love. She wasn't sure that she and Adam had ever really experienced it together. It would be a terrible fate to grow old and die without ever having experienced it. But loving a man was not the task before her.

"Can we just sit here like this for a while?" she said.

"Of course."

They sat together without speaking. She closed her eyes.

He was running his hand through her hair. My white and gray and brittle hair, she thought.

"How's your daughter?" he said. "I haven't even asked you how she's doing."

She wasn't sure she wanted to talk about it, but she couldn't think of a graceful way to evade it. So she told him about Maud. He hadn't even known she was in the hospital.

After she said something about how close Maud was to getting her Ph.D., Patrick asked a question about it, and she realized that he didn't know what subject Maud was studying.

"We don't really know each other very well yet, do we?" she said.

Eleanor told him more about Maud, and then she talked a little bit about Carl and Josh, and Patrick talked about his daughters, and soon the two of them had moved on to the subject of their marriages, speaking with more ease than they had in all these past months. For a moment she thought the evening might flow back toward the physical—she thought he might kiss her again. But he didn't, and she decided it was better that way.

She left the hotel at about two in the morning. Patrick asked her to stay, but she wanted the comfort of her own bed.

Sometimes, when she was in a doctor's office, she would look at women's magazines and read articles about how your sex life can be hotter in your sixties than it ever was before. She wasn't sure she believed it, and even if she could believe it, she wasn't sure she wanted a sex life anymore.

SIXTY-NINE

When she got back to her apartment, she walked from room to room, turning on all the lights. She was glad to be home. It was a relief not to have to think about her body anymore. When she was on the couch with Patrick, trying to have a sex life, her body was a terrible thing, a piñata, fit for nothing more than to be whacked with sticks.

But with no gifts inside. A piñata filled with pus.

Now, when she was alone, her body didn't seem like too much of a misfortune. As ramshackle a structure as it was, it was home.

She was tired, but she couldn't sleep. She wondered how Maud was doing, but it was too late to call.

She sat at the desk in Maud's old room and opened her notebook. As late as it was, she thought she would spend an hour or two in the blessed silence, trying to write.

For the last year, the thought that she was going to get together with Patrick had made her life seem rich with possibility. The other thing that had made her feel like this, that had given her a desire for the future, was that after decades of dreaming about it, she had finally begun to write. So it seemed important to write for an hour or two, to reaffirm her belief that her life had promise.

She sat there for a long time, but the words wouldn't come.

The other day, she had been in the middle of a chapter about the Thanksgiving before her sister died. She tried to keep going, but nothing came. Her sister, her mother, and her father had left the room. All she could think about was Maud.

The notebooks she had filled during the past months were stacked in a box next to the desk.

She knew it was a mistake to try to take stock of her life at four in the morning, but she took the notebooks out of the box and looked through them slowly. After she was finished, it was hard to restrain herself from dropping them in the trash.

For months she had felt as if she was finally embarking on a project that she had dreamed about when she was a girl, a project that she'd secretly persisted in considering her true life's calling. Although she'd begun so late, and might be haunted by a sense of belatedness for the rest of her life, during these months she'd at least had the satisfaction of feeling as if she had well and truly begun. But now it seemed obvious that if she'd actually thought that her writing had amounted to anything more than glorified journal-keeping, she must have been in a state of temporary derangement. It was as if she'd drunk a potion when Adam left her, an elixir of self-delusion, in order to survive being alone.

She wasn't a woman in love. She wasn't a writer. She wasn't a woman in the process of "reinventing" herself. She was a mother. If she was anything more than that, she couldn't remember what it might be.

SEVENTY

The trip to Zabar's was a pain in the ass. He made the mistake of going in the late afternoon, and it was jam-packed with nerdy-looking Upper West Siders. He looked for things that Maud might like, but who the hell knew what Maud might like? He bought some tofu spread, because he knew she used to like it, and some lobster salad, because he liked it himself. He knew that Maud was a vegetarian, but he was pretty sure she still ate fish.

He hadn't told Maud he was coming. He wanted to surprise her. He would show up with a tasty lunch and a printout of the last week of discussions from her philosophy group.

The checkout line was very long, and he had the additional misfortune of being behind a quartet of Upper West Side phonies who had just gone jogging. Two men and two women in early middle age. The women had frizzy hair and slack but curiously unlined faces; it was clear from a glance that they listened to NPR, subscribed to *The Nation,* and hoped that Hillary Clinton would run for president. The men, gangly testosterone-deprived men of the Upper West Side, with their foolish too-short running shorts and their pale white legs and their feminized bodies, were doing prissily elaborate stretches as they stood in line, rotating their heads as if working out cricks in their necks.

This, Adam thought, was how you could always spot an Upper West Side phony: sooner or later you'll see him rotating his head in a full circle, trying to loosen up his neck or upper back. Professors and social workers doing half-assed imitations of ballet dancers.

He flagged down a taxi on Broadway.

He was still in a state of shock. Every third woman on the street seemed to be Thea, except that none of them had her fire.

Perhaps the worst thing about it was how it had undermined his faith in his understanding of human nature. He had thought that the success of his new novel would buy him at least another year or two with Thea.

He had been invited to a party that night. A publication party for some hot young British novelist, it was being held at Elaine's. He'd decided to visit his daughter instead. He hoped he'd made this choice purely out of love for his daughter, not because Thea's departure had left him feeling too defeated to show his face.

The cab emerged from the Midtown Tunnel. Queens is one of those places that makes you suspect that humanity has an ugliness instinct, an innate drive to live amid hideous surroundings.

His cell phone rang.

"Adam."

"Yes?"

"This is Jeffrey. Jeffrey Lipkin."

"Hello, Jeffrey."

So this was it. He was at a fork in the road of time. Two future universes lay before him: one in which he was disgraced, a plagiarist and a fraud, another in which he remained a distinguished man. In a moment, one of those universes would flicker out and die.

"I'm writing about you. You and your new book."

An exposé? It was impossible to tell from his tone.

"I have to tell you," Jeffrey said, "that I think this is a work of genius. It goes far beyond anything you've ever done before. You've put it all together here. The lyricism and the precision. I know you don't like being compared to your friend Izzy Cantor, but, honestly, I think you've taken things that he began and taken them much further."

"Thank you, Jeffrey. Your opinion means a lot to me."

"No. Thank *you*."

He wanted to ask about the article—what? where?—but it was better to appear above such things.

"I'm really stunned," Jeffrey said. "How many writers do their best work in their sixties? Philip Roth? Yeats? Henry James, maybe? I can't think of anybody else. And now there's you."

And now there's me, Adam thought. With a little help from my friends.

"Anyway," Jeffrey said, "I just wanted to thank you again. To watch an established artist taking the kind of risks you've taken in this book. Mining your material more deeply than you've ever done before. Risking a kind of emotional openness you've never risked before. Writing in a more lyrical style . . . it's all just amazing. So thank you. Really. Thank you."

And that was that.

It was over. It was done. If Jeffrey didn't see it, no one would.

Adam was free.

He had a moment of sadness for Izzy. Not even your truest and most loyal reader could recognize your literary fingerprint. I'm sorry, my old friend. Not even your most ardent admirer could save you.

SEVENTY-ONE

The moment passed. He wanted to celebrate.

But here he was, outside a psychiatric institution in Queens.

He paid the cabbie and got out of the cab and went in. The person at the desk told him that visiting hours would not resume for another fifteen minutes. He could have talked his way in again, but he decided that today he wouldn't mind waiting. The reason was that the attractive young woman he'd noticed the day before—she was visiting the shell-shocked patient when he was visiting Maud—was here, in the waiting room, reading *The New Yorker*. It wouldn't be unpleasant to sit near her for a little while.

She looked comfortable with herself. She had an air of self-sufficiency and calm. As before, she was dressed in a simple, subtle, unadorned way, no jewelry except for her earrings, no makeup. He was sure that if he could get close enough to smell her he'd find that she was wearing no perfume either. But there wasn't a hint of self-denial about any of this. She was one of those women who was free of vanity because she could afford to be. Men would be drawn to her whether she did anything to enhance her appearance or not.

She finished her article, looked up, smiled. She had probably been waiting here for a while. She looked as if she'd be happy to talk.

"Do you work here?" Adam said. Obviously she didn't; it was just something to say.

"No. I'm a therapist, but I'm not associated with Holliswood. My aunt is a patient here."

"Do you think this is a good place?" he said.

"Yes. It's better than most."

"Are there still fashions in psychiatric institutions? Years ago everyone who was anyone spent a week or two at Payne Whitney. I'm not sure the treatment was particularly good, but if you needed to be institutionalized, you went there, because it was the place to see and be seen."

"I think I read that Marilyn Monroe spent time there."

"Marilyn Monroe. That's right. A lot of writers went there too. It was one of the few places where writers could mix with movie stars on equal terms. Robert Lowell. James Schuyler. Not that those names would mean anything to anyone your age."

"I'm not as young as you think I am. And I love Robert Lowell."

"A psychologist who reads poetry. Will wonders never cease." He thought of Ellie as he said this. He was being unfair to her—she'd always read much more poetry than he had—but he didn't care.

"If a psychologist wants to read poetry," she said, "those are the poets to read. That whole generation of American poets was interested in the line between sanity and madness. Lowell, Roethke, Plath, Anne Sexton. Allen Ginsberg."

"Allen never ended up in Payne Whitney, though. He wanted to be a man of the people. Only public hospitals for Allen."

Her expression was one of smiling suspiciousness. "You're a writer yourself, aren't you?"

"I've been known to scribble a line or two."

"I *thought* I recognized you. Are you Adam Weller?"

He nodded modestly, trying not to show how pleased he was to be recognized. It didn't happen often—perhaps once or twice a year.

"I read you all through college. I really couldn't stand your books. I hated the first one, and despised the second one, and was morally offended by the third. And I disliked them even more when I reread them." She said all of this with a sly, flirtatious smile. "I was reading a lot of feminist literary criticism, and you were one of the enemies."

It was like the moment when the cherries fall into place on the slot machine and everything starts ringing and flashing. He was certain that he could take this woman home if he wished to. He didn't wish to: after thirty-five years with Ellie, a love affair with another psychologist was the last thing he needed. But it was exhilarating to know that he could.

"Are you still the unreconstructed sexist that my women's-studies teacher said you were in 1992?"

"My prejudices aren't that specific anymore. At this point I'm just a misanthrope."

A moment later, the attendant emerged to tell them that visiting hours had begun.

The scentless beauty extended her hand to Adam and said, "Very nice to meet you." She went through the double doors and was gone.

Adam stood in the waiting room holding the Zabar's bag.

The phone call from Lipkin had elated him. And the conversation with the psychologist, as brief as it was, had dispelled his fear that he might be too old to attract anyone else like Thea. There were many young women out there who, through some mixture of ambition and father-fixation, would be happy to be seen on his arm.

As recently as last night, as recently as this afternoon, he'd thought that he would visit Maud here every day. Now he reconsidered. She had to be here, for now, because she was serving a temporary sentence in the community of the bent and the broken, but there was no reason he had to visit. Maud would either triumph over her troubles or be defeated by them, but in either case the outcome would have nothing to do with how often he saw her.

It was probably better, in fact, if he saw her as little as possible. It would probably be easier for her to work out her problems without the clutter of family complications, the burden of the paternal presence. He was sure that it had always been difficult for Maud to live in the shadow of her overachieving father, and so it would surely be an act of sensitivity and tact if he stayed at arm's length.

Ellie's habit of visiting every day was different. She could follow Maud here, into this land of the dim and the drooping, because she had trained for it all her life. She had something to offer Maud by visiting her here.

Adam had something else to offer. When Maud imagines making her way back to the world outside these walls, he thought, the world of striving and achievement, she can think of me, residing in that world, and maybe it will inspire her. Maybe it will be better for her if I *don't* visit. Maybe that will plant the idea in her subconscious that in order to see me — and in order to rejoin the world of achievement and success — she'll have to work her way out of this dreadful place.

So Adam succeeded in reasoning his way to the conclusion that it would be better for Maud if he didn't visit her again. But it was just a sort of idle mental exercise. He knew that he was merely finding reasons to do as he pleased. And at bottom he didn't believe that he needed excuses. He believed what he had always believed: if you do what you want to do, as long as you are not actually going out of your way to be cruel, you are acting within the moral law.

He dropped the Zabar's bag in a wastebasket and left the building. He walked toward the subway. You couldn't just hail a cab out here in the boonies.

The evening blossomed before him. He was suddenly free. He was going home for a shower and a drink. After that, he was going to keep his place in the world of striving and achievement, and thereby maintain himself as a model for Maud to aspire to, by appearing at the party at Elaine's.

SEVENTY-TWO

There was a knock on the door and then a staff member poked his head in.

"Rec therapy in ten minutes," he said. "Your visitor gone?"

"My visitor?" Maud said.

"Sign-in sheet said you had a visitor."

Maud shrugged. "My invisible friend."

"Anyway, rec therapy in ten. Just wanted to let you know."

Maud wanted to read another page or two. She'd been looking through the Kafka anthology she'd brought here—the bleakest, most dispirited set of musings that had ever been committed to paper.

She came across the line she'd read the day before: "One must not cheat anybody, not even the world of its triumph."

She put the book down. She would have thrown it across the room, but it was a library book.

The line had seemed mordantly beautiful the day before, but it bothered her now—the resignation it embodied, the passivity.

Dear Mr. Kafka, she thought. *Fuck you.* If the world triumphs over me, it'll be because it kicked my ass, not because I politely allowed it to.

She wasn't sure if this was just braggadocio, or if she could back it up.

Local girl in loony bin talks trash to Kafka; Kafka unimpressed.

She straightened out her room for a few minutes and then headed down the hall for the evening's activities.

SEVENTY-THREE

The best thing about being here, Maud decided, the most restorative thing, was that you could sleep. For the first time in months, she was dreaming. It was good to dream, even though none of her dreams were happy.

All of them were about Samir. In one dream, they'd arranged to meet in a Dunkin' Donuts, and she was hurrying to get there on time, but her high school guidance counselor made her stop and take a math test. She knew the Dunkin' Donuts was going to close soon, and she was afraid that Samir, newly weak and fragile now that he was dead, would end up getting locked inside.

She kept dreaming that he was alive, but dying. In one dream, he was in a floating hospital, getting blood transfused into his jugular vein. Maud was waiting for him on Ellis Island. She spoke to him on the phone but he was vague and befuddled and she wasn't sure he remembered her. She asked him to put his doctor on the phone, and the doctor, in a sympathetic voice, said, "I wish we'd gotten to him sooner. We can rescue his body but it's too late to rescue his mind."

In another dream she came home from a walk and found Samir in her apartment.

"I thought you were dead," she said.

"I was never dead," he said. "But they won't let me stay here. I asked if I could live with you, but they say I'm not allowed."

David wasn't in any of these dreams. This made her sad beyond reason. She wanted Samir to meet him, if only in her dreams.

She dreamed about Samir almost every night. Only one of these dreams left even a trace of something like happiness. He was in a hospital room; she knew this was the last time she'd ever see him. She told him how much she loved him. He smiled and said, "I noticed that."

Seventy-four

W hat have you been thinking about?" Ralph said.

They were in the activities room at Holliswood, but from his tone you might have thought that he was visiting her at a research institute, some noble center of learning, where she'd been spending a few days contemplating the higher mysteries of the philosophical tradition.

She was glad that he was speaking to her in this tone.

"I've been thinking that I need to read more about free will."

"Why's that?"

"I don't really know what put me here, and I don't really know what might get me out. Most of my fellow inmates think that everything they do and everything they can't do can be explained by chemical imbalances. That seems to be the prevailing view. The professionals here seem to believe the same thing. But I'd prefer to think that there's something about me that can't be reduced to chemicals. Call it consciousness. Call it imagination. I'd prefer to think I can think my way out of this, whatever my brain chemistry might happen to be."

"I believe that. I believe you can."

"I'm thinking of checking myself out for the weekend. Seeing how it goes."

"Can you do that?"

"I put myself here voluntarily, so I can leave anytime I want. They could stop me if they thought I was a danger to myself, but

I've talked with the doctors and they don't think I am. I don't either. In case you were wondering."

"I wasn't," he said. "But I'm glad to hear you say it. Do you know what you're going to do if you do check out for the weekend?"

"I have an idea. But I don't want to talk about it. It's too stupid."

"I'm sure that isn't true."

She left the next morning, unsure of whether she was going to go back in.

She felt guilty to be leaving the clinic without going immediately to pick up David. But there was something she wanted to do by herself.

She went to the Port Authority and took a bus to Sparta, New Jersey, where Samir had grown up.

When he'd first told her the name of his hometown, she'd felt like laughing. It was too perfect. Clenched, defended Sparta: the perfect place for a militant to come of age. He'd told her that it was actually a tranquil town—almost tranquilized: rural, wealthy, and white. But she'd always liked to imagine him growing up in a place that was not quite a part of America.

When she got there, she took a taxi to the public library. The poetry section was in the basement. She didn't think there was much chance that she'd find the book he'd told her about, but there it was. *Contemporary Arabic Poetry.* Inside the back cover was a sleeve containing a checkout card. The book had been published in 1987; three people had checked it out that year, the last of whom was Samir. She found his signature, written in a careful hand, next to the due date of November 20, 1987.

One person had checked it out in 1988, another in 1990.

Sometime after that, the computer age had reached New Jersey, and the checkout card had become a charming artifact, a relic from a simpler time, and there was no way to know if anyone had taken the book out of the library since then.

She thought about the way he had used his mind. The mask he had worn when she met him—the mask of a brusque and literal-minded man—had only been a mask. This book was proof: this book, and the story he had told her about it. He was someone who had found in poetry a door to a wider life.

The two of them had been making their solitary expeditions in libraries at around the same time. He'd been a few years older, but she'd fallen in love with reading at an earlier age. Probably there were days in which each of them, miles apart, had felt more alive in the company of some new book, and wished there was someone to share it with.

Her hand was steady as she held the book, but she felt a sort of inner trembling. He had held this book in his hands.

She found the poem he had quoted from, and she read it slowly. It was just as Samir had described it: a poem about a man whose life has been overturned by love.

It was as if he, at fifteen, were imagining her, in the future. Reaching toward her. And she, now, was reaching toward him into the past. It was almost as if they were touching.

Not really, but almost.

She thought about removing the magnetic strip from the center of the book and taking it home with her. Instead, she put the book back on the shelf, for someone else to find.

She was incapable of visiting a library without taking a look at the philosophy section. The philosophy section of the Sparta library was very small, but she wouldn't have called it bad. There was no such thing as a bad philosophy section, in Maud's view.

She spent half an hour reading an essay by William James on free will, half arguing with him in her mind, half agreeing.

She had almost forgotten the pleasure of reading philosophy, the pleasure of thinking about unanswerable questions.

She put the book down and closed her eyes.

My first act of resilience, she thought, will be to believe in my own resilience.

She could almost see Samir smiling at her. If he could speak to her, he'd probably be saying something like *It's just like you to reach your moment of truth in a library.* She could almost hear him saying it.

She took a bus back to Manhattan. The bus to Sparta had gone through local streets; the bus back to the city, an express, went up the highway.

This turned out to be unfortunate. On the highway, she was reminded why people say the things they say about New Jersey.

There is a stretch of New Jersey that smells bad in a way that no place else does. It smells bad in a way that is both industrial and weirdly animate, weirdly intimate, as if factories were living creatures that sneak out to the marshes near Paterson to take their shits.

There is no species of optimism so sturdy in construction or noble in character that it can remain unshaken during a bus ride through northern New Jersey. Her feeling of triumphant hopefulness was fading. She missed Samir. She missed herself: the person she'd feel like, the person she'd *be,* if he were still with her. She had accepted his death, but she still hadn't fully accepted the idea that they weren't going to have a future together.

Their only future together was David. But the sheer challenge of taking care of him still seemed overwhelming. Being a mother was like a psychological experiment—a rigged experiment, in which you're asked to endure a level of stress that's in fact impossible to endure.

She tried to hold on to what she'd felt in the library, but it was difficult.

SEVENTY-FIVE

The ideal homecoming party, Eleanor thought, wouldn't have taken place next to a cemetery. But it was wonderful to be having any homecoming party at all.

"Could he have changed since Thursday?" Maud said. She was holding David in her arms. "Maybe he's been changing gradually and I'm just noticing it."

"How do you think he's changed?" Eleanor said.

"I can't define it. He seems slightly more mature, perhaps. Slightly wiser, after spending so much time with his grand-mother."

The three of them were in a pocket-sized park.

"How does it feel to be outside?" Eleanor said.

"It feels good."

It was early December, but the day was mild and the sky was blue.

Maud had checked herself out of Holliswood, at least for the weekend, and maybe forever. Eleanor didn't know what she was planning to do.

"Have you been doing any writing?" Maud said.

"No. Not a word."

"That sucks."

Eleanor shrugged. "There are other things in life. This young man has been a charming companion."

A black car stopped on the bottom of the slope, a car from a taxi service. The driver came out, opened the trunk, and took out a wheelchair, and then he helped Ralph out of the car and into the wheelchair.

Eleanor hadn't seen him since Samir's funeral. He looked gaunt.

After Maud kissed him hello, she retreated to a picnic table to nurse David.

"How are you, Eleanor?" Ralph said.

"Today I'm good."

"It's good to see her back on the outside. Our beloved."

"It is good. Do you think she's going to go back in?"

She hadn't wanted to ask that question—she was sure that Ralph had no more idea of the answer than she did—but, in her anxiety, she had to. She had to look for reassurance.

"She's a fighter," Ralph said.

Eleanor wondered whether that was true. She hoped it was.

Her cell phone rang in her purse. She resisted the urge to answer it. She hoped that it was Patrick, but she didn't want to think about Patrick right now.

Maud was back. "Are we ready?" she said. She put her lips close to David's ear and said, "Are you ready to visit your daddy, little dude?"

Eleanor was tired from the walk through the park. She'd been tired out, anyway, from nearly two weeks of taking care of the little dude.

"If I can have another couple of minutes to rest, I'll be able to carry him."

"I can take him," Maud said.

"How'll you manage that?" Eleanor said.

Maud was going to have to push Ralph up the hill. His wheelchair was motorized, but the hill was steep, and the motor was only good for flat surfaces and slight inclines. Eleanor wouldn't have the strength to push it herself.

"It's not a problem, Mom." Maud settled David snugly in his carrier, picked it up, and shrugged her arms through the straps. She usually wore it so that David was in front of her, but now she put it on her back, like a backpack. "He's good ballast." She took the handles of Ralph's wheelchair.

"My daughter the Amazon," Eleanor said.

"Are you sure this isn't too much for you?" Ralph said.

"It's fine," Maud said. "I'm an Amazon."

"You're sure?" Ralph said.

"We must imagine Sisyphus happy," Maud said, and started pushing.

"If you say so," Ralph said.

Eleanor walked a step or two behind them. Maud pushed her friend's wheelchair steadily and without apparent effort. She seemed a sturdy and formidable creature.

David, riding on Maud's back, was intently hitting his rattle against the side of his carrier.

The odd little party made its way slowly up the hill.

SEVENTY-SIX

This was Maud's first look at the gravestone.

It bore Samir's name, the year of his birth, and the year of his death. Nothing more. This reserve seemed more faithful to his temperament than an inscription would have been.

Her mother and Ralph stayed with her for a few minutes, and then, at her mother's suggestion, they went back down the hill. Ralph said he'd be able to wheel himself down.

Maud spread a blanket on the soil and put David down on his stomach.

She was glad that her mother hadn't objected to her wish to have some time here alone with David. She'd been afraid that her mother would think it was morbid.

It wasn't morbid. It was the opposite of morbid, in her mind.

David was starting to gain control over his limbs. He was flapping his arms and legs, as if he were trying to swim.

One of the many things she had never known about infants is how hard they *work*. David never rested. It was fascinating to watch him struggling to master the world. He spent every waking moment absorbed in the monumental effort to become more human. With every effort to move his arms or lift his head, he was coming closer to the human world.

The law of life, she thought, was striving. David striving to learn, striving in every moment to become more human. Ralph striving to stay alive. Her mother striving to remake her life after the blows she had received.

She picked David up and nursed him for a few minutes. His mouth was working hard, but he was gazing up at her calmly.

I don't want the world to get its triumph over you, little man. Over us.

He had dark eyes, like his father's.

I wish you could have felt your father's love.

She knew that Samir would have loved this boy. She knew that his love for this boy would have changed his life.

The thing about Samir, she thought, was that he wanted to live. Whether he'd fallen asleep at the wheel or gotten forced off the road by a drunk driver or whether something had gone wrong with his car, it didn't matter: she knew that he'd wanted to live.

She wanted to call out to him. She wanted to shout his name out as loud as she could.

She cried a little, and she held David close. A foe of sentimentality, evidently, he inserted two fingers into her nostril.

His lips were parted, as if he were about to speak. Tiny, wet, shining.

The world is waiting for what you have to say, boy.

In Jewish tradition, a mourner visiting a grave will find a small stone and place it on the grave or the tombstone. Maud had read about the custom and found that its origins and its meanings were unclear. But something about it had always struck her as right. It was a gesture that was tender, solemn, and illusionless.

Holding David in the crook of her arm, she bent down and found two stones, one for Zahra and one for Samir.

They were visiting the graves of a man she had known for only five months and a girl she had never met. The graves of a father and sister whom David would never know. But that didn't seem like the truth of the matter. The truth, she thought, as she carefully placed a stone on each grave, was that the four of them, somehow, were a family.